DOUBLE-BARRELED ROMANCE

Marigold and Shaun—Separated by a dastardly twist of fate, they spent years yearning for each other across a savage land. . . .

Maranta and Ruis—Thrown together by a Brazilian family's desperate need for an heir, they spent years searching for true love. . . .

Ramanda Johnson
864 Lake Dawn Rd

Fawcett Gold Medal Books
by Frances Patton Statham:

FLAME OF NEW ORLEANS   13720-1 $1.95

JASMINE MOON   13988-3 $1.95

DAUGHTERS OF THE SUMMER STORM   14201-9 $2.25

UNABLE TO FIND FAWCETT PAPERBACKS AT
YOUR LOCAL BOOKSTORE OR NEWSSTAND?

If you are unable to locate a book published by Fawcett, or, if you wish to see a
list of all available Fawcett Crest, Gold Medal and Popular Library titles, write
for our FREE Order Form. Just send us your name and address and 35¢ to help
defray postage and handling costs. Mail to:

FAWCETT BOOKS GROUP
P.O. Box C730
524 Myrtle Ave.
Pratt Station, Brooklyn, N.Y. 11205

(Orders for less than 5 books must include 75¢ for the first book and 25¢ for
each additional book to cover postage and handling.)

Daughters of the Summer Storm

Frances Patton Statham

FAWCETT GOLD MEDAL • NEW YORK

DAUGHTERS OF THE SUMMER STORM

© 1979 Frances Patton Statham
All rights reserved

Published by Fawcett Gold Medal Books, a unit of CBS
Publications, the Consumer Publishing Division of CBS Inc.

All the characters in this book are fictitious, and any resemblance
to actual persons living or dead is purely coincidental.

ISBN 0-449-14201-9

Printed in the United States of America

10   9   8   7   6   5   4   3   2   1

Daughters
of the
Summer Storm

1

No one stirred in the Charleston townhouse that faced the battery. It was the hottest part of the afternoon, and even the sea breeze had deserted the city. Marigold, sitting in the gazebo at the end of the enclosed garden, impatiently brushed away the fly that lit on her ecru-colored dress.

If only their houseguests would leave. Because of them, Marigold had not been able to meet Shaun at the battery as she usually did. And she had had no way to send word to him. It was all she could do to avoid her cousin, Crane, who was determined to court her.

On impulse, Marigold stood up, her tawny eyes seeking the distant seawall that separated the ocean from land. What if Shaun were waiting for her at that very moment?

She stepped from the gazebo and hurried toward the side gate. But just as her hand reached to push the gate open, a voice behind her inquired, "You are going somewhere, *ma petite,* without a parasol to cover your head?"

Filled with disappointment at being caught, Marigold gazed into the wrinkled face of the black servant, Feena. "I was going . . . I was . . . Oh, drat it, Feena. Why do you have to pop up every time I try to leave the house? Has my father asked you to watch me every minute of the day?"

"Oui."

"I suspected as much," Marigold said. She retraced her steps toward the gazebo with the servant at her side. As she glanced at Feena, Marigold's petulant expression changed. The white-haired old woman looked tired.

"Go and take a nap, Feena. It's much too hot for you to be chasing after me."

When Feena opened her mouth to protest, Marigold said, "I'll be in my bed for the next hour. I promise. You'd better take advantage," she urged. "It's probably the last time I shall make such a promise."

Feena stared at the golden-haired girl and then, taking her at her word, turned to walk along the pathway to the carriage house and the servants' quarters.

Marigold tiptoed into the upstairs bedroom that she shared with her dark-haired twin, Maranta. No sound came from the other bed. Maranta was asleep, with her small foot dangling outside the netting—vulnerable to the stray mosquito that buzzed about the room.

Marigold walked to the bed and covered the foot with the thinly woven drapery. For a moment she stood, frowning down at her meek, circumspect twin. It made sense for the Condessa Louisa, their important houseguest, to take a liking to Maranta. But if Maranta had any sense at all, she would not encourage a friendship with the elderly Portuguese dowager. Far better for the girl to keep her distance, or she might find herself whisked off to the other end of the world.

Marigold made a face, remembering her first encounter with the woman and her companion, Dona Isobel. She couldn't have made a very good impression on the visitors, having made no effort to conceal her instant dislike for both of them. But Marigold didn't care what the woman thought of her. She was far too busy thinking of Shaun.

While she walked to the other tester bed, she unbuttoned her afternoon dress. She let it slip to the floor and, kicking off her soft kid slippers, she climbed under the protective mosquito netting.

Frustrated, Marigold punched at the feather pillow before she laid her head against it. She felt angry and disconcerted. To think that her father had forced Feena to spy on her. Did he imagine the old servant could keep her from seeing Shaun?

Perspiration began to form on her forehead, and in a pique at the uncompromising heat that enveloped her, she pitched the pillow from the bed and removed her

8

petticoats and camisole. Now more comfortable, Marigold closed her eyes and drifted off to sleep.

The next afternoon, Marigold sat in the carriage beside Maranta.

Only two more days, and they would both be eighteen. September's children—that's what they had always been called. The twins were as opposite in temperament as the day that had given them birth—the dark, calm serenity of early morning shattered by the restless winds of the spawning hurricane.

Marigold's mind was restless as they traveled down the cobblestoned street to Mrs. Windom's shop to be fitted for their birthday dresses. A plan to see Shaun again began to form in Marigold's mind. He would not be pleased to see her at the railway station, but that couldn't be helped. Marigold glanced at Feena and then quickly lowered her parasol to hide the mutinous gleam in her eye.

The carriage came to a stop under the shade tree in front of Mrs. Windom's shop. "Do not take too long," Feena admonished. "We must be back in time for your little brother's christening."

"Are you coming in with us?" Maranta asked.

Feena shook her head. "It is more pleasant to wait in the shade. Now, run along, and do not waste time."

Marigold said nothing as she and Maranta stepped down from the carriage and walked through the front door of the shop.

At first, the shop appeared to be deserted. The sound of voices from one of the dressing rooms, however, corrected that illusion. Maranta started to speak, but Marigold held her finger to her lips. She walked to the back of the shop, unlatched the door, and motioned for her dark-haired sister to follow.

Maranta, puzzled at Marigold's action, didn't move.

"Hurry up, Maranta," she whispered. "We don't have all day." Marigold reached out for Maranta to push her through the open door.

"Where are you going, Marigold?"

"*We* are going to the railway station—to see Shaun."

"No, Marigold. Feena'll get suspicious and come inside to look for us."

"We'll be back before she gets worried, if you'll only hurry."

"But what about Papa?"

"Are you going to be a frightened ninny all your life, Maranta? You know *I'll* be the one he punishes if he finds out. You're too much like Maman for Papa ever to be mad at you." Marigold gave her twin sister a final push and softly closed the door to Mrs. Windom's shop behind them.

Reluctantly, Maranta followed her headstrong sister in the direction of Line Street and the railway station. She couldn't understand how Marigold dared to deliberately disobey their father. What if he should catch them going where they had no business, unchaperoned? Maranta shuddered, just thinking about it.

The familiar sights of Charleston went unnoticed and unsavored as Maranta followed her sister past Calhoun Street and Vanderhorst, on past Radcliffe and Spring, until they reached their destination.

The noisy locomotive belched black smoke and soot into the air, while it gathered steam to start on its journey. Bales of cotton had been loaded on a barrier car to protect the passengers from the stray sparks and flames spewing from the engine. And the pine knots to be used as torches to light the way home to Charleston that evening were neatly stacked in one corner of the shiny new locomotive.

Relieved that the train was still in the station, Marigold left Maranta outside to keep watch while she slipped into the station house. The golden-haired girl hesitated, her eyes searching for Shaun Banagher.

Although his back was to her, there was no mistaking him. His height alone would single him out from the rest, without the familiar proud tilt to his head.

Almost as if sensing eyes upon him, the tall, well-built young man turned. "Marigold," he said in surprise, taking a step toward her, "what are you doing here?"

"I had to see you, Shaun."

He glanced toward the passenger door and quickly ushered the girl into the stationmaster's empty office.

"What's so important that you risked coming here alone?" he asked, his voice filled with disapproval.

"Maranta is with me," Marigold assured him. "She's waiting outside."

Ignoring his frown, the girl rushed on. "Oh, Shaun. Papa is in an awful temper. He found out that I've been meeting you at the battery. And now he has threatened to marry me off to the next dandy who offers for me."

The man laughed and tenderly smoothed an errant curl that peeked from under the girl's silk bonnet.

"You're just being dramatic, Marigold—as usual."

The girl's tawny eyes clouded. "Then you don't care if I . . . marry someone else?" she whispered.

The smile disappeared and Shaun's voice changed. "You will marry no one but me, Marigold. But I won't go to your father, penniless. In a few months . . ."

"A few months," she repeated, interrupting. "By then, it'll be too late. If you really love me, you will . . ."

The noise of the clanging bell muffled the girl's voice. The man gazed out the window at the locomotive and back to the girl. "Marigold, I have to go. The train is ready to leave."

"Then goodbye, Shaun," she said, turning her face from him.

She felt his arms tighten around her while his angry green eyes explored her piquant face.

"Just what do you mean by that?" he asked.

"I shan't see you again, Shaun. There evidently is no hope for us."

His kiss brushed away the trembling of her lips, and Shaun groaned with the sudden flaring of passion.

Outside the station house, Marigold's twin, Maranta, sat on the wooden bench, her face partially hidden under the ruffled parasol that shaded her alabaster complexion from the fierce September sun. With each hiss of the locomotive building up its steam, Maranta gave a start.

Her troubled, dark, satin eyes, looking for Marigold, glanced anxiously toward the station door and then back toward the street. Why didn't Marigold hurry? It was already past time for them to be at the house where the family was waiting.

The longer she sat, the more uncomfortable she became. The heat caused little rivulets of moisture to gather between her breasts, and she could feel the wetness trickle down her blue afternoon dress. And she was thirsty. Yet, there was nothing she could do except ignore both the heat and her thirst. She lowered the parasol closer to her face, shutting out everything but the view of the station door, and began to pray silently. "Please, Marigold. Please come before it's too late."

"Just as I suspected," the angry voice exploded, breaking into her thoughts and causing the young girl to jump. She looked up into the tawny, stormy eyes of her father, Robert Tabor.

"P-Papa," the girl stammered, hastily removing herself from the wooden bench.

"Go to the carriage, Maranta. I will deal with you later."

His stern tone frightened her, but her fear was more for Marigold than for herself. Maranta hesitated and then spoke, her own voice little more than a whisper over the noisy locomotive.

"Don't be . . . too hard on Marigold, Papa. She . . . she loves him, Papa."

"That is no excuse for your behavior, coming unchaperoned to the rail station."

"Yes, Papa." She stood for a moment, watching her father's back as he disappeared into the station. And then, she slowly walked to the family carriage and, climbing into the hooded vehicle, was thankful to be safe from curious eyes.

The black woman, Feena, sat on the seat with the driver. She wouldn't look at Maranta and she grumbled to herself to indicate her annoyance at the trick the girls had played on her.

"I am sorry, Feena," Maranta apologized.

But the old woman pretended not to hear. She kept her head turned from the girl and watched the locomotive with an exaggerated interest.

Poor Marigold. Why did she constantly court trouble by not only seeking out the man she had been forbidden to see again, but by staying far too long? Feena was bound to suspect something while she waited outside the dress shop for such a long time.

Fearfully, Maranta stared toward the station. And then she saw them. Her father, with his slight limp breaking his long stride into an irregular gait, and Marigold, walking beside him, her face set in an almost identical stubborn expression, her golden hair a brighter, burnished version of the man's.

Robert Tabor handed Marigold into the carriage, and the driver, waiting for them to be seated, started the horses away from Line Street at Robert's nod and headed toward the townhouse that looked over the Charleston harbor.

"Are you going to tell Maman?" Marigold asked, slightly uneasy.

"Not until after the christening," her father replied. "I don't want to spoil the day for your mother."

Marigold relaxed at his words and cast a relieved glance at Maranta. Once again, Robert Tabor's overwhelming love for his French Creole wife, Eulalie, had postponed immediate chastisement. And later, he would have cooled down enough, so that Marigold's punishment would not be too severe, or so she thought.

The horses' hooves on the cobbled streets were the only noise of the early afternoon. In the silence that enveloped the carriage, Marigold gave herself up to thinking about Shaun. A softness crept over her face as her fingers, going to her mouth, touched the delicate spot that still tingled from the feel of Shaun's lips upon hers.

At the sight of the large Palladian-design house at the end of the street, the driver slowed the carriage and brought it to a stop before the door of the two-and-a-half-story white frame house sitting majestically on its high basement.

"Take the girls up the back stairs, Feena, while I go in the front," Robert ordered the black servant. "And see that they are presentable as quickly as possible."

"Yes, Monsieur Robert," Feena replied, her dark eyes still showing her consternation at their afternoon prank.

Robert hurriedly handed down each girl from the carriage and watched them disappear through the side gate. Lightly touching the ornamental iron railing that he had added a few years previously to the house, he climbed the sweeping front steps.

He had been lucky to acquire the larger house when Robbie was born, since they had outgrown the one on Tradd Street. But it was becoming increasingly expensive to keep up two houses—Midgard, the plantation house, and this one in town—especially with the declining price of cotton.

Robert paused and, scowling, looked out toward the sea and the brilliant blue sky before he went through the front door that the servant held open for him. A tender look replaced his frown at the sight of his wife Eulalie walking toward him with the baby in her arms.

Maranta and Marigold, careful to make as little noise as possible, dashed up the back stairs. Feena was directly behind them, puffing from the exertion of the hot afternoon.

"There will be no time for a tub bath," a sour-faced Feena informed them. "Sponge off quickly and I will help you into your dresses."

Anxious to forget the unpleasant episode, Maranta rushed to the basin on her side of the room. She drank a glass of water and then poured the rest of the liquid from the pitcher into the earthenware bowl, dipping her fingers into the cool water to splash on her face.

Maranta and Marigold, in their camisoles and pantalettes, waited for Feena to lace them into their light corsets. The old woman was still mad. Marigold could tell from the way she drew the strings together and tied them. But Marigold said nothing. She stood still while Feena helped

14

Maranta into her yellow silk dress. And then Marigold felt her own pale green crepe sliding over her golden curls.

When the dresses were in place and buttoned, Feena left them so she might get ready herself; for the old servant was not about to miss the christening of the latest Tabor infant because of the twins' antics.

In silence, Maranta and Marigold brushed their hair, and with a last glimpse in the mirror to make sure nothing had been forgotten, they hurried from the bedroom. Side by side they walked down the hall to the formal parlor where everyone had gathered.

"To think—we'll soon be eighteen, and Maman and Papa are still having babies," Marigold whispered to Maranta in disgust. "You would think Papa would know better by now and leave Maman alone."

"Marigold," her twin reprimanded. "Babies come from God, and I . . . I'm happy that He has blessed Maman and Papa with another child."

"Oh, Maranta, you are so naive. Maman is thirty-eight years old—*thirty-eight,* Maranta. Most of my friends' mothers don't even *sleep* with their husbands, much less make babies with them."

At Marigold's words, Maranta's dark eyes widened in her gentle, small face. "Please, Souci," Maranta whispered, reverting to her sister's pet name. "S-Someone might hear you. We're in enough trouble already."

The door to the parlor opened, and Arthur Metcalfe, their father's best friend, quickly drew them inside. "I thought I heard your voices," he greeted the twins, taking each under his arm to lead them into the room. And not a moment too soon, for everyone was assembled and waiting; even their little brother Robbie stood patiently in his place. Maranta and her sister had time only to curtsy briefly to the guests, before the priest, in his robes, beckoned them to come forward.

It had been decided to have the christening at home rather than in the church so that the baby, Raven, would not risk being exposed to the fever that was beginning to spread once more throughout the city.

Marigold watched while Arthur leaned over and took the sleeping child from Eulalie's arms. The man stared down at the baby, and then he looked toward Eulalie with love and pain undisguised in his soft, blue eyes. Suddenly, Marigold's own eyes widened. Why, Uncle Arthur was in love with her maman! Arthur's eyes were instantly hooded, hiding the pain, while he carried the baby toward the priest, with Maranta and Marigold, the baby's godmothers, at his side.

Silently, Marigold stood, hearing little of the rites. Her mind spun with the sudden revelation. All these years—Uncle Arthur—loving her mother. Was that why he had never married?

Marigold looked at her father and then back to Arthur. Gentle, kindhearted Arthur had never been a match for Robert Tabor, Marigold knew. Robert Tabor had only to reach out for what he wanted; he was never denied. And losing something he had acquired was completely foreign to him.

So now, Arthur had to be content with holding the dark-haired baby in the white lace christening gown, and promising to be responsible, as a godfather, for the son of the woman he loved.

Marigold dismissed the twinge of pity for Arthur. Her mind went to Shaun instead—*her* Shaun now, if what she was planning worked out. For almost a year, Shaun had labored long hours, going without decent clothes and other necessities, saving every penny for the day when he and Marigold could be married.

But she knew that time had run out. They could afford to wait no longer while Shaun accumulated more money. Her father's threat to find a husband for her—someone other than Shaun Banagher—was uppermost in her mind.

The girl's chin lifted in an unobserved challenge. For once, Robert Tabor would not have his way, she decided.

". . . Lyle Ravenal Tabor, child of the covenant . . ." the priest intoned, bringing Marigold's mind back to the ceremony taking place.

Maranta, standing on the other side of the baby, looked

happily into her new little brother's face. He had the same dark coloring she and her mother had.

When the ceremony was over, Robert Tabor stepped forward and claimed his son from Arthur's arms. His fierce, possessive look encompassed not only his youngest child, but Eulalie, his wife, as well. And Maranta, seeing it, remembered what Marigold had said on their way to the parlor.

Unexpectedly, Maranta shivered. Although she loved her father, even *he* frightened her. She was glad that she would never have to submit to any man. In two days' time, she would be eighteen, and on her birthday, she planned to ask permission to enter the convent.

2

Eighteen summers, and the twins had never once set foot on the island where they had been born—Tabor Island, just off the coast of Charleston.

The old tabby house, built of oyster shells and lime, was gone, Marigold knew, leveled by the hurricane that swept the island on the day of their birth. Feena had told her that much. But everything else remained a mystery. And any effort to get her mother to talk about that summer was met with defeat. Today, on their eighteenth birthday, she was sure it would be no different.

Once, using her brother's telescope, Marigold had been able to see the ancient lighthouse rising out of the mist surrounding the island. But that was all. They had never been allowed to get close enough to see the remains of the old house, or what the island actually looked like.

Now, standing in the bedroom she shared with her twin, Marigold glanced at her mother, who waited for the two girls to finish dressing for their party. Eulalie sat in the window seat and stared out the panes of glass, miles away in thought. Marigold watched her mother for a moment. Was she, too, thinking of the island and what had happened that day so long ago?

At the rustling of the dresses, Eulalie turned from the window and gazed at her daughters. For the first time since they were babies, the twins were dressed exactly alike, in the elegant dresses that Mrs. Windom had made for them—white moire silk, with yards of matching lace around the hems. The sleeves were billowing puffs, flaring out from the shoulders almost to the elbows, and by their enormous size, dwarfing the tiny waists, before the skirts expanded in a cone shape of voluptuous proportions.

"How beautiful you both are," Eulalie said with pride in her serene dark eyes. She opened the two small velvet boxes that lay in her lap and summoned the girls to her side. "Before we go to the salon, I would like to give you your first present—from your father and me."

She held out the exquisitely shaped gold lockets on thin, delicate chains, and with a kiss for each daughter, she fastened the intricate golden clasps around their necks. "Happy Birthday, *mes petites*."

Excitedly, Maranta and Marigold dashed to the mirror to examine their gifts.

"It's beautiful," Maranta said, turning back to her mother. "Thank you, Maman. I shall always treasure it." Her serious dark eyes moistened with tears as she fingered the delicate gold chain.

"You silly goose," Marigold said, nudging her sister. "You always cry at the wrong time. As your elder sister, I command you to smile as a proper thank-you to Maman."

Maranta brushed her hand across her eyes. "Don't be overbearing, Marigold," she replied. "Just because you're a few minutes older doesn't mean you can boss me all the time."

A teasing glint came into Marigold's eyes. "You are not only younger, Maranta, but you stopped growing too soon, too."

As Maranta drew herself up to her full height, she said, "Two inches means nothing."

"Souci! Maranta!" Eulalie said, laughing. "Don't get into an argument now. It's time to go and greet your guests. And Marigold, please try to curb your tongue and be nicer to Crane. He seems to be quite taken with you," Eulalie admonished.

"Dear Crane," Marigold said, making a face. "If it weren't for nice Cousin Julie, I could easily tell her spoiled, adopted son to drop over the seawall."

"But you won't do that, will you, Marigold?" Maranta teased. "Instead, you'll have to smile prettily when he gives you his present and then suffer his not-so-cousinly kiss."

"And what about *you*, Maranta, with all the condessa's attentions these past two weeks—treating you like some pet puppy?" Marigold retaliated. "I wouldn't be surprised if she planned to put you in one of her wicker trunks to take you back to Brazil with her."

Maranta stuck her tongue out at Marigold.

Eulalie shook her head at her daughters. "If I did not know better, *mes enfants,* I would think you both about six years old! I trust you are now ready to act like young ladies?"

"*Oui,* Maman," they chorused and followed her out of the bedroom and toward the family parlor.

Marigold, her cheeks far too flushed, attempted to match Maranta's dainty steps down the hallway. Her thoughts were not on the party, but on her own plans and what was to take place later that night. And as she glanced at Maranta, she felt guilty that she had not confided in her sister. But the success of her venture had forced her to say nothing. She would make it up to her dark-haired twin later, she decided, when the family had forgiven her for her actions.

The packed valise was already hidden in the garden gazebo, waiting for the apppointed hour, late that same evening, when everyone would be asleep and Shaun would come for her. Marigold tugged at her lip as she remembered Shaun's objections to slipping away in the night. He had wanted to face Robert Tabor and ask properly for Marigold as his wife. But Marigold knew her father too well. He would never consent to such an alliance. No, this was the only way—to elope—and then it would be too late for Robert Tabor to stop their marriage.

Maranta, still mulling over Marigold's teasing words concerning the condessa, did not notice Marigold's high color or unusual quietness. The dark-haired girl followed her maman into the parlor, until the noise of well-wishers suddenly greeted her, banishing her troubled thoughts and turning the frown on Maranta's face into a smile.

Hands reached out to propel the twins into the center of the room. They were surrounded by Arthur, Crane and his mother Julie, the Condessa Louisa, and their father Robert Tabor, with the family priest, Father Ambrose, standing beside him.

Two important events, within the space of two days—first the christening, and now the twins' birthday, with the same small group of people attending both.

Outside the circle, a childish voice penetrated the noise. "The presents—'Ranta! Souci! Look at all your presents. Don't you want to open them? I'll help you."

They looked toward their small brother Robbie, who stood beside the tea table where the presents rested. Already his chubby fingers were toying with the ribbon of one of the larger presents.

"Not yet, Robbie," Eulalie said, her voice concealing her amusement at his eagerness to help. "We'll cut the cake first, and *then* your sisters will open their presents."

Seeing the look of disappointment on his face, Maranta stepped toward him. "Will you help us blow out the candles on the cake, Robbie?" she asked.

He nodded and with one lingering look at the presents, he went with his sisters into the dining room where twin cakes, one at each end of the table, blazed with their eighteen tapers.

An hour later, with the birthday cakes nearly demolished, Maranta and Marigold moved back into the drawing room. And again, Robbie ran to the tea table where the presents waited to be opened.

"Open this one first. It's the biggest," Robbie urged, lifting a large box and taking it to the settee where Maranta and Marigold sat together.

It was addressed to both girls, and with their little brother helping, the twins removed the ribbons and wrapping. Inside the box were identical teakwood chests, inlaid with ivory and mother-of-pearl. One for each girl.

"To my godchild, Maranta—To my godchild, Marigold," the identical cards read, and the name, "Uncle Arthur."

Immediately the two girls laid aside the beautiful gifts and ran to where Arthur was sitting. He stood up to receive their kisses.

"Thank you, Uncle Arthur. Thank you," they chorused,

22

and his pale blue eyes showed his pleasure at their enthusiasm.

Robbie continued to preside over the presents, choosing the ones to be opened next. But just as he reached for a long, slender package, the tall, dark-haired Crane stepped forward and took it from Robbie's hand.

Crane walked toward Marigold, and leaning over, he kissed the girl on both cheeks. "Happy Birthday, Marigold," he said, handing her his gift.

With a barely disguised sound of annoyance at Crane's uncousinly kisses, Marigold moved her head and quickly lifted the lid of the small box. Her amber eyes stared in disbelief at the gaudy brooch—chips of garnets encircled by mother-of-pearl and embedded in filigreed gold. Whatever Crane had paid for the brooch was far too much. She would never be caught wearing it.

"Garnets. How generous of you, Crane."

At Marigold's polite reply, Maranta stifled a giggle. She knew how much her twin detested garnets. Then her attention turned to the package that Robbie thrust in her lap.

The old condessa, seated across the room with her companion, Dona Isobel, watched with interest while Maranta untied the ribbons.

Suddenly, Maranta's fingers became clumsy and the ribbons knotted. A coldness swept over her, and for a moment, Maranta did not want to open the package. But the feeling passed, and she continued to work with the knotted ribbon until the package was open.

The dark-haired girl gasped as she stared down at the gift—a brilliant cross that rested on a blue velvet background, its diamonds and pearls, elegant and exquisite, overwhelming her.

"Aren't you going to show us your present, Maranta?" Cousin Julie asked in an amused voice. "And tell us who has given it to you?"

Maranta lifted the heavy chain, and her troubled eyes sought out her mother. "Maman?" she whispered, as if she needed guidance. With a reassuring nod from Eulalie, the girl said, "It is a very beautiful cross—from the condessa."

23

With the murmurs of everyone echoing in her ears, Maranta walked hesitantly across the room and laid her cheek against the thin, wrinkled cheek of the aristocratic old woman.

"Thank you, Condessa Louisa. The cross is very—beautiful. But you shouldn't have given me anything so grand," she added.

"Nonsense, my dear," the woman said. "I wanted you to have it. It suits you well."

The condessa and Dona Isobel exchanged a fleeting, satisfied glance as Maranta returned to the settee.

Much later that night, Marigold sat on the high tester bed and licked the vanilla icing from her fingers, while Maranta carefully put her birthday presents away into the lowboy by the window.

"What did I tell you," Marigold said, eyeing the cross of pearls and diamonds that the Portuguese woman had given to Maranta. "The condessa clearly prefers you to me, and her choice of gifts proves it. There's nothing extravagant about embroidered handkerchiefs," she added, touching the small box at the end of her bed with her toe.

"I would rather have the handkerchiefs," Maranta said, her solemn dark eyes looking down at the cross in her hands. "I have a feeling that this is a family heirloom, and the condessa should not have given it to me."

"But if you become a part of the Monteiro family, then it won't matter, will it? We all know the condessa is shopping for a suitable bride for her son."

"But I don't plan to marry, Souci. You know that."

"Is that why you didn't bring a piece of cake to put under your pillow—so you couldn't dream about the man you're to marry?"

"That's only with wedding cake, Souci, not birthday cake. And anyway—you only have crumbs left. You didn't plan very well, did you, if you expected to dream of your future husband?"

Marigold tossed her golden hair over her shoulder and replied, "I don't need to dream about him. I already know the one I'm going to marry."

"Shaun? Or Crane?"

Marigold made a face at the mention of Crane's name. "Why, Shaun, of course."

"What if Papa won't let you marry him?"

"That doesn't matter now. I'm . . ." Marigold stopped and in an impatient voice said, "Oh, do hurry and put on your gown, Maranta. I'm tired and want to go to sleep. And the candlelight is hurting my eyes."

Surprised at her request, Maranta said, "Aren't you feeling well, Marigold? Usually you're the one who wants to keep the light burning half the night."

Marigold pulled the sheet over her head without replying. And Maranta, sensing her sister's impatient mood, quickly slipped into her gown and blew out the candle beside her bed.

With guests in the house, it had been impossible for Maranta to find time to be alone with her parents—to get permission to enter the convent. But Cousin Julie and Crane were leaving the next day, and things should quiet down. She would just have to wait for the right moment to approach her parents. Maranta knelt by the side of the bed and began her evening prayers.

"Now, what are you doing, Maranta?" Marigold's voice cut through the darkness of the room.

There was a pause, and then Maranta answered, "I'm saying my prayers as I usually do each evening."

Marigold started to reply and then changed her mind. She merely sighed. There was no need to try to rush Maranta, even though Shaun might already be waiting in the garden.

Waiting. The waiting had made the day seem interminable. Through breakfast, luncheon, the party, and then the dinner later that night—having to thank everyone for the birthday gifts—having to smile and pretend to be enjoying the day, and all the time wondering if her valise might be discovered by a servant and brought back into the house—wondering if Shaun might have trouble hiring a carriage at the last minute—and now, more waiting—for Maranta to go to sleep and the household to settle down for the night.

Marigold could hear Maranta climbing into bed. Soon, now—

She listened as the old clock in the downstairs hall wheezed its message, each chime seemingly slower than the previous one. Marigold counted until the twelfth chime sounded and died away. And then, total silence, except for Maranta's even breathing that indicated she was asleep. Good. Now she could get up without fear of disturbing her sister.

"Shaun, I'm coming," Marigold whispered, willing the message to reach him while she climbed out of bed and groped toward the wardrobe to rescue her petticoats and dress.

Marigold's hand stopped in midair in its search; for in the distance, a baby began to cry. Marigold remained frozen, listening to the sudden stirring down the hall toward the nursery. Raven's cries grew louder, and Marigold knew he would not go to sleep again until the wet nurse had satisfied his hunger. Just her luck for the baby to wake up, tonight of all nights. But she could still get dressed, Marigold decided. And when the house became quiet again, she would be ready to join Shaun in the garden.

The small bit of moonlight seeped through the curtains, but she dared not look out the window toward the enclosed garden to see if Shaun were there. Somehow, she was superstitious about that. Instead, she removed the silk petticoats and dress from the wardrobe and tiptoed back to her bed with them.

The petticoats rustled as Marigold slipped them over her head. She had never noticed how noisy it was to get dressed, especially by oneself. Each sound seemed magnified in the darkness.

Marigold glanced toward her sister's bed before continuing with her dressing. But Maranta had not stirred. Quickly, Marigold loosened her hair from its confining plait and ran her hands through it. That would have to suffice. No time for an elaborate coiffure, even if she could see.

At last, Marigold felt for her kid slippers under the

bed. First one, and then the other—and her reticule, hidden under her pillow—

The bedroom door creaked open, and Marigold, alarmed at the sound, hurriedly got back into bed, dropping her reticule on the floor and pulling up the spread to shield her fully clad body. Surely, Feena was not keeping watch at night, too. Could it be her father? Had he heard her and come to see what she was doing up so late at night?

Hardly daring to breathe, Marigold watched the door. It opened all the way, and a small form stepped over the threshold.

" 'Ranta!" the voice called softly. "I'm thirsty."

It was seven-year-old Robbie, intent on waking up Maranta.

Marigold leaped from her bed and whispered, "Robbie, what are you doing up?"

"Raven woke me," he complained. "And I want some water. I'm thirsty."

"Ssh—Don't talk so loud. Come, and I'll give you some water from my pitcher," Marigold promised. She took her brother by the hand, and with only the moonlight to guide her, she led him across the room to the stand where the pitcher rested.

"That's enough, little piglet," Marigold scolded, taking the second cup from him. "And now, back to bed, before someone catches you."

"Souci . . ."

"Hush, Robbie. Please go back to bed like a good little boy."

He hesitated. "Will you walk partway with me? The hall is awful dark."

Reconciled to seeing him down the hall to his door, Marigold put her arm around the little boy and walked with him to his own bedroom.

"Can you make it from here?" Marigold asked at the door. "Oh, that's all right. I might as well tuck you in, now that I've come this far."

Marigold leaned down and brushed the burnished gold hair from the child's forehead. "Good night, Robbie."

She planted a kiss on his chubby face and then backed away from the bed.

"Souci, I'm sorry that I . . ."

"That's all right, Robbie." Marigold cut him off. "Now go to sleep."

She disappeared and Robbie sighed. She had not let him explain about the note. He was sorry that he had lost it that afternoon before giving it to her. But maybe it wasn't so important, after all. And he would tell her about it tomorrow. With that decision made, Robbie turned over on his side and went to sleep.

3

Shaun was not in the garden. Marigold waited in the gazebo, with her valise at her feet. In the darkness, she hugged her bombazine cloak closer to her body and listened for the slightest sound that would alert her to Shaun's coming.

But there was nothing, except the occasional bark of Mr. Gammon's dog down the street. Lucky for her that Jason's hunting dogs were at Midgard. It would not have done for her older brother's hounds to be in the garden with her. They would have given her away immediately.

While Marigold watched, the moon began its descent from high in the sky. It hovered near the treetops before finally plummeting out of sight. Gradually, Marigold's head drooped against her chest and her eyes closed.

The sea breeze, rising from the ocean, spread over the coastal battery and invaded the garden where Marigold rested. With a sudden flapping noise, the wind whipped the hem of the girl's cloak against the valise. She sat up with a start. Had she gone to sleep? And if so, for how long?

Marigold rubbed her eyes impatiently and listened. Horses' hooves, clattering on the cobblestoned street, grew louder and then stopped.

It had to be Shaun coming for her. Eagerly, Marigold clutched the handle of her valise and listened for the gate to open and close. At its click, she felt relief. She had been so afraid that something would stop him from coming. But now, Shaun was here.

When the tall, dark figure started down the path, Marigold could wait no longer. Grabbing up her valise, she hurried from the gazebo to meet him.

"Shaun," she whispered, her mouth curving into a welcoming smile. But the voice that greeted her was not

Shaun's voice. Marigold stiffened when she recognized the man standing before her.

"He's not coming for you, cousin," he said, taking the valise from her hand. "He never intended to elope with you tonight."

It was her cousin, Crane—not Shaun. And what was he saying? That Shaun was not coming?

"I . . . I don't believe you," Marigold responded in a faltering voice. "Something's happened to him. I know it. Tell me, Crane. What's happened?"

A harsh laugh escaped from Crane's lips. "What's happened?" he repeated. "Do you really want to know, Marigold?"

"Yes," she hissed with impatience. "Tell me."

"Then I suggest we go where we can't be seen. It is a long tale, and *I* don't relish being caught by your father in such a compromising situation. Even if *your* reputation is ruined, I still have mine to think about," he added in a pious tone.

Marigold, swallowing the lump in her throat, ignored his barb and walked back toward the gazebo. Crane followed, bringing her valise down the path with him.

When they were seated on the bench inside, Crane, speaking more gently to her, said, "Marigold, I wish there were some way I could tell you the truth without hurting you."

She clasped her hands tightly together and said nothing, waiting for Crane to continue. Her body shivered, and she drew her cloak closer around her.

"Are you cold?" he asked, suddenly solicitous.

"Yes—no," Marigold hedged, not wanting her cousin to know the effect his words had on her.

"Shaun Banagher is a bounder. He does not deserve anyone as beautiful as you . . ."

"For heaven's sake, Crane, spare me the sympathy and get on with it," she said, forgetting to keep her voice low.

"All right, Marigold. Even though it hurts me to tell you. It was all a joke—from the very beginning. A bet

Shaun Banagher made at Keppie's Tavern last December, when he had had too much to drink."

"A bet? What kind of bet?"

"That he could get the proudest girl in all of Charleston to fall for him and agree to run away with him. He didn't even choose you, Marigold. The tavern keeper did. Shaun merely took up the challenge. And from the looks of things, he won the bet."

"I don't believe you, Crane." Marigold's voice was horrified at Crane's words.

"Would you believe me if I took you down to the tavern where he is now, and let you hear it for yourself?"

"You mean S-Shaun's discussing me—in a c-common bar?"

"Yes. And still drinking to his victory when I left."

Marigold turned to flee from Crane and his cruel words. She could not believe it of Shaun. Yet, how would Crane know that she had planned to elope that night with Shaun—unless Shaun himself had told it?

"Just a minute, Marigold," he said, putting his hand on her arm to stop her from escaping. "There *is* a solution, you know. You could marry *me*. That way, no one would believe that Shaun had jilted you. And he would have to return his winnings."

Crane's offer of marriage was the final insult. Marigold's temper overrode her caution, and she blurted out her refusal. "I would sooner be disgraced and in hell before I would consider marrying *you,* Crane."

His hand tightened on her arm. "Well then, you shall have your wish, cousin. For soon, all of Charleston will be laughing at you. You know how gossip spreads."

Marigold flung off Crane's hand from her arm, and with tears blurring her sight, she walked proudly down the path toward the house.

To get to her room before the weeping began— that was all she asked. And once inside her bedroom, she hurled herself onto the bed and smothered her sobs in the feather down pillow.

Maranta, still sleeping soundly in the other bed, was

not aware that, for Marigold, the world had come to an end.

"Miss Marigold, wake up," Feena's voice urged her. "Your papa wants to see you right away."

Vaguely, the woman's voice penetrated her consciousness, but Marigold did not want to wake up. Something too painful was waiting for her, ready to break her heart. The girl groaned and turned over, hiding her face from the light.

"No use to pretend you're still asleep, Miss Marigold," Feena remonstrated. "I don't know what you did last night to make your papa so angry and your maman so sad. But you'd better get those dainty feet out of bed and on the way to the library."

The tawny yellow cat's eyes were dull and lifeless in Marigold's face as they surveyed the people in the library—the triumphant Crane Caldwell, standing beside the drapery of the French doors; her father Robert Tabor, scowling behind his mahogany desk; and her mother Eulalie, seated quietly on the divan.

"You wished to see me, Papa?" Marigold asked, hiding her nervousness at his summons.

The man stared at her with narrowed eyes while his hand opened and closed over the gold letter opener on his desk.

"Yes, Marigold," he answered finally. "Crane has informed me of what happened last night—that you were planning to run away with the man I had forbidden you to see again. Do you deny it, Marigold?" he asked.

"No, Papa," she replied and then was silent.

"Is that all you have to say for yourself?" Robert asked, his temper rising. "No apology—no word of explanation to your mother or me?"

"I . . . am sure that Crane has . . . told you everything."

"Oh, Souci," Eulalie said, her voice showing her sadness.

Marigold waited in the center of the room and stared ahead, looking neither at her mother or father. She would not beg for forgiveness in front of Crane. Instead, she stood as some prisoner in the dock, waiting for her sentence—the punishment to be meted out for her behavior—for her sin of misjudging Shaun Banagher, thinking he truly loved her as she had loved him.

"Then, Crane's solution seems to be the only possible one," Robert Tabor pronounced, "to keep you from being utterly disgraced. No decent low country family would ever welcome you as a daughter-in-law, when word gets out of last night's escapade."

Her father's voice was heavy to match her own heavy heart. "Is that all, Papa?" Marigold asked, still standing before him.

"For now. You may go to your room, Marigold, until I can make the proper arrangements for your marriage to Crane."

Her father's words barely registered. Dismissed, she turned and walked slowly out the door without looking in Crane's direction and up the stairs to her room.

And Robert Tabor, still seated at the desk, watched as Eulalie, with tears in her eyes, excused herself from the room.

Marigold's submissiveness was something new—something that Robert did not know how to deal with. If she had complained or refused Crane's offer, as he had expected her to do . . . But Marigold was like a ghost, with no life left in her—a fact that chilled Robert much more than Marigold's wayward behavior.

Huddled in the window seat, Marigold stared out the window into the garden. No sun was visible. The sky was overcast, with clouds hovering in the distance. A suitable day for what had taken place—the burial of all her dreams, the complete destruction of her considerable pride. How could Shaun do this to her—jilt her and then laugh about it, broadcast it to the world? Marigold put her hands over her ears to drown out the imagined laughter. And it was in this position that Eulalie found her, after knocking at her door and getting no answer.

"Souci," Eulalie called in her soft, gentle voice, waiting for Marigold to take her hands from her ears.

Marigold looked up, seeing her mother before her.

"You do not have to marry Crane, you know," Eulalie assured her daughter. "If you wish, I will talk with your father. Perhaps I can persuade him to let you wait, at least."

"I don't care about anything anymore," Marigold replied. "I only know I can't stay in Charleston." Marigold's voice broke, and she looked out into the garden again.

"Do you love Shaun Banagher that much—to leave your family and the life you know, just to avoid seeing him again?"

Feeling the intensity of her mother's question, Marigold stared at Eulalie. How could she know the feeling inside, unless. . . ?

Eulalie's lip trembled. It seemed little more than yesterday that she was busy packing her own valise to escape Columbia, the state capital, and Robert Tabor. Her mind, skipping over the years, was brought back to the present by Marigold's words.

"I . . . love no one."

Despite her denial, Eulalie was not convinced. Yet, if Marigold wanted to leave Charleston, it might be best for her to marry her cousin.

"Crane loves you, Marigold. He would be . . . kind to you, I am sure. And Julie is pleased to think she might have you as a daughter. I would miss you, of course. But daughters have a way of getting married and leaving their mothers. I knew it would happen some day, but not quite this soon." Eulalie's attempt at lightness belied the sadness in her eyes. "And even Maranta. There is a possibility that she will leave us, too," Eulalie added.

"Then Papa has given her permission to enter the convent?" Marigold asked.

"The convent? No, Robert would never consent to that . . ." Troubled anew, Eulalie hesitated. "But we were speaking of *you*, Marigold. The other can . . . wait—for the moment."

34

"Where is Maranta?" Marigold asked, realizing she had not seen her twin that morning.

"She went with Julie and the condessa to . . ."

"Souci," the voice interrupted, as her twin pushed open the door to their bedroom. "Is it true? Are you actually going to marry Crane? But what about Sh—?"

Maranta stopped, putting her hand up to her mouth when she saw her mother. "Oh, I'm sorry, Maman. Did I interrupt something?"

"I was just leaving," Eulalie replied. "But I wish you would come into the room in a more ladylike manner, Maranta."

"I am . . . sorry, Maman," the girl apologized. "I shall . . . try to remember."

Eulalie turned back to Marigold. "Then you have no objections?" she asked, finishing her conversation with Marigold.

Marigold shrugged her shoulders, indicating her lack of interest in the question. And her mother, forced to consider it as her final answer, left the room.

"What was that all about?" Maranta asked. "Is it true that you're really going to marry Cousin Crane?"

"It would seem so," Marigold answered.

"But what about Shaun? Aren't you in love with him?"

"It appears that Shaun does not love *me*. That puts a stop to any plans I might have had, doesn't it?" Marigold said, with no attempt to hide the bitterness in her voice.

"Souci," Maranta murmured, "I'm so sorry." She leaned over and kissed her sister on the cheek, seeking to comfort her.

"For heaven's sake, Maranta. Can't you be anything but sorry? That's all you've said from the minute you came into the room."

"I'm s—" She stopped herself from saying it again. Maranta, silent, moved to the wardrobe and took off her morning dress. She hung it up carefully and then removed the pins from her long, dark hair. Maranta began brushing the thick, black strands, while her troubled thoughts

35

dwelled on her golden-haired twin, still huddled miserably in the window seat.

The hurried preparations for Marigold's wedding began, with invitations hand-delivered by the servants to the Tabor friends who were in residence in Charleston.

The choice of the Tabor garden was not a surprise. It was much healthier for friends to gather in the open air, because of the fever. To many, it was not even surprising that Marigold was marrying her cousin—only that the wedding was taking place in such a hurry—three days from the time the invitations were issued. Some speculated that the bridegroom was impatient to get home to upper Carolina, since a new lode had been discovered in the Caldwell gold mine during his absence.

The day before the ceremony, a small trunk was brought from the attic of the plantation house. It contained the fragile veil of Alençon lace that Eulalie had worn in her own wedding to Robert Tabor.

The trunk was carried into Marigold's room, and Eulalie, tenderly lifting the veil, for a short moment closed her dark eyes and held the lace against her breast. And Marigold, choosing not to watch her mother and her remembrance of joy on her wedding day, turned her head. For Marigold, there was no joy, no love. Shaun had jilted her, forcing her to save face by marrying her cousin, whom she disliked.

On the morning of the wedding, another carriage arrived from Midgard, loaded with magnolia leaves and jasmine to decorate the garden. Throughout the day and up until that afternoon when Feena came to help her get dressed, Marigold had hoped that Shaun would send her some message, some excuse for not appearing, or even come, himself, to stop the marriage. Each time the giant brass knocker on the front door sounded, the golden-haired girl held her breath and waited for the sound of footsteps coming to her room.

Now, it was too late. Crane was waiting for her. Father Ambrose was waiting.

Marigold, thinking of the tragic ceremony that would link her forever with Crane Caldwell, pushed away the veil that Feena held for her.

"I cannot desecrate Maman's veil. I don't love Crane. Let Maman put the lace back into the trunk with her memories. I will do without it."

The old woman snorted. "The veil will soften your stubborn chin, *petite,* just as it did for your maman over twenty years ago."

Marigold looked at Feena in surprise. "Maman was reluctant to marry Papa?" she asked. "But how could that be? He adores her—and she loves him. Wasn't that true when they married?"

"Your maman had never set eyes on Monsieur Robert. How could she be expected to love him?"

"You mean—they met as strangers at the altar?"

"Worse than that, *cherie.* It was a proxy marriage. Another man stood in his place. And she didn't see Monsieur Robert for over a month after the ceremony."

While Feena talked, she pinned the veil in place. And Marigold, pondering Feena's information, said in a soft voice, "I . . . didn't know that."

"And I shouldn't have told you, *petite,* even now. But I wanted you to know that you are not the only woman who has protested the marriage bed."

Marigold stood before the mirror, staring at the white birthday dress, the veil of delicate lace covering her face. "Did Maman love someone else?" she asked.

"How do I know?" Feena's voice was suddenly irritable. "You will have to ask her that yourself."

Eulalie came into the room, and Marigold rushed to her mother. "Oh, Maman, I don't want to go through with it. I'm afraid."

Eulalie's sympathetic, dark eyes took in the golden beauty of the girl. No wonder Crane was in love with her. "Every girl is afraid on her wedding day," Eulalie said in a soothing voice.

"Even you? Were you afraid, Maman?"

"Oui, ma petite. I trembled from head to toe." Eulalie

smiled in a conspiratorial manner as she continued. "And I was even more frightened when I saw your papa for the first time. But Feena has probably already told you."

Marigold laughed. But a few minutes later, as she walked into the garden with her father, Marigold's topaz eyes became solemn, and her nervous hands almost crushed her bouquet; for standing beside Father Ambrose was Crane Caldwell—her future husband.

4

"Did you get the note to her, Chad?" the young man asked, painfully turning his body to face his friend.

"Aye, man. That I did. I gave it to her small brother, standing inside the gate. He promised to take it up to her right away."

The man dropped his head to the pillow again, and the pain in his face eased somewhat at Chad's reassuring words.

"Marigold—it's a beautiful name, isn't it, Chad? You know, they call her Souci at home. That's the French name for the flower—all golden, like her hair."

"Don't talk so much, Shaun," the man fussed. "You've got to save your strength to get well." He took the empty bowl from the bedside and placed it in the sink. "I'll be leaving you for a while now, so go to sleep, man."

Chad could not bear to listen to Shaun talk so lovingly about the bitch. He was in this condition because of her and still, she had run out on him, marrying her cousin.

But wasn't that the way the aristocracy lived? Marrying each other, not thinking an outsider's blood was good enough for them? But God! How was he going to tell Shaun Banagher that the girl he loved had married someone else and left Charleston?

And the final blow was to hear the Caldwell fellow brag that the girl had played Shaun for a fool, as well. Chad just hoped that no one at Keppie's Tavern would ever make the mistake of mentioning it in front of Shaun.

Shaun was a big man and strong. That was why he had gotten the job in the first place. Too dangerous for the slaves to load the unwieldy equipment onto the flatboat. Replacing an Irishman was so much cheaper than buying another slave. But Shaun had not minded, for he had

39

wanted the extra money. If only the other man's foot had not slipped, causing Shaun to be caught against the protruding metal spike.

When the pain in his chest returned and his breathing became labored, he gripped the sides of the bed with his hands. He had lost a lot of blood, but he would not die. He had so much to live for. Marigold—her face loomed before him, her long, golden hair catching the glint of the afternoon sun as it had that first time he had ever seen her, sitting in the train like a golden goddess. The image stayed with him until his vision blurred and he lost consciousness.

Maranta sat in the garden with her brother Robbie. A pall had descended on them ever since Marigold had left for Cedar Hill with her new husband Crane Caldwell and his mother Cousin Julie.

But at least today, Maranta was getting a respite from the condessa's constant demands—to fetch her shawl, or smelling salts, or digitalis that had been prescribed for her heart condition; for Eulalie had taken the Portuguese woman with her for a visit into the countryside to see a friend's magnificent gardens, and they would not be back until late.

Robbie, his attention on the last of the sticky, candied apple he was eating, finally stood up and rubbed his hands down the sides of his linen suit, until reprimanded by Maranta.

She took her handkerchief to wipe the rest of the caramel from his upper lip, and as she did so, Robbie looked at her and said, " 'Ranta, I . . . I don't like Cousin Crane. Do you?"

Startled at his confidence, Maranta did not answer immediately. She folded her handkerchief and placed it again in the pocket of her dress.

"Cousin Crane is our brother-in-law, Robbie," she explained. "We should all learn to like him, because of Marigold."

"But Marigold doesn't like him either," Robbie stated, with an obstinancy in his voice.

"Of course she likes him, Robbie. Otherwise she would never have married him."

"But that's what I don't understand. She told him that night in the garden that she'd rather be disgraced and in h-hell first. He just laughed when she ran back into the house. But then, she married him anyway. Do you think it was because Shaun didn't come that night?"

Maranta was surprised at her brother's question. But then she saw before her the lackluster Marigold—deep hurt revealed in her gold-flecked eyes. Maranta shivered as she remembered other things—Marigold's certainty that she would marry Shaun Banagher, despite their father's disapproval. And Marigold's impatience to cut off the light and go to sleep.

Had she planned to run away with Shaun Banagher that night? Had Crane stopped them? No, Robbie said that Shaun had not come. But had Marigold been expecting him?

"How do you know so much, Robbie? Were you out of bed that night?"

"Raven woke me," he said, "and then I got thirsty. I came to your room, but you . . ."

The words tumbled out, one after the other, while Maranta sat and listened with a sinking heart. Robbie left nothing out. For it had been a heavy burden on his mind, especially about the note he had lost.

". . . The man gave it to me at the gate. Only I dropped it, and when I went back to look for it, Cousin Crane had it in his hands and he was reading it. I tried to tell Marigold, but she wanted me to go on to sleep. 'Ranta, do you think it was *my* fault that Marigold had to leave Charleston?" Tears hovered on his golden lashes, threatening to spill over at any minute. "Cousin Crane said that everybody was going to be laughing at her."

Maranta comforted her small brother as best she could, putting her arms around him and hugging him. "No, Robbie. It was not your fault. But you *should* have taken the note straight to Marigold. You know that, don't you?"

He nodded and pressed his face closer to Maranta.

41

"But perhaps Crane gave her the note himself," Maranta added, although she knew that possibility was slim.

"Yes, maybe he did," Robbie said in a relieved voice, turning from Maranta to take up the blue and white ball that rested on the gazebo floor.

While Robbie kicked it down the path toward the house, Maranta remained seated, trying to decide what to do with the information her brother had imparted to her. What if the note had been from Shaun? Would it make any difference now that Marigold was already married to Crane?

Almost as if she saw Marigold standing before her in silent supplication, Maranta knew what she must do. Find out the truth from Shaun Banagher. But after that, what?

Maranta walked toward the carriage house to give instructions to the groom and then went in search of Feena. Even though her father had left for Taborville immediately after the wedding, Maranta would not risk his wrath by going out unchaperoned.

She found the black woman in the hall outside the nursery, but when confronted by Maranta's request to come with her, Feena shook her head.

"No," the woman stated emphatically. "Shaun Banagher spells trouble where your papa is concerned. Better for you not to get anywhere near the man. And besides, I'm busy." She continued folding the white squares of linen for the baby Raven.

"You will not go with me?"

"Not while your maman is out," Feena answered.

"Then I . . . I will have to go by myself." Maranta turned from the woman and began walking toward the stairs.

"Now, Miss Maranta, lamb," the woman said, putting down the folded squares and following the girl down the stairs, "you can't go by yourself. You know the trouble you and Miss Marigold got into last time."

Maranta paid no attention to the woman but opened the door and hurried toward the small landau that was waiting in the street in front of the house. She climbed into it with Feena directly behind her, grumbling all the time at the girl's waywardness.

"I always thought Miss Marigold was the headstrong one. Now you're acting just like her."

"I *have* to do it, Feena—for Marigold. You understand, don't you? Because of the note . . ."

"I understand we're *both* going to get into a peck of trouble. And what if you're right? Miss Marigold is already married, and nothing's going to change that."

The landau creaked as Feena settled herself beside Maranta, with the hastily snatched parasol opened to protect them from the sun.

Feena's French accent had diminished little over the years, even though her speech had taken on some of the subtleties of the low country. Maranta looked at the light-skinned woman who had traveled from New Orleans with Grandmère and Maman many years before to the Carolina plantation. Even though Feena's words might be true, Maranta could not back down now. She guided the pony toward the station house, while Feena mumbled her discontent.

"He's going to skin us both when he gets back from Taborville. And looking exactly like Miss Eulalie did when she was young isn't going to help you a bit with Monsieur Robert."

Maranta continued to her destination on Line Street. When the landau stopped, Feena got out with Maranta. She walked into the rail station a few paces behind the girl, and then out again, for Shaun Banagher was not at the station. So Maranta climbed back into the landau, crossed the tracks, and slowed the carriage, her eyes searching for Shaun Banagher's abode. Maranta came to a stop in front of one of the shanty cars.

With Feena beside her, Maranta knocked at the door and waited, but there was no answer from within.

"I don't like this a bit," Feena whispered. "If the man is ill, as the stationmaster said, then you have no business going inside. No telling *what* he has."

"If you're afraid, you can remain outside," Maranta suggested.

"Oh, no. You're not getting out of my sight," Feena

declared. "I'm sticking closer to you than molasses in a finger-poked biscuit."

Maranta knocked again, this time a little louder. "Chad?" a man's voice called out weakly, and at the sound, Maranta pushed open the door.

"It's . . . it's Maranta Tabor, Marigold's sister," she said, standing at the threshold. "May I c-come in, Mr. Banagher?"

"Maranta?"

The girl moved into the darkened shanty car, and Feena followed.

It took a moment for the girl's eyes to become adjusted to the darkness. And then she saw him, lying on a cot in the corner of the small room. A fetid air pervaded the closed space—the stench of the sick room.

The man, staring at the two women who had invaded his quarters, attempted to raise himself. At his sudden movement a red stain appeared on the linen wrapped around his chest and began to grow rapidly.

"*Mon Dieu*," Feena said, taking one look at Shaun Banagher. "The man is bleeding."

Feena, with a protective motion, waved Maranta back and headed toward the figure on the cot. With a swiftness that denied her age, the woman was beside the cot and lowering the man's head to the pillow.

"Do not move," she ordered. "You will make the bleeding worse."

Pieces of stained linen were heaped high upon the chair beside the cot. As Feena searched for fresh linen, Maranta spied some beside the window. Not heeding the woman's order to stay back, Maranta moved forward, handing the fresh strips to Feena.

In horror, she stared at the injured man. When had it happened—this accident? Was this why Shaun had not come that night, as he had evidently promised Marigold?

Shaun, oblivious to Feena's ministrations, gazed anxiously up into Maranta's startled face, his green eyes glazed with fever.

"The message—Marigold—she . . . understands?" the man inquired.

44

Maranta tried to keep her voice from quivering. "The message," she repeated. "We . . . we will talk about it later. When you are stronger."

So now she knew what the note must have contained. Marigold had not been abandoned by Shaun. But Crane Caldwell, taking advantage of the situation, had deliberately convinced Marigold otherwise. And Shaun Banagher, hanging on so desperately to life, was too weak to be told of the deception.

Maranta, belatedly reacting to the sick room and the sight of the bloodstained linen, felt dizzy. The closed room, the shallow breathing of Shaun Banagher, drove her to the front door for fresh air. With her hand over her mouth, Maranta collided with a stocky, brawny figure walking up the steps.

Chad, surprised to see the young girl before him, reached out to steady her. Then as he recognized Marigold Tabor's sister, his eyes became hostile and his body stiffened.

"What are you doing here?" he sneered. "Gloating over what your sister has done to him?"

At his harsh words, Maranta shook her head and reached for the railing. "What happened?" she asked in an anguished voice.

"A spike pierced his chest when he was loading a flatboat at the docks. It was a deep gash, and it's healing very slowly."

"When did it happen?"

"Why should that matter to you?"

Undeterred by his frosty manner, Maranta whispered, "Is he . . . going to die?"

Chad swallowed and a muscle twitched in his jaw. "He might, unless he can be kept still. He keeps trying to get out of bed to go to your sister—and each time, the bleeding starts again."

"Has a doctor been to see him?"

Chad's harsh laugh indicated his contempt at her question. "And who would pay for a doctor?" he asked. "You—Miss Tabor? Or your wealthy parents? Maybe you would, at that—to ease your guilty conscience.

Shaun won't spend a blasted penny on himself, even for getting a doctor, because he thinks Marigold Tabor is still waiting for him, and he'll need the money for her. And I can't tell him any different. Shaun would sell his soul to the devil for your sister's sake. But I guess he just couldn't make money fast enough to suit her."

"You don't talk to my Miss Maranta that way," Feena said, suddenly thrusting herself between Chad and Maranta. "Come, *ma petite*," she said to the girl. "We have done all we can for today."

Feena took the girl's arm and led her to the landau. The servant drove home, handling the reins, while Maranta, pale and silent, rode beside her, unable to get Chad's words out of her mind.

Robert Tabor, with the front door still open from his arrival home, heard the carriage. At first, he thought it was Eulalie, coming home with the condessa, and he stepped outside to assist them. But then he saw that it was the small landau and Feena was driving it, with Maranta beside her. Callie had not told him that she was out, also.

Quickly, Robert bounded down the steps when he saw Feena helping Maranta from the carriage and half-supporting her.

"What is the matter, Feena? What happened?" he asked, taking the woman's place at Maranta's side.

"Miss Maranta saw something that upset her."

Gently, Robert put his arms around his daughter and walked beside her up the stairs, Feena trailing along behind.

Robert frowned. Where had they been? Had Maranta seen a carriage accident? Or had the two, in their drive, stumbled upon a duel? He would find out later—after Maranta felt herself again.

"Callie," Robert Tabor called. "Bring some brandy upstairs to my daughter's room."

Maranta's color returned after she sipped the fiery liquid that her father had ordered.

Feena, fluttering around the room, aroused Robert's

46

suspicions. The old antagonism between the servant and the man who had married Eulalie Boisfeulet had not lessened over the years—the war between them was constant, and Feena was still banished back to Midgard whenever she did something to displease Robert Tabor.

He would like to have gotten rid of her altogether, but it was far too late for that. She had spent her entire life with the Boisfeulets, taking care of Eulalie as a child, and then Jason and the twins, Marigold and Maranta. She was quite old, but her loyalty was as fierce as ever, and it displeased Robert that he had seldom been included in that loyalty.

Robert looked at his young daughter, sitting in the big chair, her long, black hair spilling over her shoulders. So like Eulalie when he first knew her. And Feena, standing like some dark Valkyrie by her side, daring him to reprimand her for—he knew not what.

"You may go, Feena," Robert said to the woman. "I wish to talk with Maranta alone."

Feena's eyes widened, and she looked at Maranta, giving a silent warning to the girl before she obeyed Robert Tabor and left the room.

"Where did you go this afternoon, Maranta?" he asked.

Her hands fluttered against her skirts, and she cleared her throat. "To . . . to . . ."

"You'll have to speak louder than that, Maranta, for me to hear you."

She cleared her throat and started again. "Papa, don't be angry with me. I . . . I *had* to see him. It was not his fault that night that he didn't come. Marigold had no way of knowing, but Crane knew what had happened . . ."

The puzzled look gradually gave way to a slow angry red that crept over Robert's face to mar his handsome features.

"You are speaking of the man that Marigold had been forbidden to see?"

"F-Feena went with me. I . . . didn't go inside alone."

Robert moved and slapped his hand against his thigh. "What is it about this . . . this Shaun Banagher that

47

causes even an obedient daughter like you to lose every ounce of discretion, to . . . to follow in her wayward sister's footsteps? Does he have you mesmerized too, Maranta?"

"N-No, Papa."

He did not hear her; for he noisily paced back and forth in the room. "I'll teach that young pup a lesson he'll never forget. I'll have him horsewhipped."

Maranta, her face losing its color again, hurried to her father's side. 'P-Papa, I beg of you. Please don't harm him. He . . . he is ill."

"I care not for the man. It's *you,* Maranta, that I am concerned about." Robert stared down at the tiny pleading figure, and his terrible visage softened.

"What am I going to do with you, Maranta? Do I have to marry you off, too, to keep you away from the fellow?"

Maranta looked up into her father's tawny eyes with her own soft, dark doe eyes and replied, "That will not be necessary, Papa. I . . . I have wanted to tell you for a long time. Now that I am eighteen, I wish to enter the Convent of Our Blessed Lady."

The wind suddenly rose and whipped through the open window, and in the distance, a rumble of thunder beyond the battery announced the storm sweeping from sea to land. Maranta, standing in the middle of the room, watched as the stunned look on her father's face gave way to a frightening granite hardness.

Forgetting Shaun Banagher for the moment, he asked, "You could give up your family as easily as that?" His voice rose with the gathering intensity of the wind. A shutter flapped and the drops of rain pelted the bedroom window.

But neither Robert nor his daughter made a move to let down the sash.

"You would be content, shut away with your prayer beads and your 'Hail, Marys'—shut away from everything that you have ever known—your mother, Robbie, and the baby?"

"I . . . I would miss all of you, Papa," she assured

him. "You and Jason—and Marigold, too," she added in a small voice. "But I would be happy in a certain way, too—apart from the world."

His eyes narrowed and the years dispersed. Instead of Maranta, it was Eulalie who stood before him as she had years ago in her chaste nun's clothes. And the old feelings spawned themselves inside him. He shook himself to rid his mind of those emotions that he had thought were absolved—guilt, sorrow, jealousy—but his face remained set and hard.

"Then, you shall have your wish, Maranta . . ."

"Oh, thank you, Papa." She placed her hand on his arm, but he carefully removed it.

"I have not finished. You shall have your wish—to be separated from your family. But it will be to no convent that you will go."

Maranta looked up in alarm.

"I thought you were too sensitive to be removed from the bosom of your family," he continued, "but now, I see that I was wrong. It will come as no surprise to you, Maranta, that the Condessa Louisa wants you to return to Brazil with her—as the bride chosen for her son. I hesitated before, but when the woman returns this afternoon, I shall give my consent."

With those frigid words, Robert Tabor left the room, his limp more pronounced. And the frightened Maranta, kneeling by the bed, nervously twisted the fringe of the white canopy spread while her agitated voice prayed over and over again, "Help me, Blessed Lady."

5

Marigold uttered an epithet under her breath.

She sat at the crude dressing table in the bedroom of the inn and attempted to arrange her golden hair to hide the bruise on the right side of her face. She ignored the man eying her so insolently with his coal black eyes.

Finally he spoke and she could no longer ignore him. "It's a wasted effort, my dear," he said, "to try to conceal it. I will give you five more minutes to stare at yourself, and then we'll go downstairs. Mother is already waiting for us."

Marigold whirled from the dressing table bench and faced Crane, her husband, her snapping tawny eyes matching the golden flecks of her dress. "Won't it embarrass you for your mother to see what you have done to me?"

Crane laughed. "So you're going to blame it all on me, are you? If you had not been in such a hurry to escape me, it would not have happened."

"I . . . I hate you, Crane Caldwell," Marigold said and turned her back to him to take up the hairbrush again.

The man roused himself and came to stand behind the golden-haired girl, his eyes seeking hers in the mirror. "At least you're beginning to feel *something* again," he conceded, "even if it's hate."

His fingers tightened on her shoulders. "But don't think you'll be able to shirk your duties, Marigold. I intend for you to become a meek and obedient wife. And to show your gratefulness to me for rescuing you from a disgraceful situation."

Marigold bit her lip to keep the retort from spilling out. She was seething at his harsh treatment of her. How could she have been such a fool as to marry him? There

51

was something malicious about this cousin—no, no cousin of *hers*. They were not related by blood.

Marigold arose from the dressing table, and taking the lightweight evening shawl from the chair, she went toward the door and stood aside for Crane to open it.

Her mind was busy as she walked to the small private dining room that lay to the right of the larger, main dining room of the inn. She hated *all* men, Marigold decided— especially Shaun Banagher and Crane Caldwell.

Cousin Julie's dark eyes lit up when she saw her adopted son and his wife. Then noticing the swollen, discolored area of Marigold's face, she expressed her alarm. "My dear, what has happened to your face?" Julie asked, hastening to Marigold's side.

Her first thought, to denounce Crane, quickly died when she saw Julie's concern. She could not hurt the woman like that; for Marigold could not be absolutely sure that Crane had done it deliberately.

"A s-small bruise, Cousin Julie," Marigold explained. "You remember when the carriage almost turned over yesterday. I must have hit my cheek then."

"I believe they are ready for us, Mother," Crane said, indicating the innkeeper, who stood waiting to seat them.

Julie's concerned eyes returned to Marigold's face as soon as they were seated. Seeing this, Crane leaned close to his wife and gently touched her bruised cheek.

"Poor Marigold. Already I can see that I will have to take better care of you. I will tell Sesame to go slower tomorrow. We cannot risk marring such a beautiful face."

His hand lingered, caressing the smooth, silky skin just below the bruise, until Julie, noting the loving gesture, relaxed.

"Do that, Crane," Marigold whispered sarcastically under her breath. "I am sure that will help."

Julie looked up with a puzzled expression, but Crane smiled at his mother, and Julie returned the smile, although her troubled eyes retained some of their uneasiness.

Marigold barely remembered the man that her mother's cousin had married. He had been dead for such a long time, Desmond Caldwell had, but she knew from her own maman that he had loved Julie very much. So much so that he had brought home a dark-haired eight-year-old orphan for her to mother, since she was childless.

Now Crane was twenty-six years old, no longer an orphan, but a man of means, having inherited Cedar Hill Plantation and the gold mine adjacent to it. And this same man sat beside her as her unwanted husband.

"I plan to move into the cottage, Crane, when we get back home," Julie's quiet voice informed her son. "You and Marigold shall have the big house . . ."

"No," Marigold interrupted. "We cannot allow her to do that, can we, Crane?" she implored. When he did not respond, Marigold turned to Julie. "Cedar Hill is your home. We cannot push you out of your own house."

The girl was panic-stricken to think that she would be alone in the big house with Crane.

Julie merely smiled and brushed aside Marigold's objection. "When you are newly wed, you don't need an old woman in the house with you constantly."

"But—"

Marigold's objection was cut off. "Don't protest so much, Marigold," Crane said. "I think it's a good idea, Mother. And we are appreciative that you are so understanding. Aren't we, Marigold?"

Her hesitation prompted a hand on her arm. "If you do not agree, Mother will think that you are afraid to be alone with me, Souci," he purred, his soft, teasing voice at odds with the increasing pressure of his fingers on her arm.

"T-Thank you, Cousin Julie," Marigold managed to say. "You are very thoughtful."

The meal was set before them, and Crane released Marigold's arm.

For the next three days the pattern was the same. Stopping at an inn each night and arising early the next morning, they made their way up the Cherokee Trail. Then, at Nelson's Ferry, the carriage left the trail to proceed northward toward the land of the Waxhaws in upper Carolina.

To Marigold, looking out the window of the carriage, the frenzied, moving landscape echoed her own restless

53

spirit. Frantic drifts of leaves, caught up by the wind, sailed through the air—colors of red and yellow and deep purple torn from their moorings, with no certain destination but downward, where they were crushed by carriage wheels and horses' hooves. And the farther north the carriage went, the more alien the land seemed to the golden-haired girl who stared out the window.

Gone were her sandy dunes, the black water verging the roadway. In their place were flamboyant red hills, catching the glare of the afternoon sun, and bloodred puddles of water, drained from the adjacent hills—treacherous patches spread over the road, waiting to imprison an unsuspecting carriage wheel in the gripping, grasping mud.

"Close the window curtain, Marigold," Crane ordered. "You're apt to get mud spattered inside the carriage."

The voice of her husband, who was seated across from her, brought Marigold out of her oblivion. Before she could respond, Julie's gentle voice pleaded, "This is Marigold's first trip to the up country. I am sure she is anxious to see as much along the way as she can. Let her keep the curtain open, Crane."

"I was only thinking of you, Mother," Crane explained. "I did not imagine you would enjoy having mud ruin your dress."

"I am already travel-stained, son. It won't matter to have a little more dirt added to it."

But already, Marigold was closing the curtain. Julie turned to Marigold and said, "Keep the curtain open if you like, my dear."

"Thank you, Cousin Julie. But I . . . I have seen enough for now." Marigold yawned and leaned her head against the seat.

"I expect you are tired of traveling," Julie commiserated. "Sometimes I think the road will never end, and just when I despair of ever seeing Cedar Hill again, then the landscape becomes familiar and I'm home again."

Home again. Would Marigold ever feel that way about Cedar Hill? Could it ever take the place of Midgard Plantation where she had grown up?

The malaria season would be over soon, and her maman and papa would close up the townhouse and return down Biffers Road through Emma's Bog to the old plantation house that had been in the family for almost a hundred years—Robbie and baby Raven, and Maranta. And Jason, her older brother who would be returning home in another month from the Grand Tour, would join them, too.

Marigold closed her eyes, the image of the plantation house impressed upon her memory—and the little river house, hidden in the maze of honeysuckles and yew, high up on the river bluff where she and Maranta had played with their dolls.

Shaun Banagher's face invaded her memories, and sadness was mixed with anger. Because of him, it would be years before she would feel free to go home again—to enjoy the St. Cecilia Balls, the race season in February, the theater, and the socials from house to house at Christmastime.

An exile—that's what Shaun Banagher had made her. But no. He would not get away with it. Who was he to cause her to spend the rest of her life on some godforsaken plantation in the up country?

She would show him. If she played her cards right, she would once again be the toast of Charleston. No one would ever believe she had been jilted by Shaun Banagher.

The plans began to formulate. Unconsciously, her hand went up to her cheek, and Marigold winced. It was still sore and discolored. What a fool she was to antagonize Crane at the very beginning of their marriage—to fight him. She would have to learn to handle him better than that if she wanted her plans to succeed.

The monotonous swaying of the carriage lulled the girl to sleep. Farther north the carriage moved, the horses straining in the uphill climb. Then the road leveled off, and the vehicle began its gradual descent to the rich bottomlands next to the long, winding Catawba River.

With a jerk, the carriage stopped, and Marigold was immediately awake. "Are we at Cedar Hill?" she asked. She remembered to smile at Crane, and the dark-haired man, surprised at her friendliness, returned her smile.

"Not yet," Crane answered. "But it won't be long now. Jake has only to take us across the river on the ferry, and then it's less than a mile.

"If you would like to get out and stretch your legs, Marigold—you and Mother—I'll go and signal Jake that we're here."

Crane stepped down from the carriage, and in a cavalier manner, he placed the footstool on the ground and helped Marigold and Julie to alight from the vehicle that had held them for so long.

At first, her legs were stiff from the constant sitting. So Marigold stamped her feet on the ground and brushed the dust from her green silk crepe dress. The dust rose up in a cloud and Marigold coughed.

Julie laughed at the surprised look on the girl's face. "It will be nice, will it not, to soak in a soothing hot tub of water tonight?"

"I don't think I will ever get all the dust off," answered Marigold, who removed the matching silk-ribboned bonnet and shook her long, golden hair free of restraint. Despite herself, Marigold gazed over the land with interest.

The Catawba River, red and swollen from the recent rain, was no replica of her gray, civilized Ashley River that pulsed gently with the tides and only misbehaved occasionally when a coastal hurricane unleashed its strength to push the water out of bounds. *This* was raw power, impatiently hemmed in by the rugged banks, threatening to spill over into the bottomlands at any moment. Primitive, pagan and restless—

And guarding this angry red water was one lonely sentinel on its banks—a weathered gray post with a bell at the top.

Marigold watched as Crane walked toward it. His hands reached out to the bell rope, and Marigold jumped at the ominous clang that echoed up and down the deserted river.

In the nearby bottomlands, with the old cornstalks bent and bleached by the early autumn sun, a covey of brown and white quail flew off in a whirr of wings. And then, the landscape was silent again.

An excited shiver passed through Marigold's body, and Julie, beside her, mistaking the movement for one of fright, explained to her. "Crane is calling old Jake to let him know we want to cross the river. If you look hard, you can see the ferry."

Marigold, shading her eyes against the late afternoon sun, peered in the direction that Julie pointed. In fascination she watched the small, wooden, raftlike structure leave the opposite bank. Attached with a rope to the taut metal cable stretched from one bank to the other, the craft looked fragile and unstable. When it swung too far downstream, the man took his long pole and guided the raft back upstream. Each time it went too far downriver, the man used the pole to correct its course, digging the pole into the water and pushing, as if he were a Moses calling on the water to obey him.

The raft finally slammed into the riverbank, and a violent rattle filled the air as Jake flung the chains from the end of the raft and proceeded to jump onto the bank. He quickly attached the metal hooks at the end of the two chains into rings embedded in the wooden planks, securing the ferry to the bank.

When the man had finished, Sesame moved the carriage forward, and Marigold, standing to the side, held her breath. There was nothing to keep the horses from going too far—from pitching the carriage over into the river beyond the raft. Nothing except Sesame's steady hand.

Just when Marigold thought the carriage was lost, Sesame yelled and pulled on the reins. Finally the carriage stopped, and Marigold began to breathe easily again.

Crane stood on the bank, his hand out to help Julie and Marigold down the slippery planks onto the ferry.

"Is this . . . the only way to get to Cedar Hill?" Marigold asked, trying to keep the alarm from showing in her voice.

"No," Crane answered, "but it's the shorter way. And we're lucky to get here when we did. Old Jake doesn't cross the river after sundown. Would you like to get back into the carriage?" Crane asked.

It mattered little to Marigold. Being in the carriage seemed just as dangerous as standing by the railing, but at least it was a place to sit down, and Marigold's knees felt unsteady.

6

The carriage wound its way up the hill, leaving the river-bank behind. Jake had not wasted any time; for almost as soon as the carriage wheels left the ferry, the man cast off to return to the shack on the other bank for the night.

Marigold could feel the unspoken antagonism between her husband and the black man, Jake. And she wondered what had happened in the past for Crane to resent the old man so much.

Her curiosity overcame her reticence to question Crane about it. Impulsively, she said, "Why do you and Jake not like each other, Crane?"

The man's fingers gripped the strap hanging on the side of the carriage, and even though his voice was controlled, he could not keep the animosity completely out. "Jake is that oddity—a free black man. He is too proud—bad influence on the slaves. They might get the idea that they would like to be free, too."

"Slaves? You mean you have slaves at Cedar Hill?"

"Don't look so surprised, Marigold. What do you think Sesame is?"

"I n-never thought about it. But back when Maman and Jason visited Cedar Hill, there weren't any slaves."

"You'll find that many changes have been made since I became master," Crane emphasized. "It was a matter of expediency—because of the gold mine. As long as we did the placer mining—getting the gold from the top of the ground—the Indians didn't mind helping. But when we started underground blasting, they refused to work in the shafts and tunnels."

Repugnance was evident on Marigold's face, and seeing it, Crane lashed out. "You act as if you disapprove; yet, your father has many more slaves than I do."

Crane had misunderstood. It was the idea of being

forced to work in such a dangerous situation—with the frightening possibility of being buried alive—that had caused the look on Marigold's face. But her husband's remark about her father acted as a goad, and she felt honor bound to defend him. For Robert Tabor would never deliberately place his slaves in such danger.

"Not through choice," she replied. "If my father could afford it, he would free all his slaves tomorrow."

Crane's laugh dispelled any desire for Marigold to be nice to her husband.

"And if *I* could afford it," Crane said, "I would import some of those out-of-work iron miners from Cornwall, as the owners have done just over the state line. I am like your father and have to use the cheapest means available. It matters little to me whether the slaves till the soil or work in the bowels of the earth getting the gold out."

The look on Marigold's face made him angry. "And you can remove that snobbish look from your face, Marigold," he said, lowering his voice. "Do you think your sand hills are the only ones that matter? Take a good look at the red clay earth around you. For this raw Carolina up country produced both the President *and* Vice-President of these United States."

"Yet, even Vice-President Calhoun felt it necessary to secure his bride from the low country," Marigold countered, not content to let Crane boast too much at her expense.

Julie seemed oblivious to the whisperings of Crane and Marigold. It was as if she were reliving another time, with her gaze directed to the woodland area.

Even the horses were behaving differently, snorting impatiently as they plunged along the last stretch of road that separated them from Cedar Hill. And Sesame, pulling back on the reins, was hard put to control them.

"The horses are impatient to get to their feed bags," Crane said. "They sense it won't be long before they're home."

Marigold's mind came back to Jake and the words

60

Crane uttered concerning the man. "Was that why Jake was in such a hurry to get across the river? To eat his dinner, too?"

"Jake has to obey the curfew," Crane said. "He is not allowed out after dark."

"Oh." The exclamation hung in the air for a while, until Marigold, still curious, asked, "What would happen if he didn't get home? Before dark, I mean."

"He could be arrested by the authorities."

"But you just said he was free. That doesn't sound free to me, if he has to be home by a certain time."

"It's the law, Marigold," Crane stated impatiently. "Just as it's the law that *you* no longer exist as a separate person. Now that we are married, you are *my* property and subject to me."

Marigold laughed at his words. "And will you shut me up in the barn tonight, along with *your* horses and *your* carriage?"

"Only if you're difficult, beautiful one, and keep bothering me with all these questions," he whispered in her ear, drawing her close to him. "As soon as we get the dust washed off of you, I have a better place for you to go— in my bed."

The girl pulled away from Crane. "That isn't funny," she said, lifting her chin to glare at her husband.

"It wasn't intended to be."

Marigold gritted her teeth. How long could she stand being married to Crane—being forced to share his bed, when she ached to be in the arms of another man?

She was trapped. Not only by the vows she had taken, linking her to the wrong man, but also by the river. What if she ever sought to escape Crane Caldwell and Cedar Hill?

There was the business of the bell. Jake would not be the only one to hear its clang. And even if the ferry were on the right side of the river, Marigold knew she would not be able to handle it by herself, if she ever needed to do so.

"Please, God. Don't let it ever come to that," Marigold

61

whispered silently—one of the few times she had ever uttered a prayer, for Maranta had always been pious enough for the two of them.

"Look, Marigold," Julie said, breaking into her thoughts. "Beyond the row of cedars, you will see the house any moment."

Marigold leaned forward, peering through the golden autumn haze that had settled thickly on the land. With the last remnants of the sun framing the house, the structure came into sight. Cedar Hill—the sprawling country house, built upon the red clay earth—miles from her beloved low country and the man she had thought to marry. Cedar Hill, her home now—hers and Crane's. At its sight, Marigold felt no warm welcome, no respite from the long journey. Instead, a coldness invaded her body, matching the suddenly cold premonition that gripped her heart.

To seek comfort, Marigold reached up, her hand clasping the golden locket around her neck—the talisman of her eighteenth birthday and her coming of age. With the metal growing warm in her hand, she felt some measure of confidence return. Cedar Hill would never get the better of Robert Tabor's daughter. *That,* she promised.

7

Maranta stood on the dock and waited for the dinghy to take her to the ship anchored in Charleston harbor.

Her father was the only one to see her off; for Feena had been sent back to Midgard, and Eulalie was nursing the sick Robbie, who had suddenly come down with fever.

The Condessa Louisa stood with Dona Isobel, her middle-aged companion. Drawing Dona Isobel into conversation, the white-haired condessa discreetly moved down the wharf to allow Maranta and Robert Tabor time to say goodbye.

"You have not forgotten anything?"

"No, Papa."

He was ill at ease with this dark-haired child of his who so resembled his wife. And seeing her bite her lip, trying to keep the tears back, he was half inclined to put her in the carriage and inform the condessa that he had changed his mind.

But the idea of having her shut away in a nunnery was galling to him. She was meant to be loved—to bear children. And the condessa had promised him that Vasco Monteiro would treat her gently. So he resisted the urge to wave the Portuguese woman on and instead, leaned over and kissed Maranta on the forehead. "Maranta . . ."

The whistle sounded.

"Papa?"

"God go with you, daughter." He backed away from her, and with her vision blurred by the fullness of tears, Maranta walked blindly toward the condessa and her companion.

Over an hour later, Robert Tabor was still standing on the wharf. The *Beaufort* was now completely out of sight, having disappeared over the horizon.

Another part of him was gone, and he grieved for the loss of his dark-haired child.

The ship traveled to the Bahamas, taking on fresh water and supplies in Nassau. Then, on through the West Indies and the Caribbean, past Venezuela and Guiana. Onward the ship sailed, through rough seas and placid waters, until finally, Brazil, the land of rain forests and deserts, mountains and valleys, diamonds and gold, sugar and coffee, was sighted.

Yet, for Maranta and her companions the trip was far from over. For now the journey along the Brazilian coast began. Southeast, past the mouth of the Amazon, on to Fortaleza, and rounding the northeastern tip, the *Beaufort* headed southwest past Rio, the capital. Two months from the day it had set sail from Charleston, the *Beaufort* brought its steam-propelled paddle wheels to a stop—in a natural harbor with the blue mountains of the Serra do Mar hovering in the distance.

To the constant beat of the music, they came—one after the other—with the heavy sacks of coffee beans over their shoulders. Black and strong, the bodies—slaves parading from the warehouses to the dock. And everywhere the heavy, penetrating odor of coffee infiltrated the air. There was no place where Maranta Tabor could be free of it; for this was Santos, the port city of São Paulo, the coffee kingdom.

"It will not be long now," Dona Isobel assured Maranta. "As soon as the coffee is loaded and the slaves are gone from the dock, we will be allowed to leave the ship."

Maranta, in a secluded part of the deck, nodded and watched while ropes drew their pungent load high into the air and then lowered the sacks onto the ship. The ropes sank out of sight and then swung the empty cradle back to the dock to repeat the procedure until all the coffee was loaded.

Maranta's fears swung back and forth in rhythm to the ropes and the chant of the strange music coming from the wharf. She had been on the ship far too long and she

64

ached to feel solid ground underneath her feet. But she was afraid to leave the vessel, for she would be that much nearer to the man who waited to make her his wife.

What if he were disappointed in her, as he was sure to be? Would he send her back home on the same ship as his coffee beans?

Frowning, Maranta picked at the small, downy, green feather that had floated through the air to lodge against her pale blue silk dress.

For ten days, the ship had been in quarantine because of the death of one of the sailors. But no one else had become ill, so they were all being allowed to go ashore.

During their time of forced quarantine, fresh fruit had been delivered to the ship and enough water, not only to drink, but to bathe in, as well. Even though she had washed her long, black hair the evening before and soaked luxuriously in the tub that the condessa had ordered aboard before leaving Charleston harbor, Maranta was already hot and uncomfortable.

No change of seasons for her. Now that she had survived another sweltering Carolina low-country summer, with its dangers of malaria and yellow fever, Maranta could look forward to no cold winter. She was destined to live through another summer season, this time in an uncivilized foreign country where seasons were turned upside down and the Brazilian heat had just begun.

Dona Isobel, dressed in black from head to toe, began fanning vigorously. "This trip has been hard on the condessa," she confided to the girl seated beside her. "And the journey from Santos to São Paulo and upriver to the *fazenda* will be even more taxing for her." The woman's troubled face brightened, and in a kind voice she said, "But I know she counts her trip a success because of you, senhorita."

Maranta's dark eyes became even more solemn, and she folded her hands listlessly in her lap and kept quiet.

"It won't be long before we disembark. I think I had better see if the condessa needs me," the woman said, getting up from the makeshift seat. "I shall not be long and I know I can rely on you not to wander about. You

65

promise to stay seated here on deck until I return, Senhorita Maranta?"

"Yes, senhora," the young girl replied, knowing it would be futile to try to run away. She knew no one who would help her. And the little of the Portuguese language she had learned from Dona Isobel on the ship was not enough. *Fazenda.* She had recognized the word for coffee plantation. That was easy. But all the other alien words. How would she converse with the man who was to be her husband if he did not speak English?

A fresh wave of fright swept over Maranta, and for comfort she touched the golden locket she was wearing around her neck—that bit of gold that had been blessed by Father Ambrose on her birthday and presented to her by her maman and papa, now half the world away.

At that moment, devastation overwhelmed her, and to keep the tears from becoming reality, Maranta shut her eyes.

The man's booted foot, perched carelessly upon the railing next to her, was the first thing she saw when she opened her eyes again. She did not know how long the man had been staring at her. With a sudden start, Maranta stood up, ready to flee the arrogant, dark-haired stranger who met her glance boldly and continued to look her up and down as no gentleman in Charleston would ever think of doing.

"Senhorita Tabor," he called when she had taken only a few steps from him. "There is no need to run away. I promised Dona Isobel that I would not ravish you here on deck."

His laugh followed her as she fled to her cabin. He knew her—knew who she was. And that thought frightened her more than anything else.

Breathlessly, Maranta closed the cabin door and sank onto the large cushion on the floor. Her bonnet—her reticule—she had left them on deck. But she would not go back for them. She would willingly give up her new blue silk bonnet and all that she possessed never to see the man again.

"What is it, Maranta?" the old condessa's voice questioned. "You look as if you have met with a ghost."

The adjoining door was open, and the condessa stood, looking down at the small, frightened figure fighting for her breath.

"Not a ghost. I . . . I think it was a devil, instead," she managed to answer.

The puzzled expression on the condessa's face cleared when the deep laughter sounded behind her.

"Ruis, what a bad boy you are—to frighten Maranta so. And what are you doing with her bonnet and reticule?"

"The frightened child with the sorrowful eyes left them on deck," he answered nonchalantly, walking into the room to rid himself of Maranta's belongings.

"Maranta," the condessa said, while the girl struggled to her feet, "I wish to present my elder son, Ruis Almeida José da Monteiro, the Count of Sorocaba. He has come to help us disembark. Ruis, my son, this is Vasco's *noiva*, Maranta Tabor."

He took her small hand in his and, bowing before her, he brought her hand to his lips. As quickly as she could, she withdrew her fingers from his grasp. Her dark eyes betrayed her relief. He was not Vasco, but his older brother, the *conde* and *fazendeiro*, master of the plantation.

"I . . . am sorry to have been so frightened on deck," the girl apologized. "It was just that . . ."

"And I, too, am sorry, *menina*. I should not have startled you—especially when you had been dozing in the sun."

"I was not asleep, senhor," she protested. "I had merely closed my eyes for a moment."

His white teeth were in contrast to his bronzed skin as he smiled at her answer.

"You are ready, Mãe?" he asked, turning to the white-haired woman.

"*Sim,* Ruis. We are more than ready to leave this ship."

Maranta, with her blue silk bonnet now covering her dark hair, felt foolish as she walked beside Dona Isobel.

For Ruis da Monteiro watched their progress with an undisguised amusement.

The little green bird chirped loudly in its swinging cage, held gingerly by Maranta—almost as if it were protesting the disparaging glances of the important *fazendeiro* standing impatiently to help them across the plank.

The condessa had already been ushered across and into the open carriage, where she sat with her spine stiff as a farthingale. When their turn came to cross onto shore, Maranta hung back to let Dona Isobel go first. The woman required little help in negotiating the gangplank. But when it came Maranta's turn, the swinging cage overbalanced her, and had it not been for Ruis, she would have fallen into the water.

His arms enclosed her and steadied the cage, while a green feather floated upward to land on his lapel.

"Th-thank you," Maranta uttered in an embarrassed voice.

Ruis, still with one arm holding her, took his other hand and disdainfully flicked the stray feather from his immaculate coat. "You must have much regard for this silly, molting bird—to risk falling into the water for it."

Maranta's eyes immediately darkened into a stormy glint. "Fado is *not* molting," she declared. "He was merely shaken up by the sudden movement. And I *do* have much regard for him, since it was the captain of the ship who gave him to me."

"So you are not quite so meek as I had thought," Ruis said, still laughing. Then he leaned down and whispered in her ear, "Does the condessa know how quick and fierce you are—to defend another?"

"Ruis," the voice sounded from the carriage, "don't keep the child standing there. I am in a hurry to get to the hotel."

"We are coming, Mãe."

"Is . . . is Senhor Vasco at the hotel?" Maranta inquired on her way to the carriage.

Ruis frowned at her question and took his time in answering. "Vasco has not been well. We thought it best for him to remain at the *fazenda.*"

His look discouraged any more questions that she might have had concerning her future husband, and besides, they were at the carriage.

"If you will trust me with Fado," he said, reaching out to take the cage, "I will see that he is securely placed."

There was nothing to do but hand over the little green bird. But Maranta's eyes remained on the cage until it was safely wedged in the seat beside the driver.

Ruis followed Maranta into the carriage and eased himself beside her, in the seat facing the Condessa Louisa and Dona Isobel.

"Would you like to swap places with me, senhorita?" Dona Isobel asked the girl. "You cannot see anything of the city when you ride backward."

"Oh, yes, please," Maranta answered eagerly, not so much from wanting to view the city as to escape from the conde's side.

As soon as the switch was made, Ruis nodded for the driver to leave the wharf. Already sent ahead were the many trunks belonging to the condessa and two belonging to Maranta and Dona Isobel. All that she possessed was in that one large trunk, the last tie with her life in the Carolinas, with the exception of the small valise tied to the back of the carriage.

In the evening, Maranta sat at the little table near the window of her bedroom. She picked at the food on the tray that had been sent to her. Finally she gave up trying to eat the unappetizing, hot food, and with her fingers, she crumbled the bread into small bits to set inside the cage for Fado.

"Poor Fado. I know how you feel," she said aloud to the little green bird. "A prisoner too—just like me."

Maranta stood up and peered out the balcony window. The gaiety in the street was disturbing, and she longed for the quiet of the chapel she had seen on the way to the hotel, where she could have prayed without being disturbed.

She would be glad to leave Santos early the next morning; for Dona Isobel had promised that the weather would be more to her liking, once they left the coastal tropical city and climbed upward onto the plateau where São Paulo was built among the clouds.

The condessa was not well, and Maranta, kneeling to say her evening prayers, remembered to pray for her and her weak heart—and to be thankful that Ruis Almeida José da Monteiro, Count of Sorocaba, already had a wife. With his dark blue eyes, resembling black sapphires, still haunting her, Maranta's mind wandered from her prayers. He had left Dona Isobel the responsibility of attending to the ailing condessa and even now was somewhere in the city, enjoying the gaiety. Suddenly, the uneasy thought struck her. What if Vasco were a carbon copy of his brother? "No, please let him be different," she whispered, returning to her prayers.

Finally Maranta stood up, her knees stiff from the time spent by the bedside. Her legs had not seemed to want to obey her ever since she had left the ship that afternoon. Even now, Maranta steadied herself by holding onto the giant post of the jacaranda bed. Then, she blew out the light and climbed into bed, making sure to close the mosquito netting.

And outside, the noise continued, until Maranta's tired brain finally filtered out the noise and she drifted to sleep.

As the tap at her door became more insistent, the dark-haired girl sat up, brushing the long tresses from her face. She yawned and rubbed her eyes and, in a husky, small voice, called out, "Come in."

The door remained closed and the knock sounded again. Maranta frowned, pushing the mosquito netting out of the way. Of course. Whoever was at the door did not understand English. She slipped out of the bed and, in her bare feet, she walked silently to the door to open it. A servant with her breakfast tray, more than likely.

The quick intake of breath alerted the man to her distress, but he paid no attention after a summary glance at her state of undress. With the tray in his hands, Ruis walked into the room and set it upon the table where, the evening before, Maranta had eaten her lonely meal.

70

"Do not continue hiding behind the door, *pequena*," he admonished. "The carriage is outside, waiting to leave the city before the heat of the day. You have little time to dawdle."

"B-but I am undressed, senhor," she replied. "I did not expect you to b-bring my breakfast to me. Please leave the room, and then I will come from behind the door."

The small bare foot, partly visible below the long white gown, made no attempt to move. Impatiently, Ruis said, "Do not be so modest, Maranta. In that long shroud of yours, you are safe from even the most lecherous of eyes."

Ruis removed the cover of Fado's cage, and the bird stirred and gave a tentative chirp. "Fado is hungry this morning," he announced. "Don't you think you'd better attend to him before he loses *all* his feathers?"

Smiling, Ruis left the room and closed the door behind him. Later, when Maranta spied the small sack of seed beside her tray, her attitude toward the man softened.

She fed Fado first, and then Maranta hurried through her own breakfast, eating little more than she had the evening before. She quickly dressed, for her mind was on the conde's words. He was waiting impatiently, as usual, for them to leave the hotel.

"You are ready, senhorita?" Dona Isobel asked, coming into Maranta's room just as she finished tying the pale yellow sink organza bonnet under her chin.

"Yes, senhora," Maranta replied. She lifted the bird cage from the table and followed the dark-clad woman in her voluminous skirts down the hallway to the lobby that was already filled with cigar-smoking men.

She felt as if she were running a gauntlet. For each man, in turn, laid his cigar on the table and gave undivided attention to the progress of the small, dark-haired girl with the green bird in hand. A murmur followed her—smacking sounds and conversation—and she felt the slow, pink blush cover her face as an insinuating laugh sounded directly behind her.

"Pay no attention to them, senhorita," Dona Isobel

advised. "They have nothing better to do, it seems, than to point out your obvious attributes and to speculate what you are doing in the conde's care."

It was worse than she had thought then—what the men were saying openly about her. Did they usually treat all women that way, even when they were adequately chaperoned? Or was it just Maranta?

What a failure she was—Maranta decided, with a sad expression giving poignance to the large, dark eyes—to have to rely on someone else to protect her. First, Feena, and now, Dona Isobel.

Men did not hesitate to insult her to her face. But her twin Marigold would not have taken it. With one quelling glance, Marigold would have stopped their bawdy remarks. Even Shaun Banagher's friend would not have dared speak to Marigold in such an abusive tone as he had used with her.

Shaun Banagher. Was the man Marigold had loved already buried in some obscure cemetery on the outskirts of Charleston? Maranta had no way of finding out if he was dead or not. That had made it so difficult to compose a letter to Marigold.

Aboard ship, in the long hours when there had been nothing to do, Maranta had attempted to write a letter to her twin—dozens of times—only to have the proper words elude her each time.

Would Marigold feel comforted, even if Shaun were dead, to know that he had not abandoned her that night after all? Or would it cause an irreconcilable breach when she realized that her husband Crane Caldwell had deliberately deceived her?

Maranta, absorbed in her dilemma, followed Dona Isobel through the massive brazilwood doors and onto the street where the heavy, ornate, black coach with the golden crest emblazoned on its side waited.

Ruis was standing near the carriage, his eyes fixed on Maranta as she approached. Remembering their earlier encounter, the girl blushed and lowered her glance to the bird cage in her hands.

Unintelligible words were spoken in low tones between

Ruis and the black-clad woman, and to Maranta's consternation, Dona Isobel hurried back into the hotel, leaving her alone with the arrogant man.

"Are you ready to get into the carriage?" Ruis asked the girl who stood hesitantly beside the footstool that had been placed by the vehicle.

"I . . . I think I'll wait for Dona Isobel . . ."

"It will be a long time to stand in the sun, *menina*," Ruis replied. And in a teasing voice he continued, "Vasco might not be pleased to have a freckle-faced *noiva* delivered to him."

"I don't freckle, senhor," she informed him, but already Maranta had switched Fado's cage to the other hand and placed one foot upon the stool.

Strong arms encircled her, and Maranta, lifted bodily into the coach, protested this close contact with the conde.

"Please, senhor," she said, "I can manage by myself."

"Can you, little one?" he said, his eyes taking in the pale yellow dress, the delicately shaped face, and the small hand that fluttered nervously in distress. "I wonder . . ."

He sounded almost sorry for her. And then, abruptly, his tone changed to the familiar disparagement. "This trip will be no delightful picnic excursion into the country, Maranta. Someone should have informed you, so you could have dressed appropriately."

"You do not approve of my dress, senhor?" she asked, meeting his bold, dark eyes with her angry ones.

"Oh, I approve, all right. Probably even more than my *charuto*-smoking friends inside. But that has nothing to do with it. You'll see what I mean before the day's over."

Fingering the delicate streamers of ribbon attached to the skirt of her yellow dress, Maranta turned to gaze in the direction of the ships in the harbor. The *Beaufort* was nowhere in sight. It had already sailed with its load of coffee. And that knowledge made Maranta forlorn.

The breach was complete. Despite her wishes, Maranta was in an unfamiliar land—a present for a man who would probably turn out to be just as arrogant as his brother.

73

In relief, Maranta saw Dona Isobel appear with the condessa at her side. And the conde's attention turned to the two women, leaving Maranta to nurse her bruised feelings.

Whatever she did was wrong. But why should it matter to the conde about her dress? She would be sitting inside the coach, while he, in his rough shirt and pants and polished boots, would more than likely ride the large black stallion that was tied to the back of the carriage.

Maybe the conde would like it better if she were clad in black like the condessa and Dona Isobel. But she possessed nothing that color in her wardrobe. Besides, black was for mourning.

Perhaps it *would* be appropriate, Maranta thought, biting her lower lip unconsciously. For had she not lost everything now that was dear to her—her family *and* her dream? Despite the humidity and heat of the morning air, Maranta shivered.

Into the carriage, Ruis helped the condessa and then Dona Isobel. But to Maranta's consternation, he stayed inside the carriage, also.

Out of the port city they went, heading for São Paulo, fifty miles away. The ornate wheels of the Monteiro family coach rolled in a lumbersome motion over the rough road that constantly disappeared under green vegetation. With umbrella leaves blotting out the sunlight at times, the carriage moved through the rain forest. And the conde, his mind preoccupied, ignored the other three passengers and the constant bumping of the carriage, while Maranta, gritting her teeth, took care that she was not thrown into the arms of Ruis Almeida José da Monteiro, Count of Sorocaba.

8

For almost an hour they rode, meeting no one. Then, suddenly, men on horseback appeared out of nowhere, blocking their path, and beside them were fierce-looking dogs, their spiked collars glinting in the sun.

Ruis, reaching underneath the carriage seat, casually took the gun from its hiding place as the carriage slowed and then came to a stop.

Maranta was frightened. But Ruis, displaying no outward fear, jumped from the carriage and walked forward to meet the men.

"Do you think they will harm him?" Maranta whispered to Dona Isobel.

At her question, the condessa laughed. And before Dona Isobel could explain, the condessa answered, "No, Maranta. They are some of Ruis' best gauchos."

"He . . . knows them?" the girl asked doubtfully.

"Of course. They take care of the Monteiro cattle on the pampas. But they have come to help with the carriage. It is very rough from now on until we reach the plateau."

"But the dogs . . ."

"Are an added protection," the condessa finished.

Now relaxed, Maranta leaned out the carriage window to get a better view of the lush, tropical growth. She reached over to touch the velvet-soft leaves just beyond the window, when a giant hand seized hers and pushed it away from the foliage.

"Keep your hands inside the carriage, Maranta," the man barked.

"But I only wanted to touch the leaf . . ."

"*Meu Deus!*" he said, slapping his forehead. "Do I have to *show* you every danger before you'll believe me?"

The leaves rustled as a large snake unwound itself from the tree trunk and slithered away.

"Senhora," Ruis directed to Dona Isobel, "kindly see to this child. And make certain she *stays* inside the carriage until I tell her she can get out."

"I will be more watchful," the woman promised. "Do not worry."

Muttering angrily to himself, Ruis rode away on his black stallion to catch up with the gauchos.

Despite the recital of supposed dangers each time they stopped, Maranta saw no dread venomous snake called the *jararaca,* nor a single jaguar—that sleek, silent predator of the forest which Ruis had warned her about. Instead, she saw the tiny, green, harmless hummingbirds and beautiful flowers that decorated their journey.

Hundreds of variegated blossoms covered entire shrubs, and Maranta, unable to keep silent, exclaimed over their exotic beauty. "Oh, look at the flowers," she said, only to see the blossoms take wing and fly away.

"Not blossoms at all, Maranta," the condessa said, amused at her puzzled expression. "They are *borboletas.*"

In amazement Maranta watched as they flew through the air to settle on another unadorned shrub, giving instant beauty to it, also.

"Butterflies," Dona Isobel said, translating for Maranta.

After that, the landscape began to change. The tropical coastal rain forest was left behind. With ropes attached from the carriage to the pommels of the gauchos' saddles, they began the climb over the Great Escarpment, or Serra do Mar. One misstep of the horses and the carriage could easily plunge over the precipice and be lost forever. And Maranta, for the first time, began to feel a physical fear of this uncivilized land.

Once, Maranta looked out, and then she immediately closed her eyes and gripped her seat, as if, by her actions, she could keep the carriage safe from harm.

Into the clouds they traveled, and the lightweight cloak that Maranta thought she would never use again she hugged around her body and was grateful for its warmth.

By the time they reached the *estallegen,* the crude inn where they were to spend the night, the hem of Maranta's delicate dress was in shreds. Her long, silken hair was knotted—tangled—and already she could feel the swelling underneath her eye where an insect had bitten her.

But they had stopped for the night, and Maranta was thankful to give her body a rest from the constant jolting of the carriage.

The odor of food cooking in the open air pervaded her senses, tantalizing her. She was ravenously hungry and she would make no protest over anything that was served. All day she had subsisted on fruit and nuts, but now she was ready for heavier fare, even the *feijoada,* the rice and black beans that seemed to be a part of every meal.

When the food, cooked by the Indian woman, was ready, Ruis and the gauchos, with the black driver of the coach, took their plates and sat apart from the women. It was only later, when the meal was over, that Ruis came toward the women. Probably to give them *more* instructions for the night, Maranta decided.

She knew there was no possibility for a bath. Ruis did not have to tell her that. And she had no desire to explore outside the *estallegen* either, because of the dogs and the remembrance of the gigantic snake wrapped around the tree trunk.

Maranta's hand went up to the area under her eye to trace the outline of swelling. The movement caught Ruis's attention, and before she knew it, the man was beside her, removing her hand to examine the swollen area for himself.

"When did this happen?" he asked in a displeased voice.

"I . . . I don't really remember.'"

"And I suppose you don't remember," he added sarcastically, "that you were to inform me immediately if something like this happened?"

"A mere insect bite? I do not make a habit of complaining over something so small. I am used to the gnats and mosquitoes of my own country, senhor."

The sapphire eyes flashed their displeasure at her answer. But instead of responding to Maranta, the conde turned to Dona Isobel and the condessa. "I am taking the naughty *pequena* to the river to bathe her face in the cool water."

77

The two women nodded, making no protest. But Maranta pulled back, saying, "It is not necessary, senhor."

His grip tightened on her arm, and in a furious voice he whispered, "*I* am the one to decide if it is necessary, senhorita."

Prodded and pulled along, with no chance even to get her cloak, Maranta was propelled away from the rude hut and toward the distant gushing water.

It was still light, but the land had taken on an eerie glow. The mist around them resembled smoke from some witch's boiling cauldron, and the sky was brushed with streaks of carmine red. Having heard his whistle, the fierce dogs with their dagger-sharp collars obeyed the conde's summons and ran before him, their legs disappearing in the layers of mist that clung close to the ground.

The fury was still in the conde's voice when he spoke to Maranta. "*Brazil* is your country now, Maranta. And that I will *not* allow you to forget."

For a moment, she was puzzled. And then it came to her—what she had said about her own country. Fighting against the conde's domination of her, Maranta momentarily became brave. She pulled back from him, and with her dark eyes flashing, she said, "*Vasco* will be the one to instruct me. *You* have no jurisdiction over me, senhor —only over your own wife. And I pray that you will have no trouble remembering *that*."

His deep laughter destroyed her bravado, and she trembled at her own temerity.

"I see why the condessa was so entranced with you, Maranta. The small, pious São Joana going out to face her enemies, with her knees knocking together in fear."

The laughing eyes hardened, and in a sterner voice, the *conde* said, "Let me explain once and for all so that there will never be any doubt. You are wrong when you say I have no jurisdiction over you. As Vasco's intended wife, you are already a part of the Monteiro family, and *I* am head of that family. Do you know what that means, Maranta, here in Brazil?" He did not wait for her to answer, but continued. "I am the ruler of a vast area of land. The laws are ones made by me. If I should choose to have a slave whipped or even killed, that is my right, with no one to dispute it. If I should choose to have a member of my own family . . . punished, it is within my rights. I am the *fazendeiro* and king of my own land. And *you,* Maranta, are still subject to me. *Now,* do you understand why you must obey me?"

The words numbed her. It was worse than she feared. Not only Vasco to please, but also this . . . this arrogant lord who stood above her, demanding obeisance.

With one last rebellious action, Maranta curtsied before him, and in a soft, muted voice answered, *"Sim, Dom Ruis."*

His white teeth flashed as his hearty laugh echoed over the land. "You do not have to address me in that manner, Maranta. You may reserve *that* title for our own Dom Pedro, emperor of all Brazil. As a member of the family, you will call me Ruis. Now, let us see to your face before the eye closes."

The river was within sight, and Ruis led her to the bank where the water splashed noisily over the rocks. Motioning for her to sit on the rock that projected out of the water onto the bank, Ruis took the wicked-looking knife from his side. He swished it in the water several times and with a lightning motion, he caught her face to hold it toward the sun, while the knife point flicked the skin under her eye.

Maranta took one look at the knife. "No," she whispered. And that was all she remembered—that and his dark sapphire eyes . . .

The distant sound of voices bothered Maranta. She wished they would go away so she could sleep. With a tiny moan, she moved, trying to find a position to relieve the ache in her body.

"She is coming around, Ruis," Dona Isobel's voice sounded next to her.

But when she opened her eyes, only the conde stood over her, his tanned face showing a sympathy and something else that Maranta could not fathom.

"Do not look at me like that, *pequena.* I intended no harm to you."

He sat beside the pallet on the floor where she lay, and in the dim light of the fire, she saw the hesitant movement of his hand as he brushed the tangled black hair from her forehead. As if soothing a frightened child, he talked in gentle tones, explaining, "I had to use the knife, Maranta —for it was no ordinary insect bite. A beetle had burrowed under the skin, and it was imperative that I remove it."

A regretful tone crept into his deep voice. "I can understand how frightened you were, after my speech, to see the *faca de ponte* coming at you. But I have not marred your porcelain face. The tiny imperfection will be healed before Vasco sees you."

Maranta closed her eyes. She was too tired to respond.

Gently, Ruis covered her with the blanket, and as he left her side, he whispered softly, "*You* should be the one named Innocencia."

The next morning, Maranta changed clothes. She worked with her long, tangled hair, brushing it furiously until, at last, it was smooth. There was no need to place the tattered yellow dress in the valise. It was ruined, as Ruis intimated it would be. So she balled it up and discarded it instead of packing it.

But the dress was of no concern. It was the condessa who required attention. Her drawn, ashen face was almost the color of her snow-white hair, and Maranta was worried that she might not survive the trip.

Offers by the girl to help were negated by Dona Isobel, who followed behind the conde. He carried the frail, old condessa gently in his arms. Placing her in the carriage, he turned to Dona Isobel and inquired, "You have her medicine, Isobel?"

"*Sim*, Ruis. It is here in the brocade bag. I will give it to her when she needs it."

"*Obrigado*, Isobel."

"*Não tem de quê*, Ruis."

Maranta's attempt to translate the polite exchange caused her brow to wrinkle.

"There is something bothering you, *menina?*" the conde asked.

She blushed, as if she had been caught eavesdropping. Hastily Maranta said what had been on her mind previously.

"If the condessa wishes to lie down, Fado and I could ride part of the way up front with . . . with the driver. That would give the senhora more room."

Her subdued rust-colored dress peeked from under the cloak and came under his scrutiny, the sturdiness of material seeming to meet with more approval than the flimsy yellow dress of the day before.

"We will tie the cage to the back of the coach, Maranta," Ruis announced. "Rico has enough to do, without watching out for some worthless bird."

"But I would watch out for Fado, senhor. It would not be necessary for . . ."

"You will not be riding beside Rico. You may ride on the stallion with me this morning."

"But . . ."

His sharp look quelled her protest. The last thing she wanted to do—to be near him. Miserably she waited while he tied the cage securely and then spoke through the window of the coach in the nasal language that she found so hard to follow.

"Come," he said in English to Maranta.

Dejectedly she followed his order, walking behind him to the stallion that was tethered to the post. Before lifting her on the horse, Ruis examined the area under Maranta's eye. "It looks much better this morning, *pequena*."

In silence they cantered along the trail, and Maranta, trying to avoid the conde's touch, sat stiffly away from him.

"Relax, Maranta. I am not going to eat you," he said, taking his arm to draw her against his chest.

A minute or so later he inquired, "Is that not more comfortable, hm?"

She ignored his question and asked one of her own. "Who is Innocencia, Dom Ruis?"

"You are not to call me by my formal title, Maranta. Have I not instructed you to call me Ruis?"

The silence lasted for quite a while until Ruis finally answered her. "Innocencia is my wife. She is a cousin of the family that acts as regents for our child emperor, Dom Pedro II."

"Child emperor? How old is he then?" Maranta inquired, forgetting about Innocencia for the time being.

"He is five years old—which means Innocencia's family is assured of power for many years, unless they continue to squabble among themselves and kill each other off."

The irony was apparent in his voice. The conde, seemingly unwilling to continue the conversation, rode in silence, and Maranta asked no more questions.

After they had ridden some distance with the gauchos ahead of them, he said, "You were kind to think of Mãe's comfort and give up your seat in the carriage. Her illness is far more serious than she will admit. I only hope that Vasco will appreciate her sacrifice in finding you for him."

The conde sounded as if he blamed *her* for the condessa's illness, and that hurt Maranta. She had not wanted to come to Brazil. And she would have been far happier if the condessa had chosen someone else.

"I am sure anyone would have done equally as well, R-Ruis." Maranta stumbled self-consciously over his name. "I do not flatter myself that the condessa made the trip to Charleston specifically to . . . to interview me."

"You are wrong, Maranta. It was precisely for that reason that Mãe changed her plans and sought you out."

"But why?"

"You are of the same religion, Maranta. That was important. And then, after she saw your little enameled painting that your brother Jason carried with him, Mãe's interest in anyone else subsided."

"She saw the painting?"

"Yes. And I have to agree with her—a beautiful little portrait of twins as opposite in nature as Oxalá is to Iemanjá."

"But I don't understand . . ."

"The sun from the dark moon goddess or 'mother of waters.' I keep forgetting, Maranta, that you are not familiar with our special Brazilian deities."

"No, it isn't that. It's what you said about the painting. *You* saw it, too?"

"Of course. I was with Mãe in Lisbon, at the home of friends. Your brother was invited to dinner one evening, and he had the miniature with him. He was proud of you for painting it for him. A talent you inherited from your French grandmother, I understand."

"You mean—just one glimpse of an unknown girl's face, and the condessa . . . ?"

"Not quite so dramatic," Ruis corrected. "Mãe made a point of getting to know Jason during that visit. She questioned him very closely. And so, instead of returning to Brazil with me, she booked passage with Dona Isobel to Charleston."

"I knew that the condessa brought a letter from Jason for Maman and Papa," Maranta mused aloud. But then, her thoughts turned inward. Maranta couldn't believe that the condessa had chosen her over Marigold. She must have come to Charleston because of her golden-haired sister. But once there, the woman had changed her mind.

"You are noticing the landscape, *sim?* How it is now turning to reddish purple clay, with fewer trees? It will be good to store it away in your mind, so that on afternoons during the rainy season, you may have something to occupy your time. The pigments and brushes for you are already purchased and stored at the *casa* in São Paulo."

At the thought of the paints waiting for her, Maranta did not know whether to be displeased or grateful. For it meant that the conde had already planned her leisure time, as well. But also, that *she* was the one, not Marigold, who had been selected as Vasco's *noiva,* even before she knew of the existence of the Monteiro family.

Maranta frowned, trying to sort out her emotions. Her pleasure in the paints dulled as she realized that it had evidently not occurred to the arrogant Count of Sorocaba that the Condessa Louisa might have come back to Brazil without Maranta Tabor.

The dogs began to bark excitedly ahead of them, and at this sound the conde said, "They have caught the scent of a jaguar. It is time, *menina,* for you to get back into the carriage."

9

Down the Avenida Paulista the heavy coach went, into the heart of São Paulo. The magnificent mansions belonging to the coffee barons stood on both sides of the street, framed in the dusk. Maranta shivered at the coolness of the evening air and cast a worried glance toward the condessa who sat upright with effort.

The gauchos, with the dogs, had disappeared at the entrance to the city, and the coach, driven by Rico, possessed only one rider beside it as it crossed the viaduct, passed through the *praca,* with its fountain in the middle, and made its way to the Monteiro *casa.*

The small wrought-iron balconies curved outward from the second-story windows, and the red, tiled roofs with ornate decorations at each corner—their curves and scrolls turning upward—proclaimed the wealth of their owners.

It was before the largest house that the coach stopped, halfway down the street. And within minutes, the iron gates had been opened by servants with lamps in their hands. At last, they had reached civilization.

To remove the dirt and grime from the journey in a tub filled with warm water—to sleep in a soft bed again instead of pallet and hammock—that was what Maranta thought of, until she looked at the condessa in the light.

She could not hide her alarm, and the condessa, seeing the girl's reaction, touched her hand and whispered in a weak voice, "Do not worry, my child. I shall be all right now that I am in São Paulo. The mineral waters have restorative powers, you know."

"I trust you will feel much better, senhora, after you have rested."

"Thank you, Maranta."

The black stallion was covered with foam, and the

conde, climbing from the saddle, handed the reins to a servant who led the animal away to be unsaddled and cooled down.

Then, with the condessa and Dona Isobel taken care of, Ruis gave orders for the carriage to be moved—not realizing that Maranta had stayed in the courtyard and was now seeking to unfasten Fado's cage from the back of the carriage.

As the vehicle rolled away, leaving Maranta alone on the pavement, she called out, "Wait, Rico," and hurried to catch up with the disappearing carriage.

The conde's hand reached out and stopped her. "What is so important that you have to chase the carriage, *menina?*"

"Fado," she gasped. "He is still tied to the back."

"Your little bird will be rescued, Maranta," he said gently. "Go now with Pará. She will show you to your room."

Much later they sat at the table in the huge dining room —the conde, Dona Isobel, and Maranta—with the empty chair at the other end of the table where the condessa should have been. Silver glittered under the candles' power, and dancing shadows appeared on the fine linen cloth with its inlay of delicate lace.

Maranta sat in silence, toying with the *doce da marmelo,* the hard quince jelly that was served as the last course. She waited for the conde to indicate that the meal was over; for it was very late and she wanted to escape the oppressive air that had threatened to ruin her dinner.

Surrounded by the accouterments of his wealth, the conde had subtly changed. He seemed more remote and restrained than ever. Gone were the rough clothes he had worn on the journey from Santos to São Paulo. Gone was the sense of camaraderie between them when she had ridden on the black stallion with him.

A mere change of clothes, and Ruis had become the imperious conde again, the proud head of the Monteiro family—and absolute ruler in his own domain.

At last, Ruis moved his chair back, giving the signal that the meal was over. He stood up while Maranta with her white shawl draped over her shoulders followed Dona Isobel from the room.

The man took his seat again, and as Maranta lingered in the hall, she saw the conde remove a *charuto* from the box offered him by the servant standing beside the chair, hold it to his nose for a moment before lighting it with the candle. Seeing him in his gold velvet chair that almost resembled a throne made Maranta feel very small and insignificant.

Pale silks and brocades draped the huge bed where Maranta was to sleep. Already, the covers had been turned down and a gown laid out for her.

For a week, the conde had said. That was how long they would stay in São Paulo before leaving on the last segment of their journey—up the Tietê River to the *fazenda*. And if the condessa were not well enough to travel by then, they would remain in the city for a longer period of time.

Maranta walked about the room, touching the fine draperies and unconsciously rearranging the objects on the table beside the gilt chair. Next to her bed, her jewelry case lay, and taking off the locket from around her neck, Maranta opened the case to place the locket inside. On top lay the elaborate cross of pearls and diamonds that the condessa had given her on her eighteenth birthday.

For the first time, a desire to try it on came over her. Would it make her look as imperious as the conde—with their fine family jewelry around her neck?

Maranta unclasped it, and when she had put it on, she tiptoed to the small mirror to see the effect. The magnificence overwhelmed her. No—she still looked the same. She was Maranta Tabor. And the necklace looked as if it belonged to someone else.

If she had become a nun, her cross would have been made of silver or some lesser metal—much more suitable —and she would be dressed in black, not white, as she was tonight—black like Dona Isobel and the condessa.

Maranta wandered around the room, forgetting about the necklace, since her mind had returned to the sick woman. Hastily, Maranta put her shawl about her shoulders, and picking up a candle, she left the bedroom to seek out the family chapel that was attached to the house. She had seen it earlier that evening when she had lost her way to the dining room.

No one was about in the hall to deter her or give her directions. Down the marble steps she went, intent on remembering the way she had gone earlier, walking through the maze of corridors toward the back of the house, stopping and then changing directions until finally she saw it—the door still ajar, and the candle burning upon the altar, with the Blessed Virgin smiling in welcome.

Maranta took the shawl from around her shoulders and placed it over her long, black hair. Reverently she carried the candle and approached the altar where she knelt.

Her lips moved in silence, and for a long time she remained, her knees sheltered from the cold marble floor by the velvet cushion. She prayed not only for the condessa, but for her own family as well. And with the recalling of each one dear to her, her heart grew sad and a tear escaped and dropped onto the velvet cushion.

There was a noise behind her, and alarmed, Maranta quickly stood up, searching the shadows. She was not alone, and her dark eyes, resembling limpid pools, widened in fright.

"You do not have to be afraid, *menina,*" he said, coming to stand before her.

In relief, she recognized the conde, who gazed at her in sympathy, taking in the tears that still clung to her lashes. But his sapphire eyes, latching onto the cross at her breast, underwent a sudden transformation. He took a step toward her, and in a hoarse voice croaked, "By what right are you wearing the *Cruzamento da Monteiro?* Take it off at once, Maranta. It is a sacrilege for you to have it on."

He made as if to jerk it off, and in defense, her hand went to her breast as she backed away from him.

"It . . . it was a gift—from the condessa," she answered in a whisper.

Her words brought a tense, incredible look to his face. "*Mãe* gave you the cross?"

"Y-Yes—before we left Charleston."

The conde closed his eyes, and the pain that filled his face was unmistakable.

Maranta realized then that the condessa had made some terrible breach in giving her the heirloom. Fumbling at the catch, she said, "I will gi-give it back, senhor."

"No, Maranta. If the condessa gave it to you, she . . . meant for you to have it."

He turned and fled from the chapel—leaving the puzzled Maranta alone before the Blessed Virgin.

More unhappy than ever, Maranta wandered around the *casa* by herself. The doctor came often, and Dona Isobel seemed totally oblivious of the lonely girl because of her nursing duties with the condessa.

And the conde. Ever since their encounter in the chapel, he had looked as if he hated her.

The only time Maranta saw him was in the evenings at dinner, and she felt so self-conscious that she made no attempt to join in the conversation but stared at her plate throughout the meals.

Maranta would have liked to see to have seen something of the city, but everyone was too busy for her to suggest it. It was almost like being confined to the ship again, with nothing to relieve her boredom. And she dared not go back into the chapel.

It was mid-morning and Maranta sat on the bench in the secluded garden. With nothing to do, she made up a game, trying to imagine what each place that the condessa and Dona Isobel had told her about, looked like—the spa outside São Paulo where the hot sulphur springs bubbled and where people went to improve their livers—

At the idea of some fat woman flushing out her overindulged liver with glass after glass of sulphur water, Maranta laughed aloud and then quickly turned her head to make sure no one had heard her.

She must be more careful—especially with the condessa lying sick in the massive bedroom upstairs.

The frown soon disappeared as Maranta's mind skipped to Ypiranga—where Dom Pedro I had given the cry of freedom, separating Brazil from Portugal, the mother country. There would have to be a fountain in the square, of course, where the people came each day for water. And perhaps there would be a statue of Dom Pedro, himself, astride his horse.

Maranta closed her eyes, attempting to conjure up a suitable statue, but instead of the emperor, her imagination gave her Ruis da Monteiro on his black stallion.

Suddenly a feeling of terror swept over her. If the condessa died, then Maranta would be entirely at the mercy of the conde, with no one to protect her from him.

Her lip quivered and her trembling hands folded in supplication. Penha—the shrine in the hills where miracles were made. If only she could go there, she would pray for a miracle. But Dona Isobel was too busy, and there was no one else she could ask to take her to the shrine.

Maranta sighed and she hid her troubled face in her hands. The long, black strands of hair hung over fragile shoulders.

"There is something wrong, senhorita?" the voice behind her asked.

A startled Maranta jerked her head up, and she turned in the direction of the voice to see the man who had evidently been watching her. His eyes were narrowed, and Maranta could see the same antagonism, with no hint of pity or concern for her. It was the same as it had been since that night in the chapel.

"Penha," she whispered, not realizing she had said the word aloud.

She could not move. His glance pinned her against the garden walls as effectively as if she had been one of the captured *borboletas,* skewered to its velvet casket.

"You wish to view our famous shrine in the hills?" he asked politely.

Maranta quickly nodded. "To . . . pray for the condessa," she said in a distressed voice, barely audible.

Again his eyes narrowed and Maranta dared not move.

"If you wish to go, I will take you, senhorita. And while you are there, I think it would be wise to pray for yourself, as well as for Mãe."

He turned his back to her, but halfway down the path, the conde stopped. Facing in her direction, the dark-haired man ordered, "Be ready in a half hour."

"Yes, senhor," she replied to his back, for already he had turned and was disappearing toward the stables.

10

She saw the conde reach out and take the basket from Pará, the Indian girl. Maranta hesitated at the edge of the courtyard, but Ruis, seeing her, placed the basket on the mosaic-tiled pavement, and with bold steps, walked toward Maranta.

"You are looking for the carriage?" he asked, standing before her with his long, black cape swinging over his shoulders.

Maranta nodded.

"A wheel is being repaired," he explained. "Besides, the road is too narrow for the carriage. We will take Diabo instead."

At the sound of his name, the black stallion snorted in impatience. Maranta took a step backward, but the conde's hand reached out to guide her to the horse. "You object?" he asked, gazing down at her with his superior, haughty mien.

"Yes," Maranta answered defiantly. "If . . . if we are to go by horse, then I wish to have one of my own. It is . . . degrading to be treated like a . . . a sack of coffee beans, hoisted in front."

"My apologies," he said, the coldness still evident in his eyes. "I was not aware that you rode."

"We are still strangers, senhor, so there are many things . . ."

". . . that I have yet to learn about you," he finished. "Well, today, it will be how well you can follow a donkey path up the hillside.

"Xangu," he shouted. And when the boy appeared, the conde said, "Saddle the mare with the condessa's saddle, immediately. The senhorita wishes to show off her horsemanship."

Even his choice of words antagonized her. But she

would not let him know it. Instead, Maranta would show the superior, arrogant conde just how good she was at sitting a horse.

When the mare was brought out, Maranta was perplexed. No sidesaddle, as she had been used to, but a smaller saddle similar to the conde's had been placed on the mare's back. Maranta looked down at her blue dress, and then to the saddled mare. Inadvertently, she caught the glint in the conde's eyes.

"There has been some mistake, senhor," she said, now furious at his joke. "You *know* I cannot ride in that type saddle."

"The only mistake, *pequena,* is in your dress. I suggest you run inside and borrow one of Mãe's riding habits. It will be much more suitable. But hurry, the wine is already getting hot."

So he thought he was going to get the better of her. Well, she would show him. And it would be his own fault if *everything* in the picnic basket were spoiled before she came out again.

Dona Isobel was helpful, even to finding a hat to shade Maranta's face from the sun. Luckily, the black divided riding skirt fit, even though it was quite old. And the hat, black also, was trimmed in silver, like the skirt.

Maranta hurried back into the courtyard where the conde waited. "Good. That is much better," he voiced, giving his reluctant approval to Maranta's costume. "And it did not take you forever, as I feared," he added.

Awkwardly, Maranta sat astride the little mare. "Do not worry, *pequena,*" Ruis said, sensing her uncomfortable feeling. "There is no one to censure you for riding like a man. And once you are used to it, you will see the advantages. Unlike Innocencia, you have much courage."

Hearing the man speak of his wife was reassuring to Maranta, even though his words were not flattering. Yet, he never mentioned Vasco, his brother. And Maranta, too shy to ask anything about the man who was waiting for her, said nothing but followed the conde out the gates into the street.

The little mare, ridden by Maranta, trotted alongside

the black stallion—up the hilly path away from the city of São Paulo.

She was still not comfortable, riding astride, but the girl gave no indication of it to her companion, Ruis da Monteiro. Her black, three-cornered suede hat, a smaller, more elegant version of the gaucho's hat, shaded her pale complexion from the sun and hid from view her serious, dark eyes with their worried thoughts mirrored in them.

For a long time, they met no one else on the road. Occasionally, a group of pilgrims made their way down the path from the hills—some on foot, some in litters, or palanquins, similar to the pictures Maranta had seen in the court of the Great Khans.

And for this occasional greeting when they met, Maranta was thankful. It had not occurred to her that she would be so alone with this arrogant, dark man. And she wondered why Dona Isobel had not objected to her journey. But then, Maranta remembered. Ruis da Monteiro made his own laws. And if he decided to ride off, leaving her in the hills, or even to take her virtue, there was no one to condemn him.

The wind whipped a strand of hair into Maranta's eyes, and the mare slowed her gait when she felt the slight tug on her reins. By the time Maranta's vision cleared, and she had righted her hat, Ruis and the black stallion were nowhere in sight.

Panic seized her, and as Maranta urged the mare on, her voice called out, "Ruis, Ruis." Around the bend in the road she went, and then she saw the black stallion, waiting.

The conde's eyes were on Maranta's face, and when she caught up with him, the terrified girl saw a strange expression flicker across the man's features. "You thought I had left you, *pequena?*" he asked.

"My hair got in my eyes, and when I looked up . . ."

"The bend in the road is sharp. And I did not realize you had stopped," he explained.

Ruis got off Diabo and, surveying the ground near the road, he said, "This is as good a place as any to have our lunch. You are hungry, Maranta?"

95

His sudden use of her name made her wary of him. She had become used to his calling her *pequena* or *menina,* as if she were a child and beneath his notice. And she was not sure she liked his reverting to calling her by her proper name.

"I am very thirsty," she acknowledged. She blushed as he continued staring at her; for now she had to decide how to get down from the horse.

Ruis suddenly laughed, as if he had become conscious of her dilemma.

"You swing one leg over the horse, *pequena,*" he advised.

"Well, you don't have to stare at me while I attempt it."

He ignored the petulance in her voice, and before she knew it, Maranta was lifted off the horse and placed on the ground by the arrogant conde in his black cape. "This will solve your problem," he said, "until you have practiced."

The hard object at the conde's side dug into her flesh and made Maranta aware of the wildness of the countryside. He was wearing a gun.

"Are there . . . jaguars in this area?" she asked.

"An occasional one," he answered, "although snakes are far more prevalent."

Maranta shuddered and looked toward the group of rocks not far from the road.

"We will avoid the rocks," he said, following the direction of her gaze. "There is a spring not far from here—a more suitable place to spread our lunch."

With the mare's reins in her hands, she walked behind Ruis until he ordered her to stop. "Wait here," he said, "until I see that the area is safe."

Soon he was back without Diabo. From Maranta's hands he took the reins of the mare and tied them to a nearby sapling. "It would not do to have Diabo tied too close to the mare. He might forget that this is a religious pilgrimage we are on."

The conde's dark eyes swept over her, and Maranta, disconcerted at his manner, stared at the ground. But the conde continued, "I shall wait here for a while,

Maranta. But do not linger too long—or I shall come to find you."

She walked past him, her head held high, even though her cheeks were burning. Why did he have to embarrass her so? Somehow, with the condessa and Dona Isobel, it had not seemed so bad when they had stopped to take care of the necessities. She was almost sorry now that she had asked to come.

But then, Maranta thought of the condessa. And it seemed more urgent than ever to get to the shrine at Penha.

"I should tell you, *menina*," the conde said as they finished their lunch, "a little about the shrine.

"Many of the people who come to pray are simple, trusting people—unsophisticated in their knowledge. They clutter the altar with representations of any parts of the body they wish to have healed. You might see a foot of clay, or a heart, or any other . . . organ that needs attention—But they believe in miracles. For them, that is the important thing," he said, his voice suddenly taking on a harsh and condescending tone.

"And I, too, will pray for a miracle, senhor," Maranta's voice affirmed with a slight tremor.

"Then, come. Let us not waste any more time."

As soon as they reached the place, Maranta felt at peace. There was something comforting about the shrine high on the hill, with the wind blowing, making a slight whistling sound. And as she knelt before the statue, which was aged from the weather and the constant wind, Maranta forgot the objects on the altar, forgot all else but the condessa. Her lips moved silently, while the statue seemed to smile at her and give her courage.

The hand on her shoulder finally brought her mind back to her surroundings.

"It is growing late, *menina*. We must leave before darkness sets in." The conde's impatient words held no tinge of apology for having disturbed her.

He took Maranta's hand and led her toward the horses. As he lifted her upon the mare, Ruis looked into her eyes, and in a dry tone, he said, "And did you pray for yourself as well, Maranta?"

"Did I need to, senhor? With the great Count of Sorocaba protecting me?"

His lips tightened into a thin line, and he made no effort to reply to her impertinent question. Instead, he moved Diabo toward the road and began to canter, leaving Maranta to follow as best she could on the little mare.

The lamps were lit by the time they reached the *casa*. Dona Isobel stood at the door, and her worried frown lifted when the two came into sight.

No one noticed that Maranta could barely walk—for all eyes were on the condessa seated in the salon.

"Mãe," the conde greeted her with surprise. "You are feeling better?"

"*Sim,* Ruis. The doctor has given me permission to get up. I have rested in bed long enough."

It was a coincidence, Maranta thought. For it was too early for a miracle. Perhaps the condessa had not been so ill after all—just exhausted—and the trip to the shrine had been unnecessary. Although her soul did not protest the wasted journey, Maranta's body rebelled. It was an effort to get up the stairs by herself, and when Maranta saw the warm bath that Pará had prepared for her, she stumbled toward it.

Later as she sat painfully in the tub, Maranta wondered if this was why Ruis had suggested she pray for herself. And she was sorry that she had not done so.

The tray of food remained on the table—untouched. And the room was filled with silence. Not even Fado in his cage interrupted the quiet by as much as a chirp. Sighing, Maranta covered the cage and blew out the light.

The tears came slowly, staining the embroidered pillow cover, while her body ached from the long, hard journey into the hills. Never had she felt more alone—in a house of strangers. It was as if she had been swallowed up—completely forgotten by anyone who had ever spoken her name with love.

11

"Marigold . . . that was her name—Marigold Tabor."

The man stood at the long counter in Keppie's Tavern and ordered another mug of rum. "Robert Tabor was seeing her off today on the *Beaufort*—with those two foreign women. Promised to some Portugee bigwig on a coffee plantation in Brazil, I was told."

At the mention of the Tabor name, Shaun Banagher put down his mug. Chad, seated beside him, paled. He got up noisily from the table and began to say something to Shaun, but the auburn-haired man, interested in the conversation at the counter, motioned for Chad to be quiet. He reluctantly sat down again.

"No, it was the other twin," someone corrected. *"Marigold* is the one that married that fellow from the up country—her cousin—several weeks ago."

Chad, afraid to look at Shaun, closed his eyes and groaned.

"Now, I've got to hand it to that Robert Tabor," the second man continued, "Marrying his daughters off so well. One to coffee and the other to gold."

The first man scratched his head and replied, "I reckon so. Only if *I* had such beauties in my house, I'd be real slow to hand 'em over to some other man to enjoy—'specially that one with the golden hair."

The other men laughed at his comment and drank to his sentiment. But Shaun left his unfinished drink on the table and blindly headed for the door. Chad rushed to catch up with Shaun, but the three men weaving their way into the tavern impeded his progress.

"Shaun," Chad called. "Wait for me, man."

But Shaun, oblivious to anything but his own pain, kept walking, his feet moving along the wooden pathway from the wharf.

A few minutes later, Chad matched his stride to that of his friend, who had slowed down and was now breathing rapidly from the exertion. It was Shaun's first venture out after the accident, and at the corner, with the street lamp illuminating his friend's face, Chad glanced at Shaun and was appalled at what the light revealed.

In a low, dangerous voice, Shaun said, "You lied to me, Chad."

The anger that Chad had curbed for Shaun's sake overflowed at the sight of the man's pained, twisted features.

"Forget about her, Shaun. The bitch isn't worth worrying over."

Suddenly, Chad found himself on the ground, nursing a bruised jaw, while Shaun disappeared haltingly from sight. Shaun's newly healed chest wound was of far more concern to Chad than his own bruised jaw. He should have kept his temper, rather than risk damage to the recuperating, auburn-haired giant. He should have known that Shaun would defend the girl no matter what she did.

Damn! Why hadn't he kept Shaun out of the tavern? Especially on the very day that the other Tabor girl had left Charleston with those two foreign women. He could kick himself. He should have known that the men in the tavern would be talking about the girl and discussing her twin sister as well. And after he had been so careful to assure Shaun that Marigold Tabor was visiting relatives in the up country.

Now, Shaun knew that she was not only visiting her cousin, but had married him.

He picked himself up from the ground and headed for the rail shanty, where Shaun sat at the table, his head in his hands. The man did not look up when Chad entered. And Chad, afraid to say anything that would antagonize the man further, made a fire in the stove and heated the stew for their supper.

"I didn't believe her, Chad. I thought she was being dramatic when she told me of her father's threats."

The unfilled earthen plate was hurled from the table to break into shards against the wall. "Damn Robert Tabor!" Shaun said, standing up. "Damn his soul to hell!"

At least no one in the tavern had accused Shaun of being jilted by the girl. That was Chad's only consolation as he sat by himself at the table and ate his stew, already cold.

The gate swung noisily behind her. Marigold, avoiding the path of the black-and-white-speckled guinea hens, gathered up her skirts and walked quickly toward the big house.

True to her promise, Cousin Julie had moved her things to the cottage. She remained at the big house during the day, but after supper each night Julie would go back to the cottage. And Marigold, feeling more vulnerable than ever, was forced to spend the evenings alone with Crane.

The main meal was in the middle of the day, and already, Marigold was late for it. She found Julie and Crane seated at the dining table, finishing their soup. Marigold, with a breathless apology, took her place at the end of the table.

"You seem to have no conception of time, Marigold," Crane scolded. "And because of that, you will have to forgo the first course."

"I am not hungry anyway," Marigold announced as the servant began clearing the table of the soup plates.

"We are having quail—one of your favorites," Julie spoke up, attempting to soften the harshness of Crane's words to his wife. "You'll enjoy that, I'm sure."

Marigold smiled and nodded. Crane still looked at his wife with a frown on his saturnine features, and Marigold, afraid he would question her as to where she had been, turned her tawny eyes to him and asked, "Did you bring up much gold from the mine this morning?"

The frown remained on Crane's face. "Not as much as I hoped. One of the slaves drowned in the underground water. I had to have the others whipped before they would venture back down again. Damned inconvenient, since we have only a short time to blast before winter sets in."

Not one shred of sympathy did he show. And Marigold, instead of revealing her antipathy to his lack of feelings, casually asked, "Did the man who drowned have a family?"

"Yes, Marigold. But I forbid you to take one of your goodie baskets to them. An interfering wife can be a scourge to her husband and spoil everything he has worked for."

"Crane . . ."

"Now, Mother," he said at the woman's protest, "Marigold has to learn, like Floride, not to barge into her husband's affairs."

Floride Calhoun, Vice-President Calhoun's wife, was a sore spot with Marigold. Crane was constantly harping on the damage the low-country woman had done, accusing her of bringing about the estrangement between Andrew Jackson and his vice-president, John Calhoun, because of her snobbish ways.

"I expect there was more to it than Floride's snubbing of the barmaid," Marigold answered, refusing to be cowed by Crane's behavior.

"Peggy O'Neal is no longer a barmaid, but Secretary of War Eaton's wife. And any insult to Eaton is a double insult to the President," Crane said. "Calhoun should have kept his wife locked away. Then maybe Jackson would not have reorganized his cabinet and removed every Calhoun member. Now, he has no influence in Washington at all, because his snobbish wife thought she was too good to associate with Mrs. Eaton."

"He seemed to have enough influence to keep the Senate from approving Mr. Van Buren as minister to England," Marigold answered, her voice unusually sweet.

"Marigold, a knowledge of politics is not becoming in a woman. Your father may have allowed it at Midgard, but here at Cedar Hill, it will not be a subject for discussion."

"Yes, Crane."

Soon the ground was covered with a layer of snow and ice, and work at the gold mine was suspended.

But the cold weather heralded a new activity—one that Marigold tried not to think about. She knew it was necessary, but the high-pitched squeals of the hogs as they were slaughtered brought nightmares to her sleep. The making of sausage, the hanging of hams underneath the house in the cellar went on with Julie supervising, and Marigold was glad when it was over and that she had had no part in it.

Even though Julie did not sleep at the big house, Marigold was aware that Crane still considered his mother mistress of the plantation. All he seemed to require of Marigold was to frequent his bed and look pretty, as some inanimate fixture he could claim as his own.

And although she had little prior knowledge of the way most men treated their wives, Marigold soon realized that their relationship was a poor one, not like the marriage between her mother and father. However strong and stubborn Robert Tabor might be, he had never openly subjected Eulalie to ridicule or degradation, as Crane seemed to take delight in with Marigold. For Crane never let Marigold forget for one day that Shaun Banagher had jilted her.

The fire was low on the bedroom hearth, and Marigold hurriedly finished brushing her hair as she heard Crane's footsteps on the stairs.

He walked into the room. Marigold, wary of his glazed, dark eyes that passed over her, gathered her peignoir closer to her body and turned her back to Crane.

With a sudden violence that stunned the golden-haired girl, his hand reached out and pushed her onto the bed. "Crane," she protested, but already he was on top of her.

Jerking her head back by the long hair, he said, "Call me Shaun."

So now it was to begin all over again—that degradation that gave him such pleasure.

When she did not obey his command, he pulled her hair tighter from her scalp and ordered, "Say it, Marigold. It's Shaun you want, isn't it, Marigold? Admit it. Not Crane, your husband—but that lusty, Irish animal, Shaun Banagher."

Marigold kept silent, refusing to say the name. Deliberate and slow, Crane removed his robe. Marigold's arms were taken from the sleeves of the open peignoir, and then she heard the splitting of the matching gown.

"So beautiful," he murmured, kissing her breasts, and then pulling at the tender nipples with his teeth, hurting her. Gratefully, she felt his mouth move lower, but then the real teasing began, and her body grew warm under his actions, in spite of herself.

"Is this the way he aroused you, Marigold? Made you desire him?"

Suddenly she felt his hardness on her thigh, before he found the vulnerable moist softness. At his insistence, she put her arms around his neck and finally whispered, "Shaun," for she was now beyond any turning back.

Succumbing to Shaun's name, she said it over and over, until she felt Crane begin the slow, rhythmic movement. Faster and faster it came—frenzied and passionate. At last, something exploded inside her, and she moaned at the fulfillment.

After his success, Crane kept her pressed to him as he taunted her. "You are a wanton and a slut, Marigold. A proper wife feels nothing. I don't know why I took pity on you and married you."

And Marigold, with tears in her eyes, was shoved aside, while her husband turned his back to her and went to sleep.

The next morning, Marigold hid her fresh bruises under a long-sleeved, high-necked velvet dress—a practice in which she had become adept since marrying Crane Caldwell. One day, he would not get away with it, she vowed.

"Is there something the matter, my dear?" Cousin Julie asked. "You seem so sad this morning."

Marigold turned to the woman, who sat in the rocker and embroidered the dainty, delicate baby bonnet by the warm fire in the parlor. She tried to smile, but tears came to her eyes instead.

"I'm afraid I miss my parents—and the rest of my family," the girl confided.

At once, Julie's dark eyes were sympathetic. "Perhaps Crane will take you for a visit when warm weather comes —unless of course, you are . . ."

Julie smiled and looked down at the tiny hat in her lap.

"Although I'm sewing this tiny garment for a friend, it may not be long before I can begin one for my own grandchild. It will be such a joy when you and Crane . . ."

"No," Marigold said, her face losing color. She jumped from the chair, and seeing her distress, Julie attempted to right her indiscretion.

"Forgive me, Marigold. I did not mean to upset you. You and Crane have been married such a short time. Please forgive an impatient old woman for dreaming aloud far too soon."

Marigold could not help it. She ran from the room, forgetting her manners, only aware of the repugnant thought that ran through her brain. She did not want Crane Caldwell's child. But already, his seed might be growing inside her.

She knew Feena had secretly concocted potions for some of the slave girls to keep them from becoming pregnant. Why had she not thought to ask Feena about it before leaving Charleston? There must be somebody at Cedar Hill who had the same knowledge as Feena. She would begin a subtle inquiry, starting with Juniper, the cook. Perhaps she would confide in Marigold the name of the *mauma* who made amulets and possets for the slaves. But she would be careful not to reveal the real reason for seeking the information.

The black woman stood in the middle of the kitchen, kneading bread on the rough table. She looked up as Marigold entered the kitchen.

"You want somethin', Miss Marigold?" the woman asked, still punching at the dough with her flour-covered hands.

"Not really," she answered, undecided now on how to approach the woman. "I just . . ."

"Oh, Juniper," the feminine voice sounded behind her, "I neglected to tell you that Mr. Crane wants syllabub for supper tonight. Will you have time to make it?"

"Yes'm. But the milk needs to be took out'n the . . ."

"I'll do it myself," Julie said, changing her mind. She reached for the apron hanging behind the door. "You just

105

keep on with the bread-baking," she continued, tying the large white apron around her waist.

Julie looked at Marigold and said, "It's Crane's favorite dessert, and I know you'll want to learn how it's done. It might be good for you to watch, my dear."

Disappointed, Marigold stayed in the kitchen and watched Julie as she prepared the congealed dessert. The opportunity of speaking privately with Juniper was lost.

Two days later, Marigold gave up trying to talk with Juniper alone. She had not realized how closely Cousin Julie supervised the kitchen. Marigold would just have to find someone else, outside the big house. And she could not wait any longer.

With her cloak sheltering her from the cold wind, the girl slipped out of the house and walked toward the barn. She passed the corn crib and continued in the direction of the slave cabins.

Although it was the middle of the afternoon, the sky was beginning to grow dark. Marigold glanced up at the gray, clabbered clouds that obscured the sun. A storm was in the making. And as if to give credence to her thought, a gust of icy wind whipped through the bare branches of the giant poplar tree behind the barn. Like some grotesque puppet, manipulated by an unseen hand, the tree danced in a lumbersome, menacing movement, bowing its branches toward the ground, and then lifting them awkwardly into the air.

Faster, Marigold walked, heading in the direction that Crane had forbidden her to go. And Sesame, standing at the door of the barn, followed the girl's progress with dark, troubled eyes.

Billowing smoke drew Marigold toward the cabin at the end of the path. She hesitated at the door, painted blue to keep the evil spirits out.

"Hello," Marigold called. There was a surreptitious movement from within. Yet no one answered her or came to the door.

Marigold knocked this time as she called out. Still, no one came.

Shivering from the long walk through the icy wind,

Marigold decided she would not wait. She pushed open the door and stepped inside.

"So—you have come to spy on me."

Her husband, Crane, sat up in bed, a quilt gathered around his bare chest, while a naked black child hovered uncertainly in the corner.

A puzzled Marigold looked toward her husband and then back to the child. And a wave of sick disgust suddenly swept over her.

Silently, she turned to walk out, but Crane jumped from the bed and grabbed her by the wrist. "You cannot go, yet."

Crane, looking at the boy, ordered, "Put on your clothes and get out."

And Marigold, her knees unsteady, sank into the chair by the fire and shut her eyes. A few minutes later, the door closed, and Crane, fully dressed, stood over her. She was now alone with her husband.

"You should not have opened the door, Marigold," Crane admonished.

"You are . . . despicable," she uttered, her voice unable to hide her disgust at her husband's actions.

"Did I not forbid you to come to the cabins?" he said, his voice displaying a growing rage at her disobedience.

Marigold, paying no attention to his rising anger, replied, "Yes—and now I see why."

"You saw nothing, Marigold. Nothing, at all."

"I saw . . . enough. You and that child—together —naked."

"And is that a blow to your pride, my aristocratic wife, to learn that I seek comfort in an earthier setting?"

"I don't care how many wenches you take to bed with you, Crane. But to . . . to molest an innocent little boy. You would be hanged if anyone found out."

"But no one's going to find out, Marigold. Simply because you're going to keep quiet."

"The blow to Cousin Julie when she learns . . ."

"You will never tell my mother what you have seen, Marigold!"

All at once, his voice rose and fear clouded his dark

eyes. And Marigold, seeing it, recognized the weapon she now held in her hands.

"For a price, Crane. I will keep silent—for a price."

He hesitated. "And your . . . price?"

"You will stay out of my bed," she said. "You won't ever touch or taunt me again."

Suddenly, Crane laughed, and the fear disappeared from his eyes.

"And you think that will be such a harsh punishment for me? I hate to disillusion you, Marigold. Even though I have been more than satisfactory for you, *you* have never been able to give me much pleasure."

She flinched at the words that matched his cold, hard eyes.

"And remember one thing, Marigold. You are still my wife. If you are ever unfaithful, or if you ever try to leave me, I will kill you."

There was nothing else to say. Marigold, her heart heavy, got up from the chair. And Crane, putting on his coat, walked out into the chilling wind with Marigold, his wife, unwillingly at his side.

In silence, they walked back to the big house. A devil's bargain Marigold had made. Now, it was no longer necessary to seek out the brewer of herbs and possets.

12

The Tietê River—Maranta stood on its banks and looked at the painted canoes loaded down with the trunks and supplies. The prows rose out of the water, and the faces carved on them seemed to stare at her.

"How long is the river?" Maranta asked, her soft voice barely loud enough to be heard by Ruis, who stood beside her.

"Between seven and eight hundred miles," he answered.

Maranta gasped. "You mean . . ."

Ruis laughed. "We will not be going the entire way. Only to the falls at Hitû. The *fazenda* is not far from there."

She looked again at the *monsoon,* the canoe fleet that was almost ready to start on its journey.

"And . . . is there much danger?" Maranta asked.

"The pilots know the river. Don't be afraid, Maranta. They are familiar with all the shallows and rapids along the way. And you will have ample protection when we portage around them. The condessa has gotten you this far. She would never forgive me if I allowed some *guaicurú* to sweep you onto his horse and carry you off into the plains."

Maranta, undecided whether the conde was teasing her or not, refrained from asking any more questions.

Huddled under the *poncho* that the conde had forced her to wear on top of her clothes, Maranta stared miserably at the figure seated in front of her. The conde's back, so formidable, not only emphasized his aloofness, but cut off Maranta's view ahead. She could only gaze toward the banks as they passed by rapidly.

From the canoe, Maranta could not distinguish the

jataí trees from any of the others. For they were all a blur of green viewed through the steady drizzle of rain.

Such a small thing to be annoyed about. But all day Maranta had experienced the discomforts of traveling, without really seeing much of the countryside. Earlier in the journey, Dona Isobel had told her how the Indians made their canoes from the bark and even took the resinous substance from the roots of the *jataí* trees to burn in their lamps. How she wished she were in the same canoe with Dona Isobel. Then, she could talk with her along the way.

But Ruis had arranged their seating. And once again, Maranta was paired with the arrogant, silent conde.

Her leg grew numb, and the girl tried to change her position. Immediately, the conde turned his head. "Be still, Maranta. We are entering a dangerous section of the river. And I do not wish to fish you out of the water if the canoe should overturn."

Again, she stared at his back and sank to the same uncomfortable position, afraid to move because of his warning.

Tents, horses, carts, and all manner of supplies followed behind them in separate boats. And alongside them were additional canoes rigged with guns, manned by alert guards.

As the rain gradually subsided, Maranta kept her eyes on the nearer bank, certain that she saw lurking figures watching their progress. But she was mistaken. It was only a group of anthills in the distance. And recognizing them, she relaxed.

She remembered that Dona Isobel had told her that once a priest had excommunicated a group of ants because they had eaten up an altar cloth. Without realizing it, Maranta laughed aloud.

"You find the trip amusing, *menina?*" the conde asked. As he turned his head and waited for her answer, the cold water dripped from his hat onto his soaked *poncho.*

Maranta felt as if she had been reprimanded by Father Ambrose, his look was so stern.

"I was . . . thinking of a story that Dona Isobel told this morning," she said, her smile no longer on her lips.

"So?"

Was that an invitation for her to relate it to him? Maranta grew visibly smaller under the heavy black cloak.

"I do not think it . . . would amuse you," she apologized.

He shrugged his shoulders and turned around. Again, Maranta gazed at his broad, unbending back that obscured her view.

They made camp for the night not far from the riverbanks. The men strung their hammocks between trees, extending a circle around the two tents that they set up for the women.

Small and cramped, the tents were only large enough to cover two hammocks and no more. And so it was that Dona Isobel was alone in one tent, while Maranta shared the other with the condessa.

Maranta was glad that she did not have to be alone, like Dona Isobel. She was still frightened from seeing the huge snake swimming in the river that afternoon and overturning one of the canoes loaded with supplies.

What a terrible sight, seeing it thrash in the water when the guards turned their guns on it. She had felt the shakiness of their own canoe in the waves the snake had generated. What if it had been *their* canoe instead that had overturned? Now, Maranta knew why the conde was so stern with her when she moved about. There was no telling *what* was lurking under the water.

But he was still overbearing—forcing the women to get ready for bed much earlier than usual and bringing the water into their tents for the nightly footwashing because of the *chiguas* that could burrow underneath the toenails and cause painful swelling of the feet.

It was not even dark yet—and Maranta could hear the men laughing and talking a short distance away, where the mules and horses were corralled.

Dona Isobel came into the condessa's tent to help her. Since there was not enough room for the three of them,

111

Maranta slipped out to put water in Fado's cage, which hung in a tree immediately outside the tent. When that was done, Maranta forgot about the bucket on the ground and stumbled against it, spilling the rest of the water. In exasperation, the girl stared down at the ground, as she righted the empty bucket. Now, there was no water to wash in. And Maranta, afraid of what the conde would say if she requested more water, decided to go to the river herself. It would take only minutes. She would be back before anyone missed her.

Maranta walked carefully past the campfire where they had cooked their supper—black beans and rice, with fresh fish. Between empty hammocks she went, with the bucket over her arm. She could still hear the men laughing and talking and could smell the odor of tobacco that wafted through the air. Soon she was at the water's edge. Gathering up her skirts, Maranta knelt to fill the container with river water.

The sky, in that brief period between twilight and total darkness, was aflame with wisps of gold and purple, and as she stood up, she observed its beauty with her artist's eye, capturing the scene for some future painting.

Ruis had not mentioned the pigments or brushes again. Maranta hoped they were packed in one of the crates in the canoes. But what if they had been in the crate that was lost that afternoon on the river?

Maranta frowned as she walked back toward the camp. There was no sound from the men in the distance. And the shapes of the trees and shrubs—no longer highlighted by the last rays of the sun—loomed before her.

Maranta increased her pace. She had lingered far too long at the river. The landscape had lost its sense of peace and beauty and was now a colorless gray-black that was becoming increasingly darker—alive with dozens of moving winged creatures. And they looked as if they were heading straight for her. Maranta stopped and brushed her hair back to get a better view of them. In panic, she remained rooted to the same spot, not knowing which way to turn to escape this menace that had appeared so suddenly.

Ruis, taking Diabo to the water's edge, looked up as the sky blackened with winged creatures. Vampire bats —he might have known they would smell the scent of horses and mules and come out of the caves in search of fresh blood.

His one thought was to get Diabo out of danger, but as he wheeled the horse around, his eyes spotted the small, vulnerable figure standing directly in the path of the bats.

Maranta? But she was supposed to be safe in her tent. A small hand went up, brushing the long, black hair from her face. It *was* Maranta.

Instantly Ruis spurred Diabo toward her and shouted, "Maranta! Cover your face! The bats!"

She screamed as the first creature attached itself to her arm, biting into her flesh with its vicious teeth. She hit at it with the bucket, spilling the water. But in a split second, the bat was gone and she was lifted from the ground.

Into the sheltered copse Ruis rode with the girl in his arms, as the bats, their victim suddenly snatched from them, continued their flight toward the corral.

Hysterically, Maranta clung to the man who had rescued her. And the conde, forgetting to reprimand her for disobeying him, held her in his arms—quietly soothing her until her sobs subsided.

"I am s-sorry," she finally whispered. "I was seeing to Fado and I spilled the water. I didn't want you to know."

"Are you so afraid of me, *menina,* that you could not ask me to get more for you?" he asked in a sad voice.

"Y-Yes," she affirmed.

Ruis da Monteiro's jaw clenched at Maranta's apologetic confession. And in a voice harsh and cynical, he warned, "Someday, Maranta, that worthless little bird will be the death of you."

Dona Isobel, staring out of the tent, was relieved when Ruis brought Maranta back to camp. In the language that was foreign to her, Maranta vaguely heard the exchange between the conde and the woman.

But when Maranta was placed in the hammock in Dona Isobel's tent, Ruis explained, "Isobel will stay with Mãe tonight. Because of her heart, I do not want the condessa

113

to know what has happened. . . . You will remain here where I can attend to your arm."

"I am sorry . . ."

"It cannot be helped, *menina*. But soon, you will learn that I do not give orders for my own gratification."

Ruis sat beside the hammock until the girl went to sleep. And then, he left the tent to find his own hammock to rest for what remained of the night.

The next morning, Maranta's arm was sore, but she tried to dismiss the unpleasant episode by thinking instead of the journey ahead. She went down to watch while the cargo was reloaded for their continued trip on the river.

Maranta was now able to tell when they were approaching another cataract, with the distant rumbling of water growing gradually louder, and the canoes gliding more swiftly along the river without benefit of the long spear paddles. And even though she was conscious of the hazards, Maranta was glad to leave the canoe at intervals and walk on the banks while the horses and carts were unloaded.

As she trudged behind a cart or sat inside with the other two women to be jolted over the terrain until the Tietê became navigable again, Maranta's mind turned more and more to Vasco—the unknown man she was to marry—who was waiting for her at the *fazenda*.

When, finally, they left the canoe fleet near the falls at Hitú, the girl realized she would never be able to find her way back to civilization. She was trapped by mountains and jungled forests, vampire bats and anacondas—insurmountable obstacles.

With a shiver, Maranta clutched the bird cage closer to her. Her one small consolation was the cheerful little green bird, Fado, who had miraculously survived the watery trip without losing a single tail feather.

13

With the condessa and Dona Isobel, Maranta sat in the garden of the café in Hitû. The town was a welcome surprise to the girl; she had believed there would be no settlements beyond São Paulo.

"There are many *aldeas*—Indian villages—scattered throughout the area too, Maranta," Dona Isobel explained. "The Jesuits were quite productive in converting the Indians to the faith."

The condessa laughed. "That is a matter of opinion, Maranta. And when you meet Patû, you will understand. There never was a more pagan *mameluco* than he. Sometimes I wonder if he still shrinks heads as his grandfather did before him."

"Patû?" Maranta repeated. "Who is that?"

"The Indian servant who takes care of Vasco," answered Dona Isobel. And at her reply, the condessa frowned, as if the woman had been indiscreet.

The white-haired condessa suddenly tapped her cane, and a waiter immediately poured coffee into their cups that were already half-filled with sugar.

The beverage was much too sweet for Maranta, and she sipped little of it. But it went unnoticed, for Ruis soon returned with transportation to the *fazenda*.

It was a palanquin, the shaded litter similar to the ones Maranta had seen in São Paulo and Penha.

If it had not been for her increasing anxiety in meeting Vasco da Monteiro, Maranta would have enjoyed this new experience—sitting back on the soft cushions and feeling the soothing sway as the palanquin, attached by poles to the mules' harnesses, was carried along the shaded slopes of the *terra-roxa*, that purplish red earth that produced the finest coffee plants in all of Brazil.

"You are very pale, Maranta. Is the swaying making you seasick?" the old condessa asked.

The girl quickly shook her head, but her voice revealed its telltale tremor. "I am f-fine, Dona Louisa."

"You may begin calling me 'Mãe,'" she said matter-of-factly, "for by this time tomorrow, you will be my daughter."

The closer they got to the *fazenda,* the more alert the old condessa seemed, while Maranta grew visibly paler.

By this time tomorrow. Maranta closed her eyes and rested her dark head against the pillow. So she was to be given no chance to get to know Vasco before she was pushed into being his wife. But she would not think of that now. She was so sleepy . . .

The voices were low and near. Vaguely, she recognized the deep voice of Ruis, but not the words he spoke.

"*Sim,* Dom Ruis," another male voice answered, and as Maranta opened her eyes, she gave a sudden cry, for a savage-looking man was bending over her. She moved quickly to avoid him.

"Do not be afraid, senhorita," Ruis said. "Patû is merely curious to see what Vasco's *noiva* looks like. He did not mean to startle you." Ruis reached out to help the unsteady Maranta to her feet.

"Shall I carry you to your room?" the conde asked.

"I can walk," she assured Ruis and pushed herself away from him.

He let her go and spoke again to the Indian, whose dark features revealed no emotion at Maranta's reaction to him.

"We are at the *fazenda?*" Maranta asked the conde when the Indian was no longer in sight.

"Yes, *menina.* And Mãe and Dona Isobel have already gone inside." The conde seemed amused, treating her once more as he would a child.

Eager and curious faces peeked around the corner of the *fazenda.* Maranta self-consciously brushed her skirts down to smooth them, and her hand went up to her disheveled hair.

The house was like a fortress, built on a high elevation —its walls of *pisé,* that claylike white stucco, and its roof of red tile. And on the left, in front of the chapel, a tall crucifix shadowed the ground beneath it.

As Maranta stood on the sheltered veranda of the *fazenda,* she looked down upon miles of sloped terraces, with green bushes jutting out in symmetrical rows.

"I have never seen a coffee plant before," Maranta confided.

The conde, following her gaze, said, "It is a beautiful sight when they are all in bloom. Like a vast, endless field of snow." The pride in his voice was undisguised. "But you will have ample opportunity to see it, so we need not stand here any longer."

The conde clapped his hands, and a young black girl appeared.

"Sassia is to be your personal maid, Maranta. Go with her, and she will see to your needs."

"But how will I get her to understand me?"

"She speaks English. That is the reason I brought her here."

The black girl smiled and took a few steps, expecting Maranta to follow. But Maranta hesitated and looked back toward the palanquin. "Fado?"

"Is already in your room," Ruis assured her, his voice only slightly irritated.

Maranta followed Sassia through the reception hall and up the stairs to the second floor where the family's sleeping quarters were situated.

Maranta's room was in the center of the house. Almost like a prison, she thought. But she soon forgot that at the sight of the tub that had been loaded onto the *Beaufort* in Charleston. It was sitting in the corner of her bedroom, and Maranta looked longingly toward it.

"I will bring the hot water," the girl said, "and wash and brush your hair until it shines. Then, Dom Vasco will not be able to take his eyes off you tonight."

At the mention of Vasco's name, the same anxiety that she had felt earlier swept over her. Only a short reprieve

117

—and then she would be face to face with her intended husband.

Silently, she let Sassia attend her, her mind on the dreaded evening ahead.

"And which dress will you wear tonight, *yayá?*" she asked Maranta, who stood in her petticoats beside Fado's cage.

Maranta shrugged. "I do not care. *You* choose one for me, Sassia," she said.

The girl's hands eagerly riffled through the row of dresses and stopped at the cream-colored silk, with its wide bands of brocade braid around the bottom of the skirt.

"I think . . . this one," Sassia said, shaking it to remove the last wrinkle. "And the tortoiseshell combs for your hair."

"But I have no combs."

"They are a gift from the *sinhá-dona,* the Condessa Louisa," Sassia explained.

And Sassia, taking over the arranging of Maranta's long hair, appeared satisfied with her work. As she led Maranta down to the main *sala,* Sassia's eyes shone with pride for her mistress, the girl who was to be Dom Vasco's wife.

But Maranta's eyes showed her dismay and nervousness. Everything was strange and alien—Sassia's calling her *yayá,* the parlor labeled by another name. Would she ever become used to the foreign words, the foreign food, and most of all, the foreigner who waited for her?

Maranta licked her dry lips and forced her hands to be still, for the condessa was walking toward her to draw her into the room. The white-haired woman's black dress was very formal, and her manner gave no indication of the long, hard journey she had suffered.

"Maranta, how lovely you look tonight," she said, taking her hand. "Vasco has been waiting impatiently to see you."

The man sat in a chair across the room—a younger version of Ruis, with his blue eyes, his hair that shone like satin. Yet, he was different, too, a paler version upon close inspection, like a reproduction of an original with lines

118

not quite so well defined. He watched her hesitant progress with an amused look on his face.

Vasco made no effort to rise. Like a haughty king he sat and waited for Maranta to come to him. And when she stood before the man, he held out his ringed hand to her. He brought her delicately shaped fingers to his lips, but instead of releasing them, he grasped them tighter, so that Maranta could not step back.

"You have done well, Mãe. I compliment you on your selection."

And to Maranta, he spoke quietly. "My apologies for not rising, Maranta Tabor. But you see, my legs have been no use to me since the accident."

"Vasco—"

The young man interrupted his mother. "Better for the girl to know now, so that she can back out if she does not want a cripple for a husband."

Pity rushed into Maranta's heart at the sight of the handsome man, so young and so tragic. And the pity was mixed with relief. The marriage would be in name only, and for the first time since her departure from Charleston, Maranta was at peace.

"I will not back out, senhor. I have already given my promise."

A sudden noise from the shadows at the far end of the *sala* caused Maranta to look in that direction. And she stared into the cynical eyes of Ruis da Monteiro as he walked forward into the light.

Patû picked up Vasco and carried him into the dining room, where Dona Isobel joined them for dinner. And Maranta, forgetting her shyness, talked with Vasco to show him that she did not care that he was not so healthy as his brother Ruis, the arrogant *fazendeiro*.

There was only one thing that disturbed Maranta. Ruis's wife, Innocencia, had not made an appearance; and yet, no one bothered to explain her absence.

When dinner was over and Maranta was again in her room preparing for bed, she questioned Sassia about Innocencia.

"Dom Ruis's wife was not at dinner tonight, Sassia. Is she away?"

Sassia stopped brushing Maranta's hair for a second. "She doesn't eat with the rest of the family very often. The young senhora is delicate and has headaches much of the time."

"Is she very . . . beautiful?"

"Oh, yes. Pale eyes like a summer sky—and hair like moonbeams."

Maranta did not know why that knowledge pained her —that Innocencia was beautiful. Of course she would be —chosen by someone like Ruis da Monteiro.

"Does she . . . do they have children?"

"They were expecting one at one time, according to the Indian girl, Floresta. But something happened, and Dona Innocencia lost the baby. Floresta says she doesn't think the senhora can ever have another child."

"How sad."

"But Dom Vasco—" Sassia stopped abruptly and began to brush Maranta's hair more vigorously.

"What were you going to say about Dom Vasco?"

Sassia, looking confused, acted as if she could not remember. But Maranta had a feeling that the black girl had merely changed her mind about confiding in her.

"There are so many people here, Sassia, and so many names. I'm not sure I'll ever be able to learn or remember them all."

Sassia nodded. "Anyone who is born in the *fazenda* can remain for life. That is the custom, *yayá*. But it makes it awfully crowded sometimes," she said. "Especially when the *fazendeiro* has a black wife as well as a white wife, with two sets of children."

"What? You mean Dom Ruis . . ."

Sassia laughed and shook her head at Maranta's incredulous expression. "Not Dom Ruis. But some of the others on the neighboring *fazendas*. Is that not true in your own country where there are slaves?"

"No," Marenta refuted. "A man can't have two wives in my country. It's true that a man may have a . . . a

120

mistress, but if she has children, they are not . . . ac-knowledged."

Maranta blushed, but Sassia did not notice. "Then Brazil is better than your country, senhorita—for here, *all* the children are acknowledged and share in their father's estate, even when he is not married to their mother."

"It is a . . . a disgrace to be illegitimate. I feel sorry for any child who is born of such . . . such sinful parents."

When Sassia was gone, Maranta knelt by her bedside for a long time before she finally laid her head on her pillow to go to sleep.

Even the morals were different in this strange land. To think that a man would have the effrontery to keep his mistress in the same house as his wife. But at least with Vasco da Monteiro as her husband, Maranta would never be subjected to *that* disgrace.

14

Late the next afternoon, Maranta stood in the middle of her bedroom, while Sassia placed the white lace mantilla over her dark hair.

Maranta wore her birthday dress—that voluptuous-skirted white moire silk that Mrs. Windom had made for her eighteenth birthday. Little did Maranta and Marigold know at the time that those dresses would also serve as their wedding gowns.

The mantilla had been delivered to her room with the message that the priest had arrived and was waiting in the family chapel to perform the ceremony that would link Maranta Tabor forever with the Monteiro family.

She thought of Marigold in the identical dress, saying her unwilling vows to Crane Caldwell. And now, it was *her* turn. But somehow, things had not worked out so badly for her, as they had for Marigold. At least, Maranta would be spared the indignity of sharing her bed with her husband.

"And what jewelry will you wear, *yayá?*" Sassia asked, adjusting the mantilla in graceful folds over Maranta's creamy white shoulders.

"The locket, I think," Maranta said.

Sassia walked to the open jewelry case. "The cross is beautiful . . ."

"I will *not* wear the cross, Sassia. Please put it back."

"Yes, *yayá.*"

Maranta waited for Sassia to fasten the golden chain around her neck. She did not see the black girl as she pulled the *figa,* the tiny amulet resembling a closed fist, from her apron pocket to stick it to the underside of the locket before placing it about her neck.

When the knock sounded on the door, Sassia went to answer it.

"Is the senhorita ready? I have come to escort her to the chapel."

"*Sim,* Don Ruis. She is ready."

The man surveyed Maranta from head to toe, much as he had done with his bold eyes on the ship, the *Beaufort.* Once again, Maranta felt the staining of her cheeks and the swift flutter of her heart.

Ruis did not speak but held out his arm for her hand. Maranta walked with him from the bedroom. But instead of going down the stairs, Ruis led her through the second-story parlors and the library to the gallery above the chapel—opposite the bedroom wing of the house.

"It is more private this way, *menina,*" he finally said. "The priest is waiting to see you before the ceremony."

Maranta nodded. To hear her confession, before she received the marriage sacrament. That was the custom.

And when that was done—when she had confessed her anxieties and her mild displays of temper on the long, hard journey—she met Vasco at the altar. While she knelt, Vasco sat beside her in a chair, with Patû directly behind him.

Vasco placed the heavy gold band on her finger and the bracelet upon her arm, showing his ownership. And Maranta knew then that she was no longer the same. She was a married woman—no longer the *yayá,* the pampered young daughter of the household.

The statues glittered with magnificent jewels—emeralds, diamonds, and gold—for the chapel of the *fazenda* was not only a place for prayers and sacraments. It was the repository for anything of value that belonged to the family. Hidden under the marble squares of the floor was the strong box that contained the Monteiro money. And the jewels, in plain view, were completely safe, guarded over by the saints that no one would dare to rob, upon pain of eternal damnation.

In vain, Maranta searched for Innocencia, but she was not present. The only ones to witness the ceremony besides the conde were the condessa and Dona Isobel—they and the barefoot Indian girl who fled when Maranta saw her hiding in the gallery above.

"Welcome to the Monteiro family, my daughter," the condessa said, kissing Maranta on both cheeks.

"Th-thank you, Mãe," she answered with affection. And the condessa's face showed her pleasure in Maranta's acceding to her wishes in calling her *mother*.

Dona Isobel kissed her and wished her well. Dom Ruis stood apart from them all, offering no words of congratulations to his brother, Vasco—no words to indicate he was happy to have Maranta Tabor as a member of his family, living in his *fazenda*, perhaps for the rest of her life.

His attention focused on the priest instead, who was anxious to return to an old man who lay dying in the hut at the northern boundary of the Monteiro property. Ruis ignored the wedding party to accompany the man to the carriage waiting at the steps of the chapel.

The quiet celebration came at dinner late that night, with the wine and the love cake that had been specially prepared in the kitchen.

Vasco, with Maranta at his side, watched as she spied the marriage symbols made of sugar and cinnamon and manihot flour that decorated the top of the cake. When she recognized what they were intended to be, Vasco laughed at her obvious embarrassment.

He leaned toward Maranta. "Do not blush, my beautiful bride. It is the servants' way of saying they wish a happy marriage for us—with many children." Again he laughed and tweaked the loose curl at her neck.

"You must cut the first piece and give half to me, wife." He handed the silver knife to her. Obeying him, Maranta closed her eyes while she sliced through the suggestive decoration.

Was she mistaken? Was Vasco capable of being a real husband—of sharing her bed and siring children?

At the thought, her hand trembled, and she dropped part of the cake. No one seemed to notice, with the exception of Dom Ruis, who sat at the head of the table and sipped his wine, while his dark sapphire eyes remained on Maranta.

"I am tired, Patû," Vasco said suddenly. "I would like

125

to go to my rooms." He turned to Maranta. "Sleep well, and I shall see you in the morning."

Visibly relieved, Maranta smiled at him. "Good night, Dom Vasco."

The Indian lifted the man from his chair, and Maranta watched as they left the dining room.

"Vasco," the Indian girl whispered, emerging from the hallway. Through the open door, Maranta saw her new husband reach for the girl's hand, and somehow, Maranta's relief was dulled by his action.

"If you will excuse me, Ruis, I think I shall retire, also." The condessa looked tired and strained. Ruis, concern for his mother showing in his dark-tanned face, nodded and stood while the condessa departed with Dona Isobel behind her.

Now there were only the two of them left—Ruis and Maranta. And the girl, panicking at the sudden change, hastily pushed back her chair to flee from the room. "If you will excuse me, also . . ."

"Sit down and finish your wine, Maranta," he ordered.

"But I . . ."

"There is no need for you to leave so abruptly—even though your husband has deserted you on your wedding night."

Reluctantly, Maranta sank to her chair. Tears came to her dark doe eyes. It was obvious to everyone that Vasco was not overjoyed to have her as his wife. But did Ruis have to be so cruel as to voice it aloud?

Maranta made a pretence at sipping her wine, but it remained at the same level. She could not swallow anything for the lump in her throat.

Noticing how upset she was, Ruis dismissed her. "You may go, Maranta, if you wish. I see that you will never succeed in finishing your wine."

When she was almost to the door, he asked, "You know which direction to take to your new rooms, *menina?*"

"New rooms?" She stopped. "Don't I have the . . . the same room as before?"

"No. You have been given the apartment next to the

126

library—adjacent to the gallery of the chapel. I will ring for Sassia. She will show you."

The girl had evidently been expecting the summons, for it took her little time to reach the dining room.

"The senhora wishes to go to her rooms. Will you please show her the way, Sassia?"

Maranta felt at a disadvantage, with Dom Ruis giving orders. Once again, she felt insignificant, realizing how completely she was subject to the whim of the arrogant Count of Sorocaba, who had the power of life and death in his hands.

The candles of myrtle wax lit the way along the hall—taking her farther from the main part of the house.

"Is this the portion of the *fazenda* where Dom Vasco lives?" Maranta asked, retracing her earlier steps when Ruis had escorted her to the chapel.

"No, senhora. Dom Vasco sleeps in the guest chambers on the ground floor. He has a rolling chair that he can push onto the veranda when he pleases. He is carried upstairs only for meals."

"Then n-no one else is in this part of the house?"

"Dom Ruis spends much time in the library across from your apartment. That is where he works—and reads. He has many fine books, senhora."

"But at night . . ."

"Do not be afraid, senhora. The *fazenda* is well guarded at night."

Maranta, walking into the apartment, was so entranced at its beauty that she forgot her fear. The fine, heavily carved furniture gleamed in its waxed luster. And the silken draperies, of pale lilac, matched the sofa before the ornate fireplace that was now filled with greenery.

She opened the door to the bedroom and sank almost to her ankles in the luxurious white fur carpet. The massive bed of dark wood took up a major portion of one end of the room. Like a mammoth version of the palanquin, it was oriental in character, its fretwork reaching to the ceiling, where the thin white silk draperies hung, ready to be closed against the drafts, protecting the one who slept there.

The only contrast in color came from the clutter of pillows—mauve and aqua, pale lemon, and deep pink—that invited Maranta to lay her head against their exquisite softness.

"It is beautiful," Maranta whispered, awed by the magnificence of the room.

So different in design from the rest of the house. So different from the nun's meager cell that Maranta had thought to occupy in the Convent of Our Blessed Lady.

"Was this the Condessa Louisa's apartment, Sassia? Have I taken it from her?"

"No, Senhora Maranta. The young conde had it redone for his wife, Innocencia, but she never slept here. She preferred . . . another part of the house."

The eyes, blue as a summer sky—and hair the color of moonbeams. Yes, Maranta could see how it would suit a woman of that coloring. The knowledge that it was originally intended for the conde's young wife caused Maranta to lose part of her pleasure in being given the beautiful apartment.

"But the room suits you much better, senhora," Sassia said, as if she could tell what Maranta was thinking. "For you are like the 'mother of waters'—with your skin made of pearl and your black hair."

But Maranta shook her head. Marigold—or Innocencia. The apartment was meant for a golden-haired woman, not for a girl whose tresses were black like the night with no stars shining.

Maranta sighed. It had been a long day and she was tired.

"Shall I help you with your dress?"

"Yes, please."

Maranta started to protest when she saw the lace gown and peignoir that Sassia laid on the bed. Designed for her trousseau—her wedding night—and purchased by her own maman.

She had no need to look beautiful tonight, for she would spend her wedding night by herself. But was that not what she had wanted? Why then this feeling of loneliness and isolation?

128

With her long hair loose and flowing down her back, Maranta walked to the jewel case where Sassia had placed the locket. Once again, Maranta pulled out the cross of pearls and diamonds and examined it. Why had the condessa been so lavish with her gift? Surely, even then, on her birthday, the senhora had known that she could never be a true wife to her son.

Carefully, Maranta returned the gift to its case and knelt by the bed for her evening prayers. She heard the steps past her apartment—once and then twice. Maranta lifted her head from her prayers and listened. But then a door opened and shut—the library, more than likely. Relieved, she closed her eyes again and continued with her prayers.

The candles burned low, and Maranta, ready for bed, stood up and removed the peignoir to place it across the chair near the bed.

A dark shadow in the doorway moved, and the startled Maranta recognized the tall, masculine figure of Dom Ruis staring at her with his strange dark sapphire eyes.

"R-Ruis, what is the matter? What are you doing—in my room?"

She drew her arms across the thin lace gown to hide the outline of her young, high breasts.

"Have you not guessed, Maranta," he said, his voice bitter and cold, "why the condessa brought you here?"

"To . . . to marry Dom Vasco," she replied, her face now the same color as the white silk draperies that lined the massive bed.

Ruis gave a harsh laugh. "Do you think Mãe risked her life for that? No, Maranta. It was for the sake of an heir to the Monteiro fortune—a child to be worthy of the proud Monteiro name. You were selected as the mother of her grandson."

"But Vasco . . ."

"Can never sire another child. He has only Tefe, the half-breed, the *mameluco,* by the Indian girl, Floresta."

"No," Maranta said, backing away from him.

"Yes, Maranta. The only reason you have been brought here is to bear *my* son."

"But you . . . you are already married, senhor."

"Do you think I do not know that? Do you think that it has not haunted me that I am tied for the rest of my life to a wife who is barren—and insane?"

"Please, Dom Ruis," Maranta said, her trembling hand pushing back her long, black hair from her cheek. "There has been some mistake."

"There is no mistake, Maranta. Did I not see with my own eyes the *Cruzamento da Monteiro* about your neck and hear your confession that it was the condessa who gave it to you?"

His hand grasped her arm, and he stared fiercely into her frightened eyes. "The cross is always given to the mother who has borne the Monteiro heir. My father gave it to Mãe the day I was born. And I had hopes of presenting it to Innocencia—"

His voice was filled with pain and a rage that Maranta did not understand. "How do you think I felt that night in the chapel when I saw you with the cross on your breast and realized, for the first time, what the condessa had planned?"

His grip became tighter, and Maranta gave a tiny cry. "I shall . . . s-scream, senhor, if you dare to t-touch me."

"You are already in my arms, *menina*. And there is no one to come to your aid. Will it be more of an embarrassment for the servants to think you spent your wedding night alone? Or will it cause you even more grief for them to learn you have spent it with me?"

She was trapped. Maranta trembled as the conde lifted her into bed and closed the delicate silk curtains to shut out the rest of the world . . .

15

Halfway across the world, the lamps burned bright in Mrs. Stark's boarding house on Chalmers Street.

Shaun Banagher was tired. He stretched his large frame and ran his hand through the thick auburn-colored hair, as the knock sounded at the door.

"Come in," Shaun called out. "The door isn't locked."

Chad opened the door, and Shaun, recognizing his friend, stood up to greet him.

The man seemed ill at ease as he eyed the comfortable bed, the bright room that was in such contrast to the dark, cramped shanty car that he had once shared with Shaun.

"Sit down, Chad."

The man shook his head. "I'm on my way to Keppie's Tavern for a mug of beer. Thought you might like to come."

Shaun smiled. "Not tonight, Chad. I still have work to do."

Chad glanced at the books and papers on the table and frowned. "You can't work every minute of the day and night. Everybody needs a little time off for some fun."

But Shaun refused, and as soon as the disappointed Chad left, he went back to his work.

He could not tell Chad of the important business meeting the next morning. But if all went well, and his prospective financial backers approved his plans, then he would be assured of success.

It was ironic, thought Shaun, that the inheritance from his Cousin Edward had come too late to enable him to marry the beautiful golden-haired girl, Marigold. Now, he could only seek redress against Robert Tabor by accumulating enough wealth and power to challenge him in the marketplace.

Shaun thought of the plans he had outlined—to buy

cotton from the farmers all along the rail line; to sell it at a good profit; and then to purchase manufactured goods that the same farmers needed to buy. A double market could be quite profitable. And if that went well, he had a plan to expand the rail lines with the iron from local foundries. His backers would be pleased to hear what could be done using trains to carry goods from the back country to the port of Charleston.

For some time, there had been fewer and fewer ships in the harbor. The prosperous country above the fall line had preferred sending its cotton and other exports to Savannah, instead. But if Shaun had anything to do with it, Charleston would once again be a thriving port with ships waiting in the harbor—some which he himself would own one day. The building of rails would make the difference, covering the entire state and eventually running all the way from north to south, and east to west, leaving the waterways and wagon trails obsolete.

But his inheritance was too small to accomplish all this. He needed much more money at his fingertips. If the financial backers approved his plans the next morning, then he would be in a position to buy out the major stock in the same railroad that had once hired him as a worker.

Remembering his rough work clothes, Shaun glanced down at the clothes he was wearing, which were much more suitable for a man on the way to success. Beneath the close fit of his fine linen shirt, his powerful muscles rippled. And because of them, Shaun realized that he gave the appearance of being a little less civilized than the slender town dandies who spent their time gambling and horseracing. But he didn't mind; his studies and labor had paid off.

One afternoon, a month later, Shaun sat in the Exchange with his personal banker, Mr. Pettigrew, and two planters who had come to town for supplies. Shaun's meeting had gained him the backing he had desired, and now, important men were taking notice of him, accepting him as a business, if not social, equal. Conversation focused on the high tariff that had plagued the planters ever since its passage three and a half years previously.

"Something will have to be done and soon," Mr. Pettigrew was complaining. "It's choking us economically, shutting off most of our trade with Europe."

"Never thought I'd see responsible men behaving like asses in Washington. Just hope John C. can do something about it this term," one of the planters responded and then in a cautious voice added, "It's a touchy situation, though, now that he and President Jackson don't see eye to eye. But 37 percent! I can't afford to pay such a high tariff, especially with the price I'm getting for my cotton."

He took a sip of brandy and then turned to Shaun. "How are *you* making such a good profit, Mr. Banagher?"

With a twinkle in his eye, Shaun replied, "Buying from the better New England factories and weeding out the items that fall apart at first use."

"Well then, you're doing better than John Henry here. He's spending all his money on *glue,* just trying to keep the parts together."

The men at the table laughed at the teasing banter.

"You may be joking, Malcolm," John Henry, the other planter said, "but it's about the truth. Even paying the high tariff on the imports, I'm actually coming out better in the long run. Domestic goods just can't touch the ones made in England."

"You think there's any chance of the tariff being lowered this session?" Malcolm asked Mr. Pettigrew.

"If it isn't, I fear it's going to split apart the nation," the banker responded in a sober voice. "Congress can't keep favoring the North to the economic detriment of the South."

Robert Tabor and Arthur Metcalfe walked into the Exchange and joined a group at another table. Robert's tawny eyes narrowed at the sight of Shaun Banagher, but he gave no other indication that he recognized the man who had caused him such grief.

"Now there's a man who's hurting worse than I am," John Henry whispered. "Hear tell Robert Tabor even has his townhouse up for sale."

Shaun turned thoughtful when he heard that piece of information. He sat quietly, listening to the rest of the conversation, and occasionally lifted the snifter of brandy to his lips, until it was time for him to leave. But he thought only of what John Henry had said about Robert Tabor.

The winter months passed and at last, the first jonquils at Cedar Hill announced that it was spring in the Carolina up country.

Marigold looked out over the field of yellow, adjacent to the house, and she became suddenly homesick for the scent of jasmine at Midgard. But there was no possibility that Marigold could leave Cedar Hill for a visit to her parents; for Julie had become ill during the winter months and had gradually worsened. First, it was the mild but plaguing cough that refused to go away. But over the months it had turned into a debilitating illness, with a steady loss of weight and a feverish flush to the woman's face.

At Marigold's insistence, Julie had been moved back into the big house, and a large part of the girl's day was spent in taking care of the woman. But regardless of her careful attention and regular visits from the doctor, Cousin Julie did not improve.

One afternoon, Marigold, as was her custom, sat with her mother-in-law.

"You are so good to me, Marigold," Julie said in her weak voice, as soon as she recovered from her coughing spell. "I hate to be so much trouble."

"Nonsense," Marigold replied. "I *enjoy* sitting with you. I'm only sorry that you're ill."

Julie closed her eyes and rested her head against the pillows. Her face, once beautiful, now showed the strain of her long illness. A sad-hearted Marigold tiptoed from the room to let the woman sleep.

"No hope." The words of the doctor echoed in the girl's mind. "Only a matter of weeks. We'll just have to make her as comfortable as possible until the end."

Why did she have to die? Cousin Julie was the only person who made life bearable for her at Cedar Hill . . .

besides old Jake at the ferry. And she had not been able to take any more food to him lately because of Julie's illness. She hoped he was now well enough to cook his own food. Marigold brushed the tears from her eyes as she made her way into the kitchen to supervise the supper.

For several more weeks, the sick woman lingered, becoming weaker each day. The telltale sign of bright red blood on her handkerchiefs could not be disguised, and Marigold dreaded the day when a massive hemorrhage would take her life.

On a late May afternoon, when the only sounds to be heard were the mules returning from the fields, Julie, in the downstairs bedroom, beckoned Marigold to her bed and in a weak voice whispered, "Marigold, be kind to Crane. He . . . he hides his emotions under his quick temper. But I'm sure he . . . loves you very much."

The girl took the woman's hand. "I will . . . try, Cousin Julie," she promised.

"He was such a dirty little urchin when Desmond brought him home. And the words he spoke." A faint smile formed on Julie's lips as she remembered earlier days. "I had to wash his mouth out with soap more than once."

The coughing started again, with a fresh spurt of blood, and Marigold, alarmed, called Juniper to sit with the woman while she hurried to find Sesame.

It was at that moment Crane came into the house. "What is wrong, Marigold?"

"Cousin Julie is much worse. She needs the doctor."

Crane's face turned pale, and rushing down the hallway to Julie's bedroom, he left Marigold to find Sesame and give him the message to go for Dr. Kellie.

Far into the night, Dr. Kellie and Crane kept watch by Julie's bedside. Lights remained on throughout the house, and the steady hum of the whistling tea kettle belied the happy sound it had been earlier in the day.

Toward morning, Marigold, sleeping in a chair in the nearby parlor, stretched. Her arms and legs felt cramped, and the back of her neck was tense from the uncomfortable position in which she had slept.

The stirrings along the hall next to the parlor prompted her to leave the chair. As Marigold walked toward Julie's door, the figure of Dr. Kellie came forth. He closed the door, and with a sad expression to match the anxiety in Marigold's eyes, he shook his head.

The girl, alarmed, hastened inside the bedroom. Crane stroked Julie's hand that now lay limp against the coverlet, and by his action, Marigold knew the worst had happened.

"Crane?" the girl whispered softly.

He raised his anguished face toward her. "She's dead, Marigold. There is nothing you can do. Please leave me alone with my mother."

The low, plaintive singing in the slave quarters began that morning and continued throughout the day and into the night. Sesame, his eyes moist with tears, kept repeating, "I just knowed somethin' bad was gonna happen when Mr. Crane cut down that cedar tree in the middle of the cotton field. You don't cut down a cedar. It'll bring bad luck ev'ry time."

The news spread quickly over the countryside that Julie was dead. On the day of her funeral, the tiny country church was filled with friends and neighbors who had come from miles around to pay their last respects to the gentle, brave woman who had survived the slave uprising in Santo Domingo and had been brought from Charleston to the up country as Desmond Caldwell's bride.

Marigold and Crane stood in the cemetery in a downpour of rain. Through the fine weaving of the black mourning veil, Marigold peered out onto the dismal landscape and concentrated on the water dripping from the yellowed leaves of the stunted magnolia tree several feet in front of her.

The droning voice of the rector blended into the cadence of the rain, while the somber, black-clad people stood on the other side of the tree and served as a silent chorus, occasionally nodding in agreement at the words spoken by the man at the grave.

The black wrought-iron spiked fence jutted up from the earth behind them, enclosing the rows of white gravestones planted in the hallowed ground. Beyond that, the carriages and horses stood at attention, with even the horses seemingly aware of the solemnity of the occasion.

"Dust thou art, to dust returnest . . ." The girl closed her smoky topaz eyes when the first spade of dirt was cast into the six-foot chasm before them. As it hit the pine casket, Crane gave a moan, and Marigold reached out for his hand to comfort him. His grip tightened, and for the first time, Marigold felt pity for Crane in his obvious grief.

When the grave was filled, they were shepherded back to the carriage, where Sesame waited to take them home.

Some of the neighborhood women had remained behind at Cedar Hill, and as soon as Marigold and Crane changed from their wet clothes, they went into the parlor, as was the custom, to receive the condolences of the people who had returned from the cemetery.

The dining room buffet and table were filled with food—cakes and pies, ham and chicken and vegetables—brought from the neighboring plantations to feed the family and visitors. Marigold ate little—and Crane, even less.

Eventually the carriages dispersed, leaving Crane and Marigold alone with the steady, unrelenting patter of rain on the old plantation roof.

There was a chill in the air, and by nightfall it was necessary to build a fire in the parlor. Soon, Marigold, tired and sleepy from the long day, went upstairs. Crane sat for a long time and stared into the embers on the hearth. Then he banked the fire and retired to his own bedroom—the one across the hall from Marigold. Ever since the episode in the slave cabin, they had not slept in the same room.

Marigold, ready to climb into her bed, leaned over to blow out the lamp. It was then she heard the muffled sobs from across the hall.

Troubled, she took the lamp and, walking between the rooms, she knocked at Crane's door. "Crane, it's Marigold," she said.

The door opened and her husband stood before her. Julie's request to be kind to Crane was uppermost in her

137

mind. "I cannot go to sleep," she explained, "while you are so troubled. Can I get you anything? A glass of warm milk, perhaps—or a brandy."

"Marigold." His voice broke and he reached out for her. As if she were soothing the dirty little urchin that he had once been, Marigold stroked the dark head that rested against her breast.

"Stay with me, Marigold," he begged. "I cannot bear to be alone tonight, knowing that she is in a rain-soaked grave . . ."

"Hush, Crane. You must not think of that."

As she talked, he led her to his bed and covered her with the down-filled comforter. He held her in his arms until his body, growing warm, stopped shivering.

Marigold, surprised at her tenderness for Crane in his grief, remained in his arms, with the lamplight flickering in the room, while the storm outside gathered in intensity and then subsided.

It was toward morning that the nightmare began. She did not know why she awoke. Perhaps it was the lamplight in her face. Or it could have been the feeling that she was being watched. Sleepily, Marigold opened her eyes. Her husband, Crane, sat upright, his arms folded.

He stared at her, and in his dark eyes, she saw something that reminded her of a wild predator relishing the imminent subduing of its victim. And she was afraid.

"Crane," she murmured. "Is it time to get up?"

"No, Marigold."

"Then, why do you have on the light?"

"I have been watching you, Marigold—and waiting for you to wake up. I will have to punish you, you know."

"Punish me? What do you mean, Crane?" Marigold sat up, pushing a strand of golden hair behind her ear.

"I have been lying here, thinking of the threat you have held over my head these past months. But Mother is dead. Now, it no longer matters that you discovered my secret in the slave cabin."

Marigold threw back the comforter and tried to leave the bed, but Crane grabbed her arm and jerked her toward him.

"I cannot allow you to get away with threatening me, my beautiful, haughty wife."

The girl fought to get loose, but Crane tightened his grip and threw her back against the pillows. He reached for the small bamboo cane and began to beat her. At the first blow, she screamed.

Listening to her cry, Crane's eyes took on a glazed appearance. "Scream all you want, my dear," he crowed, his breathing uneven. "There is no one to hear you, save your husband."

16

She waited until she was certain he was asleep. Marigold, barely able to stand, put her hand over her mouth to keep from crying out.

It was the last time Crane would ever violate her body like that, she vowed. Never again would she take pity on him. His kisses and pleas for forgiveness afterward could never erase the violence of his actions.

Marigold crept into her own room and, with trembling hands, she dressed and packed a few clothes in the valise that she pulled from underneath the bed.

She had little money for the journey, but it did not matter. She would manage somehow. She could not stay another day with Crane.

It was still dark as the girl groped her way to the barn. She could not afford to wake Sesame, and so she saw to the horses herself. They whinnied when she removed them from their stalls to hitch to the carriage.

Marigold listened, but no one came to see about the noise in the stable yard. While everyone else at Cedar Hill slept, Marigold opened the gates and started down the road away from Cedar Hill and toward the river.

The tall cedars, blue gray in the semidarkness, gave way to green full-leafed hardwood trees that lined the road to the ferry. The sun came up, spreading its glittering light over the road and filtering through the trees.

Would Jake be awake? Marigold wondered. Would he cross the river in time to get her safely on the ferry before Crane could stop them?

The horses, sensing her urgency, rushed down the road and stopped at the water's edge. Marigold, her unruly hair hanging down her back, stepped toward the bell to give the signal to Jake.

She jumped as the peal magnified itself, the air carrying its dismal clang over the whole countryside.

Oh, please hurry, Jake, she pled silently while her wary eyes turned to the road to make sure she had not been followed. Back and forth she paced on the muddy red bank while she waited for some sign of movement across the river.

The rattle of chains on the opposite bank told her that Jake had heard her signal and was now casting off. Marigold watched as the raftlike structure came slowly over the swollen waters of the river. The rain of the previous evening made it more difficult than usual for Jake, and Marigold's heart missed a beat each time the ferry was dragged off its course by the swiftly running current. But each time it happened, Jake took the long pole and guided it back.

Again Marigold glanced at the road behind her. More nervous than ever as the time lapsed, she could not tell if the sudden pounding was a horse galloping down the road, or her own heart beating in her ears.

Then, she saw the figure on horseback in the distance. It was Crane, she knew, coming to take her back to Cedar Hill. The bell had awakened him.

The raft was almost to the bank. Marigold ran to the carriage, and before Jake had time to finish hooking the last chain to the planks on the bank, she moved the carriage forward.

"Cast off, Jake," she shouted. The horses cantered down the bank, pulling the carriage behind. With all her strength, she tugged on the reins, and the horses drew up only inches from the end of the raft.

"Miss Marigold, what's the matter?"

"It's my husband. He's after me, Jake. Hurry!"

The black man took his pole and shoved the ferry from the bank. His muscles rippled in the early morning sunlight, and Marigold began to tremble.

The shout came from Crane. "Stop, Jake," he ordered. "Bring the raft back."

"No," Marigold whispered.

Jake's hands became slack on the pole. His worried face looked at the man on the bank and then to Marigold, and his look reflected his indecision.

On the opposite shore, Crane stood, a smile on his lips and a relaxed air to indicate his certainty that Jake would obey him.

"Miss Marigold?" Jake questioned.

"If you take me back, he'll—he'll kill me."

Her words had the desired effect. Jake's eyes narrowed at the sight of her swollen face, and his muscles began to work again, digging the pole into the water to continue the journey across the river and away from Crane Caldwell.

Seeing the movement away from him, Crane became livid. "Jake, didn't you hear me? I order you to return my carriage and my wife to me immediately."

Jake continued to move the ferry in the opposite direction.

"You'll spend the rest of your life in irons, Jake. That, I promise you," Crane shouted, his raspy, hoarse voice carrying over the water.

Marigold, hearing his threat, realized the dreadful position in which she had placed her friend, Jake.

"Oh, Jake, I'm so sorry, I didn't mean to get you into trouble because of me."

"Where're you goin', Miss Marigold?" he asked, ignoring Crane's words and the girl's apology.

"To Charleston—to my parents."

"You plannin' on drivin' that distance all alone?"

"I . . . I have no choice," she answered.

Marigold glanced again across the river. The horse was still in sight, but Crane had disappeared. Then she saw her husband pushing a canoe into the water.

"He's following us, Jake," Marigold's distressed voice announced.

The black man turned to look toward the wobbling canoe and, in a reassuring voice, said, "He won't get across the river in that, Miss Marigold. The water's too swift."

A few feet from the bank, the canoe overturned. And minutes later, a waterlogged Crane crawled out onto the muddy bank, while the overturned canoe drifted down-stream.

Jake's strength propelled the ferry to the other bank, but before he fastened the chains to the metal rings, the man took one last glance at Crane, who stood shaking his fist at them. Turning to Marigold, he said, "Wait, Miss Marigold, at the top of the hill, while I get some things out of the house. With Mr. Crane so mad, I can't stay here. I might as well come with you."

A few minutes later, to Marigold's relief, she sat back on the cushioned seat of the carriage, while Jake crooned to the horses, urging them at top speed down the road.

Each time they stopped, Marigold hid her face from view with the long, black mourning veil that she had worn to Julie's funeral.

Curious people turned to look at the slim girl dressed in black from head to toe. But the mystery of the obviously bereaved figure, with only her driver to accompany her, went unsolved.

"Not even a maid to travel with her," one elderly woman commented at the first inn. "Looks as if she's running from something, if you ask me. Wonder who she is?"

Marigold ignored the speculative comments and kept to herself, wearing the disguising veil until she and Jake were on the road again.

By the third day, the routine was well established with Jake seeing to the lodgings and paying from the small metal box he had brought with him.

"My father will reimburse you, Jake," Marigold assured the man as she climbed into the carriage.

The sun was already up, and it promised to be a good day for traveling as they left the yard of the inn.

"I'm not worried about the *money*, Miss Marigold," Jake said.

Neither one spoke of the worry that served as a goad to hasten them on their way—the knowledge that Crane might be directly behind them.

It would not go well with either the black man or Marigold if Crane should catch up with them before they reached the safety of Charleston.

By mid-morning, Jake stopped in a clump of trees to give the horses a rest. Unhitching them from the carriage, he led them down to the old Indian springs hidden from the road by a small, grassy mound.

Marigold, glad to stop for a while, flicked the dust from her dress and walked in the opposite direction of the springs. When she returned to where the carriage had been, she was surprised to see that Jake had moved it so that it could not be seen from the road.

"Jake?"

"Cain't be too careful, Miss Marigold," he admitted.

"You think my husband is following us?"

"Could be. I got this feelin' in my bones. Woke up with it this mornin'. And my bones is usually right."

The light went out of the girl's eyes. "I . . . won't go back with him, Jake, if he finds us."

Jake nodded, showing no surprise at Marigold's avowal. In another half hour, the black man had the horses hitched to the carriage, and he pulled out onto the road.

Because of Jake's words, Marigold began to glance regularly at the road behind her. The sight of other carriages did not alarm her. She looked for a lonely rider on horseback—a rider with coal black hair and cruel eyes.

They were on the old peltry road north of Blacksfield when the left wheel of the carriage developed a wobble. The carriage jolted and tilted to one side. Marigold held onto the strap inside the vehicle until Jake could bring it to a stop in the middle of the dusty, lonely road.

The girl climbed out of the carriage and watched as the black man ran his hands over the wheel to assess the damage. Marigold waited for him to speak.

The orioles in the trees sang their summer song and darted in and out of the woodland, while the horses jerked their heads up and pawed the ground.

Finally Jake said, "We cain't go no farther on this wheel, Miss Marigold. It's done for, good and proper."

"Can't you fix it?" she asked, trying hard to keep the mounting anxiety from her voice.

The man shook his head. "Looks like somebody deliber-

145

ately damaged it, Miss Marigold. And the pothole in the road musta done the rest. We was lucky to get this far."

While Jake talked, the dust in the road behind them began to clear. And as it did so, Marigold saw in the distance the large roan horse with its lone rider bearing down upon them.

Stifling the exclamation, Marigold's hands went to her mouth, and at her actions, Jake looked back.

There was no mistake. The distinctive riding posture of Crane Caldwell could not be duplicated by another rider.

"Mr. Crane's caught up with us, Miss Marigold." The man's voice was sad at his pronouncement.

But Marigold was not about to wait like a trapped animal for Crane to apprehend them. She had gotten this far. She would not give up now.

"Quickly, Jake. Help me unhitch the horses," she ordered and ran to the horses' heads.

"What you plannin' to do, ma'am?" he asked, following her.

"We'll ride the horses into the woods. Crane hasn't won yet."

"We got no saddles," he objected. "You won't get far, Miss Marigold. Me—now I'm used to ridin' bareback on a mule, but a lady has to have a saddle."

Marigold laughed as she climbed upon the horse's back and urged the animal into the woods. How many times she had ridden like this in growing up, giving her brother Jason a good run down the narrow road through Emma's Bog. Of course, she had always gotten a good tongue-lashing from Feena afterward, but now it did not matter that her petticoats were showing. The important thing was to hide before Crane Caldwell spotted them.

Into the wooded forest they rode, away from the carriage and the rapidly approaching figure. When the two had reached the safety of the canebrake, Marigold led her horse into cover and watched as Crane got off the roan to survey the carriage with its injured wheel.

He glanced to the back and to the front of the abandoned carriage and looked to one side of the road and then the other, as if undecided what to do. Finally he climbed back on his horse and galloped south, leaving a cloud of dust in his wake.

Marigold's elation plummeted when Jake spoke. "He'll be waiting for us at the next inn."

The girl pulled at a long strand of golden hair, twisting it around her finger as she thought. "Then we won't stop at the inn, Jake," she said aloud, and again lapsed into silence.

The train. How far had the tracks been laid? She tried to remember what Shaun had said—something about when it was finished all the way to Hamburg in 1833, it would be the longest rail line in the world. It could not be helped if she risked coming face to face with Shaun. That was preferable to being caught by Crane. They should have come this far by now.

"We're taking the train, Jake," she announced. "We'll head southwest until we find the tracks. And if you don't have enough money to buy our tickets, we'll sell the horses."

Crane Caldwell waited at the inn until it became apparent that Marigold was not going to be stopping there. Blast the girl, he thought, as he tried to decide what his next stop should be. He could not afford to let her get to Charleston before him. His one hope lay in getting there first, to intercept her before she had a chance to talk with her father.

Convinced he was wasting his time staying at the inn, Crane paid his bill and asked for his horse. He would ride all night to make sure he arrived before Marigold.

"But Mr. Caldwell, aren't you going to use the bed for the night?"

"I've changed my mind. I shan't be staying. Kindly have my horse brought from the stables at once."

"Yes, sir," the innkeeper answered, still puzzled at the man's sudden change of plans.

"I am sorry, ma'am, but I have to abide by the rules. No Negroes riding on the train except those that have their master's children in their care."

Marigold glared at the ticket agent. "It's unfair," she countered. "Can't you make an exception for my driver? We have to get to Charleston tonight."

"I can sell you a ticket for yourself, ma'am—but not for your driver." The man was noticeably uncomfortable, and he coughed several times while Marigold stood waiting. "Perhaps the man could get your carriage repaired and bring it on later," he suggested.

Marigold finally realized there was no dissuading him. And after talking it over with Jake, she purchased her ticket and left the horses with Jake.

Now alone, she was subjected to the curious stares of the other passengers who sat waiting for the train to leave. She had tried to clean her face and smooth her black traveling dress, but it was hopeless. And with no comb to control her unruly golden hair, she looked like a hoyden instead of a lady. Yet, Marigold did not care what they thought of her. She was impatient for the train to start.

But she heard no familiar hiss of steam that would announce their departure. Everything was quiet except for a baby that alternately fretted and then went back to sleep.

"Why don't we leave?" Marigold asked the stout woman sitting next to her on the hard bench.

"Can't—until the stagecoach comes in from Columbia."

"When will that be?" Marigold's voice questioned again.

"Don't rightly know. Maybe one hour—maybe as long as four."

Marigold sighed and settled down for the long wait. Already the darkness had consumed the light in the sky and partially obliterated the rails in front of the engine.

When the girl had almost given up hope that the train would ever leave, workmen appeared and poured fresh sand on the platform car in front of the locomotive and placed pine knots in the urn-shaped rods. She strained to see if Shaun might be with them, but there was no giant with auburn hair and green eyes.

Steam began to hiss in the engine, and the pine knots outside were ignited to be used as flares in the darkness.

148

The bell clanged and the passengers from the coach and everyone else with a ticket scrambled into one of the three pleasure cars. Soon the train was on its way to Charleston, the engine hopping over creeks, scattering sparks on both sides and making noises like a rocket in a Chinese fireworks display.

They stopped at Midway and again at Summerville, and as the sun came up, the train finally slid into the little station on Line Street.

The sight of the familiar wooden station where she had last seen Shaun Banagher brought pain to Marigold. But it was mixed with anger, too . . . not only at herself, but at the man who had deceived her and brought her to such a point that she had been forced to flee an abusive husband.

It was too early in the morning for the street vendors to be out, singing about their fine wares. Along the deserted familiar streets she walked, from Spring to Radcliffe, Vanderhorst and Calhoun, on her way to the Tabor townhouse situated on the battery.

The malaria season had started at Midgard, so the family would be in residence here at the townhouse.

Marigold, her appearance even worse because of the smoke and soot of the train journey, knew it would be hard to explain her disheveled state to her mother and father. If she could slip into the house before they awoke . . .

The Palladian-design house loomed before her at the end of the street, and the strong, salty odor of the ocean invaded her senses. Sea gulls flew along the battery and Marigold, tired and hungry, quickened her steps toward the white house and hurried through the side gate and up the back stairs to her old room—hers and Maranta's.

The room was not the same. The twin beds had been replaced by a larger mahogany bed, with the mosquito netting pushed back at each side. And the twin bowls and pitchers of water were now on the opposite side of the room, away from the window.

Marigold quickly shed the dirty black dress. She poured

water into the basin and leaned over, splashing the cool water on her travel-grimed face. With no further thought except that she was safe at last, she climbed into the mahogany bed, pulled the mosquito netting around her, and promptly fell asleep.

17

The man walking along the hall was engrossed in his thoughts. He walked past the open door of the guest bedroom, but it was not until he had reached the stairs that the crumpled heap of dark material on the bedroom floor registered in his mind.

He stopped abruptly and retraced his steps to investigate. From the doorway he stared at the black dress on the floor and then to the bed. His eyes narrowed as he saw a slight movement behind the mosquito netting. And with a quick, angry stride, the man crossed the room, jerked back the netting and pulled the girl from the mahogany bed.

"Just what do you think you are doing?" he demanded.

Marigold stumbled at his rude treatment. "No, please," she cried and put up her hands as if to ward off a blow. Her tawny eyes flew open, expecting to see her husband Crane. But instead, there was another man glaring at her—one with green eyes and sinewed muscles held in check under the fine linen coat.

The girl, now wide awake, stiffened. Staring at her, making her aware of the thin camisole and petticoat that barely covered her, was the man responsible for all her pain, all her disgrace.

"You!" she said, and pushed his hands from her arms as she took a step backward.

"Marigold?" His voice was incredulous. He reached out, to touch her, to make sure that the girl was not a mirage standing before him. But she again knocked his arm away.

"What are you doing in this house?" she asked, her voice rising in agitation. Without waiting for a reply, she ordered, "Get out at once, Shaun Banagher, or I'll have my father throw you out."

At the hostility in her voice, Shaun stood, rooted to the floor. He saw the flushed cheeks, the smoldering look that changed the girl's normally beautiful eyes into the glittery, spitting ones of a cat.

"That would be rather hard to do, Souci," he said, "since this house now belongs to me."

"I . . . I don't believe you. My father would never allow you to . . . to take anything of his."

He continued staring at her and said, "Put on your clothes, or I shall take something else that belongs to Robert Tabor. I won't be responsible for my actions if you continue to stand before me, displaying your obvious charms."

With heaving breasts, Marigold fled across the room to the wardrobe and opened the door. It was empty. Of course, if what Shaun said was true—that he owned the townhouse—then her clothes would no longer be in the room.

Marigold turned to see Shaun poking at her unfortunate black dress with the toe of his boot. He leaned over, picking the dress up, and then he dropped it to the floor as if it were too sullied for him to handle.

His action made her furious. "My dress, if you please," she said in her haughtiest manner.

Shaun made no effort to give it to her. "You do not have another dress with you, Marigold?"

"The carriage broke down. My . . . my luggage is still in it."

"Then, how did you get here?"

"I . . . took the train—from Blacksfield."

"Alone?"

"That is none of your business, Shaun. Now, please give me my dress."

"No, Marigold. It is not fit for anything but the garbage heap. Wait here until I bring you something to cover yourself. Then we'll decide what to do."

"Shaun," she called after him. But already he was out the door, taking her only dress with him.

Much later she sat at the breakfast table across from

Shaun Banagher. Although her face was still sullen, her hair was clean and shining, with the golden curls in place.

The sleeves of the dark blue silk robe were rolled up, and the sash that held together the long, flowing robe was knotted twice about her waist.

Shaun watched the girl while she satisfied her hunger, buttering yet another hot biscuit and spreading the damson jelly over it.

"Where is my father?" Marigold asked between bites. "If you own his house, you must know where he is."

For a second Shaun stared at her, lifting his brow in a quizzical expression. "He's on Tabor Island for the summer. You know it?"

Marigold nodded. "I was born there—in the middle of a hurricane."

Shaun suddenly grinned as if she had said something amusing, and she scowled at him.

A servant came into the dining room and handed a note to his master. After reading it, Shaun said, "Good. Take everything up to the guest bedroom." When the man had gone, Shaun said, "I hope everything I ordered will fit, Marigold. When you finish your breakfast, you will need to get dressed."

She stopped eating and glowered at Shaun. "You ordered clothes—for me?"

He nodded.

"But you had no right. If you had not been so . . . so contrary, taking my dress, I could have managed. I didn't need your help, Shaun Banagher."

The stubborn words brought a look of displeasure to Shaun's face. "You will always need help, Marigold—to protect you from your own impulsiveness."

Angry now, Shaun leaned forward. "Why did you marry Crane Caldwell? Was it because you knew you could do as you pleased with a husband like that?"

Marigold lifted her chin. "You know very well why I married Crane."

"No, I don't. But perhaps you can explain it to me. I gather it was not completely your father's fault. No one could ever force you into something you didn't want to do."

"I married Crane because I . . . because I . . . loved him," she said, her eyes flashing with angry sparks.

He quickly masked the hurt that her words brought. "If you've finished your breakfast, then I think you'd better get dressed." His voice was suddenly cold and distant. "Are you planning to go to Tabor Island?"

"Yes."

"Do you need me to make the arrangements?"

"No—thank you. I . . . I have enough money to hire a boat," she lied, her eyes blinking back the tears.

"Then I will be on my way. I am already late for an appointment." Shaun got up from the table, and Marigold, with her back to him, heard the door close.

"Damn him," she said to herself, brushing the tears from her eyes. It had not mattered that almost a year had elapsed since she had seen him. The same overwhelming love for him was still there. It had only taken his touch for Marigold to realize that she would never be free of the burning passion that would keep her from ever loving another man.

But she would not let Shaun suspect it. Her pride would see to that.

Marigold was suddenly weary. The last frantic days had taken their toll. And she still ached. But she had to get out of the house and find some way to sail to Tabor Island before Shaun came back.

Up the stairs to her old room Marigold walked. And on the bed lay a number of boxes—the clothes that Shaun had purchased for her, as if she were some charity child. Dainty underwear—petticoats—and an Indian muslin dress of pale green with satin sash—and slippers, too. The man had forgotten nothing, even to the matching parasol to shade her face from the sun.

Taking off the blue robe, Marigold dressed in her new finery and went to the mirror to survey herself. Only the shoes were a little large. Everything else fit.

She would pay him back, she promised herself—Shaun, as well as Jake.

154

Jake—she had forgotten that she had given him this address. He would be bringing the carriage and horses to this house, now owned by Shaun Banagher. Why had her mother and father not written to let her know the house had been sold? Now, the only thing she could do was to leave a message for Jake with one of the servants.

A half hour later, Marigold walked down the front steps and started toward the wharf. She would have no trouble getting someone to take her across the sound. Her father would pay when they reached the island.

The main trouble would be in finding a boat that was not in use. She might have to wait for some time before one became available.

Marigold walked down the street, her parasol shading her face and golden curls from the sun. A group of children, watched over by their nursemaids, played games on the green. Emerald green, the grass—like Shaun Banagher's Irish eyes—darker than the dress he had purchased for her. Mad with herself for still thinking of him, she deliberately put the man out of her mind and thought instead of the trip to the island.

Crane was worried. Marigold should have shown up at the wharf long before now.

He sat looking out from his vantage point, surveying the entire length of the wharf and watching the dock workers with their rhythmic hoisting of the bales of cotton onto the boats.

Could Marigold have gone to Midgard first? But no, she knew better than that, with the malaria in full epidemic on the low country plantations—the miasma ready to lay low any white person who ventured into the bogs or swamps.

But even if she went to the townhouse, it should not have taken Marigold this long, since she had such a head start.

It must have been a shock to her, Crane decided, to find the house on the battery occupied by strangers. He smiled grimly to himself, glad now that he had not told her of the letter he had received from Robert Tabor, saying that the townhouse had been sold and they had gone to Tabor Island for the summer.

Crane's smile disappeared and a frown took its place. Could the people in the townhouse have taken Marigold in and given her shelter? He had not thought of that possibility.

If she did not show up within the next hour, he would go to the house and inquire. Since there were no boats to the island for another two hours, she could not slip past him if he left the wharf for a time.

It did not suit him, having to be in Charleston. The blasting in the gold mine would have to be delayed, just when he had discovered another rich vein. If it had not been for Jake—

His anger at the black man overwhelmed him. Not only to take Marigold across the river in spite of her husband's objections, but to disappear, leaving Crane to travel the much longer route, since the ferry was on the wrong side of the river. Crane felt sure it was Jake, too, who had paid for the girl's lodging on the way. Marigold had no money of her own. He had seen to that.

The knowledge that Jake would soon be apprehended calmed him. Crane determined that once caught the black man would never again be free to come and go as he wished. The penalty for horsethieving was hanging, and Jake would soon be swinging from the gallows.

The hour was almost up when Crane left the café and walked out onto the wharf. Still no sight of Marigold. A coldness suddenly pervaded him. What if Marigold had never reached Charleston?

Suppose some man had seen her and desired her? It would have been so easy for someone to break the lock on the door at one of the inns—if indeed the door even had a lock. And Jake would have been too far away to hear her cry for help.

In agony, he saw the scene before him—the man slipping into her room, the muffling of her scream, and the struggle between them, before the man took his pleasure of her, caressing her soft young body and doing things that

156

no man had a right to do with Crane Caldwell's wife. Even at this moment, he might be taking his pleasure of her.

Crane broke into a cold sweat, and his hand gripped the wooden railing. He would kill him. No one would get away with taking Marigold from him. He would hunt the man down if it took the rest of his life . . .

The slender figure in the pale green dress walked down the steps that led to the wharf. With relief, Crane realized it was his wife Marigold.

He took his handkerchief from his coat and wiped the beads of perspiration from his forehead. Nothing had happened to the girl. She was safe. His imagination had run riot, as it had done so many times before.

Crane walked rapidly toward her, stepping out from behind the stack of cotton bales into full view. "Marigold," he said, "thank God you're safe."

Marigold gasped at the sudden appearance of her husband. "C-Crane," she said in dismay, backing away from him. But he did not seem to notice her aversion to him.

"I have been so worried about you. You should not have come all this way alone. If you had waited a day or so, I would have come with you."

Marigold could only gaze at him in disbelief. He acted as if nothing had happened between them to make her run away from him.

He drank in her elegant, stylish appearance—the new dress and parasol to match. And then he smiled. "So you have been shopping," he said. "That accounts for your delay in getting to the wharf."

"What are you doing here, Crane?" she croaked, determined not to let him get away with his innocent badinage.

"Why, waiting for my wife. Where is your luggage, my dear?" he asked in a solicitous tone. "A boat leaves for Tabor Island in another hour."

She stared at him and did not answer.

"Come now, you didn't leave it by the side of the road, did you? If that's the case, then we'll have to postpone

157

our trip until we see about a new wardrobe for you. I cannot have your parents thinking that I do not provide properly for you."

"I'm not going anywhere with you, Crane. Not to Tabor Island. And certainly not shopping with you. Kindly remove your hand and let me pass."

"Oh, but you *are* going with me, Marigold."

"No, Crane. I've left you for good, and nothing you say will make me change my mind."

An ugly glint invaded his coal black eyes. "Not even to save Jake?"

Marigold's face turned pale. "Leave Jake out of this, Crane. He has nothing to do with us."

"You forget easily, Marigold. You see, Jake not only helped my wife run away from me, he stole my horses and carriage, too. A horsethief is always hanged. And when Jake is apprehended, that's what will happen to him."

"No," she cried. "*I* was the one who took the horses and carriage. Jake had nothing to do with it."

"It would look a bit ridiculous, would it not, if I went to the sheriff and accused my own wife of stealing my horses? No, I think I prefer to have Jake hanged instead."

"Crane, please . . ."

"Shall we take a carriage back to the hotel and discuss this in privacy? Your distress seems to be disturbing the dock workers."

Marigold looked in the direction of the men who had stopped their loading to stand and watch. With a sinking heart, she allowed Crane to help her into the waiting carriage. Her mind was in turmoil, trying to think of what to do.

It had not occurred to Marigold that Crane could be so vindictive as to accuse Jake. Unless she could persuade Crane to drop the charges against him, the black man would be hanged for helping her escape. Whatever sacrifice she had to make, Marigold knew that she could not allow Jake to be hanged.

18

Through the streets of Charleston in the carriage, Marigold and Crane rode from the wharf to the hotel. Marigold made no attempt to converse with her husband but stared from the window at the turkey buzzards cleaning the wharf and streets of the garbage left by the street vendors and fishermen. And Crane, appraising Marigold's appearance, did not like what he saw. She should have purchased a black dress, not this sinfully revealing green one. It was an affront to his mother for Marigold to be dressed so frivolously.

The carriage stopped in front of the hotel, and Crane led Marigold inside, where he engaged a suite of rooms for the night. After getting settled, it was soon time for lunch, and the two left the sitting room for the dining hall downstairs. Through the meal, Crane continued to stare at Marigold in her green dress and to look displeased. But he would not reprove her about her choice of costume until they returned to the suite. Recalling the scene the girl had made at the wharf, he was not anxious to see it repeated in public, if she should lose her temper again.

As soon as lunch was over and they had returned upstairs, Crane closed the door to the sitting room and spoke. "Marigold, I don't like your green dress. It's not appropriate, and when we have purchased others for you, I hope you'll pack it away."

"What's wrong with it?" Marigold asked, knowing that it was far more becoming than any of her other clothes, especially the drab black dress she had left behind at the townhouse on the battery.

"It's not suitable for mourning. You should have thought of that when you purchased it. I shall have to buy you several black dresses this afternoon."

"Black?" Marigold repeated in horror. She hated black.

It made her skin too white and her golden red hair far too brassy. And besides, the weather was too hot.

"You can save your money, Crane. I'll never wear another black dress."

"We are in mourning for at least a year, Marigold. I'll expect you to abide by tradition and dress appropriately."

Marigold's topaz eyes glittered and her chin lifted in defiance. After a moment of silence, she capitulated. "Then let's go, Crane, to purchase this . . . this mourning wardrobe. But I want to go to Madame Reynaud's shop instead of Mrs. Windom's."

Crane relaxed at her acquiescence. "You may go to any shop you wish, my dear, just so you make sure to select clothes suitable for mourning."

"Madame Reynaud is quite expensive," the girl warned.

"That does not bother me. I am well able to afford it."

It was a small shop on the second floor of a dilapidated building that needed repainting. When Crane saw its location, he gazed at it in distaste. "It doesn't look very elegant."

"Madame Reynaud's clients care only for the way her clothes look on them. They don't give a fig for the way her workroom looks."

Marigold stood aside to allow Crane to open the door. When the bell clanged, a little gray-haired woman came forward almost immediately. Crane, looking condescendingly toward the woman, said, "I am Crane Caldwell. My wife is in mourning. And she wishes four or five dresses suitable for the next few months, together with the proper accessories."

"*Oui*, monsieur." The woman smiled and launched into French at the sight of Marigold and then turned back to Crane. "What is your price limit, monsieur, for this wardrobe of mourning?"

"It is of no concern to me. I will leave that up to my wife."

"And what type of mourning dresses do you wish, *ma petite?*" Madame Reynaud asked the girl.

160

"Why, the French, of course," she said in a sweet, demure voice. "And we must have them by tomorrow."

The woman threw up her hands in horror. "Then I suggest we begin right away. I will send for Natalie. And you, monsieur, may call for your wife in three hours."

Crane, irritated at the woman's dismissal, hesitated. But since Marigold seemed so amenable and the room so small, he left.

When Crane returned at the designated time, several boxes were packed and ready to be taken with them, with the promise that the others would be delivered the next morning. Madame Reynaud's girls would have to stay up all night, finishing the order, but she would personally see to their delivery at the hotel the next morning.

"*Bon soir*, monsieur," the gray-haired woman said, "*et* madame." And once again, Marigold and Madame Reynaud spoke in French, further irritating Crane, who could not follow the conversation between the two women.

They had dinner in their sitting room. Afterward Crane, curious that Marigold had made no effort to remove her new clothes from the boxes, said, "I want to see what your redoubtable Madame Reynaud has selected for you."

Marigold's hands tightened on the chair in which she was sitting. "Certainly, Crane. The boxes are on the bed."

He stared at her and she stared back. She was certainly not going to model the clothes for him. Finally, he moved into the bedroom, and Marigold, still sitting in the chair, waited and listened for the tirade that was sure to come. From inside the bedroom, Crane's voice called out, "Marigold, will you please come into the bedroom? I want to hear the explanation for your obvious disobedience to me."

Sighing, she pushed herself from the chair and slowly walked toward the bed where Crane stood, holding up the white evening dress and gazing at it in distaste.

"I don't understand, Crane, what you mean by my obvious disobedience."

"The dress is white—not black, as I requested."

161

"Oh, but I thought that was understood. You asked me to get something suitable for mourning, and I did."

"Marigold." His voice rose in anger.

"But Crane, you were in the room when Madame Reynaud and I discussed it."

Marigold managed to look hurt as she continued. "I am half French, Crane, and I have chosen to mourn Cousin Julie in the French way."

"What does that have to do with this dress?" he demanded.

"White is the French color for mourning," she explained. "I did as you asked, Crane, and chose a wardrobe suitable for mourning." Her eyes filled with tears, and Crane, seeing her reaction, was uncertain. Had the girl deliberately done this to irk him? Or was it because of her foreign ways? He remembered he had not always understood Julie, his foster mother, either.

Seeing Marigold looking at him with such innocent, wide, tearful eyes, Crane finally said, "Well, it's too late to do anything about it. But I'm not pleased, Marigold. Somehow, I have a feeling that you deliberately misled me."

He went back into the sitting room and took up the *Courier* to read. And Marigold, with nothing to do, paced up and down the room like a caged cat.

"You're going to wear yourself out if you continue this nervous walking back and forth. Why don't you take a nice, relaxing bath?"

Marigold paused and glared at the man. "Not while you are in the room, Crane."

He smiled. "So modest. And yet there is not an inch of you that I would not recognize."

Marigold muffled her angry response, and Crane, pretending not to notice, turned a page of the newspaper. "I see where the widow of the late Bishop Nance is reported to have separated from her second husband. Do you know them, Marigold?"

"Yes. She is very beautiful."

"Then he must be a fool to allow her to disgrace him like this, with such notoriety in the newspaper."

Every word that Crane uttered made Marigold even more irritable. She picked at the threads of the drapery and gazed out the window.

"You might as well settle down, Marigold. We're here until tomorrow. And there is nothing you can do about it."

She continued standing at the window. In a few minutes Crane, still looking at the paper, said, "The new oriental drama of Mr. Hart and Mr. Young is playing tonight on Queen Street. *Cataract of the Ganges*. I think I'll go out to purchase tickets—and that will give my modest wife an opportunity to calm her nerves and get dressed in privacy."

"I thought we were in mourning," Marigold accused. "Surely you don't intend going to the theater. Aren't you afraid of what people will say?"

"Because of the way you have chosen to dress, no one will ever suspect that you are in mourning, Marigold. And since I prefer a pleasant evening to watching you pace back and forth, wearing out the carpet, I shall buy tickets for the performance. Besides, I'm not well known in Charleston, so I won't be censured for any impropriety."

Getting his coat, Crane remarked, "I'll send a maid with bath water, Marigold, and leave you for an hour."

She splashed the sponge over her body, not caring that the excess water dripped to the floor. She was so angry. Crane had her hands tied because of Jake. But once Jake was safe—

Marigold smiled, and in a better temper, she hurriedly finished her bath and put on the new dress. At least, Crane had not gotten the better of her in that.

It was a beautiful dress—of sheerest Indian muslin. And the shoulders were dangerously low cut. As Marigold moved before the mirror to look at the gown shimmering in the light, she remembered Shaun's disparaging look at her ruined black dress, her hair in tatters and tangles. She knew that was why she had vowed never to wear another black dress. If he could only see her now. What a different appearance she made from the hoyden Shaun had dragged from his bed.

But he was not apt to see her again. Shaun had washed

163

his hands of her and left her to find her own way to the wharf. He was no gentleman, she fumed. A gentleman would have left a carriage at her disposal, rather than force her to walk all the way in the hot sun.

Marigold heard the steps along the hall, and Crane, coming into the room, held up the tickets in his hand. "We're lucky," he said. "These are the last two tickets for the performance tonight. The man behind me was turned away. If you're ready, Marigold, we will go. The carriage is on the street."

As Marigold walked through the lobby of the hotel and down the steps to the street, heads turned to look at the golden-haired girl dressed in white. Marigold did not notice the stares and approving looks, but Crane did.

She kept her silence as they traveled in the carriage to Queen Street. It did not take long to arrive at their destination. Marigold, stepping from the carriage in front of the theater, recognized many of the people waiting to go inside. In answer to their nods and tipping of hats, she inclined her head discreetly, keeping her proud bearing, for she remembered her near disgrace because of Shaun Banagher.

Despite the rumors of cholera that had swept from Europe to New York and Albany and that was reportedly on its way to Charleston, the theater was filled. Already late, Marigold and Crane had no more than found their seats before the lights lowered and the curtain went up. An excited murmur of approval moved through the audience at the opulent scene before them, and the roar of applause greeted the beginning drama.

At intermission she saw him—Shaun, dressed in elegant evening clothes, and with one of the insipid Henley sisters at his side, with her wispy hair, her childish figure disguised by the oversized sleeves, the ridiculously wide skirt, and her parents hovering approvingly in the background.

How dare he embarrass her this way! Marigold was furious. But then, her anger turned to chagrin. Shaun had every right to escort the girl. Marigold was the married one—not Shaun.

164

She smiled at Crane as he returned with the glasses of sherry, and for the first time during the evening, Marigold began to converse animatedly with him, while turning her back to Shaun Banagher and his party. Soon the signal sounded, and Marigold and Crane went back to their seats for the final act.

Marigold, now aware of Shaun's eyes on her from the nearby box, took an exaggerated interest in the happenings on stage, laughing daintily behind her fan at some of the more amusing elements, and leaning over to comment to Crane off and on.

But then, she became engrossed in the exotic scene before her. Marigold gripped her chair as the drama rushed to its breathtaking ending. The dark-haired girl on stage, dressed in a minimum of clothing, teetered over the cataract. The audience gasped, but the heroine was suddenly dragged to safety by her dark-skinned lover. And Marigold, with the others, gave a sigh of relief.

The final curtain went down on the embracing lovers, and there was complete silence in the theater. Then the applause began, mounting higher and higher, until the whole theater shook from the intensity of the applause.

The crowd swarmed from the theater, and on the pavement outside, Marigold, clinging to Crane's arm, passed by Shaun without speaking. Into the waiting carriage she stepped, and through the darkness she sped, with Crane at her side, and her heart left with the man she had deliberately snubbed.

That night, Marigold slept in the sitting room, while Crane retired to the bedroom. He was pleased with Marigold's behavior toward Shaun Banagher. He had known they would meet someday but was not sure how Marigold would react. Now he knew he could rely on the girl's pride to keep them apart.

Marigold tossed and turned in her sleep. And her troubled dreams awoke her—the vision of her twin Maranta, hanging precariously over the cataract of the Ganges. But no. That was the dark-haired actress in the theater—not Maranta.

She sat up, feeling the heat of the room closing in on

165

her. Creeping to the window, she raised it higher for the cooling breeze of the sea. And the stars in the sky beckoned to her.

Could Maranta see those same stars on the coffee plantation where she lived? What was it like for her in Brazil? Marigold wished she had paid more attention to the geographer at Miss Denison's Seminary.

The girl left the window and crawled back onto the sofa, where she remained for much of the night, thinking of her twin and their separation from each other. And her heart was sad.

The next morning, Marigold packed her clothes in the new valise and was ready to leave when Crane came into the sitting room.

"We will have breakfast downstairs," he stated, "and then it will be time to take the boat."

All at once, Marigold remembered Jake. He would be coming with the repaired carriage—to the house on the battery.

"You go ahead, Crane, and order for us. I will be down in a moment."

"Make sure you don't dawdle. The boat won't wait."

As soon as he left, Marigold searched for writing paper and pen. At the desk in the sitting room, she sat and quickly penned a message to Jake—and addressed it to the black man in care of Shaun Banagher. She could do nothing else.

The messenger boys that hung about in the streets were congregated around the shoeblack in front of the hotel. Taking one of her meager coins from her new reticule, Marigold pressed the money and the letter into one of the outstretched hands, and she watched the boy running down the street before she joined Crane for breakfast.

Azure blue—with the sparkle of gold sprinkled over its white-tipped edges—the sea that Marigold loved surrounded her, lifting the boat in the rolling swells. The white sea gulls flying about with their punctuating cries—these were the sights and sounds that she loved.

Crane, slightly ill from the rolling of the water, eyed

166

Marigold resentfully for her obvious enjoyment of the trip.

She gazed out to sea, her hand shielding her amber eyes from the burning sun. They were nearing the island where she had been born—she and Maranta—and a feeling of excitement obliterated the pain and unpleasantness of the previous days.

They would be surprised to see her, with no message to prepare them for her coming. But she had never been much to write. Her parents knew that.

The old lighthouse stood tall and formidable in the distance—the sentinel that had been used by her father as a watchtower for the British ships, the structure that had sheltered her mother from the hurricane as she gave birth that stormy night. And now, Marigold would get to see it up close, walk up its winding steps, and gaze out its broken windows to sea, to the miles of water where the ships sailed in a line across the horizon, where Maranta herself had sailed half a world away.

Raven and Robbie, Feena, her parents, perhaps even Jason—Marigold was impatient to see them all.

The palm trees, the palmettos came into view, some of the taller ones growing at a strange angle along the sandy beach, bent that way by the buffeting winds. And then, the dock appeared, and the boat slowed, drifting and gliding over the glassy waters.

The boat stayed barely long enough for Marigold and Crane to disembark, before it started up again for the next stop in its journey through the barrier isles off the coast.

Marigold, not certain how far she would have to walk, left her luggage near the wooden pier for a servant to fetch and walked toward the path that was edged with cassina bushes, recently clipped. Crane had rung the bell at the pier to alert everyone of their approach. Marigold shivered, remembering the sound of the other bell near Cedar Hill.

What would she tell her mother—to explain her sudden visit? Because of Jake, she had made her bargain with Crane not to divulge his mistreatment of her. And they need not know about her harried flight in the carriage, especially now that she had left the money for Jake with Mr. Pettigrew at the bank, and the note at the townhouse. Madame Reynaud had been quite helpful, advancing her the money and adding it to her bill for Crane Caldwell.

"Do not be embarrassed, *ma petite*," the woman had said. "Many husbands are that way—willing to make an outward show, but so very stingy with the household money. You are not the first, and you will not be the last."

Nevertheless, Marigold had held her breath when Crane examined the bill for her clothes. And she had tried to conceal the visible relief when he pulled out his money clip and paid the woman without a fuss.

19

"No," she whispered. "Please—" Her mouth was covered with kisses. She struggled against him, attempting to push him away.

And then Maranta awoke. Alone—with the silken sheet tangled around her arms. She sat up, trying to separate her nightmare from reality. But they were the same.

Her wedding night had been spent, not with her invalid husband, Dom Vasco, but with his arrogant brother Ruis da Monteiro, Count of Sorocaba. He was gone, but his presence remained with her. The imprint of Ruis's head on the pillow beside her was not the only evidence that he had stayed in her bed through the night. Her body felt it, too—his total mastery of her. She tried to rid herself of the feeling of his flesh upon hers, of the half-awakened senses and the shame. But it was impossible.

With a cry, Maranta gazed down at the white lace gown on the floor, barely visible through the still-closed silken draperies of the bed. Just when she leaned over to retrieve the gown, the door opened, and Maranta hastily scrambled under the covers to hide her unclothed body.

"I have brought your breakfast, Senhora Maranta," Sassia said, pulling back the draperies of the bed. "The tray is in the sitting room, with hot *yerba mate* to drink."

"I . . . am not hungry, Sassia," Maranta said, moving still farther down in the bed. Her cheeks were flaming. Did Sassia know?

The girl ignored her comment and continued. "I shall bring hot water for your bath as soon as you have finished your breakfast."

Sassia picked up the gown from the floor and nonchalantly laid it on the bed with the lace peignoir, before leaving the bedroom.

The sob escaped Maranta's lips. She knew. They all

knew. Maranta was the only one who had not known. Even the priest—for had he not made it clear to her before her wedding vows that she was to obey Dom Ruis in all things, even above her husband?

Her wedding vows were broken, and she felt wicked. Tears fell silently as she dressed herself in the lace gown that Ruis had removed with his own hands, and then she covered it with the matching peignoir.

Through her tears she saw the blurred outline of the open jewelry case. The *Cruzamento da Monteiro*. Why had she not given it back to the condessa, or at least let it remain unworn in the jewelry case? But already she knew the answer to that. It was her pride that had made Maranta put it on, her feeling of insignificance before the arrogant conde. If Dom Ruis had not seen her in the chapel with it around her neck, this might never have happened.

"And did you pray for yourself, *menina?*" His words at Penha came back to her. And now she knew why he had asked her that at the shrine in the hills where miracles were made.

Forgetting the breakfast tray waiting for her, Maranta snatched up the cross of precious jewels. She would take it to the chapel and hang it on one of the statues for safekeeping. And there it could remain forever. She would never wear it again. She could not bear to have it in her sight, to remind her of her humiliation.

Clasping the peignoir around her body, Maranta ran barefoot down the deserted hall, across the gallery, and down the steps into the chapel itself.

The white flowers near the altar were wilted—a sad reminder of what had taken place less than twenty-four hours previously.

She could not even kneel to pray. She felt too unworthy.

The row of saints stood in silent splendor before her. Maranta walked among them until she came to the Dolorosa, the sad-eyed madonna that echoed her own hurt and sadness. Standing on tiptoe, she hung the cross around the statue's neck.

As she made her way back up the stairs, her shoulders

drooped and her steps were slow. A door closed nearby, and Maranta, aware of her scanty attire, hid in the alcove until the heavy steps grew lighter along the marbled hallway and then made no further sound.

With a sudden urgency to get back to the safety of her room, Maranta rushed from her hiding place, her dark hair flying behind her, her small, silent, bare feet sprinting along the cold, black-and-white tiles of the hall.

At her suite, she grasped the golden handle, pushed open the door, and then, leaning against the closed wooden panel, she struggled for her breath; for she had run as if the devil's legions had been on her heels.

The breakfast tray lay where Sassia had left it—on the table beside the pale lilac sofa. The tea was already cold, but Maranta gulped it down to assuage the terrible thirst that had come upon her. She left the rest of the breakfast untouched.

From the bedroom door, Sassia appeared, and Maranta, seeing the black girl, put down the delicate porcelain cup and asked, "Is my bath ready?"

"Yes, senhora. It is ready."

Suddenly shy at undressing before the servant, Maranta said, "I . . . I do not need any help, Sassia. Just put my dress on the bed, and then you may go."

"Yes, senhora," the girl replied.

Maranta went behind the screen and removed her gown. As she climbed into the tub of warm water, there appeared to be no telltale signs that her body was any different from the day before. Yet, Maranta knew that was not true. The spots of blood on the silken sheet acknowledged that she would never be the same again. She was no longer the virgin bride brought to the *fazenda* to marry the younger brother of the conde—but a girl taken by the wrong man on her wedding night. Yet, she had meant nothing to him. She was a means to an end. Without any emotion or love, she had been selected to bear the heir of the Monteiro family.

Now she knew why Marigold had not been considered a suitable candidate by the condessa. Her sister would never have allowed such a thing to happen to her.

171

But with Maranta, it was different. She was too shy, too intimidated by the entire family to assert herself. Perhaps now that the conde had had his way with her, he would leave her alone.

Maranta, feeling suddenly ill and weak, decided not to put on the dress Sassia had laid out for her. Instead, she put on a fresh gown and barely brushed the tangles from her long, black hair before climbing again into the dreaded bed that she had shared with Dom Ruis. The soiled sheets had been removed, and in their place, fresh white silken ones covered the mattress.

For the rest of the morning, Maranta remained in her room—too tired and disheartened even to see about Fado, who chirped in his cage by the window. When the bell signaled that luncheon was served, Maranta did not respond. Too embarrassed to face Dom Ruis and his family, she drew the bed draperies around her and hid in her cocoon of thin, gossamer silk.

Later, Sassia came into the room and stood at the foot of the bed. "You are not feeling well, Senhora Maranta?"

"I . . . I have a headache, Sassia."

"Do you wish me to bring some food to you?"

"No, thank you. I . . . am not hungry. But I am very thirsty. Could you please bring me some water to drink?"

The girl left the room and soon returned with a glass, holding it for Maranta as she drank. When the glass was drained, Maranta asked, "May I have more?"

The servant's troubled eyes stared at Maranta, and then, backing away from the bed, she took the empty glass with her.

But it was not Sassia who entered the room later. It was the conde, Dom Ruis. He thrust back the curtains, and Maranta, just on the edge of sleep, opened her dark doe eyes, and at the sight of the man, she gave a cry.

"Be still, *menina*. I will not hurt you," he said in a stern voice.

His face was solemn—almost angry. And in a commanding tone he said, "Let me see your right arm."

Obediently, Maranta held it out, and Ruis bent over, examining the faint teeth marks left by the vicious bat. His

172

hand ran up her arm, and she protested, "Please, Dom Ruis. There is no cause for concern."

His frown denied her affirmation. To her forehead his hand moved and then brushed back the slightly damp tendrils that clung to her perspiring skin. Under his breath he muttered words that Maranta could not understand. And in English he said, "You are running a fever, Maranta. Do you have a headache also?"

"Yes," she replied. "And . . . and my throat hurts." She swallowed painfully.

At her confession, Ruis became terrifying to see. Never had she seen his face so angry, so filled with wrath, his eyes flashing with a malignant light. He swept out of the room like a whirlwind, but before Maranta could stop shivering from fright, he was back again, thrusting something toward her.

Leaves—of some unknown plant. And he was forcing them into her mouth. "Chew them," he ordered, but Maranta, shaking her head, struggled against him and tried to spit them out.

Was he trying to poison her? Had she displeased him so much that he had decided to get rid of her?

"*Pequena,* I pray you. Do not struggle against me. Do as I ask," he begged in a hoarse voice. And Maranta, too tired to keep up the battle, accepted the leaves between her small, white teeth and tasted their bitterness on her tongue. If Dom Ruis wanted to get rid of her, there was nothing she could do to stop him.

A strange, floating feeling came over the girl. In and out of consciousness she drifted, while she murmured in her delirium. And at times, when she awoke, she saw Ruis sitting by her bed. Never Sassia—never the condessa or Dona Isobel. Always the dark-haired conde. Completely deserted, with no one in the world but Dom Ruis to soothe her hot forehead with the damp cloths, to force the bitter leaves into her mouth, to hold her and make her drink the water—always the cool water.

Once, she thought she saw an angel with long, golden hair and pale blue eyes gazing down at her. Was she dying and at the gate of heaven? But no. That was impossible. Maranta was too wicked to go to heaven. Her tears clouded her vision, and the angel disappeared.

The quietness in the room was disturbed by the chirping of a bird. Fado—and she had not fed him or given him water.

"Fado," Maranta murmured, trying to lift her head from the pillow.

The deep voice was assuring. "Fado is all right, *menina*. Can you hear him singing for you?"

"Y-Yes," she whispered, and the effort of speaking left her exhausted. The girl's eyes closed and she slept.

The demons rapidly multiplied, invading her mind and body, sending pain and agony, numbing her legs. Her throat was on fire. Maranta cried out, and the man held her against his chest, rocking her back and forth.

"What is bothering you, *menina?*" he inquired gently, pushing back the long, dark hair from her tiny, pale face.

"My legs," she answered. "They're numb."

His hand stopped abruptly. And before she could object, Ruis had jerked back the bed cover and was examining the slender legs, the tiny feet.

"Move them, Maranta," he urged.

"I . . . don't think I c-can," she said, too ill to feel any embarrassment at Dom Ruis's intimacy.

"You *will* move them, Maranta. I order you to do so."

His command meant nothing to her. She lay still, with only the fluttering of her hand to show that there was any life left in her body.

"God—no!" Ruis groaned and stumbled from the bedside.

Far into the night, the candles of myrtle wax burned, and the low chant of the family priest intermingled with the shallow breathing of the small figure that lay in the massive oriental bed.

As the pale sun finally slipped through the window, the priest arose from his knees. He took one last look at the girl on the bed, the sleeping conde in a chair beside her, before walking out into the hall. His steps led him along the gallery, down through the chapel, and to his own room at the back. Three nights they had kept watch together, and he was exceedingly weary.

The room was warm—much too warm for Maranta. She stirred and kicked off the heavy white comforter that covered her. And a laugh of jubilation filled the room.

The man smiling down at her was a stranger. Bloodshot eyes and a heavy growth of beard. And yet, there was something familiar about him too.

"Ruis?"

"You moved your legs, *pequena*," the conde said, his deep voice sounding relieved.

Maranta frowned. Why should that make him happy? she wondered. A moving of her legs. Did he think she was immobile?

In a few days, Maranta's fever had vanished, and she sat up, with pillows in embroidered lace propped behind her. Every two hours she was brought nourishment and urged to eat. But it was Sassia who now attended her. Dom Ruis had disappeared at the same time as her fever.

20

A week later, Maranta left her room for the first time since she had become ill.

On the veranda she sat, content to be lazy and do nothing more strenuous than gaze out toward the slopes of coffee plants in the distance.

"So you finally decided not to make a widower out of me."

The voice spoken from behind prompted Maranta to turn her head. Vasco pushed his rolling chair toward her and stopped. His calculating inspection of her thin body in the aqua dress that Sassia had altered and the dark circles under her eyes made Maranta nervous.

"D-Dom Vasco," she said, surprised to see her husband on the veranda.

"You gave Ruis quite a scare. And now I see why. There isn't much left of you, is there?"

At his brutal frankness, Maranta paled and could not think of a reply.

Evidently, Vasco expected none. "He thought you had rabies, you know. From the bat."

"I . . . did not know."

"Of course, Ruis said nothing to Mãe about his fears. It would have shattered all her carefully laid plans. And I doubt she could have stood that."

"What . . . what do you mean?"

"Come now, Maranta Monteiro é Tabor. Do you think I do not know why you were brought to the *fazenda?*"

He leaned toward her and with relish, he whispered, "Ruis loves Mãe too much not to give her what her heart desires—even though it means taking to bed a girl he has no feeling for."

Maranta's hand went up to her cheek, and she fled from

the veranda, the sound of Dom Vasco's taunting laughter following her.

All the time Ruis had taken care of her, he had been doing it for Mãe. Maranta meant nothing to him. And she meant nothing to Dom Vasco either, except as someone to taunt and tease in her humiliating situation. Why had the conde not allowed her to die? She did not belong on the *fazenda*. She would never belong. Even if she should bear the child the condessa wanted, Maranta would still have no official place in the Monteiro family. She might even be sent away later.

Maranta thought of her little brother, Raven, so sweet in her arms. How she had enjoyed holding him and singing to him. And what a wrench of the heart to leave him. How much more heartache if Dom Ruis should be so cruel as to send her away after her own baby was born.

But Maranta was not with child. The night spent with Ruis had accomplished nothing but the taking of her maidenhead.

"Hello," the blond girl called out to Maranta as she passed through the *sala*. "You are Maranta, Dom Vasco's wife, are you not?"

"Yes, and you must be—Innocencia."

The tinkling laugh was musical and refreshing after the harsh, cynical laughter of her husband. "I have been so bored today, playing only with the pickaninnies. Come into my room and have tea with me," the girl invited.

Unable to think of an excuse not to do so, Maranta followed Innocencia through the *sala* and into the large room whose iron-grilled door stood open.

The draperies were drawn, shutting out the sun. As her eyes grew accustomed to the darkness, Maranta realized she was in the nursery. On the floor mat, several small black babies crawled.

Innocencia clapped her hands and said to the approaching servant, "Take them back to their quarters. I am tired of them."

The woman scooped up the babies under her arms and disappeared.

"Come sit down and I will ring for tea and cakes."

Maranta obeyed, fascinated by the beautiful girl in her loose garment and bare feet. Innocencia sat on the ornately embroidered hammock and made room for Maranta. With one foot, she started the hammock into motion and then tucked both feet under her, as a child might do. The swinging back and forth was disconcerting to Maranta.

"If you don't mind, I think I'll sit in the chair," Maranta said to the girl. "I've been ill, and the swinging motion is making me dizzy."

Innocencia stopped the hammock for Maranta to get off. "Vasco said you were going to die, but you didn't, did you?"

"No."

The pale blue eyes stared at her in a curious manner, until the cakes and tea brought into the room diverted Innocencia's gaze.

"I have sweet cakes with cream every day," the girl confided. "All I can eat. Dona Isobel says it is not good for me to have so many, but I know why she tells me this. The black crow does not like me. But I do not care. I don't like her either."

Unaware of the shock her words produced, Innocencia tore into the cake, breaking it into small pieces. Her hands became sticky from the cream, and impatiently, she wiped them on the loosely fitting robe.

She was still a child—just like Robbie with his candied apple, thought Maranta. And yet, she was married to the Count of Sorocaba. And that made her the young condessa —the mistress of the household.

As soon as she could politely do so, Maranta stood up to leave.

Innocencia's voice was petulant. "Do you have to go?" she asked.

"I'm afraid so. Sassia will be looking for me. It's past time for me to rest."

Innocencia lay back on the hammock and pouted. "I'm beginning to get a headache, anyway." Then, she sat up. "But tomorrow. You'll come and see me again tomorrow?"

"If you wish," Maranta replied.

The smile lit up the angelic face. "We can have sugar cookies tomorrow. And I shall let you play with one of the pickaninnies . . ."

As Maranta disappeared, Innocencia scratched herself with the wickedly sharp three-inch fingernail on her little finger and reached for another sweet cake.

Two nights later, Maranta lay in bed. Moonbeams sifted through the soft, silken draperies and touched the gold band on her finger—the circlet put there by Dom Vasco in the chapel. But they had shared nothing more than a few sentences since that time. To Maranta it was a sacrilege to continue to wear a symbol of deceit and emptiness. Yet, she was afraid to remove it on her own.

The girl was exceedingly lonely. Innocencia behaved so strangely that she could not be depended upon as a companion. And Dom Ruis had left the *fazenda* to see to the vast property that was his. From the conversation between Dona Isobel and the condessa at dinner, Maranta gathered that he had ridden southwest to the pampas where his gauchos watched over his cattle herds.

He had been away for two weeks, and each day he was gone emphasized his dominance over the Monteiro family. What a difference it made to all of them—the condessa and Dona Isobel included—to have Ruis absent from the coffee plantation. It was almost as if they were all asleep and waiting to be awakened at his return.

On one day, Maranta was grateful that he was away. And then, the next day, she had changed her mind. Puzzled at her ambivalent feelings toward this dark-haired man, a troubled Maranta finally fell asleep.

The breathing beside her bed awoke her. The moon no longer lavished its beams upon the bedcovers but, with a frugality, had nearly vanished, leaving the room in darkness.

Beyond the silken bed draperies, a shadow moved. Someone was in her room—watching Maranta as she slept.

How long had the person been there, staring at her? Had Dom Ruis returned from the pampas, and was he coming to her bed again?

180

Maranta shrank back against the pillow. Her voice, trembling with fear, called out, "Who's there?"

The shadow moved but did not answer.

Maranta sat up and again she called out. "Please tell me who you are."

The high tinkling laugh sounded at the same time the door opened, revealing Dona Isobel in the flickering candlelight.

"Come, Innocencia," the woman said. "It is time for you to go back to your room."

"No," the stubborn voice resisted. In the candlelight, Innocencia resembled a petulant angel with her beautiful blonde hair slightly awry.

"I have a sweet cake for you in your room, Innocencia. Go with Naka and she will give it to you."

The servant appeared directly behind Dona Isobel. At the promise of a sweet, Innocencia became docile, and the frown left her face. She allowed Naka to take her by the arm and lead her out of Maranta's room.

"I am sorry that Innocencia disturbed you, Maranta," Dona Isobel said. "I think she will not bother you again tonight. But to make certain, come and lock your door after me."

Maranta obediently climbed out of bed and followed Dona Isobel to the door of the sitting room. She stood, watching the woman walk down the hall with the unsteady flicker of the candle beside her.

No wonder Dona Isobel had been able to find Innocencia so quickly. The girl had left a trail of shredded flower petals and stems all the way to Maranta's door.

Turning the lock, Maranta groped her way back to bed, where she lay, unable to go to sleep until the horizon became red with a new day rising.

After that night, Innocencia was confined to her room. Evidently, she had inherited her madness. And some times it was worse than others, Dona Isobel explained later in private.

Such a tragedy—Innocencia, so beautiful, yet with a mind less than a child's. Maranta felt a great pity, not only for the girl, but for Dom Ruis. It must be heartbreaking for him, seeing a beloved and adored wife in such a state. Was it the loss of their child that had shattered Innocencia's mind?

Maranta, suddenly restless, got up from her chair on the deserted veranda. She had not taken a footstep outside the enclosed compound the entire time she had been at the *fazenda*.

In the distance, she heard the faint roar of the falls of Hitû. And the perfume of exotic plants filled the air. A scent—almost like jasmine at Midgard. Could it be the coffee plants on the slopes? Already, the bushes were forming berries that would be harvested in July and August. But some of the limbs still held the beautiful white blossoms. Like cotton, Maranta thought, with various stages of development on the same plant.

She felt a need to get beyond the *fazenda,* to see the land that produced the pineapples and oranges, the vegetables that she enjoyed at mealtimes. Yet, she had been told by Dom Ruis not to leave the grounds alone.

Dom Ruis was not at home. He could not know how confined she felt with nothing to do. If he had unpacked the artist's supplies, he had not bothered to mention it to her.

Opening the gate, Maranta slipped out. She would not go far. Only a few feet beyond the wall. It would be perfectly safe there, within calling distance of everyone in the house.

The air was heavy, promising more rain; for it was the rainy season when, at will, the skies opened and saturated the rich earth that nurtured the coffee plants.

The small shelter in the grove attracted Maranta. She headed for it, thinking there would be a place to sit—and a roof to protect her from the rain if she should happen to be caught in it.

Someone had gotten there before Maranta. She stopped, watching the figure—an Indian, in tattered clothes. He began to eat from the tall wooden shelf. Was it a shelter for travelers? Did Dom Ruis make a habit of leaving food for the people who journeyed through his land?

The Indian turned and stared at Maranta. And she

gasped in revulsion. His skin was covered with scales—thickened, rough scales that resembled the amphibious-like skin of some creature who had crawled from the sea.

Away from the shelter and back through the gate she sped, all the time trying to deny what she had just seen. He did not even resemble a human being—ugly—covered with lesions—a man to be pitied.

Maranta hurried toward the steps. She would not feel safe until she was in her own apartment with the door locked.

So intent on blotting out the horrible vision, Maranta did not at first see what lay in front of her, curled up by the steps. Her eyes widened. No, not in the compound. It was impossible. The danger was beyond the gate—out in the wilderness—the *mata*. Yes, that was where it belonged. But as Maranta stood there, frozen in motion, her eyes reaffirmed her terror. Blocking her way was a giant snake, black and glistening and making no move to disappear as the snakes on Midgard Plantation did when a human approached. Maranta tried to cry out, but no sound came from her throat.

A rumble of thunder resounded through the sky, and several drops of rain pelted Maranta's face.

"You will get wet, *pequena,* if you keep standing there."

Dom Ruis leaned over the veranda and watched her with amused dark eyes. His clothes were dirty and rough, and the suede three-cornered hat was slung carelessly at his back.

With a trembling finger, Maranta pointed to the snake, and her eloquent dark satin eyes begged Ruis silently for deliverance.

"The *muçurana* is harmless, Maranta," he assured her. "He will not mind if you walk past him."

Still mute with fright, Maranta shook her head and remained where she was.

"Now if you were a venomous *jararaca,* that would be different," he said, laughing, as he walked toward her. "He would have you for a meal, and then go to sleep for two weeks."

183

Ruis took her by the hand and led her past the snake. Maranta edged closer to Dom Ruis as they went up the steps to the veranda. And she continued to stand close to him, trembling at her unnerving experience.

Feeling her body still shivering, Ruis said, "Surely our family pet has not upset you, *menina?* It must have been something outside the gate that made you so fleet of foot."

Maranta nodded. "The Indian. His s-skin."

"Ah, so you saw one of the Tupis on his way to the Lazar House in Hitû. Leprosy is not a pretty sight, Maranta. I am sorry that you had to come face to face with it, so soon after your own illness."

His eyes examined her closely. "Despite your paleness, you look better, Maranta, than you did when I left two weeks ago. And I see you have gained some much needed weight, too."

Hating the way he was staring at her, bringing back to her mind those days when he had taken care of her so intimately, she quickly replied, "I have been eating too many cream cakes with Innocencia."

"You have made friends with my wife? While I was away?"

"Yes. We visited together until . . . until . . ." Maranta stopped.

"Until what?" Dom Ruis prompted.

"Until . . . she became ill again."

Dom Ruis's dark brows collided into a massive frown. "Yes. Innocencia's . . . indisposition," he said bitterly and then walked away from Maranta, leaving her to bite her lip and take one last fearful look at the *muçurana* before she fled to her apartment.

21

By evening the *fazenda* had taken on new life. It was true, then. Dom Ruis, by merely returning, could sharpen the steps of the house servants, could bring a fresh glow to the old condessa's wrinkled face.

Even Dona Isobel, the penniless cousin who acted as companion to the condessa, reacted to Ruis's presence with her coy looks only partially hidden by the black lace fan.

But Maranta, seated opposite him in the *sala,* was nervous at the conde's attention. His eyes bored into her, making her feel as if she had on nothing more than the white lace gown of her wedding night, or worse—nothing at all.

"She is looking much better. Do you not think so, Mãe?" he said.

The condessa's eyes rested on Maranta for a while before answering. "Yes. Much better," she agreed. "Sassia has taken good care of her while you have been away."

"Good."

"Please," Maranta said, embarrassed that the two were talking about her as if she were not even in the room.

"Yes, *pequena?*" Ruis said, his voice soft and lazy.

"I . . . I don't like to be stared at and talked about."

His amused expression remained on his face while he continued to stare at her, watching her cheeks turn crimson. And then he shifted his attention to Dona Isobel.

"Would it disturb you, Isobel, to be in Maranta's shoes?"

Dona Isobel lowered her fan. "For myself, I would not mind being young again. But as the condessa well remembers, I never had Maranta's beauty—so consequently never knew what it was like to be stared at and talked about."

Her quick glance toward Maranta was apologetic.

Ruis pursued the subject further. "But you think you might have enjoyed the attention, Isobel?"

"Almost every young girl's ambition," Isobel admitted, "is to stir a man's interest, Ruis. It is in a woman's heart to wish to be the subject of some man's love."

"I wonder," Ruis said, more to himself than to anyone else in the room. His sapphire eyes were once again on the slight figure seated on the sofa.

"What about you, Maranta? What is your ambition, *pequena*? To be a great artist?'

The teasing made Maranta angry. Her lips trembled, but she replied in a firm voice. "I had only one ambition, senhor. But for me, it is now too late."

"And how is that?"

"I wished to become a nun, senhor—in the Convent of Our Blessed Lady."

His dark eyes were disbelieving at her avowal. His face hardened. "And who pushed you in that direction, Maranta?"

"No one, senhor. It was only natural. My own maman was a nun at one time, before my father . . ."

Dom Ruis's laugh filled the room. "But instead, she became the mother of how many children, *menina?*"

"F-Five." Maranta's cheeks burned at his inquisition.

"Mãe tells me that you resemble your mother very much." In an intimate tone intended only for her ears, he whispered, "Is that not a lesson for you, Maranta? Your destiny does not lie in a nunnery, as you are well aware."

Angry at his insinuation, Maranta jumped from the sofa. She walked to the condessa, and kissing her on her cheek, Maranta said, "I am very tired, Mãe. If I have your permission, I will retire to my room."

The condessa kissed the girl and nodded. Maranta then laid her cheek against Dona Isobel's cheek, and unable to face Dom Ruis, she left the room.

But she was not to escape him. Ruis remained standing and, bidding the two women good-night, he headed for his library opposite Maranta's apartment.

"One moment, Maranta. And I will walk with you."

"That is not necessary, senhor."

He caught up with her and placed his hand on her arm. "My name is Ruis. Have you deliberately forgotten?"

His touch made her tremble. She moved away from him.

"Do not be so skittish, Maranta. From the way you are behaving, people would think we were strangers."

"We *are* strangers."

"No, Maranta. You may speak for yourself. But you are no stranger to me. From the small curves of your body to the formation of your toes—even to the birthmark on your . . ."

"Please," Maranta croaked, tugging at his coat sleeve. "Someone might overhear."

"And if someone does?"

"I will die of shame."

"Then, if you want no one to hear, I shall have to come into your apartment. For there is a question that I wish to have answered."

They were at the door of the sitting room, and Ruis opened it to allow Maranta to precede him into the room. She walked to the hearth filled with greenery and stood with her back to Ruis—waiting to hear the words he would utter.

"Turn around and face me, Maranta."

"I . . . can't."

She felt his hand reach for her and lift her chin upward. But Maranta closed her eyes.

"You know what I am going to ask?"

"Yes."

"Well?"

If she said that she was expecting his child, he would soon discover it to be a lie. But if she admitted that her wedding night had not been fruitful, then the same thing could happen again.

"I'm waiting, Maranta. Are you with child?"

The tears slipped from under her closed eyelids. "No," she murmured, shaking her head.

She was in his arms, and he stroked her hair gently. "Do not be so fearful, *pequena*. If there were an alternative you know I would not force my attentions on you."

187

Maranta opened her eyes and saw the pain reflected in his face. Of course. If only Innocencia could give him his heir, then he would never come to her bed.

She heard the door close. Maranta was now alone; for Ruis had disappeared to his library across the deserted hall.

Relieved, Maranta rang for Sassia. And soon, the girl was relaxing in the brass tub of warm, soapy water, with her black hair piled high on the top of her head.

She had forgotten to ask Ruis about the paints and brushes, she'd been so intent to get away from him. But she could do that tomorrow at lunch, if he were not off somewhere on the *fazenda,* too far to return in time for lunch.

Maranta slipped her toes under the pile of suds at the end of the tub and lifted her foot into the air. And at that moment she looked up into the amused face of the conde, standing over her.

Quickly she lowered her foot into the water and held the sponge in front of her.

"Shall I bring you a toy from the nursery, *pequena?*"

"I am no child, senhor."

The pink-tipped nipples of her breasts peeked through the suds, in spite of the sponge she held in front of her.

Ruis's eyes narrowed. "Yes. I can see that you are no child, Maranta. And so it is time to stop playing games."

He reached for her hand. "Climb out of the tub, Maranta," he ordered.

"Sassia . . ."

"Has gone to bed. She will not be back tonight."

"My gown—"

"There is no need to put on what will only be removed in a few minutes."

Maranta's lip quivered, but Ruis ignored her look of distress. He held the toweling for her and wrapped her in it. She trembled as his knowing hands dried her body and then pulled the ribbon loose, making her hair tumble to her waist.

She was swept up in his arms, with the towel left on the floor, and Ruis carried her across the room to the bed.

His dark hair was still wet from his own bath, and his tanned body glistened in the candlelight. Maranta attempted to pull the sheet over her, but Ruis's hands stopped her. His eyes traveled the length of her body, and Maranta whispered, "The candle. Please blow out the candle, senhor."

He shook his head. "Ruis. My name is Ruis. And after tonight, I dare you to call me senhor. You'll never be able to think of me as a stranger, Maranta. For you will know my body as intimately as you know your own."

"R-Ruis."

"That's better, *pequena*." He took her hands and placed them on his muscular body. And at the feel of his firm flesh, she shuddered and closed her eyes.

"Keep your eyes closed, if you must, Maranta," he taunted. "It matters not." He pressed his mouth against her ear and whispered, "Tonight, I shall make you forget that you ever had the desire to become a little nun."

Her body was not her own—but *his* to do with as he wished. Under his gentle assault, Maranta responded against her will to this new world of sensual pleasure—feeling his hands caressing her body and his lips covering her with kisses.

Not realizing what she was doing, Maranta ran her hands through his hair and touched the tanned cheek that lay against hers. And at the moment his body met hers, filling her with a promise of ecstasy, she encircled him with her arms, drawing him closer.

In a primitive response to the rhythmic motion of his body, Maranta moved. Her need overwhelmed her—this feeling that possessed her body and mind, driving out all fear, all guilt, everything but her desire.

Her body tensed, and she clung to Ruis, her hands entwined around his neck.

"Do you still wish to become a nun, Maranta?" he whispered, stopping his lovemaking for a brief moment.

In agony, she denied it. His cry was triumphant as he began again, bringing her to the precipice. In waves, the alien feeling came, so that no part of her body escaped from it. And then she was lost in eternity, with the man who demanded her very soul. Willingly she gave it to him.

"Maranta," he cried. His body gave a giant shudder, and Maranta gasped at the intensity.

Her rapid breathing matched his, her breasts moving against his chest, while the air he breathed invaded her mouth. He drew her close and held her. Face to face they remained, while the candle flickered its last remnants of light and was extinguished.

She awoke in the middle of the night and sat up. Ruis was beside her, breathing steadily. In the darkness, Maranta felt a terror that she had never encountered in her life. That night, she had denied ever wanting to become a nun. Ruis's kisses and caresses had made her forget every precept that had ever guided her life.

The terrible truth struck her. She had not wanted him to stop his lovemaking. She had welcomed Ruis's advances as ardently as some slave mistress in love with her master. The sin was multiplied—a double sin—hers as·well as Ruis's, because of her own desire.

With a tiny groan, Maranta climbed out of bed. Groping for the peignoir at the foot of the bed, she wrapped herself in the garment and sank to her knees, where she prayed for forgiveness for the rest of the night.

In the distance, over the slopes of the *terra-roxa,* the sun came up. Ruis, restless, reached out for the girl beside him, but she was not there. He opened his eyes and looked down on the small figure kneeling by the bed. Her long silken hair spread over the white coverlet, and Ruis captured a strand in his giant hand.

"Climb back into bed, Maranta," he said in a gruff voice. "It is too soon for morning prayers. Besides, the chapel is the place for religion—not here in the bedroom."

When she did not respond, Ruis climbed out of bed and lifted her from the rug. "You are cold, *menina,*" he said with an irritated tone. "Do you wish to become ill again?"

Under the coverlet he placed her, drawing her to the warmth of his body. As she struggled against him, Ruis's strong arms held her.

"Let me go, Ruis," Maranta begged.

"No, little Iemanjá. You cannot escape me until I know you have the seed of my son planted within you."

At his frank words, Maranta moaned.

"You did not object last night, *pequena*. What has happened? An attack of conscience in the little nun's mind of yours this morning?"

"It is wrong—"

"I have no patience for confession," the man snapped. "Save that for the family priest."

"Ruis, please. I beg of you . . ."

"Hush, Maranta." His voice brooked no opposition, and she became silent as Ruis's hands began their exploration afresh. But Maranta, determined to show her unwillingness, lay passively in his arms.

Angered at her behavior, Ruis sat up, his cold eyes glaring at the petite girl beside him.

"Do you think it is a pleasure to take a woman against her will, Maranta? I am sick of this, as you are. And I promise when you are with child, I shall be happy to leave you alone with your maidenly prayers."

He leaped from the bed, grabbed his robe, and departed from the room, leaving a weeping Maranta more desolate than ever.

She loved him—not Dom Vasco, her own husband who ignored her, but Ruis da Monteiro, who had just made it plain how distasteful it was to take her to bed, and that it was all for the sake of an heir.

Maranta rubbed her arm where the bat had left its mark upon her. A pity that it had been only a fever and not the deadly rabies that had invaded her body.

And yet, despite his harsh words, had it not been Dom Ruis who had braved danger to himself to save her? He had allowed no one else to be exposed to her illness.

But it was for his heir—not for Maranta. She must remember that. A grieving Maranta turned her face to the pillow and finally slept.

22

Maranta knew that she would never be able to claim her bed as her own until Ruis had accomplished his purpose. Each night she lay in his arms and felt his body upon hers. And the more he drew her to him, the more she fought —for her survival and her pride.

Each time the old condessa looked at her, Maranta shrank in shame, remembering the lovemaking of the evening before. But it was no lovemaking on Ruis's part. It was a cold, calculated plan. Yet, she would never let Ruis suspect the effect he had upon her heart and mind. How much longer was it to go on? How much more disgrace could she bear, sealing her lips—so not to whisper his name in ecstasy? For he must never know she had lost her heart to him as well as her body.

Once again, Maranta remained cloistered in her apartment—too upset to seek the company of anyone in the *fazenda.*

"Maranta?"

Ruis's voice disturbed the girl, and she started at his sudden appearance in her sitting room. He frowned at the dejected figure on the pale lilac sofa. "It is not good for you to sit and mope in this apartment, *menina.* You must get more fresh air—not only for your own sake, but for—"

She jerked her head up and glared at him with her stormy dark eyes, daring him to continue, to put into words what she had tried so hard to forget.

At her behavior, a coldness pervaded his voice. "I have set up an easel on the veranda for you, Maranta, with your paints and brushes. I won't have you behaving as if you have been walled into this room, like a martyr waiting for death. In fifteen minutes, I expect to see you on the veranda."

He turned heel and slammed the door. Maranta closed her eyes and knotted her hands into small fists.

Every action—every gesture. Like a marionette, she was forced to move and behave, with Dom Ruis manipulating the strings. As if she did not have a mind of her own, or as if it mattered not that her very soul was in mortal danger.

Sighing, Maranta arose from the sofa and slowly walked down the stairs, out onto the shaded veranda of the plantation house. A perverseness had kept her from changing her dress. If she ruined it with the paints, then it would be Ruis's fault.

Maranta found the easel, and setting aside her anger at Ruis, she explored the box at her feet. Delighting in the abundance of colors, she began the absorbing task of mixing the paints to her specifications, and in quick slashes, she brushed a light wash over the white linen canvas that stood before her. All her frustrations she put into her painting, using the brushes to blot out her unhappiness. Soon the canvas began taking shape as she remembered the landscape from Santos to São Paulo.

Abruptly, Maranta wiped her hands on the cloth. Fado would enjoy sunning himself on the veranda. And the little green bird could keep her company while she painted, for no one else seemed to be about. Even the conde, certain in his arrogance, had not waited to see that she obeyed him. Maranta hastened upstairs, and with the chirping Fado in his cage, she returned. Innocencia was on the veranda and leaning over the canvas that Maranta had left. Was it curiosity to see what she was painting? For a moment, Maranta watched her. Then she saw that the girl had a brush in her hands, dabbing paint on the canvas, spoiling what Maranta had already done. But instead of becoming angry at her, Maranta felt a gentle sympathy. At least she must be better, to be able to leave her room.

At Maranta's approach, Innocencia, looking guilty, dropped the brush on the floor. "It's all right," Maranta assured her. "Do you want to paint, too?"

The girl's eyes indicated she was far away. "The forest —it is evil," she announced. "It frightens me. I have hidden it so it can't harm me."

When Maranta came closer, she saw that Innocencia had slashed the scene with black, ruining the careful color of the sunset that was beginning to take shape.

Aware of Naka coming toward her, Innocencia fled from the veranda, colliding with a servant who balanced the *tigre* on his head. It was lucky for both of them that he had already been to the river to empty the barrel that held the waste collected from the bedrooms, which was stored under the stairs until it was full. Innocencia shouted at the man as he retrieved the rolling *tigre*. And Maranta, wrinkling her nose, seated herself again at the easel and took a cloth to dip into the turpentine. Rubbing gently across the canvas, she removed the ugly black color. But in doing so, she could not save the beautiful hues of the river sunset. She would have to start over.

For the rest of the afternoon she worked, forgetting all sense of time, until a wave of nausea assailed her. Impatiently, Maranta brushed her hair back and surveyed the canvas. She had worked too long, sitting in one position. It had tired her. That was why she did not feel well.

Sassia in her bare feet approached the girl. "It will soon be time for dinner, Senhora Maranta. I will bring your things inside for you."

The idea of food was repulsive to her. And she did not look forward to dressing or facing the family at dinner, especially Dom Vasco, with his amused expression each time he looked at her.

Maranta stood up and stretched, bringing her hand to rub the tense muscles at the back of her neck. A warm bath would make her feel better. "The canvas is easily blurred, Sassia. Make sure it does not rub against anything."

"I will be careful, senhora."

Later, as darkness overtook the *fazenda,* Maranta proceeded directly into the dining hall. The bell had already clanged, indicating it was late. But the only one ahead of her was Dom Ruis.

His eyes took in her appearance, the pale, ice blue dress that gave such contrast to her alabaster complexion and her liquid dark eyes. And his possessive look reached out to snare her.

Maranta put her hand up to her cheek in defense, but already, Ruis had turned to greet the condessa and Dona Isobel. Soon, Patû lifted Dom Vasco into his chair, and the meal began.

The conversation went on around her, but Maranta sat silently, toying with her food.

"You are not eating, daughter," the old condessa said, peering at the girl with curious, expectant eyes. "Has something happened to take your appetite?"

"No, Mãe," she assured her, spearing a piece of meat to put into her mouth. But the taste was not pleasant, and Maranta had difficulty swallowing it. She reached for the glass of wine at her place to help wash it down. The glass suddenly blurred in front of her, and in her awkwardness, the wineglass spilled its red liquid over the embroidered lace tablecloth.

Immediately a servant came to mop it up, and Maranta, lightheaded, pushed her chair from the table. Her one wish was to get to her room and lie down. "If you will excuse me, I . . ."

On unsteady feet, Maranta left the table. She did not know what was the matter with her.

"Ruis," the condessa's voice sounded. "The child is not well. I think you had better follow her."

She had gotten as far as the *sala* before her knees gave way. *"Meu Deus,"* the deep voice proclaimed, while strong arms caught her before she reached the floor.

She was on the bed, with the cool cloth draped over her forehead. The odor of ammonia assaulted her nose, and Maranta moved her head to avoid it. As her eyes fluttered open, she saw the man's face hovering over her.

"What . . . happened?" she asked, attempting to get up.

196

"Lie still, *menina*," Ruis ordered. And with an unfathomable expression, he stated, "You fainted, Maranta."

Indignantly, Maranta protested. "I . . . couldn't have fainted. I'm fine, I . . ."

"I assure you, *pequena*. You fainted, right into my arms —and it was not the first time. Only this time, I do not believe it was in fright."

"Is the fever returning?"

"No, Iemanjá. I think perhaps there is another reason. I think more than likely that you are with child."

Maranta's face paled even more, and unable to meet the dark sapphire eyes that held a satisfied gleam, Maranta pushed the cloth from her forehead and burrowed her face into the pillow.

For the first time in weeks, Ruis did not come to her bed that night. Maranta lay in the darkness—alone and unable to sleep. If it were true—what Ruis had said, that she might be with child—then it was no longer necessary. Dom Ruis Almeida José da Monteiro, Count of Sorocaba, would have his heir in less than nine months' time.

Morning sickness soon affirmed Ruis's suspicions. There was now no doubt. Maranta was with child, and there was no way she could keep it secret—from the servants, from Vasco, or Innocencia—

Innocencia improved, and Naka relaxed her constant vigil over the girl. The episode concerning the canvas was forgotten, and although Innocencia showed no interest in what Maranta was painting, at least she made no attempt to destroy it with the black paint.

One day, Maranta sat at her easel and occasionally glanced toward Innocencia who sat at the other end of the veranda. When Floresta brought refreshments and set them before Innocencia, the girl called out, "Come and join me, Maranta. Sweet cakes and tea." She turned the porcelain cups upright and waited for Maranta.

Maranta realized she was hungry. She put her brushes aside, and removing the apron that protected her turquoise dress from the paints, she cleaned her hands and walked to the far end of the veranda. It was her pregnancy that gave her such an appetite, Maranta decided, especially after the morning sickness disappeared for the day.

Innocencia filled one cup from the teapot and pushed it toward Maranta.

"Are you not going to have some, too?" the dark-haired girl asked, when Innocencia left her own cup unfilled.

"Later," she said, "when I have finished my sweet cake."

Between bites, Innocencia watched Maranta expectantly with her pale blue eyes. The liquid was not tea. Maranta could tell from its odor. Holding up the cup, she asked, "What is it?"

"*Aguardente*," Innocencia replied, giggling.

Maranta knew that the servants were partial to an alcoholic drink made from sugarcane juice, but she was not anxious to try it. She wrinkled her nose at the odor.

"Don't be a prude, Maranta. Drink it," Innocencia urged.

Maranta took the cup in her hands but lowered it at the sight of Ruis riding in from his inspection of the slopes. He had seen them and was coming toward them on the veranda. A pretty sight for him, Maranta thought bitterly—his wife and his pregnant *comadre* having tea together. Only it was not tea.

Ruis's boots sounded on the stone floor, interrupting the chirp of Fado in his cage. The man was almost upon them when Maranta determinedly raised the cup to her lips.

Ruis lifted his head like some dark panther sensing danger and sniffed the air. That peculiar odor. Where was it coming from?

"*Que Diabo!*" he said, reaching out and knocking the cup from Maranta's lips. The liquid spilled on her dress, and the delicate porcelain cup tumbled to the floor where it shattered.

His violent action alarmed Maranta. With trembling hands, she jumped from her chair and tried to brush the liquid from her skirts.

"You—you had no right to do that," Maranta said, her voice as unsteady as her heartbeat.

"I have every right," Ruis corrected, with a fierce gleam overtaking his sapphire eyes. "Where did you get that drink, Maranta? I demand to know. Who gave it to you?"

He looked at the silent Maranta and then toward Innocencia. The blonde-haired girl put her hand to her mouth to stifle her giggle.

Ruis's gaze narrowed at the girl's nervous gesture. "Was it you, Innocencia?"

She giggled again and nodded.

The thunderous look echoed in the man's voice. "Go to your room, Innocencia. At once!"

The girl got up from the table, and turning her back on both Ruis and Maranta, she snatched the rest of the sweet cakes, before running inside.

Maranta, now angry at Ruis's harsh treatment of both of them, defended Innocencia. "Surely, there was no need to frighten Innocencia like that, over a little harmless *aguardente*."

Ruis took the silver teapot and, opening the lid, stared at the remaining liquid. Flipping the lid back in place, he repeated, "A little harmless *aguardente*. Is that what you imagined it to be, Maranta?"

"Isn't it?"

"Poor little innocent. You did not drink any of it, did you?"

"You gave me no time to do so."

"Bem!"

"It is not . . . *aguardente*?"

"No, Maranta."

"Then what is it?"

She watched him empty the liquid onto the ground beyond the railing of the veranda and then hurl the beautifully engraved silver teapot over the surrounding wall. He stood at the railing for a minute before coming back to the table.

"You remember the day the Indian outside the gate frightened you?" Ruis asked.

"How could I forget—especially with the snake coiled up by the steps to frighten me, too."

"But the Indian, Maranta. You remember his appearance?" Ruis insisted.

"I am not likely to forget those horrible lesions on his skin," Maranta said, shuddering.

"The same deadly drink that caused his skin condition, Maranta, was in your teacup."

Her face turned pale, and she held onto the chair at her sudden dizziness.

"You are never to eat or drink anything that Innocencia offers you. Is that clear?"

"Yes, Ruis."

He walked with her into the house, his dark face still brooding. "Who served you, Maranta? Who brought the teapot to the veranda?"

Reluctantly, Maranta answered, "It was . . . Floresta."

The man's lips tightened into a thin line. "I shall have to speak to Vasco about that."

A subtle change spread over the *fazenda,* and Maranta became more of a prisoner than ever, with constant attention lavished upon her. She was waited upon, hand and foot—not allowed to lift the lightest pillow, move the easel one inch on the veranda, or carry Fado's cage up and down the stairs. Sassia remained at her elbow, seeing to her food, and Maranta, despite her scare with Innocencia, felt stifled at all the attention given her—from everyone, except Ruis. His duty was done. She was pregnant. And so he could afford to stay away for days at a time, seeing to his vast estate.

Ruis had been gone for over a week before Vasco deemed to speak to Maranta alone. He wheeled his rolling chair out onto the veranda and inspected the painting that Maranta had nearly completed.

"I understand that you are soon to become a little mother. Is that true, my faithless wife?"

Maranta, dropping the paintbrush at his question, marred the stone floor with the red paint. Vasco's harsh laugh mocked her attempt to clean it up.

"What shall I do, Maranta? Announce to the padre

your terrible sin? Or keep silent and pretend that the child is mine? What would you have me do, wife?"

Maranta was voiceless. The blood drained from her face. "Dom Vasco . . ."

"Upon second thought, I think I might enjoy playing the role of a proud papa. Floresta has become too possessive of late. And then, too, it will bother Ruis, since he can never openly acknowledge the child as his. . . .

"Yes, that is what I shall do, Maranta. It will save you from being labeled an adulteress. And I will receive satisfaction, seeing Ruis denied *something* in his life. And what will be harder for him than to deny his own son?"

Maranta twisted the paintbrush in her hands. "The child may be a girl," she said in a timid, low voice.

"Oh no, my dear wife. Ruis would never allow that. It will be a boy, and to the world, I shall be its father—

"Do not look so glum, little one. We shall get along very well together. From now on, I intend to see to your welfare, as a true husband should."

Sassia, bringing a glass of cool water for Maranta, frowned as the laughing Dom Vasco rolled his chair back into the guest chambers on the first floor of the *fazenda*.

With a trembling hand, Maranta took the glass from Sassia and downed the water in quick, nervous gulps.

From that time on, Vasco gave her every attention. Each afternoon, with the help of Patû, Vasco presented himself at the upstairs apartment, across the hall from the library belonging to Ruis. And each afternoon became a war of nerves for Maranta. It was difficult to make conversation. But Vasco did not seem to mind. It was as if he were waiting for something to erupt, and his eyes, so like Ruis's and yet so different, were bright with anticipation.

In the silence between them, the sound of footsteps along the hall alerted the two that someone was coming.

"It is too soon for Patû," Vasco said. "It must be that Ruis has finally returned from Sorocaba."

The door to the sitting room opened, and the tall, dark

201

man, walking inside, stopped at the sight of Vasco seated on the pale lilac sofa.

Vasco looked at the travel-stained Ruis. "You take liberties, brother, walking unannounced into my wife's apartment. I would appreciate it if you would knock from now on."

Ruis did not respond to Vasco's taunt. He eyed Maranta, as if to assure himself that she was all right, and without a word to either of them, retraced his steps, closing the door behind him and proceeding to his library.

"The day has wearied me, Maranta," Vasco said. "Please find Patû and tell him that I am ready to go back to my own chambers."

Glad to escape, Maranta obeyed. Fighting back her tears, she found the Indian and gave him Vasco's message. But Maranta could not go back upstairs. Instead, she fled from the *fazenda,* opening the gates to the wilderness, not caring where she ran.

To be the source of contention between the two brothers—like a bone, to be fought over and torn apart—this was what Vasco had been waiting for.

On and on she ran to escape the taunting voice of Vasco and the disturbing visage of Ruis. Her hair tumbled down into her face, her combs were lost in the matted green underfoot. The river falls roared in her ears, obliterating any other sound, while the alien landscape snatched at her dress and pricked her bare arms with its thorns. Bits of lace torn from the hem of her lavender skirt, mixed with the blood the thorns had claimed, left a trail behind her.

She continued to run, and the sound of the falls diminished. Maranta stumbled as she caught her foot against a root but righted herself, cutting off her fall.

Sobbing and with a catch in her side, Maranta sank to her knees at the base of an umbrella tree. With little moans, she rocked herself back and forth and reached up for the locket that could comfort her. But the locket was not around her neck. It was gone, lost—the last link left with her own family. She was alone in an alien world that she could not understand.

Gradually, her sobs subsided. She was so tired. Her eyelids drooped and closed, and under the shelter of the tree, the slight figure in the shredded lavender dress went to sleep. . . .

23

Guiding Diabo, Ruis plunged into the matted forest. "Maranta," he shouted, and the sound echoed, unanswered, through the sleeping, dangerous vegetation. It had been over two hours since Ruis had seen the dark-haired girl run across the courtyard and through the gate—disappearing completely.

Far to the west, the sun was beginning its descent. Soon, the velvet darkness would envelop the green earth, making it impossible for him to find her. And each moment increased the danger for Maranta.

A cold anger gripped Ruis's heart. It would be his fault if Maranta and his unborn child did not survive the night.

What must she feel, this young girl, uprooted from her family and placed into this nightmare? Ruis was sorry that he had been influenced by Mãe's wish. It was not his right to take his brother's wife and make her the mother of his heir. But it was done. He could not change that now.

"Maranta," he called again, diverting the horse in a new direction and searching the ground for evidence that she might have fled in that direction.

The bit of lace, which he'd spied on the thorned bush, was in his pocket. For an hour now, there had been no other sign. The matted undergrowth had sprung up under her light step, denying any sign of her passing.

Back to the thorned bush Ruis rode, using it as a landmark and fanning out in a circle from it. The cry of a wild animal in the distance spooked Diabo, and Ruis, with a calmness he did not feel, coaxed the horse back into obedience.

Finally the last rays of sunlight caught at an object hanging on the broken limb of the bush before him. Ruis stopped the horse and jumped down to examine it at closer range.

It was Maranta's locket—the one she always wore around her neck. The clasp was broken. With a worried frown, Ruis added the golden chain to the piece of lace in his pocket. Leading the horse, he walked carefully, looking downward for another bit of evidence in his search for the runaway girl.

If the jungle decreed it, she would never wear the *Cruzamento da Monteiro* about her neck, as she had that time in the chapel when he had first recognized Mãe's purpose in bringing the girl to Brazil. How angry he had been—with Mãe and the girl, too. But Maranta's haste in disposing of the family heirloom, hanging it on the madonna in the chapel, had dispelled any hint of her collusion with the condessa. The girl was innocent of Mãe's machinations. He should have realized that from the scene aboard the *Beaufort*—her sweet, innocent face looking up into his with fright. But did not Innocencia have the same look? He had been wrong about her. It was no wonder that he was wary about being taken in for the second time by a woman's outward appearance.

Diabo suddenly reared and jerked his head, tearing the reins from Ruis's hands. Across his path, the *jararaca,* the deadliest of all snakes, with its white tail, bellied over the matted undergrowth and then disappeared.

Diabo did not go far. A whistle from Ruis summoned the frightened beast, and, too well trained to ignore his master's call, Diabo sidled back to the waiting conde. Ruis patted the horse and crooned his approval, and again took to the saddle, thrusting on into the jungled wilderness.

The voice in the distance aroused Maranta. She lifted her head and listened. Ruis? What was he doing calling her name? How had it suddenly turned so dark?

And what was she doing, in the middle of nowhere, tired and hungry and heartsore?

The sounds around her took on a sinister meaning. She shrank against the tree base at the soft wailing sound

206

of a wild animal in the thicket. Almost like a child's cry. Could it be a . . . jaguar?

To be eaten alive by the predator of the forest. Was this her destiny? She and her unborn child? Maranta brushed her scratched hand across her tear-grimed face and looked toward the thicket.

What stupidity, to run away because of the hostile atmosphere created by the two brothers. All at once, Maranta's desire for the welfare of her child made her alert. She did not want to die, did not want to harm the baby that grew inside her—Ruis's son—a part of her and the man she loved, even if she had denied loving him.

Regardless of the pain and shame, Maranta realized she wanted to bear Ruis's child, to hold the baby in her arms. Surely the priest could give her some penance that she alone would have to pay, without exacting the child's life for her sin.

A protective feeling encompassed her, and she clasped her bloodied arms around her stomach, as if she could ward off the danger that threatened the child's life. The sight of the dried blood on her arms made her weak, but she was determined not to give in. Her body, poised to run, waited while her breathing grew more rapid.

At the crashing sound from the thicket, Maranta fled, too terrified to look back to see what had emerged.

"Maranta," the voice called again, and with a scream, she answered, plummeting into the undergrowth, with her arm, stretched out to break her fall, twisting under her.

The twigs crackled beside her, but she could not move. It was too late. She screamed as the animal made contact with her terrified body.

It was a human hand, not an animal, that touched her, and Maranta's wide, frightened eyes looked up into sapphire eyes that were dark and brooding. The man's fierce look matched the forbidding landscape, but Maranta did not care. Ruis had found her.

His gentle hands wiped away her tears, and he clasped her to his chest. "I could not bear it if something had happened to you, little Iemanjá."

With a firm but kindly tone, he scolded her. "You must

207

never run away again, *pequena.* I might not be so lucky to find you next time. Promise me," he said, "that you will never do this again."

"I . . . I promise."

"And I swear to you, for the sake of our child, Maranta, I will no longer cause you heartache. Vasco can claim you and the child as his own, and I will do nothing to antagonize him."

For the sake of the child—yes, she must remember.

He lifted her onto the horse and began his journey over the darkened terrain to the *fazenda* with only the stars to guide them. Feeling Maranta still trembling in his arms, Ruis attempted to take the girl's mind off the dangerous trek homeward.

"The constellation of the twins, Maranta," he said, looking up into the sky. "Do you see it in front of you?"

Maranta lifted her head from his chest and gazed upward, thinking of her twin, Marigold, as far away from her as the stars in the heavens.

At Maranta's continued silence, Ruis volunteered, "Castor and Pollux—the twins. They are the brightest in the constellation. You know the legend?"

"No."

Undaunted by Maranta's apparent lack of interest, Ruis explained, "Pollux was supposed to be immortal; for he was the son of Jupiter."

"What about Castor?" Maranta asked, suddenly becoming interested in what Ruis was saying. "Was he not immortal, too?"

"No, *pequena.* Castor was different. He was the son of Tyndareus, and therefore, mortal."

"But you said . . . they were twins."

Ruis laughed. "The Greeks were never hampered by ordinary facts of life. They broke natural laws to suit their own whims and fancies."

Maranta lay in Ruis's arms, conscious of the seed he had planted within her, even though, in the eyes of the world, she was Vasco's wife. The Greeks were not the only ones to shape their world to suit themselves.

Maranta sighed and relaxed against Ruis's chest, and

the man, feeling the tension dispel, forged ahead, his entire body conscious of the fragile young girl whose destiny was irrevocably intertwined with his own.

The condessa, her face drawn, stood by the gate, with the black shawl covering her shoulders.

"Do you see anything, Isobel?"

The companion held the lantern high and peered out into the darkness. "Nothing, Dona Louisa. I'm sorry."

"Ruis won't come back until he has found her. I know my son."

"You've stood out here far too long," Dona Isobel said, glancing at the tired woman. "Don't you think it would be more comfortable for you inside? I'll stay and keep watch."

The condessa shook her head and drew her shawl closer to her. "I'll wait for Patû to return with the dogs from the river."

The gate remained open, with the two women peering into the blackness surrounding the *fazenda*. A pale flickering light appeared momentarily in the distance and then was snuffed out.

"I thought I saw a light," Isobel said, interrupting the silence, "but it's gone now."

"Where?"

"Beyond the trees—to the right."

The condessa strained to see, but her eyesight was not so good as Dona Isobel's. "I can see nothing," she grumbled in disgust. "But *you*, Isobel. You must keep looking. Tell me if you see it again."

The woman continued watching, and after a while, the light appeared again. "It *is* a light," Isobel stated.

"Then Patû must be coming home." The old condessa's voice quivered, and Dona Isobel reached out to take her hand.

The torchlight grew stronger and steadier, while the women waited. "There are two horses," Isobel finally cried out in a jubilant voice.

"Does Ruis have the girl with him? Can you see?"

Again, Dona Isobel held up the lantern and gazed toward the movement in the darkness. "I can't tell. It is too dark—but wait. I believe I can make out something."

The pain in the condessa's neck increased and slowly spread down her arm, but intent upon the figures coming toward the gate, the woman ignored her discomfort.

"Yes. He has her," Isobel said and lowered the lantern.

Through the open gate Ruis rode, with Patû holding the torch, directly behind him. And at the sight of her son with Maranta in his arms, the condessa stepped forward. "You found her," she whispered in relief. "Is she all right?"

"*Sim,* Mãe. She's all right, I think."

"Praise the merciful Father!"

A servant boy came running to hold the torch. Patû, taking Diabo's reins in his hand, led both horses to the stable, while Ruis, with his burden, disappeared up the steps and through the doors of the *sala da entrada.*

The old condessa, still by the gate, clutched at her heart and, in a breathless gasp, croaked, "My medicine, Isobel," and staggered toward the woman at her side.

Ruis's muddy boots tracked across the black and white tiles of the upstairs hallway that shone from its recent cleaning. At the door of the apartment, he handed the girl over to the waiting Sassia.

"Get her some water, Sassia," Ruis instructed. "And when you have bathed her and put her to bed, see that she eats some food."

"Yes, Dom Ruis."

Maranta, in a tired voice, said, "Thank you, Ruis."

He nodded and began to walk from her just as Dona Isobel called his name. Ruis hastened toward the woman, and his frown deepened on his rugged, tanned face. "What is the matter, Isobel?"

"The condessa has had another seizure."

"You gave her the medicine?" Ruis asked, walking rapidly, making it difficult for the woman to keep up with him.

"Yes, Ruis. But I am afraid it is having little effect, as the doctor in São Paulo predicted. I have sent for the priest, but she wants to see you first."

210

With giant strides, Ruis walked past the nursery with the iron-grilled door, past his own room, and down the hall to the end room. Cleaning his boots outside the door, Ruis stepped inside and knelt by the condessa's bed. Her dress had been loosened, but no attempt had been made by the servants to undress her. Ruis took her hand in his and held it to his lips. "So you are misbehaving again, Mãe," he scolded in a gentle voice.

She smiled. "I am a perverse old woman, Ruis—and too wicked to join the saints yet." Her smile turned into a grimace at the sudden pain, and she clung to Ruis's large brown hand until it passed. In a weak, urgent voice she whispered, "My son, you must not let anything happen to Maranta. Take care of her, and see that she and the child come to no harm. Promise me, my son."

"I will watch over her carefully, Mãe."

With his promise, the condessa relaxed, loosening her fingers around his hand. The priest appeared, and Ruis, bending over to kiss Mãe on the forehead, nodded to the padre and left the room.

The *fazenda* was astir, with servants running back and forth to attend to both Maranta and the condessa. And it was well after midnight before Ruis, already weary from his journey from Sorocaba, had a chance to discard his travel-stained clothes and soak his frame free of grime and dust.

After assuring himself that the condessa was as comfortable as possible, he removed his things from his quarters in the bedroom wing and spent the night on the leather couch in the library, directly across from Maranta's apartment.

Two vows he had made that day—not to antagonize his brother concerning Maranta's welfare, yet promising Mãe that he would watch over her to make sure no harm came to her or the child.

He would have to be extremely careful and on guard. For the *fazenda* contained potential enemies of the girl. There was no telling what someone might do for spite or in a fit of temper—Floresta, or Innocencia—or even his brother, Vasco.

24

Riding into Charleston with the repaired carriage and the horses, Jake was careful when he stopped to ask for directions to the house on the battery. He did not trust Crane Caldwell, and he would be glad to hand over the man's property to Miss Marigold. His money was almost gone, and he needed to find work and a place to stay. His papers declaring him to be a free man had been scrutinized more than once on the way.

It had taken longer than he had thought to get the wheel repaired. Two days had passed since he had left Miss Marigold at the train station.

When Jake arrived in front of the imposing townhouse, it was already late afternoon. As he stopped on the street —not certain whether to take the vehicle into the drive and to the carriage house—he saw a tall, auburn-haired man walk down the front steps. Certain that it was Marigold's brother, Jake smiled and said, "I be Jake, bringin' Miss Marigold's horses and carriage to 'er. Might she be at home?"

"You have made a mistake, Jake," the man said. "Miss Marigold is not staying here, but there is a note for you inside. Wait, and I will get it."

Puzzled, the old man waited outside. He gazed down the street at the lawman coming. And he was suddenly nervous.

"Here is your letter, Jake," Shaun said and made to walk on down the street. Jake, turning the paper over in his hands, hesitated. Then he began to follow the man.

"Suh, I never learned to read," he apologized. "I would be much obliged if you would open it and tell me what Miss Marigold says to do." He glanced at the man waiting

213

at the corner, and then turned his attention to the auburn-haired man.

Shaun broke the seal and began to read aloud.

> "Dear Jake,
>
> "Get rid of the carriage and horses as fast as you can. Take them to Little Jim's Livery Stables and tell him I will get them later. The money I owe you is with Mr. Pettigrew at the bank.
>
> Thank you, Jake. I owe you more than money for the help you gave me. Be careful of Crane.
>
> Sincerely,
> Marigold Tabor Caldwell"

"Thank you, suh," Jake said after Shaun had finished. "If you could just tell me where this place is—Little Jim's—I'll be takin' the carriage out of your way."

Shaun gave the man directions and then remained standing on the sidewalk, watching the man turn the carriage and start down the street. The note bothered Shaun. Jake had understood Marigold's warning and was clearly frightened. But why? Seeing the carriage stopped a short distance down the street by the sheriff, Shaun hurried toward it. There *was* something wrong. The man was in trouble—and it had to do with Crane Caldwell.

"Is anything the matter, Sheriff?" Shaun asked, coming up behind him.

"Mr. Banagher." The sheriff tipped his hat and explained, "I have a warrant to arrest a horsethief and I believe I have the man."

Shaun laughed. "You mean my man here?"

"He is yours?" the sheriff asked in surprise.

"Of course. I'm afraid you have the wrong one." Shaun turned to Jake and, careful not to use the man's name, said, "Take the carriage where I told you, and then return to the house. I have something else for you to do before evening."

"Yes, suh. That is, if . . ." He glanced at the sheriff.

"You're not going to arrest my driver, are you, Sheriff?" Shaun asked in an amused tone.

"I guess not, Mr. Banagher. The man I'm looking for was supposed to be comin' from the up country. But the horses sure do answer to the description."

"A lot of bays look alike. You'd better get a description of the man, as well," Shaun advised.

He stood, chatting with the sheriff, until Jake was safely out of sight.

The pathway on Tabor Island forked, and Marigold stopped, wondering which direction to take. And then the decision was no longer left to her and Crane. For coming down the path was a man whose long stride was suddenly familiar, but without the limp. Jason. It was Jason. For a moment she had thought it was her father. Recognizing her brother, Marigold began to run.

"Jason," she cried, and he laughed and caught her up in his arms. And Crane, standing back, looked on disapprovingly at Marigold's unladylike behavior.

"So you were the one ringing the bell," he said, smiling at his younger sister, and then holding her away from him as he extended his hand to Crane. "Hello, Crane. It's good to see you again."

"You also, Jason. But I'm surprised to see you. I thought you were still abroad."

"I'm leaving in a few days to return to England. The Grand Tour is over, and now I must settle down to studying law at the Court of Assizes."

"Oh, Jason. You can't go just when I've arrived. It's not fair," Marigold protested.

"You should have come sooner, Souci. But we'll have lots of time together the next few days. You've never been here before, have you?"

"No, and I'm surprised that Maman and Papa decided to come back. I thought it was off limits to everybody."

"I'm sure the white-foot oysters and the shrimp wish it were. We've had a feast each night. That's about the only thing I remember from that one summer spent here when Neijee and I were little—the oyster roasts on the beach and collecting the shells."

215

"Where is Neijee?" she asked, remembering the slave who had grown up as friend and valet to Jason.

"He's at Midgard, working with the horses."

"For the races?" Marigold inquired.

"No. The tournament comes before that. I'll miss the race season this year."

As she followed Jason to the cottage, he conversed with Crane about the gold mine, and Marigold was content to keep quiet.

"I'm thinking of putting in a rail track with cars to carry the gold ore," Crane explained. "There is one owner in North Carolina who has done this, and it seems to be working well. It will certainly beat lowering the workhorse down the shaft each day and then hoisting him out."

"Who will you get to lay the track?" Jason asked.

"There are several companies—one here in Charleston that I will talk with. That's the main reason Marigold and I came. And naturally she wished to visit her parents before we returned to Cedar Hill."

Marigold kicked at the small piece of driftwood in her path and watched it sail through the air.

Jason laughed and returned his attention to his sister. "I can't get over your being married to Crane. It seems only a month ago that you were racing me down Biffers Road at Midgard, with your hair flying behind you. Has she become more of a lady, Crane, now that she is a married woman?"

"I think she is slowly learning to control her impetuous behavior," Crane replied. "Are you not, Souci?"

She hated it when Crane called her that. It was only for her family, not Crane. "My name is Marigold," she said haughtily to her husband. "Please don't call me 'Souci.'"

"Ah, you *are* becoming a lady," Jason said, "if you object to being called by your pet name. But I see it is not a complete metamorphosis. Your tongue still runs away with you."

Marigold, in exasperation at Jason's teasing, pummeled his chest, but her tall, handsome brother just put his arm around her and hugged her as they continued down the pathway.

Eulalie and Robert Tabor were surprised to see their daughter and Crane. But they were also delighted. They quickly shifted bedroom arrangements, moving Robbie into the nursery with the baby Raven.

"Why can't Crane stay in the nursery?" Robbie asked his mother as he reluctantly moved his clothes from his own room. "Then, Marigold could stay with me."

"Married people stay together, Robbie," Eulalie explained to her son, brown from his hours spent on the beach. "It's much more gentlemanly to give up your room for a few days, than have Marigold and Crane separated."

"I don't want Crane in my room," he pouted. "He might take some of my shells."

"Robbie, don't be stubborn. It's only for a little while, darling. And I'm sure that both Marigold and Crane will be very careful and not harm your shells."

There was little Marigold could do about sharing a bedroom with Crane. She had promised, because of Jake, not to mention her husband's mistreatment and her subsequent flight. But it was hard to be civil to him in the presence of her family.

The girl took delight in being with her family again. Raven had grown so much that she would not have recognized him. Everything would be perfect, Marigold thought, if Maranta were there on the island, in the same bedroom with her, rather than Crane.

Despite Crane's friendly overtures, Robbie would have nothing to do with the man. He stared disapprovingly at him at dinner and answered Crane's questions in monosyllables.

Everyone at the table—except Crane—put it down to Robbie's annoyance at being moved into the nursery.

The wooden cottage was rustic but comfortable. Built on the opposite end of the island from where the old tabby house of oyster shell and lime once stood, it was a short distance from the lighthouse, which Marigold was curious to explore.

Early in the morning, Marigold set out, persuading Feena to accompany her. They walked along the sandy beach, and Marigold picked up a shell washed on the beach by the previous tide and held it to her ear.

"Years ago, when we were on the island," Feena recalled, "Monsieur Jason used to come to this very spot and hunt for shells. Now, it is Robbie."

"Yes. Robbie seems to be quite concerned about his collection," Marigold answered. "Afraid that something will happen to them—But tell me, Feena, what was it like on the island back then? Why have Maman and Papa ignored the island for so many years—and then suddenly decided to build the cottage?"

"Maybe they were waiting for the ghosts to disappear. The island was beautiful but treacherous—with alligators and marsh tackeys and wild boars . . ."

"What ghosts, Feena?" Marigold interrupted.

Feena hesitated. "Madame Eulalie has never told you about Jason's governess, Florilla. But I see no harm in telling you now. That woman was a wicked one. She dressed up as a ghost, frightening your poor maman. And on the same morning the British landed on the island, she locked Madame Eulalie in the spring room and left her there to die. And she would have, too, except for Monsieur Robert getting back to the island to rescue her."

"But where were all the others?" Marigold asked.

"This was war time, you remember, *ma petite*. The British had taken everyone off the island and then set fire to the house."

"Why was Papa not on the island, too?"

"Monsieur Robert had come to get me at Midgard to be with your maman, since the time was drawing near for you to be born."

More questions formed in Marigold's mind, and eagerly she asked, "Was this . . . Florilla ever caught and punished for doing this to Maman?"

"*Oui*. She was bitten by a moccasin and died in Emma's Bog," Feena admitted. When Marigold began another question, the old woman shrugged her shoulders and said, "That is enough from the past. I am tired of talking about it."

They were in front of the old lighthouse, and Marigold, realizing she would get no more information from Feena, opened the heavy door and stared inside at the steep, narrow stairway that wound several flights until it disappeared above. A feeling of excitement lured Marigold, and she hurried up the steps—anxious to see this aerie where she and Maranta had been born.

She had no need to rely on Feena for information, for Marigold knew this part of the story well—how they had barely gotten across the island from the old tabby house to seek refuge from the hurricane, how, at their birth, their father had breathed life into Maranta when she had refused to cry. All this, Marigold knew.

She gazed at the room with cobwebs hanging from the ceiling and looked out onto the sun-drenched sea with its miles of blue water fading into the sky. She turned to look at every angle, in every direction, drinking in the scenery —the sandy beach, the palmettos, and the palms.

Then she saw her brother, Robbie, stooping down to pick up a shell. "He's out early," Marigold said to Feena who stood beside her. "Adding to his collection. I don't know where he'll put any more."

"Jason and Neijee used to stack them in piles near the porch of the tabby house," Feena offered.

The two stood at the window, watching the little boy. And then Marigold noticed Crane coming down the beach. Robbie spied the man and hurried on, going in the opposite direction. Marigold watched as Crane caught up with her little brother. The man grabbed Robbie's arm and, in doing so, loosened the child's grasp on his shell. The shell fell to the ground, and Marigold's hands tightened on the railing at the window when she saw her husband kick the fallen shell into the water.

Robbie cried out, and a furious Marigold ran down the steps, out of the lighthouse. Feena, standing at the window far above, heard Marigold's irate voice as she approached the two. "Take your hands off my brother," she warned.

From the vehemence in Marigold's voice, Feena knew that her suspicions were confirmed. Marigold had no love for her husband. And by his action, it seemed that he did not deserve any.

Marigold, taking off her slippers, waded into the water and retrieved Robbie's shell. She brought it to him and, putting her arm around him, led him to the cottage, while Crane stood on the beach, watching them.

"I do not know what you were trying to prove," Marigold said later to Crane in their bedroom, "treating Robbie that way."

Crane, his face dark and sullen, snapped, "The child is insolent. He needs to be taught a lesson. Haven't you noticed how he gets up and leaves whenever I come around?"

"I think it must be because of his shells, Crane," she answered defensively. "And his dignity has suffered, being treated like a baby and moved into the nursery."

"Is that what he has told you?" Crane looked at Marigold warily as he waited for her answer.

"He has told me nothing, Crane. I only assume that's the reason. Why? Could he have another reason for disliking you?"

"Not that I know of. And I hope he won't start making up a pack of lies to gain your sympathy."

"Robbie very seldom lies. Sometimes, he does not volunteer the truth, especially if he is afraid of the consequences. Does he have reason to be afraid of you, Crane?"

Marigold remembered the fear on Robbie's face, with Crane hovering over him. Crane denied it; yet he must have done something to Robbie, to make the child so frightened.

25

Marigold rolled up the pallet from the floor where she had slept and placed it in the large chest. She didn't want the servants to know that she did not share the bed with her husband, so it was better to remove the evidence before they came in to clean the room.

She and Crane went to the dining room together for breakfast. In conversation at the table, Marigold asked Jason about his horses and the jousting tournament.

They were used to the event and did not think it strange that the young men who lived half their lives on horseback should choose a chivalrous event from the past to display their skills. The tournament had been a part of their lives for years—to gather in the green meadow a mile from the Henley plantation, with hundreds of others from neighboring plantations, and watch the tents, the crossbars, and knights, pages, and squires appear, transforming the quiet meadow into an Arthurian fantasy. And each year, the fairest belles of the city watched and secretly hoped to be crowned Queen of Love and Beauty at the ball that always followed. All except Marigold. She had always wanted to be a page or squire for her father when he had engaged in the lists with his horse as finely adorned as he. But Robert Tabor had chosen his son, Jason. And Marigold had to be content with second best—to be chosen queen of the ball.

Now Jason was to take her father's place to represent Midgard, with Robbie as his page. Mr. Henley and her father had always paired as a team, because of their size. But Mr. Henley had no sons to ride in his place this year—only six daughters, including the wispy-haired Docia Henley, who had been with Shaun that night at the theater. Marigold swallowed hard, trying to get rid of the lump that had lodged in her throat at the memory of that night at the Queen Street theater.

"You *are* coming, aren't you, Souci?" Jason asked his sister.

Her mind had been wandering, and she was not sure what Jason was asking.

"Where, Jason?"

"To Jackson Meadow—to watch the tournament. The officials will expect you to sit on the stand and watch the review."

"Marigold and Crane are in mourning, Jason," Eulalie reminded her son. "She may not wish to come. I am sure everyone would understand."

"Oh, but I want to, Maman—very much."

In less than an hour, Crane and Marigold, walking along the beach, were engaged in an argument. "Why would the officials expect *you* to be there, Marigold?"

"Because I was queen of the ball last year," she snapped. "The queen and her maids of honor always sit in the review stand."

Crane's lips pursed. "I do not like the idea of your being on public display—for all to see."

"For heaven's sake, Crane, the *horses* are the ones on display. And since this is the first time that Jason has represented Midgard, I'm anxious to see him."

"I can't understand how you can so suddenly stop grieving for Mother, now that you are with your family."

"Burying myself in sackcloth and ashes, or staying here on the island won't bring Cousin Julie back. I loved her, too, Crane. But life doesn't stop just because a loved one dies."

"But you have made no pretence of mourning, Marigold, regardless of your fine words and your hoity-toity French clothes. Your determination to engage in this barbaric ritual indicates that you care nothing for my feelings."

Marigold's eyes flashed dangerously. "Did Cousin Julie ask me to stop living when she died? No, Crane. And I'll mourn her in my own way. Besides, if you don't want to go, Maman will remain here with you."

"And where will you stay in town, Marigold?"

"Papa and Jason have reserved two rooms at the hotel. I can share a room with Robbie."

At the mention of Robbie's name, Crane frowned. "On second thought, I will go into the city with you. It won't look right for you to be surrounded by men. If you're bound and determined to go, it looks as if I have no choice but to accompany you."

"Then Maman might as well come, too," Marigold said.

Crane's acquiescence took away some of the pleasure of the trip to the mainland. But at least it had brought Maman with them, with only Raven staying on the island with his nurse.

As soon as they reached the city, they checked into the Planter's Hotel. Marigold and Crane went to the same small suite that Crane, unknown to Marigold, had kept. Jason, who was anxious to put his horse through the paces, immediately left for the meadow, with Robbie and their father, Robert Tabor.

It was inconvenient, not having the townhouse anymore. Her father had said nothing about selling it, but Marigold knew he must be hurting financially with cotton down to a mere nine cents a pound. It had plunged every year that the high tariff had been in effect—all the way from thirty cents—and now so low that it was hardly worth the effort to grow it.

There was an air of excitement in town that evening. The hotel was crowded, and the townhouses along the narrow streets were bulging with guests.

The next day, Marigold dressed carefully in one of her new white dresses that Madame Reynaud had made for her. And taking up the matching parasol, she climbed into the family carriage and began the journey to the meadow. Jason had gone on ahead to see to his horse.

Seeing Neijee with the horses, Marigold waved frantically. He looked up, and a grin spread across his face as he acknowledged her greeting.

"Who are you waving to, Marigold?" Crane asked at her side.

"Neijee. I haven't seen him since he left with Jason on the Grand Tour."

"You mean you're speaking in public to a servant? Have you no sense of propriety?"

Marigold sighed. "Neijee is a member of the family, Crane. But I don't expect you to understand." She walked away from her husband and took her place in the review stand.

She sat in the stand, surrounded by the maids of honor, and watched the men in armor pass by. The clanking of spurs, the plumes of scarlet and blue and green, waving in the breeze, the intricately embroidered saddlecloths of the horses—all gave the martial and festive air of knights gathered from the corners of the realm, so diverse were they in colors and appearance. And the fine-blooded horses, beautiful and gleaming, snorted and went through their practice paces like seasoned war horses—direct descendants of those fiery, fleet-footed animals that had eluded the British through the black swamps of the countryside and saved the lives of many a patriot, disappearing like foxes in the night before the very eyes of the enemy.

And now the man and his horse became one entity—a centaur, with lance in hand, to test the quickness of his hand and eye.

The horns sounded. The practice was over. Quickly pairing off, two by two in precise formation, the horses began the sedate procession, and Marigold, listening to the names being called off, watched for her brother, Jason.

"Jason Boisfeulet Tabor," the man recited, "riding for Midgard. Shaun O'Malley Banagher, riding for Crescent Hall."

Marigold's mouth dropped open. Her brother and Shaun Banagher, paired together. She turned her head and cast a quick glance toward Docia Henley, one of the maids of honor seated near her. Being chosen by Mr. Henley to ride for Crescent Hall could mean only one thing. Shaun Banagher was as good as engaged to Docia.

Marigold's spirits plunged, and the bright sunlight caught the brilliance of the girl's topaz eyes that had suddenly moistened. Blinded by the sunlight, Marigold missed seeing the two men, holding their lances high in homage, as they quickly passed the review stand.

For the rest of the afternoon, Marigold held her head high, while the tournament went on about her, but she was only vaguely aware of what was going on around her —the rings suspended in regular intervals on the cross-bars, the gallop of horses over the course, and the hurl of lances through the rings. When a rider was successful, a great cheer arose from the crowd. And later, the tilts, with the riders speeding toward each other with their blunt poles, attempting to unseat each other . . .

On and on it went, while Marigold's throbbing headache grew worse, and Docia Henley's smile grew larger.

The sound of the trumpets, the applause of the crowd . . . Suddenly, Marigold was thrust back into reality. The two riders approached the stand, and the crowns of golden leaves were pressed into her hand. It was almost over, and then she could leave.

Kneeling before her were her brother Jason and Shaun, side by side, well matched in size and skill. She saw the heads bowed before her—one a burnished gold, similar to her own, and the other, a darker shade, deep auburn, with the tendrils on his forehead wet from the exertion of the day.

And when it was over, when the two giants had walked away with their crowns of victory, Marigold searched for her parents. Her duty was done. She had no desire to attend the ball that night—to feel her pride crushed further underfoot. All she wished to do was to get back to the hotel and lie down. And pretend that Docia Henley did not exist.

To be in his arms. To bear his children—all the things she had dreamed of were to be given to someone who did not deserve him. It was more than Marigold could stand. What a cruel trick for Shaun to play on her—to push her aside and then select someone like Docia.

In the silence of the sitting room at the hotel, Marigold gazed into the mirror. She had grown up accustomed to the stares, the polite compliments, the turning of heads as she walked by. She was the same. Her golden curls, her creamy, delicate skin, the wide, tawny, topaz eyes that she had inherited from her father—and it was all for naught. The one for whom she had wanted to be beautiful had not been impressed.

Marigold lay on the sofa, the room darkened, and the smelling salts at hand. Crane came in and, seeing the girl prostrate, he walked to the sofa.

"What is the matter, Marigold?" he asked.

"I have a dreadful headache," she replied. "I think it was the dust and the hot sun this afternoon."

"What will you do about tonight? Are you still planning to go?"

"No, Crane. I don't feel up to that. If you don't mind, I'll go on to sleep."

The girl was still asleep when Jason called for her that evening. At the knock on the door, Crane tiptoed across the room and faced his brother-in-law. "Marigold isn't feeling well," Crane informed him with a triumphant expression. "She has decided to stay here and have a quiet dinner later, when she awakes."

And so Jason went to the ball without her, to celebrate his victory in the tournament that day—his and Shaun's.

By the next afternoon, Jason and Neijee were gone. Marigold, feeling better, with only a trace of her headache left, had accompanied her mother and father, Robbie, and Crane down to the wharf to see them off.

An entire year before she would see her brother again. She had kissed Jason and clung to him, not willing to see him go. And the words that she had vowed she would not speak, had rushed past her lips.

"Jason, who was selected as queen of the ball last night?"

"Docia Henley," he had replied, and noticing the unhappy droop to his sister's mouth, Jason had admitted, "but she didn't hold a candle to you, Souci. You were, by far, the most beautiful queen we've had in years."

They returned to Tabor Island that same afternoon. Marigold, subdued and quiet, watched the sun drag its trail of purple shadows over the waters. No longer blue, but a dull gray, the waters churned and rolled behind the boat. The sails of Jason's ship were barely in sight—small wings jutting from the distant horizon.

First, Maranta, now, Jason—separated by an ocean and time and age. They were all growing up, and Marigold longed for the good times when they had all been together at Midgard, with not a care in the world.

Robbie's voice penetrated her sadness, and she smiled, listening to his childish, excited monologue. His first experience as a page at the tournament had been a big event in his young life. Robert Tabor, gazing fondly at his son, reached out and ruffled the boy's hair.

"So you think you'll be able to ride in the lists next year, son?" the teasing voice asked.

"Oh, no. It will be a while before Jason gets too old. But I'm going to start practicing on my pony as soon as we get back to Midgard."

Eulalie and Robert smiled at each other at their son's serious reply.

The boat reached the pier, and Marigold, with an urgency she could not understand, rushed to the light-house, climbed the steps to the top, and there she stood, until the tiny sails of the ship carrying Jason to England were completely erased by the encroaching darkness.

"Marigold," her husband's voice called, and the girl reluctantly came down the winding steps.

For a week, a listless Marigold moped about the island, with Crane making no mention of returning to Cedar Hill. Occasionally he would ride with her father into the city—presumably to negotiate the business of laying the track inside the gold mine. And each day, she wondered when Crane would bring up the subject of her returning with him to the up country.

She did not feel any better. What was the matter with her? Surely, she had gotten over her disappointment at the idea of Shaun and Docia Henley. But her appetite had not returned. And the taste of food she had eaten for breakfast still lingered. Marigold suddenly put her hand over her mouth. No, it couldn't be true. She wouldn't let it. But Marigold could not deny the signs any longer.

227

She was going to have a baby—Crane's baby. All because of that night after Julie's funeral.

Marigold pressed her fingers into her throbbing temples and tried to think of what to do. If her parents found out, or Crane, they would make her return to Cedar Hill. Oh God, why had she taken pity on Crane that night? Why had she allowed herself to be coerced into remaining for the night in his bed? But it was too late for regret.

The cold feeling that had spread over her body, numbing her, now changed to unbearable heat, draining her of energy, of strength. Suddenly, the bilious taste of her breakfast overwhelmed her, and she rushed toward the ruins of the tabby house. Sheltered by the cassina bushes, Marigold was sick.

She was still pale as she slowly walked in the direction of the cottage. She would have to lie down for a while, but not in the room she shared with Crane. Bypassing the cottage, with its screened porch facing the ocean, she continued walking until she reached the lighthouse.

The cot. There was a cot in the room at the top. If she could rest there, then she might be able to survive another day without having her secret discovered. Crane would never let her stay if he discovered she was going to have his child.

In the room where she had been born, Marigold lay down, not caring about the cobwebs, not caring about anything. She closed her eyes, and slowly, the tension eased and she drifted to sleep.

The footsteps downstairs on the stone floor awoke her. How long had she been asleep? The sound faltered on the stairs, and Marigold sat up, listening.

Tread by tread the steps came, and Marigold knew someone was searching for her. And she could not escape.

Finally the figure became visible in the doorway. Marigold sighed in relief as she recognized the white-haired woman. "Feena," she said.

"I have been looking for you, *ma petite*," the woman replied. "You have missed lunch, and your maman is worried about you—You do not look well. There is something wrong, *n'est-ce pas?*"

Marigold could no longer control her despondency. "Everything, Feena. Everything is wrong." She burst into tears, and Feena came to sit by her and console her as she had done through the years for as long as Marigold could remember.

"You will tell Feena what is wrong?"

"I'm . . . I'm pregnant," Marigold wailed, searching in her skirt pocket for a handkerchief.

"And that is a tragedy?" Feena asked gently.

"Yes. I can't bear the idea of having Crane's baby. The child will probably grow up to be mean and malicious just like Crane."

"But *you* will be the mother, *ma chérie*. Therein lies the difference. You will teach him to be kind and loving."

"But I don't *want* to have a baby."

At her confession, Feena's voice hardened. "So you think you are the only woman to have felt this way? Soon you will get used to the idea—and even look forward to it."

"I'm afraid, Feena. I'm afraid of Crane. I hate Cedar Hill and I just know everybody will make me go back there. And I'm afraid I'll die all alone and be . . . be buried under that sickly magnolia tree next to Cousin Julie." Her weeping grew louder.

"Would you feel better, *ma petite*, if I went back to Cedar Hill with you?"

Marigold sniffed and looked up into Feena's dark eyes. "You would go—if I wanted you?"

The woman smiled. "I am sure your maman would give permission, if you ask. Now does that make you feel better?"

The girl nodded. "Yes, Feena. If you're there, it won't be quite so bad."

"Then dry your eyes and let us go back to the cottage. The lighthouse is not a proper place for you to be alone. There are too many steps, and you must be careful."

Marigold, her mind on her troubles, walked back to the cottage with Feena. And all at once, her twin assumed shape in her mind. Marigold stopped feeling sorry for herself. Poor Maranta. Even now, she might be pregnant, too. And she did not have Feena to help her. But for her sake, Marigold hoped her twin loved her husband, this Vasco da Monteiro. It would be difficult enough to have a child when she was halfway across the world from her family.

26

By the next afternoon, Crane knew he was to be a father. A satisfied expression changed his dark face at the news. Now, Marigold would be forced to go back to Cedar Hill with him. He had kept putting it off as long as he could, afraid she would refuse, but he knew the plantation had suffered from neglect, with his leaving so suddenly. He needed to get back, not only to see to the land, but to make arrangements for the work to be done in the gold mine. If everything worked out, Crane could stop farming altogether. The mine would keep him rich.

The only thing that bothered him was that Jake had not been caught with the horses. Despite his promise to Marigold, he wanted to see the man hang for his insolence. But the black man had escaped the net the sheriff had drawn around the city.

He would post a reward for information concerning the man. Someone was bound to have seen him. And Jake would have to surface at some time, to seek employment. Perhaps it was better this way. With Marigold at Cedar Hill, she would have no way of knowing that Jake had been hanged.

The cholera that Charleston had dreaded was now getting closer, already taking its toll on some of the nearby islands. The city was uneasy. And Crane, fearful for his own safety, decided to leave as soon as he could arrange transportation.

"Marigold," he said, "I realize it is not a good time for you to be traveling, but cholera is already on John's Island. It will be much safer for you if we leave immediately—just as soon as I can see to a carriage."

She had been waiting for this, so it came as no surprise. "What's wrong with the carriage I brought to Charleston from Cedar Hill?" she asked.

"You mean it's here?"

'Well, not here on the island. Actually, it's at Little Jim's Livery Stables, with the horses."

So Jake *had* gotten to Charleston, unapprehended. Now, it would be more difficult to bring him to justice, especially without his being caught red-handed with the horses.

"Why didn't you tell me, Marigold?" His voice was suddenly irritable.

"Would it have made any difference? We could hardly have brought the carriage on the boat to the island."

There was truth in what Marigold said, he had to admit. And he could not tell her the real reason why he was upset—that Jake had not been caught.

The next morning, Marigold and Crane walked to the pier, amid the goodbyes and the handshakes and kisses. Suddenly, Robbie slipped up to Marigold and tugged at her skirt. Quickly, he whispered, "Souci—ask him for the letter. He never gave it to you." As soon as he had said it, Robbie ran toward Eulalie and remained at his mother's side, as if afraid.

Crane frowned at the child's whisperings and watched Marigold's face for some sign of what the boy might have told her. But she evidently had not understood his childish babbling. So intent was he on Marigold, Crane did not realize that Feena had gotten into the boat ahead of them.

When he saw the white-haired servant ensconced with their luggage, he stopped. "What is Feena doing in the boat?" he asked.

"Oh, I thought you knew," Marigold responded airily. "Maman has been good enough to lend her to me until after the baby comes."

His dark eyes darted suspiciously back to Feena. She smiled at the man, but her eyes were no more friendly than his. And he became uneasy.

The horse that Crane had ridden into Charleston was brought from another stable and tied to the back of the carriage at Little Jim's. With a hired driver, the carriage left the city, a silent Crane staring first at Marigold, and then at the Tabor servant, Feena.

Because of Marigold's condition, they traveled in a leisurely manner. Such a difference, Marigold thought, from her hurried flight from her husband. She had vowed never to return to him and yet, she was in the carriage with him, riding back to Cedar Hill. But it was not a willing thing on her part. If circumstances had only been different. If she had not become pregnant—if she had not felt responsibility for Jake—

But what was the use? She had brought all this trouble on herself, by falling in love with Shaun Banagher. And now, she must manage as best she could—with no one's help, except Feena's.

Stopping at the same inns on their journey home, Marigold presented a far different picture from the runaway girl with her face hidden by the black mourning veil. Crane's hat was draped in black, but Marigold's costume gave no indication of a recent bereavement.

The recovered valise—the one waiting in the carriage—contained the clothes that the girl wore on the trip back to Cedar Hill. The dust, the heat, the steady drizzle of summer rain along the muddy red trail would not be kind to the elegant white dresses. And the pale green dress was carefully packed away, as Crane had suggested, but not for the reason he had given.

She had forgotten to repay Shaun for the dress, and the other things. And now it was too late. An amused smile played around the corners of her expressive mouth. Crane would be furious if he ever found out she had spent the night in the same house with Shaun. But it was his own fault. Crane had neglected to show her the letter written by her father—mentioning the sale of the house.

But had her father named the buyer? Was Crane already aware that it was Shaun Banagher who now lived in the Palladian mansion along the battery? Perhaps he knew more than she thought.

Robbie's troubled question about a letter puzzled her. Was it her father's letter he was talking about? Had Robbie sent her a special message that Crane had not given to her?

Marigold glanced uneasily at her husband, but he did

233

not seem to be aware of her. He was thinking of something else—something that gave him immense pleasure, judging by the self-satisfied expression on his face.

The river finally came into sight—that final lap of the journey that pushed Marigold on to Cedar Hill against her will. As before, the girl climbed from the carriage and waited until the vehicle was driven onto the ferry. She and Feena followed the carriage, and when they were safely on the wooden structure, the black ferryman, who had evidently taken Jake's place, cast off, directing the raft to the other side.

Marigold was determined that Feena was going to stay in the big house with her. And Crane, mindful that it was not good to upset a woman who was expecting a child, gave in, allowing the servant to have a room in the attic, directly above the second-story bedrooms.

"We'll need to get the cottage ready for the foreman who's coming to oversee the building of the rail," Crane said that evening at dinner.

"So you are going ahead with your plans?"

"Yes. The company in Charleston seemed to be reasonable in price. The man who is going to determine the roadbed layout for the tracks will be coming in about ten days. When he has finished with the plans, he will send for his workers. But you need not bother about them. They will have their tents to live in and their own cook.

"The only one you will ever see will be the supervisor. He'll take his meals with us."

The days passed quickly, and Marigold, happy to have Feena with her, was not quite so homesick as before. With Feena, she saw to the cleaning of the cottage, the removal of the bed, and the fumigating with sulphur, as the doctor had advised because of Cousin Julie's illness.

On the tenth day, the man came. Marigold was resting and did not see him, for Crane took him straight to the cottage as soon as he arrived. But he would be present for supper. And probably with a big appetite, too, Marigold guessed. She must make sure that Juniper cooked extra portions of everything.

Late in the afternoon, Marigold dressed in one of the

white dresses made by Madame Reynaud. Her pregnancy had not yet thickened her waistline, so no one would be able to tell. They so seldom had guests for dinner at Cedar Hill that Marigold was looking forward to having the man at the table. For a while, at least, she would not be forced to make polite conversation with Crane alone.

It was almost time for the evening meal when Crane returned from the gold mine. Dusty and hot and in a bad temper, he lashed out at the boy who brought water for his bath. Not wishing to hear the tirade that spread along the upstairs hall, Marigold slipped out of the house, intent on getting away from the voice that always managed to irritate her.

Taking her basket and shears with her, Marigold walked to the flower garden—one of the few things she loved at Cedar Hill. It was a short distance from the house, and in the late afternoon, the fragrance of the summer flowers hung heavily on the air. She had cut enough blossoms for the dining table and the tall vase in the parlor, earlier that day, but Marigold began to cut other flowers, not sure what she would do with them when she finished. Crane did not like flowers in the bedrooms. He claimed they took away the air and were not healthy to have around. The fragrant musk roses, the tall purple delphiniums, and the gladioli whose spikes were slightly awry from the recent rain—they didn't look like enemies to her, for they were so beautiful.

Marigold held the white musk rose in her hand, and as she started to put it into her basket, she saw the stranger come out of the cottage and walk along the path toward the big house.

Marigold's heart fluttered. Her eyes were playing tricks on her. For a moment—just a moment—she thought it was Shaun. But of course that was impossible. Shaun Banagher was in Charleston, dancing to the tune of Docia Henley.

She openly stared at the man and clutched the basket of flowers so hard that it seemed welded to her hands. He was headed straight for her. And she watched, dumbfounded, as he approached her. It *was* Shaun. He was there, at Cedar Hill, within touching distance.

"Hello, Marigold."

She backed away from the tall, muscular man who towered over her. "Shaun. What are you doing here—at Cedar Hill?"

"Didn't your husband tell you? My company is laying the track in his gold mine."

"Your company? Crane hired *you* to build the rail system?"

The auburn-haired man's mouth moved in an ironic twist. "I believe he talked with my partner. He may not have been aware of the association. I think Crane was expecting the foreman, but since the man is busy on another project, I decided to come ahead to design the system. And I will stay to oversee it myself, so your husband will not be kept waiting any longer than necessary."

No wonder Crane had been in a bad temper, having to welcome the man whom he disliked so thoroughly.

"I . . . I have never repaid you for the dress . . ."

"Forget about it, Marigold." He stared hard at her, and the girl could think of nothing to say because of the effect his green eyes had on her.

"Are you happy with Crane?" he demanded suddenly. There was anger in his voice. "If he is mistreating you—if you need help, Marigold . . ."

She saw the pity in his eyes—pity for *her*. Was her love for Shaun so obvious in her face? Did he sense the way her heart was fluttering as she stood near him?

Marigold closed her eyes and saw him with the possessive Docia, the woman he preferred. No, she would not have him sorry for her.

"Of course I'm happy with Crane," she said, lifting her chin a trifle higher. "I am expecting his child. Is that not what makes a woman's joy complete—to be expecting the baby of the man she . . . loves?"

The words almost choked her. Marigold, watching Shaun, saw his emerald eyes change. Not pity, but something else now in its place. Resignation? Disappointment?

"Dinner will be ready in a few minutes. And I expect you are hungry, Shaun." Marigold began walking toward the house with Shaun at her side.

In a daze, Marigold sat at the table, looking at Crane and then at Shaun. How could she stay and act as if nothing were wrong, when she was being torn apart? Forced to show indifference to the man she actually loved, while pretending affection for the man she hated. Her fork clattered onto her plate, and she dropped her napkin. She could eat almost nothing. Yet Shaun, seemingly impervious to the stilted atmosphere, ate heartily, while Crane watched him with narrowed eyes.

As soon as she could do so, Marigold left the table. "If you will excuse me," she said. When she left the dining room she heard Crane's gloating voice. "My wife is expecting a child, Mr. Banagher. And so she is a little high-strung."

By the next morning, Marigold had gotten over the initial shock of having Shaun Banagher at Cedar Hill—but she was not entirely relaxed. She supposed she never would be—seeing the two men together. But somehow, she had to get through the next few weeks.

When the mail for the week came, Marigold was in the parlor, reading. Feena brought three envelopes to her, saying, "A man just delivered these, *ma petite*."

Eagerly, Marigold looked at the addresses. Two were for Crane and one for Shaun. Disappointed, she saw there was no communication from her family.

Marigold turned the letters over in her hand. What business did Crane have with the sheriff in Charleston? Could it be about Jake?

Seeing the feminine handwriting on the letter addressed to Shaun, Marigold did not have to guess the name of its sender. She placed the three letters on the front hall table and went back to her reading.

27

Crane gazed incredulously at the letter in front of him. It was not possible. And yet, the detective had sworn everything he wrote was the truth—Marigold's spending the night in Shaun Banagher's townhouse, his purchase of a new dress for her the next day, and his sheltering the man, Jake.

Crane had merely wanted to find Jake, to punish him for his insolence. But here in his hands, Crane held far more incriminating evidence. While searching for the black man, the detective had stumbled onto something far more serious—Marigold's unfaithfulness.

The glint in Crane's coal dark eyes, the fist clenched around the ball of paper indicated the man's extreme anger. The longer he thought about it, the more livid he became.

Marigold had spent the night with Shaun—in the townhouse that had once belonged to Robert Tabor. She had said nothing to her husband about it the next day, or any day afterwards. And with good reason, Crane now realized. The child that he had thought was his—it was Shaun Banagher's!

He should have guessed. From all the times that he had bedded Marigold, not once had there been any hint that she was with child. Why should it have been otherwise that last time—the night of his mother's funeral?

And the green dress she had worn to the wharf. Shaun had even purchased that for Marigold. And the final insult—Jake was now working for Shaun Banagher and under his protection.

Crane's anger was now combined with fear. They must have found out that he had deceived Marigold, forcing her into marrying him. What other reason did the man have in coming to Cedar Hill but to kill him and take

Marigold? It was not the rail to be laid in the gold mine. Owners didn't come to supervise. They sent their underlings instead. No. It was for murder—to get rid of Crane Caldwell before he discovered the child his wife was carrying was not his, but Shaun Banagher's.

The man took out his handkerchief and wiped the perspiration from his forehead. He would have to be careful. The two must not suspect that he knew the truth about them.

He would have to find a way to get rid of them both. They would have to pay for their insults to Crane Caldwell—and pay with their lives.

His head began to ache from so much thinking. Crane smoothed the crumpled paper and hid it under his mattress and then left the room to get some fresh air.

Nothing had gone right the entire day for Marigold. Ever since the letters, Crane had watched her like a hawk, as if he suspected her of some witch's planning. And his constant accusing stare frightened her. If it weren't for Feena sleeping in the same house, the girl did not know what she would do.

She had not felt well for some time, and it was hard on her, trying to maintain her pretence of being happy, with Shaun sitting across the table from her each evening.

Marigold, in the meadow next to the apple tree, now stared down at the broken eggs at her feet. She was so nervous, she could not even trust herself to take eggs from a hen's nest and get them safely to the house. And Juniper was waiting for them, for the cake she planned to bake for supper.

Marigold sat on the fallen log and began to cry. She had kept it inside for so long. And her anger, her fear, her unhappiness spilled out in great sobs, with only the pigs in the nearby pen to hear her. They stood up and brushed against the rough planks that held them in and grunted several times in answer to the girl's sobs. Finally, with their curiosity satisfied, they went away to wallow in the mud on the far side of the pen.

240

"Marigold."

The voice was Shaun's, and the golden-haired girl was embarrassed for him to find her in the meadow, crying her heart out.

With a tear-streaked face, she looked up and said, "Go away, Shaun Banagher."

"What's the matter, Marigold?" he asked gently, ignoring her command.

"I . . . I dropped the eggs," she said, "if you want to know. And now there'll be no cake for supper."

The man's deep laugh startled the pigs, and again they grew curious, pressing their noses against the wire fence and sniffing.

"Is that all?" Shaun asked. "I thought something tragic had happened."

"What else could possibly be the matter?" she retaliated. "Certainly not that I'm pregnant when I don't want to be. Certainly not that I'm married to a man I hate."

He stared at her without speaking. And the log moved as he brought his giant frame down beside her.

"You have told me on several occasions that you loved your husband. Why have you so suddenly changed your mind?"

It was too much to keep up the pretence. "I . . . I've never loved Crane Caldwell."

The man's eyes bored into her. And his voice was fierce. "Then why did you marry him, Marigold? For God's sake, why did you marry the man? Did your father make you do it after all?"

To blame her father when it was all his fault—did she have to spell it out for him?

"I married Crane because you jilted me, Shaun Banagher. And I couldn't stand the thought of staying in Charleston while you bragged about it. To bet that you could get the proudest girl in Charleston to elope with you—I hope you enjoyed your fun that night, Shaun, while I waited in the garden half the night for you to come."

Her angry words stabbed him. Shaun pulled her to her

feet, and when she tried to free herself, he held on to her, so that she could not escape. "But the letter—you must have gotten my letter that day. It explained why I couldn't come."

"I received no letter from you, Shaun."

"But Chad said he gave it to your brother at the gate."

"Robbie? He gave it to Robbie?" Marigold frowned at his affirmation. Was that what Robbie had meant when he said goodbye to her on the island? *Ask Crane for the letter.*

Crane must have taken the letter from Robbie. That was how he knew that she was going to elope. That's how he knew that Shaun was not coming. Now, it was clear. Her cousin had deceived her. And her wounded pride had made her believe him. He must have threatened her little brother to keep him from telling her.

"I think . . . Crane must have taken it from him."

Shaun moaned and pressed his lips to Marigold's golden hair. "Oh, Souci—Why couldn't you have had more faith in me?"

"You didn't really want to elope, Shaun. I knew that. And I guess all the time I was waiting for you in the garden, I was wondering if you would actually come."

Marigold looked back toward the house. "I've got to go, Shaun. Juniper is waiting for me."

"I have to see you again, Souci—alone. There are too many things left unsaid."

"Crane watches me constantly. It won't be easy."

Shaun's fingers touched the small scar near her temple. "Is Crane responsible for this?" he asked.

Marigold nodded and suddenly fled from the meadow.

The workers appeared the next day, with the great wagon loads of equipment—the small rails and the spikes and the cross ties—and the shiny metal cars that would eventually carry the ore from far back inside the tunnels to the openings of the mine.

Marigold and Feena sat on the side porch, watching the procession of men and equipment as they passed by and disappeared over the bridge to the creek. The cooking wagon, with its wooden barrels lashed to the side, stopped at the well. And when the barrels were filled with fresh water, the driver urged the mules on to catch up with the other vehicles.

Into the woods they went, along the quiet stream where rocks glittered in the sunlight and vaguely promised richer treasures farther down stream.

Soon the tents covered the hillside, with the cooking wagon off to itself. A regular camp of brawny men—yet none was so tall as Shaun. It would not be easy for them inside the mine, where they had to stoop as they worked. For some, it was the first time they had ever been inside the earth. They were used to working in the open, where the sun shone on their heads—not in a dark cavity with water dripping overhead. But they were being paid well.

The blasting began that afternoon along the hillside, to make new tunnels where the track would be laid. Powder caps were pushed into overhead recesses. The new rich veins had been discovered, running at a sixty-degree angle, east to west. And when the vein disappeared into deep rock, the men had only to take a pick and trace it at that angle to find it again. But that was left for the miners. The railroaders were concerned with making the job easier for the miners.

They worked with lanterns to give them light. And at the end of the first day, Shaun was satisfied with their progress. It would get harder the farther back inside the hill they went, but they had made a good start.

Amid all the activity, Crane went back and forth from the mine to the house. And always, Feena was at Marigold's side, a fact that Crane resented deeply—as if his wife needed protection from him.

He brooded over the child, and at the first thickening of Marigold's waist, he felt anger. Her unfaithfulness had to be punished and soon. But all this Crane kept to himself. It would not do for Marigold and Shaun to suspect that he knew.

That evening at dinner, Crane exhibited no outward animosity toward the man. He was enthusiastic about the work done in the mine that day and seemed to be content with the progress that Shaun's company was making.

"If all works out well with the mine," Crane said, "I can stop wasting time with the farming and spend all my time at the mine. I'll leave it up to my neighbors to work their bones to death in the hot sun and wait for drought and disease to come along and destroy their labors."

Shaun laughed. "It seems you have acquired the gold fever, my friend."

"Not a fever—just an appreciation of what gold can mean. The whole countryside is dotted with lost gold and silver mines. And yet, few have tried to find them."

"Perhaps our neighbors have long memories, Crane," Marigold suggested, joining in the conversation.

"Memories of what, Marigold?" Crane asked, irritated at her implied criticism.

"Oh, the greed that broke so many men, and the curse of the Indians when they got tired of having their hunting grounds spoiled."

"Gold is much more important than a few measly herds of buffalo and elk, Marigold," Crane insisted.

"Xualla didn't think so."

Her words caused Crane to smile and look toward Shaun. "My wife has read entirely too much. And her sympathies seem to lie with the murdering redskins, rather than the white men who explored this wilderness. A grave error on her part, don't you think? A woman should never have a conflicting opinion from her husband."

Marigold's face flushed. "It was the white men who were the murderers," she persisted. "When De Soto and his army came to the Carolinas and visited the beautiful Indian queen, Xualla, she welcomed them gladly and treated them well. And what did they do? They made her a prisoner in her own territory. Their greed for gold caused them to act like barbarians rather than honored guests."

"Which only proves that women are too weak to rule," Crane suggested, a smug expression on his face.

"Or it may prove that a woman should never trust

244

certain men," Marigold replied, with honey dripping from her voice.

The meal was over and she stood up. "If you will excuse me, I will leave you two to your brandy." She swept out of the room pretending to be unconcerned at the bent of the conversation. But it was a long time before she simmered down.

Crane's constant derogatory remarks about her reading —as if she did not have a brain of her own to use, but must be content to parrot her husband's opinions—infuriated Marigold. Brought up in a family where each person's opinion was valued, Marigold was not used to such condescension. Of course, she didn't know much about geography of foreign countries—about Brazil where Maranta was living, for instance. But she loved the old legends of the land around her. She didn't actually believe in the curse of the Indians about the mines, and yet, all the old stories surfaced and kept her from sleeping—the avaricious gold hunters sealed into the mine by the Indians and all outward signs of the mine obliterated; the gift of two hundred horse-loads of pearls given by Xualla to De Soto to get rid of him; the gold and copper tools and trinkets that were dug up from time to time in the surrounding fields that had once been Indian burial grounds.

The next day, Marigold was still mindful of these things when Crane invited her to accompany him to the mine to see the progress that had been made. He had never wanted her to go near the mine in the past, and she had no desire to go because of her fear of dark places. But at Crane's insistence, she found herself reluctantly walking along the pathway and over the wooden bridge, with Feena directly behind her.

She lingered on the bridge and gazed down at the water, crystal clear. In the water, next to a rock, she saw several large crawdads, their tails curled under as they backed away from some danger. She smiled at the familiar sight. The cook at Midgard always made sure that the spring contained at least two of the creatures to keep the water pure.

They came to the entrance of the mine, and Marigold hesitated. "What's the matter, Marigold?" Crane asked. "You're not afraid, are you?"

"Of course not." The girl turned to Feena. "You're coming too, aren't you?"

"*Oui, ma petite*. I am right behind you."

Marigold felt comforted at the servant's words—knowing that she would not be alone with Crane inside the mine.

Her husband took a lantern hanging by the side, and lighting it, he held it for the two women to step inside the mouth of the dark mine. The entrance was fortified by crossbeams and dirt, and as Marigold went into the darkness, the light of the lantern caught the glint of the girl's locket around her neck. The shadows of the three people were cast against the far wall, giving an eerie distortion of elongated figures.

The girl shivered at the sudden coldness, and her counterpart upon the wall moved at the same time. "It feels like the cellar where the hams are kept," Marigold said, trying to keep her voice steady.

"It's even colder than that," Crane revealed. "Forty-nine degrees. Quite a change, isn't it, from the ninety degrees outside?"

A drop of water from overhead fell on Marigold and she jumped. "I don't like it in here, Crane," she managed to say. "Please don't make me go any farther."

Crane's laughter echoed down the tunnel. "You're not interested in seeing the rails?"

"No."

Just then, a noise came from in front of them, a rolling sound on the tracks. And soon, the shiny new car filled with gold ore appeared, with two men beside it. One was Shaun, but Marigold did not recognize the other.

The auburn-haired man was surprised to see Marigold standing inside the mine with Crane and Feena. He looked at Crane with a quizzical expression.

"I thought my wife might be interested in seeing your rails, Shaun, but evidently not. Marigold appears to be more anxious to return to the sunlight."

246

"A wise decision," Shaun affirmed. "The tunnels and shafts are too dangerous for her to be exploring, especially in her condition."

"You're right, of course," Crane admitted and walked out of the mine with his wife. Once outside in the sunlight, Marigold vowed that she would never go inside again, no matter what Crane said.

28

"I think, Marigold, it is time for you to consult a doctor," Crane said as she bade him good-night. It was late and Marigold was tired.

"Dr. Kellie is aware . . ."

"I do not mean Dr. Kellie," he cut in. "*He* will not be attending you."

"But I *like* Dr. Kellie," Marigold protested.

"Nevertheless, I do not plan on calling him again."

"But why, Crane?"

"He let my mother die."

"Cousin Julie had consumption," Marigold argued. "There was nothing he could do but try to make her more comfortable at the end. It was not his fault that there is no cure for the disease."

"Nevertheless, I plan for you to see someone else. I shall tell Sesame to have the carriage at the door by ten tomorrow morning. Please be ready, Marigold."

He walked on up the stairs, leaving her standing in the parlor. Why all this sudden concern for her? Crane did not seem to be that concerned at the mine earlier that day when he forced her to go inside.

Marigold took the lamp in her hands. The door upstairs closed, and at its sound, she walked to the kitchen where Feena was waiting for her. Together they climbed the stairs to Marigold's bedroom opposite the hall from Crane's closed door.

"I don't know what I'm going to do," Marigold confided to Feena, as the woman helped her with her dress.

"You are speaking about Monsieur Crane?"

"Yes. He deceived me, Feena. He took the note from Robbie that Shaun had written to me and then pretended Shaun had jilted me."

"I know, *ma petite*. You still love your Irishman. It is written on your face."

"Is it that obvious, Feena? To everybody?"

"Only to me, I hope—for your sake. Monsieur Crane is a jealous man. You belong to him, as well as the child you are carrying. And Monsieur Shaun has no claim on you."

The tears came to Marigold's eyes. "Oh, Feena, I have made such a botch of it. Shaun will be leaving here soon to go back to Charleston and to . . . to Docia Henley."

"And when he does, you will tell him goodbye like a lady."

"I don't want to be a lady. I want to go back with him. I'll die if I have to stay here with Crane for the rest of my life."

Feena's look was compassionate. "Monsieur Crane is not the only man who has acquired a wife by deception. And the child may still salvage your marriage to him, *chérie*."

"Nothing can salvage this marriage, Feena. Not even the baby." She could not bring herself to tell Feena about the episode in the slave cabin.

"Did you know that is what your maman thought when she tried to run away from your papa?"

Marigold's tawny eyes widened in disbelief. "Maman ran away from Papa? When was that, Feena?"

"I shouldn't be telling you, but so many years have passed. . . . It was after you and Maranta were born— soon after the hurricane on the island. I was against it. But your maman was headstrong and unhappy, just as you are now. We got as far as Midgard—for your maman needed the gold that Madame Julie had given her—before your papa caught up with us."

"But why was she running away? Maman loves Papa more than anything else in the world. And he adores her."

"*Oui*. But those were stormy times. Monsieur Robert was a jealous man back then. He thought Madame Eulalie was in love with someone else. And that made it hard on her. I am only telling you this, *ma petite*, because

Monsieur Crane is a jealous man, and he knows you don't love him. But even if you feel you have made a terrible mistake, you must give this marriage time to work, because of the baby."

Marigold went over Feena's confidence time and again. Was she just being childish, wanting what she couldn't have? Was this what growing up meant—to give up girlish dreams and first loves and settle down to making the best of things? She was still confused when sleep came.

Marigold was ready at ten o'clock the next morning. And Feena with her.

The old woman had trouble going to sleep the evening before. She hoped that she had not made a mistake in advising Marigold to try to make the best of things. Monsieur Crane was not her choice as a husband for the girl, but he was her husband. Still, Feena hated to see her beautiful charge so unhappy over the marriage.

Shaun Banagher should not be at Cedar Hill. As long as he stayed Marigold would be nervous and upset. It would be much better for everyone, Feena decided, when Monsieur Shaun finished with the rails and went back to Charleston. Then perhaps her *petite* could settle down and think more of the baby.

Down over the long hill, past the row of cedars, Sesame took the carriage with his three passengers inside—Crane, Marigold and Feena. The horses splashed through the water of the small creek and pulled onto the road again. They headed toward the river, and Marigold sensed that Crane had decided to take her to one of the doctors far away, rather than use the man who was close at hand— she did not have to go over the river to get to Dr. Kellie.

On either side of the road, the two women could see the subtle change of seasons—the hardwood trees with their red and yellow crown of leaves proclaiming the fall of the year, against the faithful greenery of the loblolly pines deeper in the woods.

The mist from the river was still rising, partially obscuring the ferry tied to the bank on the other side, even blotting from view the nearby wooden planks with

251

their metal rings waiting for the wooden raft to be attached as soon as it arrived.

Sesame stopped the carriage, and with the reins in his hand, he stepped to the sentinel post with the bell at the top to alert the ferryman on the other side as to his desire to cross the river. The sound clanged through the mist, and Marigold strained her eyes for some sign of movement across the stretch of water.

Marigold's attention switched to her husband, and she watched him go through the pockets of his dark coat, his embroidered vest, and then search the floor and the seat of the carriage. Evidently not finding what he was looking for, the man enlisted Sesame's aid.

"I have lost an important paper, Sesame," he said. "Will you please go back along the road and search for it, while I stay with the horses?"

Sesame obeyed, and with Marigold and Feena still in the carriage, Crane stood by the horses. The man seemed nervous, and Feena, watching him closely, caught a slight glitter in the sunlight as the man quickly reached toward one of the horses and then just as quickly jerked back.

In an instant the horse bolted, and Feena, seeing the carriage headed straight for the water, jumped from the vehicle, grabbing at the reins dragging on the ground between the two horses. Marigold screamed when she saw Feena knocked down and entangled in the reins. It all happened so quickly—the horses on their berserk run toward the river, Feena's entanglement, Sesame approaching, and finally regaining control over the frightened animals as they slowed down.

Feena was hurt and badly, Marigold could tell as Sesame backed the horses away. She ran to the woman who still lay on the ground. Crying, the girl knelt over the old woman and tried to understand Feena's incoherent words. But it was impossible. The woman's last strength had been expended. Feena's dark eyes stared straight up at the sky, and her body suddenly convulsed and then was still.

Screaming and hysterical, Marigold was finally pulled

away from the woman by her husband. "No," she cried, fighting him.

"It is too late, Marigold," he said. "You can do nothing for her."

"Feena," she screamed again, and the name rose over the mist and came back to the girl in an echo from the silent river. Her old nurse—the one she loved—her true friend. She had died trying to save Marigold from a watery grave. The girl had never thought of Feena dying. To her the old woman was invincible. But there she was lying at the river's edge with the sound of her name echoing down the river. The woman was mortal, after all.

Marigold could not be consoled. It was her fault that Feena was dead. If the servant had not come to Cedar Hill with her, she would still be alive.

What had made the horses act up so suddenly? And what had Feena tried to whisper to her as she knelt beside her? Marigold would never know, for the old woman's voice had been silenced.

In the quietness of the afternoon, Marigold sat on the porch. The black shawl draped around her shoulders was a symbol of her grief, and her dull, topaz eyes stared unseeing at the trees that were now bereft of leaves.

There was a coldness in the air—a whisper of winter to come. And the clump of gray granite rocks in the side yard held the only warmth from the late afternoon sun.

The flowers in the garden were gone. Marigold had used the last of them to place on Feena's grave the week before. Only the fall-blooming camellias on the sheltered side of the house were in bud.

Taking up her flower basket and shears, Marigold walked down the steps. As she cut the pale pink buds, she heard the rumbling of the wagons. The cooking wagon, with its water barrels lashed to the sides, lumbered by and on down the hill, followed by other wagons with the tents inside. The hill near the mine was bare of tents and men. The rail system was completed at last. And now Crane could step up production of the gold ore.

Down the meadow, beyond the old apple tree, Marigold walked with her basket of flowers in her hand and her

shawl around her head. Down to the quiet peaceful spot
that she had chosen for Feena's grave. Marigold knelt and
placed the flowers on the mounded turf where the granite
rock jutted from the earth. No fine monument, no iron-
spiked fence—merely a common rock that Sesame had
placed there with the name crudely chiseled, and corner-
stones of smaller, white-washed rocks, worn smooth from
the constant motion of the water in the creekbed.

"I have come to tell you goodbye," the voice said above
her.

He helped her from her kneeling position and continued. "I will be leaving around noon tomorrow."

Marigold nodded, and with her sad eyes, she drank in
the man's emerald green eyes, his dark auburn hair, the
cleft in his chin. The strong, craggy face that she loved
and would never see again—

"I shall . . . miss you, Shaun."

He reached out for her hand, and in spite of her protest, kept it in his strong, warm one.

"Your hand is cold, Souci," he commented.

The bittersweet smile came to her trembling lips. "To
match my heart," she said.

Shaun's face grew stern. "Leave him, Marigold. Crane
Caldwell isn't worth it. Go home to your parents. They
won't blame you."

The girl shook her head. "They have enough troubles
of their own, Shaun. I cannot add to them."

He leaned over and kissed her gently on her forehead.
And then he put into place the black shawl that had
slipped from her golden curls. "If you ever need me, I'll
come. You know that, Marigold."

She nodded and blinked back the tears. She wanted to
cry out her need for him at that very moment, but her
pride kept her from it. She watched him walk away and
then turned to get her basket from the grass.

Crane, standing at the window on the upstairs landing
of the plantation house, gazed toward the meadow, past
the bare-limbed trees, and watched the two.

Shaun had waited until his men were gone, so there
would be no witnesses, Crane decided. He clutched at the

254

window sill, his knuckles white from his intense grasp. He had only twenty-four hours to rid himself of his faithless wife and her lover. A pity that Feena had to interfere and keep the carriage from plunging into the river. Now, he would have to get rid of them both at the same time—Marigold and Shaun—a much harder deed to accomplish.

That night, a wary Crane locked his bedroom door and loaded his pistol to place under his pillow. He was prepared if Shaun should come for him in the night.

29

The old condessa sat in bed and sipped her hot *yerba mate*. Her eyes lit up at the sight of Maranta, who had come to read to her.

As soon as the woman had recovered sufficiently from her heart seizure on that day Ruis had brought Maranta back from the wilderness to the *fazenda,* the girl made daily visits to Dona Louisa's apartment.

With unconcealed anticipation, Dona Louisa turned to Maranta. "I have a desire to hear Molière today, my daughter. It has been a long time since someone has read to me in French."

"You have the book, Mãe?" Maranta asked, wondering which of the books that she had never been allowed to read, the condessa wished to hear.

"Not in the apartment. You will have to borrow it from Ruis. He will not mind."

"But if he is busy . . ."

"You won't disturb him. Go now and ask for it. And you might select a few others while you are there. Take your time."

"Which book shall I ask for, Mãe?"

Petulantly, the old woman brushed aside her question. "Get Ruis to choose." And in Portuguese, she said, "Go with her, Jésus," to the little boy seated near the window, playing with the colored yarn from the condessa's embroidery basket.

Immediately he arose, and Maranta, hesitant to face the conde, yet wishing to obey Dona Louisa, walked out of the room with the child.

The heavy wooden door to the library was closed. Before she knocked, Maranta reached up to smooth the flyaway wisps at the nape of her neck and inspected the long, flowing blue silk garment that clung to her body in loose folds. It had been a matter of necessity, because of her pregnancy, to put away her own dresses with their tiny waists. But she suspected that the beautifully embroidered wardrobe that appeared one day in her apartment had been made for another, and merely altered to fit her own diminutive figure.

There was no reply at the first tap. Nervously, Maranta knocked again, this time a little louder.

"Come in," the deep voice commanded. And so Maranta turned the handle and walked inside.

Ruis sat at his desk, and his hair was ruffled—as if he had run his fingers through it time and again.

"*Pequena*," he said in surprise. He stood up and walked toward her. "Is something the matter?"

"No, Ruis. It is just that Mãe wishes to borrow some books from your library. If that is all right," she added hastily.

His eyes boldly drank in her appearance, with her rounded stomach, her swelling breasts now more noticeable than before.

"How is Mãe feeling?" he asked, still staring boldly at Maranta.

"She is better today," Maranta answered, her body and mind more aware of Ruis's encompassing gaze than her reply.

"She has a . . . preference?"

"What?"

"Mãe—does she wish a certain book, *querida*?"

Maranta flushed at his endearment. "Molière. She wishes Molière—and several others, if you do not mind."

"Why do you think I would mind, Maranta?"

"You are busy. I did not wish to disturb you."

Once again, his dark blue eyes pierced her. "It is a little late for that, is it not?"

His manner toward her made her nervous. Glancing at the child by the door, Maranta said, "Jésus has come to help me with the books."

Ruis laughed. "And you think he might understand English?"

"It is not . . . what you are saying, Ruis. It is your . . . manner."

"Then we shall give him something to occupy him, hm?" Without waiting for Maranta to respond, Ruis went to the shelves and quickly selected several books, taking them to the child.

"Be off with you, Jésus, and take these to the condessa."

Ruis closed the door behind him, and Maranta, standing before the shelves, felt her neck prickle as the man returned to stand beside her. He was so close that she could feel his warm breath upon her neck.

"So Mãe sent you to me," he said, taking her hand and drawing it to his lips.

"Only for the books, Ruis. I think I had better go back to her."

"Relax, *pequena*. There is no hurry."

"But she is waiting for me to read to her."

Ruis laughed. "Mãe is not that fond of books. She much prefers to gossip and manipulate other people's lives."

The girl's eyes widened. "You mean, she . . ."

"She wished to give me an opportunity to see you, without the jealous Vasco at your side."

"Vasco is not jealous." Did Ruis not realize Vasco paid attention to her solely to antagonize his brother?

Ruis lifted his eyebrows in a sardonic gesture. "You think not? Then you are even more of an innocent than I imagined. Come, *menina,* and rest awhile. It is not good for you to be on your feet overlong."

Despite her protests, he led her to the leather couch and sat beside her. "The child is stirring?" he asked.

"Yes," she admitted. "Particularly at night."

"He will be a strong, healthy son."

Ruis's pronouncement upset Maranta. "I wish you wouldn't talk like that. I'm already terrified that we shall both be a . . . a disappointment to you when the time comes."

His face softened at her admission. "You think I shall be unhappy if the child is a girl?" He reached out and touched her cheek with his hand.

"Vasco said . . ."

"Forget what Vasco has told you. I am sure *he* is the one hoping it will be a boy. For then, there would be no excuse for me to frequent your bed again."

Maranta pushed herself from the sofa. "I must go. The condessa is waiting."

She rushed toward the door. "Haven't you forgotten something?" Ruis asked.

She stared at him uncomprehendingly.

"Molière. You have forgotten Mãe's book. What will she think if you return empty-handed? I wonder which she would prefer? *The Imaginary Invalid?* Or *The School for Wives?*"

"Maranta, where are you?" Vasco's impatient voice penetrated the closed library door.

"She is in here, brother," Ruis replied, opening the door, "getting the book Mãe requested."

Vasco wheeled his chair into the library and glanced first at Maranta and then at Ruis, who walked to the shelf to retrieve a book.

"Tell Mãe that I will be down to see her before I ride out to the fields."

Vasco, pushing his rolling chair, kept up with Maranta as she walked back to the condessa's apartment with the book in her hand. Ever since he had gotten Patû to bring his chair upstairs from his chambers each day, Maranta did not know when Vasco might appear.

"You are looking flustered, Maranta," Vasco accused. "Was Ruis forward with you?"

"He touched my hand as he transferred the book to me," she snapped. "Is that being forward, Vasco?"

"Probably just an accident," he admitted. "But I hope Mãe will send someone else to the library in the future. I shall speak to her about that."

What had started out as an effort to antagonize Ruis had developed into something much more serious. For now, Vasco paid almost no attention to Floresta, or his half-breed son, Tefe. And sometimes in the hallway, Maranta could feel the Indian girl's hate directed toward her.

Not only was Vasco monitoring Maranta's health, he had also taken it upon himself to teach her Portuguese. Each afternoon she was coached by the man in his rolling chair, most of the time in her apartment, but occasionally downstairs in the guest chambers that Vasco claimed as his own. Always in the background, Patû, the Indian, stood, his face emotionless, his eyes revealing nothing.

The season for the coffee harvest had arrived and additional workers were hired to pick the ripe fruit and extract the beans hidden inside.

Great baskets, brought by the mules and donkeys, were brought from the slopes of the *terra-roxa* to be emptied onto the ground and raked in symmetrical patterns so that they might dry evenly. When one side was dry, the beans were turned to the other side, to be baked in the brilliant Brazilian sun.

The beans were dumped in great mounds, and it did not seem to matter to either the animals or the men that the coffee was trampled underfoot by muddy shoes and hooves. Maranta, watching the activity from the veranda, turned up her nose. She much preferred tea, anyway.

Ruis was up early and did not return to the house until late each evening. The condessa still had her meals in her apartment, and Dona Isobel had taken to eating with her. So now there were only three at the dinner table each night—Ruis, Maranta, and Vasco.

Innocencia lived in her own world, with Naka as her keeper. At times, she seemed to be completely lucid. But when she was having one of her spells, the slightest variation in her day disturbed her.

No one mentioned the flowers torn from their vases in the *sala* and other rooms of the house and strewn over the floor. The servants, accustomed to the oddity, cleared the shredded petals almost as soon as they fell. And fresh greenery and flowers were quickly installed in the empty containers.

Maranta, on her way to the dining *sala* one evening, stopped to admire the flowers on the hallway table not far from her sitting room door. The beautiful old gilt mirror reflected the image of the flowers—making the mammoth bouquet appear to be twice as large as it actually was.

When she reached out her hand to touch a snowy white blossom to assure herself it was real and not made of silk, she was startled by the sudden opening of the library door.

Maranta drew her hand back and took a step away. "One moment, Maranta, if you please."

Reluctantly the girl halted in her flight and waited for Ruis to catch up with her.

"I have something that is yours," he explained, coming beside her.

She watched him reach into his coat pocket. In his hands he brought out the gold locket on its delicate chain —the one she had lost that day she had run away.

"Where did you find it?" she asked, her eyes showing pleasure at the sight of the necklace.

"Hanging on a broken twig, Maranta, the day you were lost."

But that had been several weeks ago. Why had he waited so long to return it to her? Had he merely forgotten about it? She was happy to see it, whatever the reason for the delay. "I am grateful that you kept it for me. Thank you, Ruis."

Maranta reached out for the locket, but Ruis made no effort to give it up. Instead, his eyes narrowed and he turned the locket over in his hand. "Someone seems to think you need protection in this house."

Puzzled, Maranta took a step closer to see what he was talking about. The tiny symbol, the closed fist with the thumb resting between the two fingers, came into view. How had it gotten there and what did it mean?

"What is it?" Maranta asked.

"It is what we call a *figa*—a charm," he explained. "Part of the voodoo cult, or *macumba*."

"Then I shall remove it," she said. "I do not wish to wear something pagan about my neck."

"Perhaps it would be wise to keep it, *menina*. Whoever put it there would be unhappy at its removal."

Frowning, Maranta said, "My father does not allow the slaves to practice voodoo on Midgard Plantation. And surely, you do not condone this . . . this *macumba*, either."

Ruis smiled. "We are more tolerant than that, *pequena*. The old pagan gods are now saints, with Christian names. It is harmless and gives the slaves comfort."

"But I cannot . . ."

"You have much to learn about Brazil, Maranta. After the child is born—and if you are well enough by New Year's Eve—I shall take you to the falls at the river to watch one of their more interesting ceremonies. But come —it is time for dinner. Turn around, Maranta, and let me fasten the locket for you."

He was impatient, and Maranta did as she was told. Silently, she stood, watching in the gilt mirror while the tall, dark Ruis placed the golden chain about her throat and fastened the clasp.

Their eyes met, and for a moment, both stood, locked in each other's glance, conscious only of each other. A sound escaped Ruis's throat, and Maranta, afraid, took a step away from the man, so he could not tell she was trembling at his nearness.

30

The warm, rainy season came to the *fazenda,* with gray clouds obliterating the brilliant blue of the sky and fresh new shoots of greenery appearing in every direction. Weeds sprouted overnight to choke the tender young coffee plants that hid under twigs and canvas from the heat; vines and undergrowth erased a path that had been there the day before. Inside the plantation house, the rain brought a restlessness that could not be contained by eating and sleeping and waiting for the sunshine.

Day after day, the morning greeted the earth with a drizzling mist, driving the old *muçurana* from his place near the steps to the distant green vegetation in search of food.

Even Fado in his cage in Maranta's room seemed to be affected by the melancholia that gripped the *fazenda.* His head drooped, and he was silent. Maranta, concerned for the little bird, asked Sassia to take him out to the sheltered veranda as soon as the clouds lifted and the sun peeked through.

Though it was now the hour of *sesta* for all in the *fazenda,* Ruis and his *mestiços* and slaves continued to work, battling against time to rescue the tender coffee plants from the encroachment of the weeds.

Maranta lay down and tried to sleep, but she could not. Now heavy with child, she was uncomfortable. She'd also been thinking about the condessa's deteriorating health. After her last seizure, Dona Louisa had failed to rally as she should, and most of her days were spent in bed. Dona Isobel, so zealous in caring for the woman, had moved her things into the dressing room adjacent to the condessa's bedroom, in case the woman should need her in the night.

Though it was quiet, it was also humid and hot. Maranta gave up the pretense of resting. She combed her hair, slipped on the loose-fitting robe of white and gold that hung over the chair, and walked down the stairs to sit on the veranda. Sassia would not be pleased that she had left her room, but she would be careful in navigating the steps.

The downstairs door was open, and as Maranta walked silently through the *sala da entrada,* a flash of green fled down the outside steps and hurried toward the gate. Maranta frowned at the sight of Innocencia—carrying something. There was no telling what the girl was doing.

Maranta looked for Fado's cage, but it was not on the veranda. Was that what Innocencia had in her hands as she ran through the gate? The little green bird?

Forgetting everything but the safety of Fado, Maranta walked down the steps and opened the gate. "Innocencia," she called.

The girl in green was swallowed up by the expanse of green outside. Angry now that the girl had taken Fado, Maranta followed her. Maranta was upset at herself for having left the bird unattended. She should have sat with him, so that no harm could come to him.

"Innocencia," she called again. Her voice startled the old vulture in the decaying treetop, and he flew to another tree some yards away.

Maranta continued walking, careful to watch her step. She could not afford to fall or be thrown off balance.

The landscape became alive with sounds—protests at some disturbance in the distance. Maranta followed the sounds, knowing Innocencia must have passed that way.

In the clearing, Maranta spied Fado. His cage was hanging on a tree limb, and inside the cage, the little green bird hopped about with a lusty chirp, answering the calls of the other birds that were free to fly in and out of the clearing.

Relieved that the bird had not been harmed, Maranta looked around for the girl, but Innocencia was nowhere in sight. Another foolish prank, Maranta thought in disgust. The girl had taken the bird just to be annoying.

Still wary, Maranta glanced to the right and left of the

cage, but there did not appear to be any danger. But just as she made a step to take the cage in her hand, the ground gave way beneath her.

Maranta screamed and clutched at the vines, while her feet struggled to gain a toehold. The animal pit had been camouflaged by a mat of greenery, and there was no telling what was beneath her in the pit.

The bird was forgotten, while Maranta tried to get free of the tangled vines and still avoid the deep chasm that waited for her. Digging her fingers into the earth, she inched upward, only to fall back as the soft earth crumbled in her hands.

Breathing hard, Maranta gripped the edge, drawing herself upward, until half of her body had emerged. Exhausted, she laid her head against the soft, green earth and rested. And then she began once more to try to free herself.

But the vines were wrapped around her right foot, entrapping it. Fighting against them only made it worse, for the rope of vines tightened around her ankle and pulled her downward.

It was no use. She had crawled as far as she could on her own. If she were to get free, someone else would have to help. The baby stirred within her, protesting the position in which her body was placed. It was impossible, though, to find a more comfortable position. So Maranta, trapped by the vines, lay quietly, listening to Fado's cheerful chirp in the forest.

She could not hope to be rescued for several hours yet, for Ruis would remain in the fields with his workers the rest of the afternoon. And there was no one else to rescue her, unless a slave should happen to pass by. But most of the slaves were in the fields. There was no one, then. Maranta closed her eyes and asked for strength to hold on until Ruis came.

Rapidly, the *jararaca* slid over the slippery green earth. The snake, suddenly sensing a human presence, slowly wound itself into a coil and waited for the human to move.

Maranta, with heart beating erratically, watched the snake. The reptile, with its malignant eyes, seemed to be assessing the figure before him—contemplating how dangerous this adversary might prove.

Lying as still as possible, Maranta made no sound. But she was concious of the pull on her foot, the tiredness of her body, and the fear that made her cold.

The soft earth underneath her began to give way, and with a gasp, Maranta struggled to take a new hold on firmer earth. From the corner of her eye, she saw the snake come to life.

"Help me," she shouted. "Someone please help me."

At the edge of the clearing, the Indian, Patû, lifted his head at Maranta's cry. Curious to see what had happened to the girl, he walked stealthily in the direction of the shout. Through the trees he peered, his eyes taking in Maranta's plight, the venomous snake heading toward her, and her efforts to free herself from the animal pit.

With a satisfied gleam in his eye, he turned his back and disappeared in the direction he had come.

The tears blurred Maranta's vision. She had no one to blame but herself. Ruis's words the day she had run away came back to her. "You must never run away again, *pequena*. I might not be so lucky to find you next time."

She had not run away this time. She'd been trying to rescue Fado from Innocencia. Unfortunately, the reason did not matter. She had come and was now trapped.

It didn't take long to die of the venom, so Sassia had said. A small consolation, Maranta decided, as she trembled and waited for the snake to strike.

Nothing happened. Fearfully, Maranta opened her eyes again and lifted her head. The subtle movement of greenery on the earth's floor drew her attention. The *jararaca,* so near, had changed direction, as if to escape.

Maranta looked up to see the *muçurana* emerging from the path and chasing toward the venomous snake. The *jararaca* was not fast enough. The *muçurana* sprang, clamping his heavy black body around the other snake. The trapped *jararaca*, with his wicked fangs, struck time and again at the body that held him. And when Maranta saw the yellow venom streaming down the black snake's back, she cried. For a moment, she had thought the *muçurana* could save her. But the *jararaca* had proved too much for the other snake.

Maranta waited to see how long it would take the *muçurana* to die. But as she waited, the black snake merely tightened his hold, until the *jararaca's* head was imprisoned.

The fight was at an impasse. For what seemed like hours, neither snake moved. Then the black snake awakened. Along the body of the *jararaca,* the *muçurana's* froglike mouth gingerly traveled and then stopped. It began again, sliding upward until it reached the head of its enemy, and with a powerful snap, the *muçurana* subdued the venomous snake.

Watching with unbelieving eyes, Maranta saw the black snake devour its prey—first the head, and then the body —until the last thing visible was the white tail of the *jararaca de robo branco*.

With a sliding motion, the ground gave way, and Maranta, losing her hold on the soft earth, slipped to the bottom of the animal pit, cushioned by matted vines and leaves.

The rain began to fall, beating down on the leaves of the trees and soaking the soft earth in torrents. And Fado, in his cage overhead, protested.

Maranta, conscious of dryness and warmth, gazed up at white silken draperies. She was in her room—safe from harm.

The man in the wheelchair sat by her bed.

"Vasco?" she said softly, stirring from her cocoon of silk.

At the sound of his name on her lips, a satisfied look passed over the man's face. "You are safe, Maranta."

"Who . . . found me?"

"Patû. In the animal pit. He thought you were dead."

"I am grateful then . . . that he found me . . . and brought me home."

"Actually, it was Ruis who brought you back. But if it

269

had not been for Patû, you would have drowned in the pit."

Much later that night, when all in the house were asleep, Maranta awakened to the insistent drops of rain striking against the window. Bolts of jagged lightning traveled across the sky, giving an eerie flash to the room. The sound of a tree crashing in the distance caused Maranta to utter a cry and sit upright.

In no time, a door opened, and Ruis's tanned, rugged face was framed in candlelight.

"The storm has frightened you, *pequena?*" he asked.

"It . . . it woke me," the girl admitted.

"But you are safe inside, Maranta," he assured her. "You do not have to be afraid."

Thunder crashed closer this time, and again, Maranta jumped. If it had not been for Ruis and Patû, she would still be out in the storm.

"I . . . have not thanked you—for bringing me home," Maranta said.

Ruis's face, so dark and fierce, nodded in acknowledgement. "You are lucky for the second time, *menina*. I warned you once before that your worthless little bird could be the death of you."

The words rankled. Ruis acted as if it were Fado's fault that she had fallen into the animal pit. She gazed anxiously toward the covered cage near the window. And Ruis, pulling the gilt chair beside the bed, announced, "I will sit with you, until you go back to sleep, Maranta."

"That is not necessary, senhor—for you to treat me like a child. I am not afraid of the storm."

Ruis's mouth showed his disapproval of her words. "Nevertheless, I shall remain," he said, settling himself in the chair beside her.

270

31

Two days later, Innocencia was dead—poisoned by someone in the *fazenda*. And Maranta had been the last one to see the girl alive.

In a state of shock, Maranta remained in her room, while the quiet preparations for the girl's funeral went on around her. Innocencia's two brothers were notified. Her burial gown was selected and the family vault beneath the floor of the chapel opened.

Innocencia was dead, but Maranta's angry words lived on. Everyone in the *fazenda* knew they had quarreled—Dona Isobel, the condessa, Vasco, the servants, and Ruis. Most of all Ruis, for he had been the one who had come in the room to stop their altercation.

And now, Maranta was ashamed that she had been unable to control her temper. Taking the handkerchief from her moist, dark eyes, Maranta sneezed and gazed inconsolably at the empty cage on the table near the window. Fado's cage.

Finding Innocencia in her apartment was the last straw. Maranta had lost her reason and lashed out at the girl at the sight of her standing before the cage—jabbing at the bird with her wickedly long fingernail.

All the hurt and horror of her day in the rain-soaked forest rose up in her throat. "You will never hurt Fado again. I promise you that, Innocencia."

Maranta had tried to grab the cage from the girl, but Innocencia in her perversity clung to it. And it was Ruis who had come in at the shouting and gently led the tearful Innocencia out of the room—the man looking at Maranta as if she were at fault.

The tears streamed down Maranta's cheeks. As soon as Innocencia was gone, Maranta opened the window. Fado would never be safe with the girl roaming about the *fazenda.* And remembering how the little green bird had reacted in the forest, twittering and chirping with the other birds about, Maranta opened the cage door. Holding him in her hand, she thrust her arm out the window and loosened her hold. For a moment, the bird remained in her hand, as if he did not realize he was free. Then he fluttered his wings and left Maranta's hand for the ledge along the roof.

"Go on, Fado," Maranta urged, her voice breaking. "You're free."

Maranta closed the window and walked to her bed. There she lay for the rest of the afternoon, feeling sorry for herself.

Later, Maranta began to be ashamed. She should not have lashed out at Innocencia so strongly. The girl was not really responsible for her actions.

Where was Maranta's sense of forgiveness? Or her willingness to show a long-suffering spirit? Had she not wronged Innocencia, also—usurping her place with Ruis? Daring to fall in love with him? Conceiving his child?

Maranta made up her mind. She must apologize to Innocencia. She washed her face and put on a fresh robe of flowing yellow silk. Leaving her apartment, she walked to the iron-grilled door of the nursery and knocked.

Innocencia, sitting on the swinging hammock, gazed in bewilderment as Maranta apologized. She was more engrossed in the sweet cakes before her than in Maranta's words of apology.

Already, Innocencia had forgotten the quarrel in the apartment. But Maranta felt better, knowing she had made the effort to put things right between them. She declined a sweet cake offered by the blue-eyed girl and left the nursery.

Dona Isobel, in the hall, appeared startled to see Maranta emerging from the nursery. Maranta coughed and sneezed, and anxiously, the woman scrutinized the girl. "'You are feeling well, Maranta?" she asked.

"Yes, Dona Isobel—much better now that I have apologized to Innocencia for losing my temper with her."

The woman fell in step with Maranta, eyeing her as

they walked down the hall of black and white tiles. At the door of her apartment, the girl hesitated. "Will you come in, Dona Isobel?" she invited, sensing the woman's reluctance to leave her.

"No, Maranta. I must go—to the chapel—to pray."

The angelic face, with the circlet of flowers around her long golden hair, was hauntingly beautiful. Innocencia lay in the chapel, with multitudes of candles, mounds of exotic flowers, guarding her bier. The long white gown embroidered with gold—similar to the one Maranta had worn—was draped in graceful folds about her body. And her long slender hands lay folded across her breast.

No one seeing the girl—her blue eyes, pale as the summer sky, closed forever—would have suspected her of a single unkind thought, much less a malignant deed. Yet, Maranta knew differently. But she would keep silent. It would not do to speak ill of the dead.

Because of the warm weather, the funeral could not be delayed for Innocencia's family to arrive. And so on the next day, the rites took place. The old condessa, supported by Dona Isobel, Vasco, Ruis, and Maranta gathered in the chapel, and the padre began the service.

As Maranta sat in the chapel, her dark hair covered by the black lace mantilla, she stopped hearing the words the padre spoke. Her mind and eyes were on the *Cruzamento da Monteiro,* still hanging around the Dolorosa's neck—that and the head of the distant, formidable Ruis, who sat in the pew in front of her. His black suit was austere to match the severity of his posture.

A fly buzzed about the ceiling, and the sickening sweet fragrance of flowers and myrtle wax candles bombarded Maranta's senses.

The nagging ache in her back, that had begun that morning, increased, tightening its ribboned pain around her stomach. A small gasp escaped her lips and she pressed her handkerchief to her mouth.

Vasco frowned at her and whispered, "What is the matter with you, Maranta?"

She shook her head and did not answer, for Dona Isobel was gazing in their direction with a censuring look.

The service continued, and Maranta, feeling the pains coming on, twisted the handkerchief tighter and tighter. Small beads of perspiration formed above her lip, and her skin took on the pale milkiness of the white candles burning.

Now, Vasco looked worried. "Maranta?" he inquired again softly. "Is it the baby?"

Her dark doe eyes, filled with pain, rested on Vasco's face. Her lips formed the word silently. "Yes."

"You mean—the baby is coming? Now?"

"I . . . think so," she whispered, and tightened her hands on the limp handkerchief in her lap.

Vasco immediately turned and motioned for Patû, who came silently to his side. "Carry my wife to her room," he ordered, "and then return for me."

Now beyond protest at the scene she was making, Maranta was lifted into the strong arms of the Indian and removed from the chapel.

The casket closed and the dead Innocencia was lowered into the family vault, while upstairs, Ruis's child struggled to be born.

Vasco stayed by her side, letting her grip his hands as the pain worsened. Then he was sent from the room, and Sassia with Naka, took over. Finally, a strange man with a red beard and dark robe put in an appearance—the doctor summoned from the town of Hitû to preside at the birth of the heir to the Monteiro fortune.

In her pain, Maranta forgot every Portuguese word she had ever been taught. And there was no one who understood her cry for help. The man answered her in the strong, nasal language that meant nothing to her.

Dona Isobel—the condessa—Ruis—all ignored her as she traveled through hell and back again.

Far into the night, the travail continued, but the baby did not come. There was something wrong. It was in that man's eyes, and Maranta feared that she was going to die—that she and the unborn child would join Innocencia underneath the stone floor of the chapel.

Would Ruis grieve for her, too? Or would he be furious with her for allowing the child to die with her?

Maranta, through the white silken draperies of her bed, was only partially aware of another figure who stood and watched her—Ruis, with tears in his dark sapphire eyes—grieving for his dead wife, and for his son who refused to be born.

The strong hand gently touched the long black hair, wet from the ordeal of a fruitless labor.

"*Amada,* you cannot die," he whispered, his deep voice alien in its emotion. "I have greatly wronged you. But I do not ask that you pay for *my* sin. *Live, amada,*" he whispered with a desperate urgency, "for the sake of my son—and for me."

White feathers lay on the table beside Fado's empty cage—with the beads, the bowl of rice, and the plaster saint. The candles glowed in the night. The room took on the same odor as the chapel.

"No, it's pagan," Maranta protested, "just like the *figa.* Take them away," she urged, thrashing deliriously in her bed.

"Marigold," she called out. "I never told you. Shaun loved you. He didn't desert you . . . The blood," she moaned, "So much blood."

Maranta held her hand to her face. "I do not make a habit of complaining over something so small, senhor. I am used to the gnats and mosquitoes of my own country. . .

"Fado, you are a beautiful little bird—*not* silly and molting. Forget what the arrogant conde has said."

Ruis suddenly changed into the man with the red beard, who leaned down to take her hand in his. Had Ruis come to see her? Or had the strength of her wish given the man in the robe the appearance of Ruis for a short time?

She was so tired. She wished to rest, but the man with the red beard would not allow it. "Senhora," he called, over and over, slapping at her, pinching her, and never leaving her alone.

"Please," she whimpered, but he paid no attention to

her entreaty. He was intent upon punishing her, making her bear the pain—the pain that would not stop.

With an agonized scream, Maranta felt her body torn apart. Before she lost consciousness, she heard a familiar voice. Sassia's—"Rest, *yayá*. No one will stop you now."

32

Maranta awoke to an empty room. The white silken bed draperies were drawn and the shutters at the windows kept the room in darkness. Was it day? Was it night? Why was everything so quiet and deserted?

The girl lifted her hand to push the coverlet back. She had lain in bed too long, her body on fire. That much she knew. Gradually, she began to remember other things—a feeling of cool hands attending her, forcing her to drink, placing cold cloths on her hot brow. The enervating fever that drew the life out of her—

Maranta touched her forehead. It was cool. She was not dead. She was alive, even though death had beckoned to her.

She had borne Ruis's baby. Maranta raised herself and pushed aside the draperies. There was no cradle in the room. She had heard no cry during her illness. Did that mean. . . ?

If only it weren't so dark. If only someone would come—to tell her what had happened.

The sounds from outside filtered through the shuttered windows. The twitter of birds and the low plaintive singing—a sad song—greeted her.

Then a door opened, and Sassia with a tray in her hands came into the room. She set the tray on the table near the window and lit a candle, casting a dim light over the room.

"Sassia?" Maranta called.

The black girl turned in surprise toward the bed. "Senhora," she said, her face breaking into a smile at the sight of Maranta's sitting up. "You are awake."

"Sassia," Maranta repeated in her weak voice as she held out her hand to the servant in a gesture of entreaty. "Tell me—the baby—"

Her voice quavered and she could not go on. Sassia took

pity on her and replied, "He is a fine one—that baby—and growing so big every day."

"It is . . . a boy?"

"Yes, senhora. A boy."

"But where is he?"

"In the nursery with Naka and his wet nurse."

Maranta frowned. Innocencia was in the nursery. Didn't they know she might harm him? But no. Innocencia was dead. She had forgotten.

"Dom Vasco is a proud papa. He is already making plans to have the baby baptized by the padre in the chapel," Sassia offered.

"But the conde . . ."

The loud voices across the hall disrupted their conversation as a door opened. Quickly, Sassia doused the light. In the darkness, she whispered, "Senhora, you must pretend to be asleep. Do not let them know that you have awakened."

Sassia drew the silken draperies around the bed and turned her back to straighten the things on the table near the window.

Frightened at the urgency in the girl's voice, Maranta lay still, her dark eyes closing as the men came to the bedside.

"As you can see, she has not recovered." It was Ruis speaking. "It has been over a week now since the birth of the child. And so the chances are slim that she will ever get well."

"A pity," another man said in his nasal voice, "that she cannot be brought to justice. She should be made to pay for the murder of our sister."

"I have told you before," Ruis growled. "No one knows *who* poisoned Innocencia. It could have been anyone on the *fazenda*."

"But this one was the last to see her alive—Floresta has sworn. And you cannot deny that they had quarreled."

"We will not discuss it," Ruis replied. "Come, and let us not disturb her further."

The door closed again, but Maranta was too afraid to

open her eyes. Did they think *she* was the one who had poisoned the girl? Innocencia's brothers?

Later, Sassia slipped back into the room. "They are gone, senhora. Now I can open the shutters and give you something to eat."

"But Sassia. They acted as if I were the one responsible for Innocencia's death."

"Yes, senhora. But Dom Ruis will not allow them to take you away."

"I had nothing to do with it," Maranta said in a disturbed tone.

Did Ruis think she had poisoned Innocencia? And if the men came back, would he give her up to them?

The desire to see her child kept Maranta from going to pieces. She must remain calm. She would not let them frighten her. "Sassia, I want to see my baby. Will you bring him to me?"

"Naka will bring him as soon as you are prepared to have visitors. Dom Ruis is pleased that you are better."

While Sassia bathed the girl and brushed her hair, Maranta said, "What does the condessa think of the baby?"

The brush stopped for a moment and then Sassia resumed working. "Everyone in the *fazenda* thinks he is a beautiful little boy."

She had to be content with the girl's answer. Later, she would see the condessa herself and ask her.

Expectantly, Maranta sat up in bed and faced toward the door. Her hair had been twisted into a coronet, held by the beautiful jeweled comb. It felt good to be between fresh sheets, to be wearing the delicately embroidered white robe, and to be waiting for the first glimpse of her son.

Naka came to the bedside with the small bundle in her arms. "He is heavy, senhora," Naka said. "A greedy one —this fine *criança de peito*." Maranta had no trouble following the Portuguese words, punctuated by the hearty laugh.

She held out her arms for the child. Pushing back the

blanket, she stared down into her baby's eyes—dark sapphire eyes—and hair, blue-black as a crow's. His skin was a shade darker than that of Maranta, she noticed, holding his tiny hand in her own. The resemblance was there—to Ruis, and to Vasco, too. He was a Monteiro. There was no mistake.

While she held the baby, murmuring endearments to him, Maranta became aware of the tall, dark man standing at the foot of the bed—watching her. The two servants discreetly disappeared.

Searching for something to fill the sudden silence, Maranta said, "The condessa—she has seen him?"

Ruis ignored her question and continued staring. With a step he came nearer the bed, and the light from the window caught the object he held in his hands—the *cruzamento.*

"I have brought something that belongs to you, *amada.*"

Maranta shook her head.

"It is yours, Maranta," he insisted.

She drew back, holding the baby against her breast. At her action, a distressed look crossed his face and he said, "If you will not wear it for me, then wear it for Mãe's sake."

Maranta could not refuse. She remained still while Ruis's hands lifted the cross of pearls and diamonds over her head, and she felt its coldness as it touched her breast. She shivered, remembering Ruis's anger the first time he had seen it around her neck. She had vowed never to put it on again. But it was for Mãe—not Ruis—that she now wore it.

"A touching little scene," Vasco's voice announced as he wheeled himself into the room. "So you have given Maranta the *cruzamento.* Does that mean, Ruis, that you have no hopes for a son of your own? Now that Innocencia is dead, I would have thought you anxious to marry again."

Ruis's face darkened and his hands tightened against his side. "The child before you is the heir, Vasco."

"A pity that Mãe didn't live long enough to see him."

"Vasco," Ruis warned, but it was too late. Maranta had

heard. The baby began crying, and Ruis took the child from Maranta's arms. "He is better off in the nursery, *pequena*," he said in a gentle tone, seeing the stunned expression on her face. Ruis disappeared with the wailing infant, and Maranta was left alone with Vasco.

"Mãe is dead?" she asked.

Vasco, disconcerted, looked at the grieving girl and apologized. "I thought you knew. I did not realize they had kept it from you."

"When did she die?"

"She collapsed in the chapel, soon after Patû carried you upstairs."

So that was why no one came near her—Ruis, Dona Isobel, or the condessa. Suddenly, Maranta was exhausted. She lay back against the pillows and closed her eyes. "I am tired, Vasco," she said.

He wheeled out of the room and left Maranta greatly troubled and grief-stricken.

Maranta grew stronger as the days went by. But the loss of the condessa continued to grieve her. Each time she held the baby, she lamented the tragedy that had kept the old condessa from ever seeing the grandchild she had waited for—even schemed for. The *cruzamento* around Maranta's neck reminded her of that fact daily.

Maranta was not the only one affected by this cross of pearls and diamonds. It held a morbid fascination for Vasco. Amused at first, he began to resent it. But then, Maranta would remind him that it was Mãe who had given it to her—not Ruis. Sometimes in the evenings, she would catch Vasco staring at it with fury. But when she tried to go without it for a day, Vasco insisted she put it back around her neck.

"It has its purpose, Maranta," he declared, "for it is a reminder to Ruis that you will never belong to him again, even for one night. You will have to be content to be my own dear faithless wife for the rest of your life—or mine."

When Vasco goaded her too far, Maranta would retire to the nursery with Dona Isobel. The woman who had cared for the condessa for so long continued to sleep in the small dressing room adjacent to the condessa's large bedroom—almost as if the woman might have need of her during the night. But gradually, the loyalty she gave to the condessa was transferred to the child, and she watched carefully over him. It was for the condessa's sake, Maranta knew.

Vasco planned the baptism for Christmas Eve, a fitting time for an infant to be blessed. And Maranta, knowing of Dona Isobel's fierce love for the child, asked Vasco if the woman might be allowed to serve as godmother.

"If you wish, Maranta," he said. "And shall we get Ruis to be godfather? It will give me pleasure to hear Ruis addressed as 'Tio' when the child begins to talk."

Christmas Eve arrived and the family gathered in the chapel. Floresta, holding onto the three-year-old Tefe, watched the proceedings from her nook in the gallery, while below, the child that Vasco claimed as his legitimate son was sprinkled with holy water.

As godfather, Ruis held the child in his arms, and Dona Isobel stood beside him. At the sight of the dark-haired baby in the man's arms, Maranta was transported back to another world—another christening—to that of her little brother Raven. All the feelings of that day, so many miles distant, overwhelmed her—the fierce, possessive look of her father toward her mother and the baby, and Maranta's own innocent certainty that she would be allowed to enter the convent.

Now, little over a year later, she wore a priceless cross about her neck, but she was no nun. Married to one man, she had borne a son to another. Vasco, watching her, saw her shiver despite the heat in the chapel, and a satisfied glint sprang into his eyes.

Paulo Alvares Honório—the names Vasco had chosen for the child. The padre pronounced each syllable distinctly. He was now properly recognized by the church. And through it all, the baby, Paulo, in the exquisite handmade heirloom christening gown, yawned in his sleep.

33

Marigold was not dressed, though it was mid-morning. Her locket was gone and it upset her. She'd looked through the small box on the marble-topped night stand and the larger jewelry box sitting on her dressing table several times, but it was not to be seen.

Where could she have left it? She remembered having it around her neck on the previous afternoon. But did she take it off? Did she drop it somewhere? She had been so distraught the night before that she had gotten undressed for bed in a daze. Shaun was leaving, and that was all she could think about.

Perhaps the catch had broken while she was cutting the flowers or arranging them on Feena's grave. At least, those were two places to begin looking.

Marigold put on the dull blue silk dress that she and Juniper had altered, adding the panel in front to make the dress larger. She made a face at her bulging figure in the mirror and then sat down to brush her hair.

After her golden curls were pinned into place, Marigold found her black shawl and hurried down the stairs. Her slippers made little noise as she stepped onto the porch and down the side steps that hid the cellar where the hams were stored. Soon, it would be time for the slaughter of hogs . . . and Julie was not at Cedar Hill to oversee it as she had done the winter before. Surely Crane would not expect *her* to preside over the killing, and the grinding of sausage, in her condition. Marigold shuddered and walked on beyond the closed cellar door.

To the sheltered side of the house she went, her eyes staring downward where she walked. She looked at the base of the camellia bush, but there was no glint of gold in her search.

Looking for the necklace assumed a disproportionate

amount of her concentration, for she was trying to keep her mind from Shaun's leaving. On toward the meadow she walked, feeling the sting of the wintry air, the odor of apples that still clung to the limbs of the old tree. She and Juniper would have to gather them soon to make jelly and cider to sip during the cold evenings ahead.

Marigold came to the grave and saw the camellias tinged with an ugly brown—their delicately painted petals no longer beautiful because of the frost. On her hands and knees she searched, until the sight of the man running through the meadow brought her to her feet.

As Crane ran up to her, the expression on his face was alarming. "Marigold," he said, gasping for breath.

"What is it, Crane?"

"There has been an accident in the mine."

The man had never appeared this concerned before, even when the slave had drowned in the subterranean water.

"Is it one of the slaves?" she asked, not yet sharing in his alarm.

"No. It's Shaun."

Marigold's face turned ashen. "What is the matter? What happened?"

"We were inspecting the rails for the last time before he left. And a runaway car filled with ore ran over him."

"Oh God, no!" the girl cried and, flinging her shawl from her shoulders, she held up her skirts and began to run.

"He's still in the mine," Crane said. "I thought it best not to move him while I went for Dr. Kellie. He's asking for you, Marigold. And I promised to get you first, before sending for the doctor."

"Then hurry, Crane. Hurry before it's too late."

She left Crane in the meadow and flew down the path as fast as her awkward body would take her. But at the bridge, she had to stop and rest. The ache in her side could not be ignored.

"Shaun—Shaun," she said over and over and began running again toward the dark mouth of the mine where the crossbeams and dirt made an unholy design against the hillside. The lantern hanging inside the cavernous hole was already lit. Marigold, brushing aside her fear of the dark, took the lantern from its hook and began the journey inside, along the tracks, to find the injured Shaun.

Deep into the mine she walked, her heart beating fast against her chest. The rails divided and the girl did not know which way to go. She should have asked Crane. To the right? Or straight ahead? She called out Shaun's name. But there was no answer. Finally she decided to turn to the right.

The air was cold and a splatter of water fell from overhead. But the girl kept on, pushing back her fright; for the love she had for Shaun was greater than her fear of dark places.

Suddenly the earth rocked amid a deafening blast. She fell to the ground, the force of the blast knocking the lantern from her hand. In the flare, Marigold saw the loosened gold-veined rock crumbling from the walls about her, and the crosspiece shifting overhead. Dust overwhelmed her, covering her, making her cough violently. The sound of the tunnel collapsing behind her, the pieces of rock splitting apart made her cover her head with her arms to avoid being struck.

For some moments, Marigold lay on the ground—stunned. Gradually, as the dust settled, she sat up, brushing the dirt from her face and reaching for the lantern that miraculously still burned.

Someone had set off the gunpowder overhead. And now she was trapped in the mine, with no way out.

Her fear of the dark gripped her. Crane had done this to her, she knew, for some reason that she could not comprehend. Shaun's accident had been an excuse to get her inside the mine. Marigold hoped with all her heart that the man she loved had gotten away safely, and was even now traveling back to Charleston, and not buried in the mine with her.

She was drained of energy and will. Sitting in the dirt, with the debris scattered about her, she wondered how long it would be before the oil in the lantern would be gone, leaving her in total darkness.

Cold pervaded her body and her teeth chattered. Hugging herself, Marigold felt the child move. Poor baby— never to have a chance to see the sun. Crane had killed his own child with her.

She watched while the rocks deep inside the tunnel moved, and a part of the wall gave way in front of her. Another cave-in? She closed her eyes and waited. She could do nothing but wait.

The pinging sound was distant at first. Marigold lifted her head and listened to the noise of a pickax striking against the rock. Someone else was in the ruined mine with her. She watched as the hole grew larger, and finally, a man covered in dust emerged from the hole. First his head, and then his body emerged, as he twisted his shoulders to push himself through. It was Shaun. Her heart sank. He had not escaped.

"Marigold, thank God you are all right." He did not seem surprised to see her.

"I had hoped that you were on your way to Charleston, Shaun." The unemotional words sounded incongruous, even to Marigold's ears. She saw the anger in Shaun's eyes as he bent over her.

"You were foolish to be lured inside, Marigold," he said.

His words made no sense to her. He acted as if he had seen her coming into the mine. But that was impossible. Shaun had to have been farther back inside the mine than she, with no way of knowing.

"Crane told me you had been hurt."

"And you came in, without using that brain of yours, without once stopping to think that he might be setting a trap for you . . ."

"I was only thinking of *you*, Shaun," she confessed, hurt at his anger toward her.

He took the lantern and helped Marigold from the tunnel floor. But Shaun could not stand up straight because of his height. If their situation had not been so tragic, Marigold would have laughed at his caveman stance.

Shaun threw the pickax through the opening he had dug and then helped Marigold, handing the lantern to her on the other side. She did not question his taking her deeper into the mine.

"How long do we have before the air gives out?" she asked as she stopped to rest.

"There should be no danger of that. The build-up of gases should be well behind us."

She started walking again. Marigold was thirsty. And hungry. How long could they last before finally starving? She must not think about it. But the small tunnel closed around her, and she felt as if she were suffocating. The fear of the dark enclosure made her arms tingle, her heart beat erratically. She could not go on. She was ready to scream out her fear, but her voice erupted into a small, dismal moan.

"We're almost there, Souci," Shaun assured her, as the last flicker of light from the lantern vanished in the darkness.

Marigold stumbled and reached out for Shaun. Almost where? Heaven? Hell? She was so frightened. In anguish, she held to Shaun and whispered, "I don't want to die."

"You're not going to die, Souci. Hold onto me. It's probably only a few more yards."

"To where?"

"Why, to the outside."

"But there's no other way out, Shaun. We're trapped."

"No, Marigold. There *is* another way out. You don't think I'm a complete idiot, do you? I never totally trusted Crane, and after that day I came upon the two of you down here—and he had obviously forced you to come— I had the men dig another exit—one that Crane knew nothing about." His voice was soothing in the darkness.

"Today, when Crane disappeared during the final inspection, I walked on and climbed out of the hidden exit —and waited to see what he was going to do. And then I saw *you*—running into the entrance. I should have shouted to you then to stay out. But Crane was directly behind you, and it was too late."

Her laugh bordered on hysteria. A vast relief swept over Marigold. Thanks to Shaun, she would see the sunlight again.

A small chink let in light from the end of the tunnel. Marigold crawled with Shaun the last few feet, holding onto his shirt, while he dragged the pickax with him.

The sun poured through the hole, and Marigold gazed up at the sky. Shaun pushed her upward, and she climbed through to the top of the hillside. Amid the bare-branched landscape, Shaun took her in his arms and held her. She dug her face into his dusty shirt front and cried.

Shaun instructed the slaves to begin digging. He told Marigold to go back to the house, but she could not. Juniper sat with her a short distance away from the mine and wrapped the heavy black shawl around the shivering girl.

Crane was inside the collapsed mine—that much she knew. The shovels cleared away the dirt; the men lifted the crossbeams and set them out of the way—and continued with their clearing of the earth around the entrance of the mine.

For an hour, Marigold sat, while they worked. Shaun and Sesame had joined in the rescue efforts. And when the big man disappeared through the dark hole that had been made, Marigold stood to protest.

She remained standing, with Juniper at her side, holding her hand. And the slaves stood back, silent and watchful.

The wind increased, soaring through the bare-branched limbs on the hillside, and overhead, the black crows flew. A cloud passed over the sun and then the wind died—almost as if it too had stopped to watch and listen.

An eternity passed, with life and time suspended, before Shaun came out of the mine. In his arms he carried the limp body of Crane Caldwell.

Marigold, seeing Shaun, gave a cry of relief. Juniper, mistaking the meaning, clasped the girl to her mammoth bosom, as if to protect her from seeing too much.

Crane was dead. Caught in his own trap, he had not been able to escape. Shaun, leaning over to cover the man with the tarpaulin, saw the locket in his hand. The auburn-haired man removed it and put it in his pocket to return to its rightful owner.

Late the next afternoon, Shaun sat in the parlor with Marigold, the fire on the hearth still unable to take away the cold.

"You have everything you need?" he asked.

"Yes."

They waited for Sesame to bring the carriage to the front. She had no wish to remain at Cedar Hill another minute. And Shaun had been kind enough to offer to escort her back to Charleston to her parents.

He looked at the girl in the pale green silk dress and he seemed satisfied. But Marigold was embarrassed. Her swollen breasts made a mockery of the neckline, and the material over her rounded stomach was tight, emphasizing her condition. But Shaun had instructed her to take nothing from the plantation that Crane had given her. "You will take no more than you came with, Marigold," he had said. "This part of your life is finished, and you need no reminders of your unhappiness."

He held the black bombazine cloak for her—the one she had wrapped herself in that night in the garden when she had waited for Shaun in vain—and its dark fabric against her golden curls presented a exotic picture.

Down past the long row of cedars the carriage traveled —and not once did Marigold look back. She expected the carriage to proceed to the river, but instead, it turned and headed in the other direction—the longer way.

With a questioning look, Marigold met Shaun's eyes. In answer to her silent question, he said, "I have business to attend to. It will not take long."

In a half hour, they had come to the little stone church a short distance from the village. The church was round— built that way to keep the devil from the corners. The black carriage came to a stop and Shaun turned to Marigold.

"I cannot be bothered with social customs," he informed her. "You need a man to take care of you, especially in the next few months. And I might as well start now, as your husband. Hurry up, or we shall ruin the parson's supper."

He held his hand for her, but she drew back. "Shaun, you couldn't possibly wish to marry me," she said incredulously.

"And why not?"

"Docia Henley's waiting in Charleston."

"And what has that to do with *us*, Souci?"

"You love her."

"Have I ever said so?"

"Well, no—not in actual words."

"Then—"

"I can't marry you, Shaun."

The man frowned. "Does it bother you what people will say if they discover you have taken another husband while the first one is being buried?"

"No. It's not that."

"Then what is keeping you from going into the church with me?"

"It's what the parson will think," she blurted out, "seeing me like this." She stared down at the tight dress she was wearing—at her stomach that advertised her advanced pregnancy.

Shaun's eyes were amused. "He will think we have waited far too long as it is."

Not knowing whether to cry with joy or embarrassment, Marigold went with Shaun. His commanding height and air of authority sent the sexton immediately to fetch the parson. In a flurried manner, the little man appeared, buttoning his black frock coat and smoothing the few strands of hair that adhered to the top of his head. Looking over the glasses, he said, "My wife will be along presently, to serve as witness."

When Shaun and Marigold stood at the altar, she kept on her bombazine cloak as the service began.

"Is there—er—any reason why the two of you should not be joined in marriage?" the embarrassed clergyman asked.

"No. None," Shaun replied.

"Yes. Well—er—"

The parson's eyes avoided looking at Marigold after the initial shock. He hurried through the ritual in the prayer book, and in five minutes, Shaun and Marigold were husband and wife.

"My son," the parson whispered to Shaun as they were leaving, "you have done the right thing."

34

Shaun treated her tenderly, seeing to her comfort as they stopped at the inns along the way to Charleston. Cold November wind whipped in from the sea as they reached the battery, and the townhouse that had once belonged to Robert Tabor welcomed then.

"We're home, Marigold," Shaun said, touching her shoulder. But she did not respond. The man smiled and, gathering up the girl in his arms, he carried her from the carriage to the door.

"Welcome home, Mr. Shaun," the black man said, holding a lamp at the entrance to light the man's way.

"Thank you, Jake," Shaun replied. "If you will light the way to the guest room, we will put Mrs. Banagher in there for the night."

Jake's eyes widened at Shaun's revelation. He looked at the sleeping girl and back to the giant of a man. But he asked no questions. It would not be appropriate for him to do so. But he knew that Crane Caldwell was no longer a threat. And he breathed easier.

That night the winter storm began, blowing in from the ocean—the white-foamed, angry waves battering against the seawall, the cold rain pelting the roof of the house, and the strong gale swinging the shutters against the windows.

The banging awoke the girl and she sat up. In the light of the soft embers still glowing in the fireplace, Marigold saw the tall posts of the unfamiliar mahogany bed—the same one from which Shaun had so angrily dragged her the morning after her hurried trip from Cedar Hill. And here she was, in it again. But she had been put there by Shaun—the man she loved. She was no longer wife to Crane Caldwell.

All at once, the enormity of her deed hit her. She had

married Shaun, even though she was soon to bear another man's child. She had been completely selfish, thinking only of her own need, not Shaun's. The girl began to shake. Not once had Shaun professed his love for her, nor given any explanation for his backing out of marrying her the first time.

Marigold began to fear that Shaun had married her out of pity—not love. And the disturbing thought kept her awake for much of the night.

Her face was drawn and her tawny eyes mirrored her distress as she sat the next morning huddled by the fireplace and drank the hot tea that Jake had made for her. There was no other woman in the house, no servants. Just Jake, and now, Sesame. Marigold had no one to help her, to turn to. Shaun had not even felt it necessary to tell her goodbye. He had gone for the day to attend to his affairs. She was left alone.

But not for long. The knocker on the front door vibrated from a vigorous hand, and Marigold wondered who could be calling at such an early hour. She heard the voices downstairs and realized whoever it was, was coming upstairs, despite Jake's protest.

"That's all right, Jake," the girl's voice said, rising above the landing. "Mr. Banagher sent me. I'm sure Mrs. Banagher will be glad to see me."

Marigold recognized the high-pitched voice of Docia Henley.

"Marigold," the girl called out, knocking at the bedroom door. "It's Docia. May I come in?"

Marigold was tempted to ask her to go away. But that would not do. Sighing, she said, "Yes, Docia. The door isn't locked."

The girl was dressed in a fashionable blue velvet cape, and tiny pointed black shoes peeked from underneath her skirts. Her immaculate appearance caused Marigold to pull her woolen robe closer to her body and run her fingers through a tangled mass of golden curls.

"My, you do look tired, Marigold," the girl said. "But I guess that's to be expected, traveling in your delicate condition."

Getting no answer, she continued in her airy, high-pitched voice. "Mama says you're in disgrace for the way you married Shaun. But I told her you were never one for convention and she agreed. . . . But since Shaun and Papa are business partners, I told Shaun I would be glad to come and see you, Marigold. He seemed to think you might need cheering."

"That was . . . kind of you, Docia, to come," Marigold said, forcing herself to be polite.

"Really though, Marigold. Do you think it was fair to Shaun to marry him when you're expecting Crane's baby?"

Marigold had already chastised herself for that very reason, but hearing Docia say it brought out a sudden perversity.

"How do you know it's Crane's, Docia?" she asked with a bland expression in her topaz eyes.

The shock registered in Docia's face. "You don't mean —you can't mean that . . . that the baby is Shaun's?" The girl blushed and quickly looked down at her shoes.

"Would you like a cup of tea, Docia?" Marigold asked, changing the subject without answering.

"No—thank you. Suzie is waiting downstairs for me. I must be going." The shocked look remained on the girl's face as Marigold walked to the bedroom door with her.

"I . . . I can let myself out, Marigold. I know you have to watch the stairs."

The girl fled down the steps, and Marigold went back to her cup of tea and brioche, suddenly feeling much better.

Marigold had barely managed to dress before she had another visitor. This time it was someone she longed to see—her own mother.

"Souci, *mon enfant*," the woman said, taking the girl in her arms.

"Maman," the girl replied. "Oh, how I have wanted you, Maman." She had kept the tears back for so long, but now she was a child again, needing comfort. Marigold began to weep, and her mother murmured soothing words, giving her daughter time to release her pent-up emotions.

295

Finally, Marigold lifted her head and said, "Is Papa very angry with me, Maman, for marrying Shaun?"

"He does not know yet, Souci. Your papa is still in Columbia at the nullification convention. I am sure he will not be happy that you have flaunted tradition. But it's too late to do anything about it." Eulalie smiled and said, "But we must not stand here and waste time. I brought Callie with me so that she can help you pack. If you will show her . . ."

"Pack?" Marigold repeated. "Why?"

"Shaun wants you to be at Midgard for the next few months. He thinks you will be safer there."

Marigold was frightened. Why was Shaun sending her away? Was he already regretting his hasty decision to marry her?

Seeing the bleak look on her daughter's face, Eulalie said, "Souci, Charleston is in an uproar, getting ready to defend itself. President Jackson has declared the action in Columbia treasonous, and his troops and ships are on their way to Charleston Harbor."

"Papa and the others vetoed the tariffs?"

"*Oui, ma petite.* The ordinance they passed prohibits the customs officials from collecting the tariffs. And if President Jackson attempts to use armed force, then we will be absolved from the other twenty-three states. It is a precipitous situation, Souci. President Jackson has called the delegates 'traitors' and has vowed to hang each one from the nearest tree."

"Not Papa. He can't hang Papa," Marigold said, upset over the news.

She had little to pack. Putting on her black cape, Marigold walked to the waiting carriage. With Callie and her mother, she traveled down the street, away from the Palladian-design house. Along the battery, men were already at work, stacking bags of sand and bales of cotton high along the wall.

The political controversy was grave. By the first week in December 1832, John C. Calhoun had resigned as Vice-President of the United States and returned to his native Carolina. The state legislature met and promptly elected him a senator, to take his seat in Washington after the Christmas holidays.

Robert Tabor, coming home from Columbia, said little to Marigold about her marriage to Shaun. He seemed to be preoccupied with the delicate political situation and voiced his concern to Eulalie.

"I have never before been impatient for Christmas holidays to end," he said, "but this impasse hanging over us makes me wish for January immediately."

"Is it because of Monsieur Calhoun?" Eulalie asked.

"Yes. No one knows what President Jackson will do when John goes back to Washington. It doesn't help matters that Jackson has just discovered that when John was Secretary of War he voted to censure him for his unauthorized military foray into Florida in '17. Some think he will allow the man to take his seat in the Senate, but there are just as many who feel sure John will be arrested for treason the minute he reaches the city."

"If there is such danger for him, then why did the man agree to go back?" Eulalie asked.

"Because he believes this issue has got to be settled, one way or another. A nation can't trample on the rights of some of its people and expect them to remain silent. If we are not allowed to veto an act that is unconstitutional and detrimental, then he fears for the Union."

A seamstress, sent by Shaun, came to Midgard to sew new dresses for Marigold, a welcome diversion from all the political talk around her.

The materials were beautiful—the rich, warm velvets, the heavy crepes. It was a shame that her figure would not do justice to them.

Madame Reynaud did not act surprised to see Marigold. She said nothing about the girl's previous visit to her workroom with Crane, nor about the dresses of white that she had made up for her. She merely draped and pinned and cut the materials to Marigold's full figure and then handed them to the two girls she had brought with her.

"Do not worry, *ma petite*," the French woman finally

297

said to Marigold. "I have a way of disguising the fullness in front. You will look very fashionable, and your husband will be proud of you, *chérie*."

"Then, that would be a miracle indeed, Madame," Marigold replied.

The woman chuckled and went about her work, humming under her breath. She matched a gold and green brocade ribbon to the cape of lime green velvet. As she pinned it, she said, "Monsieur specifically wished you to have the cape in this color. It will go well with the green crepe dress, as well as the gold one to match your eyes. But it seems, Monsieur is partial to shades of green."

Marigold smiled, remembering the first dress he had purchased for her—and how he had insisted she wear it the day he had taken her to the little stone church.

"The memories are pleasant, Madame?" the woman asked, with a knowing smile.

Startled, Marigold looked at the little gray-haired woman. "I was remembering another dress of the same color," she confessed.

Two days later, the hooded cape and finished dresses hung in the armoire of Marigold's room. She decided upon impulse to dress in the new clothes that morning. And her heart was suddenly happy.

Although she would not be seen by anyone but her family, she took great care with her hair, plaiting it with brocade ribbon to match that of her cape. In the dress, gathered high under her breasts, she resembled the girl in the Botticelli paintings. Marigold looked in the mirror and decided she could easily have stepped from some ancient Renaissance castle. What a pity that Shaun would not see her in the dress, for she was rather pleased with the miracle that Madame Reynaud had accomplished.

By early afternoon, Marigold was restless, having stayed inside the entire morning. Taking the cape, Marigold put it on and walked outside. The day was sunny and mild, and soon, she found herself on the path to the river house.

Down past the fallow fields she walked, past the fence and toward the river where the great cottonwoods towered.

She came to the maze of yew hedge and honeysuckle that surrounded the small house. It was not quite so green as in summer. Standing on the tiny porch, she looked in the window at the deserted parlor. The door was unlocked, and on an impulse, Marigold pushed it open. This was the house where she and Maranta had taken their dolls to play under Feena's watchful eye for hours at a time. The house had a certain warmth, a hospitality that the larger house did not possess. She did not know why, but everytime she walked inside, she felt a wealth of love. And it was the same today. Had anyone ever lived in it? she wondered.

Marigold remembered the time she had wanted to move into it herself, but her parents had not allowed it. If she had been a boy, it would have been all right—

The sunlight dazzled through the windows, and Marigold became lost in her dreams. The sound of footsteps on the porch alerted her to another's presence. Who had followed her? Robbie?

As the door opened, Marigold turned. "Souci," a voice called out. And she saw her husband before her.

She smiled and started toward him. "No," he said. "Stand where you are for a moment—in the sunlight."

She stopped and waited while his eyes traveled over her. "Now, remove the cape," he said. Mesmerised by his look, his emerald eyes staring into hers, she obeyed, dropping the cape over a chair.

The swell of her breasts was emphasized by Madame Reynaud's couture hand, while her rounded stomach was hidden under the voluminous folds.

"Souci," he said, with longing in his voice. His boots made a noise across the bare floor as he came to her.

In an instant, she was in his arms. His lips moved over her eyelids, kissing her cheeks on their way to her mouth. Her breath came in short gasps while he parted her lips and explored with his tongue.

Before she knew it, they were in the bedroom, on the bed, and she was encircled by his strong arms. Her dress was unhooked and his hands caressed her flesh. Her nipples became taut with longing.

299

Only in her dreams had they been together this way. Marigold strained against him, until the roundness of her stomach came between them. Shaun sat up slowly. Breathing heavily, he whispered, "Oh, God, Souci. How I wish you were not with child." He ran his fingers through his auburn hair, and in a stern voice he said, "Fasten your dress."

With trembling hands, the girl attempted to right the dress, while Shaun walked away from her, not offering to help her.

"Your mother is looking for you," the man said from a distance, not turning his head. "I think you had better go back to the house."

The girl's face was pale. Shaun walked rapidly out of the dense thicket surrounding the river house, seeming not to care that Marigold could not keep up with him.

What Crane had said was true. She *was* a wanton. And even Shaun was disgusted with her, with her lack of control. She had invited his caresses, even in her condition. But worst of all, she had heard what she feared most. Her child was not welcome in their marriage.

With pain-filled eyes, Marigold followed the path back to the house. Shaun had not even waited for her.

The sound of laughter in the drawing room greeted her. The high-pitched voice of Docia Henley penetrated the room, and Marigold, recognizing it, turned to go up to her room. But her mother, walking toward the drawing room, looked up and saw her. "Oh there you are, Souci," she called out. "I was hoping you would come back soon. Shaun and Docia are here."

"If you will excuse me, Maman, I am not feeling well. Please give my apologies to them."

Eulalie walked swiftly toward her daughter and with a worried glance, took in the girl's pale face, her trembling hands. "What is the matter, Souci?"

"I think I should not have walked so far this afternoon."

Eulalie reached out to help her daughter up the stairs, but Marigold shook her head. "I can manage alone, Maman. You need not neglect your guests because of me."

300

"Shaun is hardly a guest, *mon enfant*. He is your husband. I am certain that he will be distressed, as I am, that you are not feeling well."

Marigold went to her room and when she reached it, she tore off the green cape and the crepe dress and removed the brocade ribbon from her hair. Taking the unflattering old woolen robe from the armoire, she slipped into it and then climbed into bed. Suddenly cold, she began to shiver. But she did not call for a servant to light the fire. Later, when Shaun and Docia had gone—

So he was still seeing her. Perhaps it was just as well then. If he still wished to marry her, it was not too late. Marigold would give Shaun his freedom. It had been a mistake to marry him so hastily. She should have known he would resent the child.

Marigold didn't know when her love for her baby had begun to develop. Certainly she hadn't felt it at first, not even when Feena had talked with her about it. It could have been in the mine—when she had thought the baby was going to die with her. Yes, she supposed that was when she first began to feel the gradual acceptance that she was to be a mother, and the protective feeling for her child.

Cedar Hill was her baby's inheritance. But could she bring herself to go back there? To rear the child where she had been so unhappy?

Marigold closed her eyes and drifted to sleep. Later, when she awoke, she heard the fire crackling in the hearth and felt the warmth in the room. Someone had come in while she was asleep, and she was grateful.

Shaun leaned over to put another log on the fire and, seeing him, Marigold frowned. "I thought you had gone," she said.

"Are you feeling better?" he asked.

"Yes, thank you."

He came to her bed and stared down at her. "Marigold, I want to apologize for my behavior this afternoon. I don't know what came over me." His emerald eyes showed pain, and Marigold, seeing this, sat up.

Her voice was distressed. "We should never have gotten

married, Shaun. But it isn't too late to do something about it. I'm sure it can be annulled, especially since . . ."

His eyes kindled in anger, negating any pain that she had seen. "You expect me to leave you, now all of Charleston knows why we got married so suddenly?"

"I don't understand, Shaun."

"Don't act the innocent little girl, Marigold. Didn't you tell Docia the child is mine—not Crane's?"

Marigold blushed. "Is that what she told you?"

"Docia doesn't discuss such delicate matters with me. She merely repeated what you had said to her mother, and a few days ago Fess Henley took me aside and said I had done the honorable thing. So you see why it is impossible for me to back out now. No, my girl. You are married to me, regardless of the way you feel. And we will stay married."

"I am sorry, Shaun."

"So am I."

35

Down to the falls of Hitû they went—as Ruis had promised—to view the special offering by the slaves to the "mother of rivers and waters," the goddess, Iemanjá.

It was New Year's Eve, and Maranta and Dona Isobel rode in the palanquin, while Ruis and Vasco were on horseback.

Maranta was surprised to see Vasco astride a horse. The entire time she had lived on the *fazenda,* she had never seen him attempt to ride. He must have practiced without anyone's knowing, except for Patû. He would have needed the Indian's help in getting into the saddle and being strapped down.

Vasco handled the horse well. Over the past months his arms had become powerful—not unusual for one who had lost the use of his legs. Riding directly behind him was Patû, as always, silent and enigmatic.

The terraced slopes were lit by torches at various points along the way. And the pathway was crowded. It seemed that nearly all the slaves were taking part in the ritual. Maranta looked back toward the *fazenda.* Naka and a few Indians had remained behind at the plantation house to watch over little Paulo.

Maranta was uneasy about leaving the baby. But, of course, it would not do to take him out into the night air. He was safer with Naka in the nursery.

"This ritual," Maranta said, speaking to Dona Isobel. "You have seen it before?"

"Many times, Maranta. Even though it's quite pagan, it's a beautiful sight, especially when the candles and flowers are carried over the falls. And it is breathtaking in Rio by the sea, with the white sand and the snowy tablecloths covered with colorful gifts. Perhaps you will have an opportunity to see it sometime when you visit the royal court." The roar of the falls grew louder, making conversation difficult.

A large canopy had already been spread on the bank overlooking the falls. It was a pavilion suitable for a king, set up for their comfort, with cushions in place.

Deeming it rude to stare, Maranta did not watch as Patû helped Vasco from the horse. She took her place in the pavilion and turned to watch the slaves gathering.

The women, dressed and decorated in their finest clothes, laid out their gifts upon the banks. As they began to sing and to chant and move in rhythm to the chanting, the sound rose over the noise of the falls.

Staring at the foaming waters that rushed to cascade down the steep ravine, Maranta said, "The falls look extremely dangerous. Has anyone ever gone over them?"

Beside her, Ruis replied, "One fellow did—several years ago. But he had been drinking too much *aguardente*. It was his own fault."

"Did they . . . find him?"

"No, Maranta. But you are not to think of such unpleasantness. You are supposed to be enjoying the celebration."

Vasco, now seated on the other side of Maranta, said, "This is a mere trickle, dear wife, in comparison to Iguaçu Falls in the Paraná. It plunges over two hundred feet straight down and even carries huge trees over the precipice."

"Then I am glad we are not at Iguaçu. This place looks dangerous enough to me."

Despite the gaiety, Maranta felt there was something menacing in the waters that foamed and rushed to disappear over the abrupt precipice.

"Look, Maranta," Dona Isobel said. "They are lighting their candles. Soon it will be time."

"Offerings for a beautiful woman," Vasco commented. "The river is the same, waiting to take anything offered to her. Do you have something you wish to contribute, Maranta, so that the goddess can smile on you for the new year?" he asked.

304

"No, I have brought nothing with me."

"What about the comb in your hair? Iemanjá might be content with that."

"Do not tease her, Vasco," Ruis warned. "She is not at home with our pagan ways."

Vasco laughed and turned to Dona Isobel. "What about you, Dona Isobel? Do you not wish to appease the goddess? Isn't there some sin you wish the 'mother of waters' to forgive?"

Dona Isobel's mouth tightened. "No. Nothing," she said, glaring at Vasco.

Maranta caught sight of Sassia among the dancers. All at once, she was not the civilized young girl Maranta had known back at the *fazenda*. She was transformed by the vibrant, throbbing rhythm of the music. In a primitive ritual, she moved and swayed and chanted. Maranta kept her eyes on Sassia when the signal was given.

At midnight the sirens and bells sounded. And the shrieking began. The river was suddenly filled with rushing figures, surrounded by chains of candles, offerings swiftly rushing toward the falls. The celebrants followed to a certain point and then stopped to watch, while Iemanjá took their offerings, sweeping them over the falls and out of sight.

The ceremony was over. The people climbed out of the river. Iemanjá had been appeased for another year.

Maranta and Dona Isobel climbed back into the palanquin. As they retraced the route to the *fazenda,* the torches were extinguished along the way, one by one. Maranta took a last glance toward the falls. She could not see it, but the roaring sound of the waters stayed with her far into the night and invaded her dreams.

The night was significant for another reason. Maranta had never left little Paulo for even that short a time before. Going immediately to the nursery, she saw her son had been well cared for in her absence. The wet nurse was feeding him, and she watched for a moment, seeing his little hands curled in pleasure at having his appetite satisfied. Breast-feeding had been denied her because of her illness. Except for holding him and loving him, she realized the child could well do without her. And that knowledge hurt her.

When several months passed and Innocencia's brothers did not return to the *fazenda,* Maranta finally relaxed. Sometimes, she wondered if that frightening episode had ever taken place except in her mind—the men bursting into her room and the angry words spoken by Ruis.

The warm season gave way to winter, with a chill in the air and a promise of frost, the enemy of the tender coffee plants. Maranta could tell that Ruis was worried about the crop. He seemed preoccupied at dinner, and his face showed the strain of long hours of work and worry. But the weather cleared and the danger disappeared. The snowy white blossoms on the slopes turned into berries, and the waiting for their harvest began.

During this waiting period, Ruis decided they should go to São Paulo. "I have business in the city," he said, "that I have put off far too long. And while we are there, we might as well stay for the Intrudo season."

Dona Isobel spoke. "Then you intend for us to travel with you, Ruis?"

"Yes, Isobel. I think Maranta would enjoy seeing the festivities. The last trip was not a particularly pleasant one for her."

"I don't understand. What is this Intrudo?" Maranta asked.

"It is similar to Carnival in Rio," Dona Isobel explained. "It's the time of gay festivities and parties before Lent."

Maranta nodded. "Like Mardi Gras in New Orleans."

"Of course, only the rough elements roam the streets, throwing flour on each other. We will avoid that part and attend the private parties instead," Isobel finished explaining.

Ruis, looking at his brother, said, "And it will be good to have you also, Vasco. It is past time for you to visit the city again."

Ruis's words brought displeasure to Vasco. He frowned

and said, "No, Ruis. I will never go back to São Paulo to be stared at and pitied. You will have to go without me."

Ruis's lips tightened. "I will not force you, Vasco. But your friends in the city will miss seeing you."

"I have no friends," he answered bitterly.

Ruis changed the subject.

Preparations were made for the trip with the canoe fleet. Maranta and Dona Isobel spent the rest of the week seeing to the packing of clothes and other necessities. Vasco, still adamant, elected to remain at the *fazenda*.

On their last evening before leaving, Dona Isobel retired early for the night, and Vasco disappeared to his own apartments on the first floor as soon as dinner was over.

Maranta paced up and down in her bedroom. She could not go to sleep for thinking of her baby. It had been a wrench to leave him just for one evening. But to be gone at least a month—he was growing so fast, Maranta wondered if she would recognize him when she returned. Worse, he might have forgotten her. He was just now beginning to smile and follow her with his eyes when she was in the room, and to gurgle when she held him.

Maranta released her long, black, silken hair from the confinement of her combs and brushed it vigorously. The long white embroidered robe that she had worn when she was pregnant was more comfortable than the gowns and peignoirs that she had brought with her from Charleston. She stared in the mirror. Her figure had changed, taking on a more womanly shape after the birth of Paulo. Now, her gowns were too tight across her breasts. But she had not mentioned the problem to anyone. She did not want to ask Vasco for money to replenish her wardrobe. But neither did she feel she could request it of Ruis. Her position was too awkward.

Suddenly wanting to take one last look at little Paulo, Maranta left her apartment and silently walked down the deserted hall to the nursery.

When she entered, the lamp was burning low on the table. Maranta tiptoed to the ornate crib. Paulo was awake.

He gave her a toothless grin, and she could not resist taking him up to hold in her arms. It would be such a long time before she saw him again.

"Paulo," she whispered, "I love you." She bent down to kiss him, and he grabbed a handful of her hair, pulling it to his mouth.

Behind her, a voice said, "He is a true Monteiro male, is he not?—reaching out for what he wants."

A large brown hand removed Maranta's hair from the baby's grasp, and when she was free, Maranta gazed into the amused dark eyes of Ruis.

"I was . . . saying goodbye, since we leave so early in the morning," Maranta apologized.

A tender look replaced the amusement in Ruis's face. "There is no need to explain, *menina*. Is it not a mother's right to hold her son whenever she wishes?"

"It will be such a long time . . ."

"I know, Maranta. And I, too, will miss seeing him." Ruis stared at the child in Maranta's arms, and he reached out to touch the baby's plump cheek.

The man was too close. A breathlessness came over Maranta. She placed the child again in his crib and turned to leave. "Good night, Ruis," she said, trying to escape.

"I will walk with you to your apartment," he said, closing the nursery door behind him.

Maranta hurried along the corridor. "You have everything packed?" Ruis asked when they neared the sitting room door.

"Yes."

Maranta stopped and waited for Ruis to open the door. Instead, he took her hand in his and drew it to his lips. Maranta trembled. In the dim, deserted hall they stood, staring at each other. The tension was more than Maranta could bear. His fingers caressed her arm in a sensuous motion.

"Maranta," he whispered, moving toward her. Afraid her heart would give her away, she moaned and stepped back. Ruis, seeing her recoil at his touch, took his hand from her arm.

"Good night, Maranta."

He left her at the door and walked rapidly down the hall.

Sassia came into the bedroom with the breakfast tray in her hands before dawn. "Senhora, it is time to get up," she said, standing by the bed.

Maranta stirred but did not waken.

"Senhora," Sassia called again. "Dom Ruis is almost ready to leave."

The words woke her, and Maranta sat up, brushing her long hair from her face and yawning. Ruis would be impatient to start, just as he had been at the port of Santos. How could she forget? She must not keep him waiting for her. The candle flame sputtered before turning into a steady glow at Maranta's touch.

"I'll have breakfast in the sitting room, Sassia," she said, slipping into the robe and walking barefoot over the furry white carpet with the candlestick in her hand. The black girl followed and placed the tray on the table beside the lilac sofa.

By the light of the candle, Maranta sipped the hot tea and ate a slice of melon. She left the corn cakes on her plate and returned to the bedroom to wash her face and put on her traveling dress and cape with the servant's help.

Soon she was ready, and her excitement at the trip vied with her reluctance to leave little Paulo. "Sassia, you will help to watch over Paulo while I am gone?"

"Of course, senhora," the girl answered. "Do not worry. Naka and I will watch over him well."

"Thank you," Maranta murmured, taking her reticule in her hands.

She had to have one last quick look at her child to make sure he was all right. Maranta dashed toward the nursery and walked into the room. Paulo was still asleep. She stood gazing down at the baby and a sudden sense of foreboding swept over her.

He was so tiny. Anything could happen to him while she was away. Maranta swallowed and forced back the tears. It was unfair of Ruis to expect her to leave him for an entire month.

She did not have to go to São Paulo. Dona Isobel and Ruis could go on without her; she would stay. Having made up her mind, she hurried out to the *fazenda* steps where the wagon containing their trunks stood.

"Please," she said in her halting Portuguese to the two boys near the wagon. "Will you take my trunk and set it back inside the house?"

Puzzled at her request, the two boys nevertheless took her trunk and carried it up the steps to the veranda just as Ruis walked out of the *sala da entrada*.

"What are you doing?" he asked the boys in a displeased voice.

"The senhora wishes her trunk brought back inside," one boy said, looking toward Maranta and then back to Ruis.

"Return it to the wagon."

"*Sim,* Dom Ruis."

The boys reloaded the trunk while Maranta stared open-mouthed at the arrogant conde. With her skirts rustling from her rapid steps, she approached him.

"I have changed my mind, Ruis. I am not going to São Paulo."

His sapphire eyes in the early morning sun sparked with anger. "It is too late, *menina,* for you to change your mind. The arrangements have already been made."

"But I do not wish to leave little Paulo . . ."

"You are using him as an excuse, Maranta. Doctor Cavales will come to the *fazenda* each week while we are away to check on the child. And the padre will be here the entire time." Ruis's anger increased and his words were sharp. "I think there is another reason for this sudden attempt to back out. I believe you are afraid."

"Afraid? Of what, Ruis? Of the river, of the bats or the snakes?" She gazed at the *muçurana* that lay in a coil by the steps, and she shuddered, remembering her narrow escape from the *jararaca.*

"I believe you are more afraid of *me,*" he accused. "of having to share your bed with me again—particularly after last night. But let me assure you, Maranta. If I should feel the need of taking a wench to bed, there will be many from the finest families in São Paulo, willing to accommodate me."

Maranta was so furious at his words, she dared not speak. She flounced down to the waiting palanquin and climbed in, turning her back to Ruis, while the boys secured her trunk on the wagon.

Shane took the key to the desk and unlocked the lower drawer. Removing a set of blueprints, he spread them on the desk and studied them, a satisfied expression on his face.

Every few minutes Maranta glanced toward her husband. He seemed to be in an unusually good mood despite his secretive manner.

For an hour they traveled straight down the road. The

36

At the *fazenda,* Vasco sat in his apartment, holding the baby that he acknowledged publicly as his own. Maranta and Dona Isobel and Ruis had been gone on their journey to São Paulo for only three days.

Floresta's dark eyes glowered at the sight of Vasco with the baby, Paulo, in his arms. He had never shown such attention to Tefe, his own son.

"He looks like me, don't you think, Floresta?" Vasco said. "No one would ever suspect that I am not the father."

"You deceive yourself, Vasco, if you think your brother is going to let you play the role of father to Paulo much longer."

"What are you insinuating, Floresta?"

"Dom Ruis will get rid of you just as he did Innocencia. And then he will make Senhora Maranta his wife."

"You are stupid, woman. Ruis would not kill me —his own brother."

The Indian girl sneered. "Did brotherhood stop *you,* Vasco, from trying to murder Dom Ruis that day of your accident?"

Vasco's face showed his annoyance at the girl's words, but she continued. "If you had seen your brother in the nursery with the senhora the night before they left, you would have no doubt he wants her. Dom Ruis will soon claim your wife, Vasco, as surely as he will claim his own son—and you will be left with nothing."

Vasco took the rattle from little Paulo's hands and hurled it at Floresta. She ducked and ran laughing from the room.

The baby began to cry, and in a fit of temper, Vasco shouted, "Naka, take this bawling brat back to the nursery."

Once planted, the seed began to grow in Vasco's mind.

313

He brooded over Floresta's words. She was right—Ruis had always been the lucky one. Even that day on the pampas, as they were driving the cattle to Sorocaba.

It had looked so easy, with Ruis in such a vulnerable position, apart from the rest. Vasco's shoulders moved in pain as he remembered. The sudden appearance of the gauchos, diverting the stampede from their master—almost like guardian angels appearing from nowhere—forcing the herd in the opposite direction.

Ironically, what he had intended for Ruis became his own destiny—to be knocked from his horse and trampled underfoot. And the ultimate disgrace had been to have Ruis come to his rescue.

Vasco stared down at his useless legs and recalled, with bitterness, his aborted effort to rid himself of his brother.

No, Ruis would not have it all his way. He had been the powerful one far too long. But now Vasco realized the vast power he held in his own hands to make Ruis suffer. He would never give up Maranta to him. And as for the child—

With a satanic expression, Vasco wheeled his chair onto the veranda and sat, staring in the direction of the river falls.

The sound of the rapids broke upon the idyllic peace of the day. Maranta reluctantly gathered the black cape around her and prepared to leave the canoe. It was so much more pleasant on the water than sitting in a jolting cart, riding the rough trail alongside the river until it became navigable again. But even with the roughness, this trip was much more sociable than the last; other women were also traveling to São Paulo to take part in the Intrudo.

The women had all mistaken Maranta for Dom Ruis's wife, which embarrassed her. When she tried to explain, Dom Ruis interferred. "It is safer for you, *pequena,* if these people think you have a jealous husband to protect you. I am not sure that you would be safe, even with Dona Isobel sleeping by your side. The men are much too bold as it is." Ruis's eyes narrowed. "I had not realized that the child has turned into a woman. We will have to do something about your clothes, Maranta, when we reach São Paulo."

Embarrassed at his attention, Maranta drew the black cape about her, as if to ward off his penetrating stare.

The journey on the river finally came to an end, as the mighty Tietê subsided into a huge lake outside São Paulo. Before evening, Maranta, with Ruis and Dona Isobel, traveled up the Avenida Paulista to the tall iron gates encrusted with the Monteiro family coat-of-arms.

In early morning, Ruis set out to put his business affairs in order, leaving Maranta and Dona Isobel alone in the *casa,* to spend the day recuperating from the exhausting trip.

The older woman remained in her room for the entire day, but though she slept late, Maranta was ready to get up by eleven. Pará, the Indian girl, brought a breakfast tray to her room, and soon Maranta left the confines of the bedroom.

The *casa* was even more magnificent than Maranta remembered. Memories of the first trip returned, and as she explored the *casa,* she found herself before the door of the chapel. It was closed.

She reached out to the double doors and pressed the handle. Slowly the door opened with a faint squeak, as if it had been closed for a long time. Inside, it was dark. No candle burned near the altar. And judging from the dust, no prayers had been said in the chapel for a long time.

The chapel contained ghosts from the past, rising up to haunt her. Ruis—with his terrible anger—glaring at her with the cross at her breast. The condessa—ill with her heart malady—

"Forgive her," Maranta prayed, kneeling in front of the unlit altar and oblivious to the dust and stuffiness of the chapel.

For so long she had carried the burden of the vision engraved on her mind—the old condessa with the sweet

315

cakes in her unsteady hand, offering them to Innocencia—
the poisoned cakes that had removed danger from Maranta and her unborn son.

The condessa had not known that Maranta was standing at the other door. No one else had seen the woman, she felt sure, for Dona Louisa had used the secret carved panel to slip from the nursery back to her room. And it was only later, when Innocencia was dead, that the condessa's actions took on a special significance.

Maranta vowed she would never tell anyone about the condessa, no matter what happened. She would save Ruis from the pain of learning his own mother had murdered his mad wife so that his son would be safe from harm.

Paulo. How she missed him. Maranta now felt impatience for Ruis to complete his business, and for the Intrudo to be done with, so they could all return to the *fazenda*.

Her clothes did not reveal that she was in mourning. Dom Ruis dismissed Maranta's objections to the beautiful, frivolous Parisian fashions he had ordered in the deep, rich hues that so enhanced her coloring.

"Mãe knows that you grieve in your heart for her, Maranta," he said in a gruff voice. "It is not necessary to proclaim it to others in the drabness of your clothes." Yet, both he and Dona Isobel were clothed in black.

They started out in the family carriage that had once brought Maranta from Santos over the Serra do Mar to this city of São Paulo. It was early evening and the Intrudo had begun.

Avoiding the crowds that had started to gather in the streets, the driver controlled the nervous horses and headed for the *casa* of friends, where they were to spend the evening.

Maranta felt self-conscious in the new slate-blue silk dress, with the gigantic *gigot* sleeves falling from the shoulders to the narrowed wrists. Her shoulders were bare and revealed far more expanse of creamy skin than she liked. But Dona Isobel had approved earlier when she was getting dressed.

"You are a married woman, Maranta," she had said,

"and you are now allowed to wear dresses that would not be considered appropriate for a senhorita."

In the carriage, Dona Isobel glanced at Maranta with pride and said, "Maranta looks quite lovely tonight. Do you not think so, Ruis?"

He looked at Maranta and then at the older woman. "I think you are both very elegant tonight, Isobel."

Dona Isobel, smiling at the compliment, patted the black lace of her own new dress and settled back in the carriage.

If anyone were truly elegant, it was Dom Ruis, Maranta thought. Seated beside him, she was very much aware of his aristocratic bearing and the fine cut of his black evening clothes.

Reaching their destination, Maranta was nervous at first. But the extreme kindness of the Almeidas helped her to relax. The affair was a small, intimate gathering—much like one within her own family circle in Charleston—with the family priest, the favorite uncle, and the daughters of the house. If one of them lapsed into Portuguese for too long a time, the host would respond in English in deference to Maranta. Yet, she was able to follow the conversation more easily than she had imagined.

Seated across from Ruis, Maranta looked up to see his amused glance as she was served the first course. Ruis leaned forward and whispered, "Be careful of the soup, Maranta. It's very hot."

Maranta glanced at Ruis and back down at the steaming soup plate. When all were served, she lifted the round spoon and took a careful sip. But the second the mixture reached her throat, Maranta realized she had misinterpreted Ruis's warning.

She gasped for air and reached for the goblet of water before her to drown the burning in her throat. Everyone at the table was amused.

"Did I not warn you, *pequena*," Ruis said, "of our famous Intrudo soup?"

"I didn't understand," she apologized, taking another swallow of water, "that you meant 'hot' with peppers and spices."

"My apologies, senhora," the host said. "We tend to forget how startling it must be to one not accustomed to our ways."

"I'll remember next time," Maranta said, managing a smile.

Soon it was time to leave, and the three climbed into the waiting carriage to return to the Monteiro *casa*. The streets were crowded and noisy. Rough horseplay had begun, with people throwing flour on each other, disguising everyone's clothes and faces.

In fascination, Maranta leaned toward the window of the carriage to watch.

"You will soon find your face plastered with the stuff, Maranta, if you are not careful. I am not sure it will complement the rest of your attire," Ruis said.

The carriage was jostled by the surging crowd, and Maranta lost her balance. Ruis reached out to steady her, while his low voice growled an angry epithet. The carriage was surrounded by the unruly crowd, and with a violent shudder, the vehicle suddenly crashed to one side.

"Maranta, are you all right?" Ruis called to the stunned girl who had been slammed to the side of the carriage.

"I . . . think so," she said.

"And you, Isobel?"

"Yes."

Ruis managed to get the door open, and he pulled both women from the wrecked carriage. The horses, frightened by the crowd, were acting up, rearing and snorting. As Ruis went to the driver's aid, he called back over his shoulder, "Isobel, stay on the walkway. Don't get caught up in the crowd."

Dona Isobel reached for Maranta's hand. The curious stared for a moment at the disabled vehicle and at the two women and then drifted on. Suddenly, another wave of humanity descended, jostling and jolting, surging through the streets and engulfing the walkway where the two women stood.

Someone threw flour in Maranta's face, temporarily blinding her. She reached up to wipe her eyes, and at the same time was shoved, torn from Dona Isobel's grasp and

318

caught up in the wild, snakelike movement of the unruly mob.

"Maranta," the woman called out, but when Maranta could finally see, Dona Isobel had vanished. Maranta's elegant new gown was now covered with flour, and she was as anonymous as the others in the crowd.

A tall man beside her grinned and grabbed at her hand. Maranta drew back, suddenly afraid. On and on she was swept away by the crowd, and the distance from the disabled carriage grew greater and greater.

Another man, whom she had seen near the carriage, appeared at her other side, and a sense of something terribly wrong assailed her. It was almost as if her separation from Dona Isobel had been planned.

The stampede was relentless. Maranta twisted and turned in an effort to escape, but the two men at her side blocked the way. As they neared an intersection, a hand clamped over her mouth, shutting off her protest. She was dragged from the crowd to the dark, narrow street at her right. Her muffled cry for help was obliterated by the noise of the revel-makers, and the crowd moved on without her, leaving her in the hands of her abductors.

Despite her struggles to free herself, Maranta was lifted into a waiting carriage in the darkened, narrow street and covered by a heavy shroud that effectively curtailed her cries for help.

Why was she being taken away? Was it for herself? Or was it because of Ruis—because the villains thought to ransom her?

The carriage sped through the night—downhill, it seemed. Soon the noise of the paved streets gave way to the hollow sound of the viaduct, and then to the dull thud of earth beneath the wheels. Away from the *praça,* the Avenida Paulista, and the city of São Paulo, the carriage traveled, taking Maranta to a rendezvous of life-threatening violence.

Dona Isobel wept and twisted the handkerchief in her hands. "It was my fault. I should have held on to her more carefully."

Pará soothed the hysterical woman and gave her the glass of warm milk laced with brandy. "Dom Ruis will find her, senhora. Wait and see."

"But it might be too late," Dona Isobel cried. "O merciful Mother of Heaven, who could have done this? Who has Ruis offended enough to demand this heartbreak for us all? That sweet child has no enemies of her own, now that Innocencia . . ." Isobel's hand crept up to her mouth, and her face turned a sickly shade. "Innocencia's brothers," she whispered to herself and fell into a swoon at Pará's feet.

37

In the garden adjacent to the chapel of the deserted house, the two abductors handed over Maranta to a man whose face was covered by a monk's cowl.

"We will have our money now and be on our way," one of the kidnappers said, glancing uneasily about him.

"How do I know you two idiots haven't abducted the wrong girl? It's impossible to identify her with that mess on her face," the voice growled from behind the priestly garb. "Wait here—until I make sure she is the one we seek."

With a cruel grasp, the man pulled Maranta with him inside the chapel. Holding onto her long, black hair that had become loosened in her struggles, he shoved her face downward into the font of brackish water that had once been holy.

Maranta sputtered as her head came up. She heard the rip of her petticoats and she cried out at the harsh treatment.

"Be quiet," he ordered. And Maranta, trembling, did as she was told. He took the remnant of the petticoat and wiped her face free of the flour mixture.

In the dim light, the man scrutinized her features. "What is your name, senhora?" he demanded.

Her weak voice responded, "M-Maranta. Maranta Tabor."

He laughed at her answer. "Come now, you must have another name, as well. What is it?" he demanded, pulling her hair tighter.

She winced. "Monteiro. I am the wife of . . . Vasco da Monteiro."

Satisfied, he eased his hold on her hair and led her down the steps behind the altar. She screamed as he shoved her inside the cold, dank room. The sound of the key in the rusty lock terrified her. Maranta pushed at the door, but it was no use. She was locked inside a family burial vault with only the bones of untold generations to keep her company.

The two brothers sat at the dining table, leisurely enjoying their late meal and congratulating themselves on their success. Outside the official residence of the magistrate, a ruckus developed, and the brothers frowned at the noise that disturbed the quietness of their evening.

Suddenly confronting them stood Ruis da Monteiro, his dark, aquiline face showing its dangerous mood.

"Brother-in-law," Honório greeted him. "What a surprise to see you. Sit down and have some wine with us."

The man stood up and gestured to an empty chair. "I was just mentioning to Vincente here that I heard you were in São Paulo. We wondered if you would come to see us."

Ruis remained standing, with a hand on the pistol showing from underneath his coat. "Where is she, Honório?" he demanded.

"I have no idea what you're talking about, Ruis," he answered in a mildly censuring tone.

Honório turned to his brother Vincente. "Something seems to be disturbing our brother-in-law. Do you have any idea, Vincente, as to what it might be?"

The amused dark eyes of Vincente, the smaller of the brothers, sparkled. "None whatever, Honório."

"I am not here to play games with you," Ruis responded, with an icy chill to each syllable. "I know you have Maranta, Vasco's wife, and I will not leave without her."

Honório, finally tired of pretending ignorance, said, "You led us to believe that she would never recover from childbed fever, Ruis—after bearing *your* child."

Ruis gave a start. And Honório continued, "Oh, yes. We know that Vasco was incapable of siring the child. Maranta Tabor has borne the heir that, by right, Innocencia would have done, if you had not put her away from you. But the girl was not satisfied with that. She poisoned Innocencia so that she could take her place as the new Condessa of Sorocaba."

"You are wrong, Honório," Ruis refuted. "Maranta did not poison your sister. And you forget, she is legally the wife of my brother Vasco."

"I am sure you and she have made plans for him, too," Vincente said. "It would be so easy to get rid of a man who is already helpless. But it will never come to that. For if the girl survives the night, she will be brought to justice tomorrow for murdering Innocencia."

"God's truth, Vincente. You, as a priest of the church, should know that what you are doing is wrong." Ruis's dark eyes filled with vengeance. "If you bring Maranta before a court of justice for a crime she did not commit, then I shall let the world know what your sister Innocencia did."

Vincente looked up in surprise as Ruis went on.

"Your sister murdered her own child—our son, who would have been the heir. When she discovered she was pregnant, she persuaded one of the Indian women to help her rid herself of the child. The mutilation made it impossible for Innocencia to conceive again. I have affidavits to prove this and will not hesitate to use them. If you wish notoriety and a slur against the Monteiro name, then be prepared for the disgrace of your own."

Honório paced back and forth between the table and the window. Ruis's words had clearly disturbed him, as well as his brother Vincente.

"Very well, Ruis," Honório finally said. "You know I cannot fall into disfavor at this time, with the Regency so shaky. The girl is locked in the burial vault at the Casa de Cabrals outside the city."

Ruis's face turned white, and he immediately moved for the door, but Vincente cautioned him. "One moment, Ruis. For your sake and the girl's, I hope your brother Vasco remains in good health."

Down the dark road Ruis spurred his horse Diabo, with his armed servants behind him. They thundered across the wooden bridge and down the hillside, with no time to spare. Maranta could last for just so long in the stuffy, airless vault.

Through the grove of trees they passed, until, in the shadowy distance, the deserted old *casa,* with its tiles falling from the roof, appeared as a ghost rising out of the overgrown wilderness.

Ruis rode through the garden without halting, and he urged the horse past the door and into the tiled corridor that led to the chapel.

The sleepy old man on guard, with the lantern beside him, looked up at the avenging specter headed toward him—a black devil of a horse, with the devil himself astride the animal. It must be Exú, the wicked one, coming to punish him because of the girl inside the vault. The old man fled into the darkness, leaving his lighted lantern by the door to the chapel.

Ruis jumped from the horse and, snatching up the lantern, hastened into the chapel. Down the steps he went behind the altar, until confronted by the heavy door secured by a rusty lock.

Standing to the side, Ruis took his pistol from the waistband of his breeches. The sound of the shot reverberated throughout the chapel and heralded the breaking of the lock.

The door creaked open, and Ruis held the lantern high. "Maranta," he called, but there was no answer.

Through the dank, stuffy stone room he walked, the lantern's light catching the white bones of some poor soul's remains upon a slab. He quickly lowered the lantern and searched the floor, in all the corners, and up and down the length of the long burial room, but there was no sign of Maranta.

Had he come to the wrong house? Or had Honório told a lie as to where he had put the girl?

Frantically, Ruis continued the search, holding the lantern higher. A white form, recently dead, lay on a slab, and in distaste, Ruis walked on. A deadly spider crossed his path, and he crushed it with his shoe.

All at once, Ruis stopped and then retraced his steps. Again, he held the lantern high and took a closer look at the corpse covered with white mold. His hand reached out to touch it, but instead of the cold flesh of the dead, his hand felt warmth.

It was Maranta, covered in the white flour from the Intrudo.

With a cry he lifted her from the stone slab and carried her out of the vault and into the chapel. He knelt, breathing into her mouth, forcing her lungs to work, and willing her to live. And for the second time in her life, Maranta responded to the lifesaving breath of one who loved her.

"*Amada*," Ruis whispered, as she moved her hand and opened her eyes.

Ruis did not wait for the Intrudo to end. Concerned for Maranta's safety, he saw to the packing and arranged transportation out of the city. He would not wait for the scheduled canoe fleet. Instead, he hired his own canoes at considerable expense and manned them with guards and as many of his male servants as he could spare from the *casa*. His bluff had worked for the moment, but he did not trust either Honório or Vincente for long. He knew what Innocencia had done with Floresta's help— but he had no positive proof, no affidavits from the doctors. And Innocencia's brothers, well versed in law, could demand to see proof of his allegations.

So, on the next day, Ruis left the city with a fragile and subdued Maranta, and his penniless cousin, Dona Isobel, who had suddenly aged overnight.

Through the long hours of riding in the canoe, Maranta relived the nightmare in the suffocating vault—the spiders crawling over her in the darkness, and her search for some place off the floor where she might avoid them. And then, finally, that feeling of lethargy that came over her body at the lack of air, causing her to rest full-length upon the slab that was reserved for the dead.

She could not comprehend her situation when she first became aware of the man's mouth upon hers, drawing her back to life, making her lungs hurt at the forced intake of breath. Then she had opened her eyes to see Ruis

—his dark head bending over her, possessing her with those dark sapphire eyes—the man who had rescued her from death.

The canoe hit rough water, and Maranta gasped. "You are all right, *amada?*" Ruis called softly, shifting his body slightly to the side to accommodate the dip of the canoe.

"*Sim,* Ruis," she answered, and at her use of the Portuguese word instead of English, the man smiled and then faced ahead.

Once more, Maranta stared at the back of the arrogant *conde*. But she felt no antagonism at his blocking out her view. She felt comfort in his closeness instead—protection, by this man who had gone to great lengths to remove her from any further danger presented by Innocencia's brothers.

Honório—that was one of the names Vasco had given to little Paulo. And Ruis had said nothing in answer to Vasco's maliciousness in naming Ruis's own son after a man Ruis despised.

Sensing that Maranta was uneasy each time he disappeared from her sight, Ruis took care to keep the girl at his side as much as possible. But it was not difficult. Maranta made no more excursions to the riverbank on her own; she made no demur at Ruis's suggestions along the way. Puzzled over this new docility, Ruis, chided himself for not watching over her more closely in São Paulo.

"What are you thinking about, *pequena?*" he asked one night in a soft tone. The glow of the cooking fire burned low, framing her small serious face in its waning light. At his question, she looked up with a guilty expression.

"I was thinking of Paulo—and wondering if he is well."

"By this time tomorrow, Maranta, you will be able to judge for yourself when you see him."

"We are that close?"

"Yes. Only a few miles more and we will be on Monteiro property."

She slept better that night in the tent, by Dona Isobel's

326

side—knowing that the child she thought never to see again would soon be in her arms.

The rain began that evening and continued through the next day, slowing them down. Each mile, each small delay filled Maranta with impatience. But then, the town of Hitû rose before them. Only a few miles more.

There was no palanquin available in Hitû. Dona Isobel decided to wait for transportation from the *fazenda,* with some of the servants to keep her company, but Maranta chose to ride the mare that Ruis had brought back with him from São Paulo—the same horse she had ridden to Penha, the shrine in the hills where she had once prayed for a miracle.

Over the *terra-roxa* the mare trotted, alongside Diabo. And behind them came two of Ruis's armed servants. Over the green hills they rode, with Maranta marking off every familiar point, every obstacle that separated her from her child, until in the distance, the fertile slopes dotted with coffee plants rose before her.

She met Ruis's gaze and smiled at him, the tension easing from her body. For the first time since they'd left the city of São Paulo, Maranta felt safe.

In the stables, Vasco waited for Patû to strap him to the horse. When that was done, the man spoke quietly to the servant.

"Bring the child to me, Patû. I shall wait here inside the stables. But make sure no one sees you take the babe from the nursery."

The Indian left the stables to obey, and Vasco waited, patting the horse and soothing him as he snorted and sidled nervously, eager for his daily gallop.

To perfect his game, Vasco had taken the horse daily to the falls and pitched a bundle into the river. Each day for a week he had watched the bright bundle disappear over the falls.

But today would be different. This time, there would be no bundle of clothes floating over the precipice. A much more valuable piece—at least to Ruis—would go over the falls.

Vasco could imagine the great cry when it was discovered that the child had disappeared with no trace. Kidnappers, stealing the child from the nursery. That's what they would probably think—with Naka and Sassia blamed for their negligence. He could see Ruis searching the countryside for weeks, with no reward for his effort, unless— Yes. He just might leave one of the child's shoes where it could be found. That would be interesting to watch.

Vasco laughed. The pleasure in planning was tantamount to that in the deed. How long he had lain awake at night, planning and plotting—ever since hearing Floresta's taunting words. And now it was time to fulfill the scheme. His brother would be home in a few days.

Impatiently, Vasco waited for Patû to return. What was keeping him?

The Indian, with the baby wrapped in a white blanket, looked back toward the house and then quickly slipped across the open space to the stable door.

"What kept you so long?" an irritable Vasco asked the Indian.

"The child was fretful and would not go to sleep for a time."

"Probably cutting another tooth," Vasco said. "Well, hand him to me."

He stared down at the sleeping child, his blue-black hair in small ringlets about his head, and his dark eyelashes long against his baby cheeks. "He could so easily have been mine," Vasco whispered. And then he thought of Ruis. The small twinge of regret vanished, and Vasco gave his horse the signal to leave the stables.

Vasco frowned. The baby was heavier than he had imagined. As the horse galloped through the open gate, Paulo began to squirm in his confinement. Soon, his discomfort was voiced in a wail—something Vasco had not planned on, to call attention to himself.

Maranta was still thinking of Paulo as they neared the approach to the *fazenda*. Soon now, the house would come

328

into view. Her eyes, eagerly searching the landscape, spotted a horse coming toward them.

"Is that Vasco?" Maranta asked.

Ruis looked in the direction that Maranta pointed. He slowed Diabo, and his face took on a displeased frown.

"He is going dangerously fast, is he not?" Maranta commented to the silent man, drawing her mare up beside Ruis.

Over the green hill the angry wail of the child pierced the still air. "*Meu Deus,*" Ruis exploded, " the fool has the baby with him."

In an instant, Ruis had spurred Diabo and was racing toward the other horse. One of the servants riding behind them took off after Ruis, while the other, debating for a second what to do, stayed at Maranta's side as his master had instructed him before leaving the city.

The baby—Vasco was holding Paulo under his arm, Maranta gave a cry and pressed the mare into a gallop. The servant followed.

Vasco, furious at Ruis's untimely return, paused for a second, watching Diabo bearing down upon him. With a shout to his own horse, Vasco headed straight for the Tietê River.

38

The mud flew from Diabo's hooves as Ruis sped over the whirring green landscape, still wet from the recent rain. And at the thundering sound of the great horse behind him, Vasco increased his pace.

Did Ruis not know that he could release the baby at any moment he wished—to be trampled underfoot, just as he had been on the pampas? But no. Vasco had survived. Perhaps Paulo would also. And he could not take that chance. Holding the baby tighter to his breast, Vasco rode on toward the sound of the roaring falls. The deed must go as he had planned.

Ruis left the pathway, his jaw set in granite hardness, determined to cut off Vasco's route and turn him in the opposite direction—away from the river. But Vasco, looking to the side, saw what his brother was doing, and he headed for the more dangerous path, closer to the rocks themselves.

Blue sky and the green earth touched and merged, pinned together by shafts of sunlight falling from the sky, rippling through the trees, making an aisle of dazzling gold to blind the riders and their mounts. Vasco's horse stumbled, and the man, strapped to the animal, swayed dangerously before righting himself with a powerful arm.

"Vasco," Ruis shouted. "Stop! In the name of God, stop before it's too late."

"It is already too late, brother," Vasco shouted back. And then the sound of the cataract drowned out their voices.

The child who had wailed so loudly on the wild ride was now quiet—as if his experience had left no further tears. Small and helpless, he dangled from Vasco's arms, while the man urged his horse over the hazardous terrain.

In torrents, foaming and misting, the waters roared

331

over the rocks, their rampant spray touching the sunlight, forming an arch of rainbows to bridge the chasm separating the oneness of the mighty Tietê.

The roar of the falls, the sense of foreboding greeted Maranta as she brought her mare to a stop on the same spot on which she had witnessed the New Year's Eve ceremony of the slaves offering their candles and gifts. Helplessly she watched and waited to see if her ultimate sacrifice—the life of her child—would be offered by Vasco to Iemanjá, the pagan goddess of waters.

Ruis dismounted from his horse and crept on foot toward Vasco. The man with the child in his arms edged his horse slowly over the loose rocks along the bluff—making for the very edge.

As Ruis reached out a rock moved; the horse stumbled; and the terrified whinny of the animal rose in the wind and floated across the wild earth to combine with the never-ceasing noise of the waters.

Maranta gazed in horror as the side of the bluff gave way. The horse fell, and the white blanket drifted toward the rapidly rushing waters and then was drawn quickly out of sight.

She sank to her knees, great sobs racking her small frame. Her life was over. She had lost little Paulo.

Dazed by her bereavement and the horror of watching Vasco plunge from sight, still strapped to his horse, she was insulated from the happenings around her.

But an insistent voice demanded her attention. Through her tears, she gazed up at Ruis, his face bleeding from a cut across his cheek, his torn clothes muddy and disheveled.

But in his arms—in his arms—

"Your son, *amada*," he said, holding out the baby to her.

"Paulo," she screamed and grabbed the child to her, hugging him and kissing him. At her onslaught Paulo began to cry.

"I think you have frightened him, *pequena*," Ruis said, his voice filled with tenderness.

332

Maranta eased her hold on the child, and sitting on the ground, she rocked him back and forth until he quieted.

While he watched them both, a troubled Ruis heard Vincente's last words. *For your sake and the girl's, I hope your brother Vasco remains in good health.* And now, Vasco was dead.

Despite the servants' search, the waters had left no trace of Vasco da Monteiro. But his actions and those of Patû lived on in the memories of all those on the *fazenda*. Patû disappeared that night, and Floresta, too, abandoning her small son, Tefe.

"It is well that she abandoned him," Ruis commented. "Part of the inheritance will be Tefe's, as Vasco's son. And I would not have allowed the child to leave with her."

So it was that Maranta, dressed in widow's black, sat in the chapel with Ruis, Dona Isobel, and Tefe and heard the padre's prayers for Vasco's soul.

The child, Tefe, was moved into the nursery with Paulo to be watched over by Naka. And in the days that followed, Maranta would sit on the veranda with the two children by her side.

It was late afternoon when the little green bird appeared on the veranda. At the sight of the familiar little bird, Maranta smiled. "Look, Tefe. It's Fado," she said. "He has come home." They watched as he hopped about as if not quite sure of his welcome. "I wonder if he is hungry."

Together, they took the cage and filled it with seed and left it on the table where the bird was used to sunning himself as Maranta painted. And then, they went inside the house.

The next day, the seed was gone, and Maranta and Tefe replenished it. Now bolder, Fado flew into the cage as they watched, but Maranta made no effort to close the door. She had given Fado his freedom to come and go as he pleased.

Through the next few days, Maranta was aware of Ruis

333

watching her. Now that Vasco was dead, she was free to leave, like Fado—but she could not. Paulo was the link that chained her to the Monteiro *fazenda*.

The mourning time for Innocencia was over, and a man like Dom Ruis would surely wish to marry again. What should she do? Maranta had never been a real wife to Vasco. She had no claim on the Monteiros. Each time that Ruis looked at her in his penetrating way, she was frightened that he would send her away.

As she sat on the veranda at the end of one day and gathered her paintbrushes to take inside, she heard: "Maranta, I wish to speak with you."

She looked up at Ruis, standing over her. "I must take these inside, if you don't mind, Ruis."

She stood up, gathering them in her hand, but Ruis took them from her and placed them on the small table where her palette lay. "No, *pequena*. You cannot continue to avoid me. There are words that must be spoken."

Maranta swayed. The discussion she had dreaded was being forced on her, and there was nothing she could do to stop it.

"You are not happy, Maranta," he said. "I have watched you closely for these past weeks, and not once have I seen a smile on your face, except with the children. Do you wish to return to your family in the Carolinas? If that is what will make you happy, then I shall not stop you."

Maranta stared at the tall, dark man before her, and her heartbeat suddenly quickened. Tears came to her eyes, and she cried out, "Please, Ruis. Don't send me away. I could not bear it—being separated from Paulo . . ."

"I would never send you away, *amada*," he corrected.

But she did not hear him. In anguish she continued, "I . . . I know that you will wish to marry again someday, Ruis—now the mourning time for Innocencia is almost over—but if you will let me stay in a little cottage somewhere, not too far from the *fazenda*, I promise—I won't be a burden to you. Just to see little Paulo occasionally—that's all I ask."

She had no pride left. Her voice broke, and she turned

her head and stared unseeing toward the coffee slopes in the distance. Ruis's hand reached out, touching her arm and drawing her to him.

"You are not a burden, *amada*," he said tenderly. "You are my blessing, instead." He looked searchingly into her dark, tearful eyes as he went on, "As for marrying again, there are many obstacles to overcome. But for me, there is only one woman I love and wish for my wife—and she is the mother of my son."

Joy transformed Maranta's delicate features. "Ruis," she whispered, hardly believing his words as his lips met hers.

"Maranta," he breathed. "I love you so."

At length, he put her away from him and left the veranda. Maranta lingered, watching Fado hop about, flying to his swinging perch and then flitting to the feeder, chirping as he went.

Maranta clasped the *cruzamento* closer to her breast, savoring the feel of the pearls and diamonds against her flesh, reminding her of the fulfillment of her destiny. Soon, the stars appeared in the sky, and she spied the constellation of the twins—Castor and Pollux—looking down on her just as it had back in Carolina. With a sense of peace she realized the *fazenda* was now her real home.

39

The holiday season at Midgard was clouded by the tense political climate in the state. But Marigold was stunned to see that another relationship had taken a turn for the better—Shaun and her father were sitting in the same room, sharing a brandy and conversation. Where was all the old animosity that Robert Tabor had once exhibited at the mere mention of the Irishman's name? Her father actually seemed to enjoy his discussions with Shaun. Marigold, sitting at the far end of the drawing room, only half listened as she waited for Robbie and the sixteen-month-old Raven to appear.

"It was a sad day," Robert Tabor said, "when Adams thought more of his own political neck than the harm he would generate by signing such a bill into law. When John Randolph said the tariff bill was concerned with no manufactures except the manufacture of a president, he was expressing the opinion of the entire South. And now, we are the ones paying for the folly in Washington."

Robert Tabor, with the rest of Charleston, waited to hear how John Calhoun would fare in Washington upon his return. Although his name had never been attached to the articles of nullification, it was common knowledge that he had been the author.

But one afternoon in January, when Marigold was returning to the house from her usual daily walk, she saw a man on horseback riding up the avenue of magnolias. He seemed to be in a hurry, and Marigold suspected the man had news for her father.

"Uncle Arthur," she said, smiling when she recognized her godfather. He jumped from the horse and handed the reins to a boy waiting at the front.

"Marigold." He hurried up the steps toward her. "I have some good news. Where is your father?"

"In the library, I think."

Arthur went into the house and Marigold followed. "John has been allowed to take his seat in the Senate, Robert," the man said as soon as he saw his friend.

"Thank God," Robert Tabor replied and clasped Arthur's hand.

Henry Clay and John Calhoun began their work on a new tariff bill. The nullification act was scheduled to go into effect on February the first. If a compromise could not be worked out in the one month's time left to them, then the nation would be divided against itself.

Clay introduced the new bill, calling for a gradual reduction of the excessively high duties over the next ten years, with the proviso that after that date, no article would be subject to more than 20 percent of duty leveled on it. It passed.

In March, Robert Tabor went back to Columbia. The convention reassembled and canceled its nullification ordinance. The crisis was over, and the federal ships left the harbor.

As soon as the bags of sand and bales of cotton were removed from the battery, Shaun Banagher came to Midgard for his wife.

"No, Shaun," Marigold greeted him. "I don't want to return with you." With the child nearly due, Marigold was uncomfortable and in a temper.

They sat in the drawing room, glaring at each other, with Shaun's face unable to conceal the anger he felt at Marigold's rebellion. "You are my wife, Marigold. I have already made arrangements. Even the nurse is at the house, waiting for you."

"Then you can tell her to stop waiting. I am not coming."

Shaun stalked out of the drawing room, and Marigold, thinking he had given in, relaxed. But then, she heard the noise upstairs—coming from her bedroom. She walked to the hall in time to see the servants carrying her trunk downstairs.

"Where are you taking that?" she demanded.

"Outside, to the carriage," Shaun answered, standing at the head of the stairs, with her green cape draped over his arm. "Everything is packed, except your cape. I presume you will wish to wear it."

He walked down the stairs and held the cape for her. "Shaun," she protested.

"If you do not come willingly," he whispered fiercely in her ear, "I shall be forced to pick you up in front of the servants and carry you out. And I am not sure, because of your size, whether I will be able to get you safely down the steps."

Her topaz eyes flashed fury at his remark. "Don't tax your strength, Mr. Banagher." She grabbed the cape from him and hurried toward the front door.

Shaun quickly caught up with her and, disguising the amused gleam in his eyes, took Marigold's arm to help her to the carriage.

"Maman is not even at home," Marigold pouted. "She will wonder what has happened to me."

"I told your father I was coming for you today."

"And he had no objections?"

"It is not up to a father to object when a husband decides to take his wife home."

In surprise, Marigold looked at Shaun. He was behaving exactly like her father—having his own way, brooking no opposition. Why had she not noticed that before?

When Marigold returned to the house on the battery, Shaun paid no more attention to her than he had when she was at Midgard. But he had provided well for her comfort. She had only to ring the little bell at her chair to bring one of the new servants to see to her every whim.

For much of the time, Shaun was away, coming home late in the evenings, sometimes after Marigold was already in bed. But toward the middle of the month, he stopped going out altogether.

Though it was mid-morning, Shaun still sat in the upstairs parlor and continued to read the paper. "Don't you need to attend to your business affairs today, Shaun?" Marigold asked.

Glancing over the top of the paper, he replied, "No,

Marigold. I have arranged to be away from my office this week. Anything of importance will be brought to the house.

"Why?"

He placed the newspaper on the table by his chair. "Isn't it obvious? You look as if you can't go another day without having the baby."

There it was again—his reference to her size. Feeling clumsy and uncomfortable, Marigold lashed out, "For your information, Shaun, this is the way all women look at this time."

His glance softened. "I know, Souci." His conversation was interrupted by the heavy knock at the front door. Soon he left her, going downstairs to his library to be closeted for the rest of the morning with a man from his office.

The next day Marigold awoke to a fleeting backache, and before afternoon arrived, the nurse and doctor were hovering over her. Shaun did not come near her. Surrounded by strangers to have the child of a man she hated, Marigold had never felt more alone in her life . . . until, finally, she heard her mother's voice.

She had an easy delivery, especially for the first one. By the time Shaun came to see her in the evening, Marigold was sitting up in bed, attacking the food that she had not been allowed to eat during the day.

Shaun stared at her large tawny eyes, the golden hair falling in ringlets onto the pillow—and her full breasts outlined by the thin silk gown.

"Having a child seems to agree with you, Marigold," his impudent voice teased. "I must remember it for future years."

"Have you seen her?" Marigold asked, laying down her soup spoon.

"Yes. I can't say she looks much like you."

Marigold lowered her eyes, and her fingers brushed against the spoon. Shaun was right. The baby's hair was coal black—like Crane's. But it was also like Maranta's.

"Have you heard about Maranta?" Marigold asked, still uneasy at Shaun's presence. "She had a baby, too."

Shaun nodded.

"Maman only got the letter yesterday," Marigold said. "It was over three months in coming."

Shaun went back to his work, and the baby, whisked to the nursery and given over to the care of the wet nurse, was brought into Marigold's room only at certain short intervals of the day. It seemed to be what Shaun had ordered. But as soon as she was allowed to be up, Marigold took the infant's care into her own hands.

Since Shaun was content to remain apart from her in another bedroom, Marigold had the cradle moved into her room. The baby stayed for the entire day, being taken back to the nursery only at nighttime. Marigold began to give the little girl her baths and to dress her in the delicate lacy gowns and bonnets. Gazing at the tiny doll in her arms, she wondered what to name her.

She sat, rocking and crooning to the child, when Shaun strolled into the bedroom without knocking. For a moment he stood at the door, watching his wife with the child in her arms. Marigold looked up, and a guilty feeling spread over her. But she refused to put the child back into the cradle. She remained sitting in the chair, holding the baby possessively. She would not have her daughter treated as something to be hidden whenever Shaun came around.

"You're back early today," Marigold said.

"I've spent far too much time on business lately, but it couldn't be helped," he replied, coming in and leaning over to kiss Marigold on the top of her head. "I didn't realize you kept the child in here with you," he said.

"Only during the day. Greta takes her back to the nursery in the evenings."

"Have you named her yet?" he inquired.

"I was debating between Merle and Corrie. I prefer Corrie. But somehow, I don't like the sound of it with Caldwell."

Shaun's lips tensed. "Since her last name is Banagher, I don't see that it's a problem."

"But surely you don't mean that. You aren't her father, Shaun."

"I'm the only father she is ever likely to know, Marigold. And you are my wife."

"You haven't even . . . held her," Marigold pointed out.

"Is that a prerequisite for claiming her as my own?"

"You would do that, Shaun? Accept her as if she is . . . yours?"

"Why must you ask, Marigold? Did I not do that in the church before we left Cedar Hill? Accept you *and* your condition?"

He sat in the chair on the other side of the hearth. "If we must play this charade, then let's get on with it. I had not realized you put such store in my holding the child."

When she hesitated, he inquired, "Well, what are you going to do, Marigold? Lay her at my feet to see if I will claim her, as the wives of the chieftains of my clan have done for hundreds of years, or are you going to place her in my arms?"

Marigold's shoulders shook as she stood up with the baby. Lured by the emerald green eyes, she came to him fearfully and held out the baby.

He took the child in his arms, and his eyes clouded with consternation. Suddenly, Marigold giggled. The spell was broken.

"That's not how you hold a baby, Shaun," she instructed. "Not like a sack of potatoes. You cradle your arm to support her head."

Shaun grinned, changing his position. He looked down at the baby and said, "Well, Corrie, it seems your father has a lot to learn." At his announcement, Marigold's heart soared.

40

Shaun strolled down the street toward the battery. He was in a good mood. Thinking of his surprise for Marigold, his eyes took on a tender glow.

He was glad his quarrel with Robert Tabor was over. Shaun had what he wanted, what he had dreamed of possessing from the moment he had seen the proud tilt of the girl's head, her pert, aristocratic nose high in the air—a fiery little beauty, used to the admiring glances of every gawking youth and ignoring them all.

Yes, he had been one of them—older than most, and at a disadvantage because of his poverty. Brian Boru, his ancestor, would have been proud of him—fighting for his lost heritage and gaining the prize he had set for himself. Now the time had come for him to take possession of the prize.

He remembered the furious look, the biting, sarcastic words when he had dragged the girl from the mahogany bed—when she had not known that the townhouse belonged to Shaun Banagher.

Not true. The house had never truly belonged to him. He had used it for a time. That was all. A house had ghosts and memories of the past. He had felt the past in the townhouse, but even more strongly in the river house at Midgard. The river house had been filled with love, and that was why he had nearly lost his head there, succumbing to Marigold's allure, even though she was with child.

But now, the babe was old enough. The time had come for Shaun Banagher to consummate his love.

He walked up the steps into the townhouse and into the library as the old clock in the hall chimed five times. Any moment now, Jake would be bringing Marigold and the baby home from their afternoon ride. And when they returned—

343

Shaun took the key to the desk and unlocked the lower drawer. Removing a set of blueprints, he spread them on the desk and studied them, a satisfied expression on his face.

The sound of horses trotting down the street carried through the mild afternoon air. Shaun hurriedly folded the plans and returned them to the drawer. He walked to the window and saw the carriage stopping in front of the house, as he had requested.

He left the library and walked outside. A smile hovered about his lips as he approached the carriage.

"Greta, you may take Corrie to the nursery," Shaun said to the child's nurse.

"Yes, Mr. Banagher."

He held the baby while the woman stepped onto the sidewalk, and then instead of helping Marigold down, he gave the baby back to the nurse and climbed into the carriage beside his golden-haired wife.

"We're ready, Jake," he announced, settling his large frame into the seat. Jake turned the carriage around in the street and started away from the townhouse.

"Shaun? Where are we going?" a puzzled Marigold asked.

"I thought I might take you for a ride into the countryside," he said.

"But I've just gotten back from a ride," she protested.

"There's something that I want to show you, Marigold. Something that has taken up much of my time lately."

Marigold sighed. "The new iron foundry, I suppose."

"No."

"Then, what?" Her curious amber eyes gazed into his teasing emerald-colored ones.

"Something else I've built," he announced.

She waited for him to explain, but Shaun didn't elaborate.

Finally Marigold said, "Is that all you're going to tell me?"

Shaun took his eyes from the cobblestoned street. "Yes," he replied and then returned to watching the horses.

344

Every few minutes Marigold glanced toward her husband. He seemed to be in an unusually good mood despite his secretive manner.

For an hour they traveled, straight down the coast. The sound of crushed shells underneath the carriage wheels was magnified in the silence of the late afternoon air. Not far from the road, the sea, blue-gray, lapped softly against the shoreline and spread its watery fingers into low-lying pockets.

At times, the sea disappeared behind sand dunes and then suddenly reappeared as the land reshaped itself into level stretches. Marigold watched as, back and forth, the waves responded to the primeval tidal call. The sun, with a dying defiance, dumped its brilliant embers of gold and red onto the turbulent water, as if by doing so, it could make its load lighter for its daily journey to the far horizon.

Marigold shaded her eyes and shifted her attention from the sea to her husband.

Shaun, who had sat beside her for the past hour with an easy, lazy indolence, suddenly sat straight and lifted his head, his eyes sweeping the landscape. Marigold followed the direction of his gaze, and as Jake slowed the carriage and turned off the main road into a newly cut avenue, she saw the source of Shaun's interest—a towering structure of majestic stones and mortar, rising from the knoll that overlooked the sea, like a sprawling giant that had not made peace with its surroundings. The late afternoon sun reflected in the vast mullioned windows and cast shadows upon the thick walls.

"Shaun?"

Marigold looked at the house and back to Shaun. But the silence continued. Shaun's face revealed nothing. There was no hint of softness in either the man's face or the house. They were alike—unbreachable.

The girl knew without being told that she was looking at the object that had usurped Shaun's attention for the past months, had taken him away from her, and for a moment, Marigold was jealous.

Shaun didn't wait for the carriage to come to a complete

345

halt in the courtyard. With a sudden impatience, he left the vehicle and stood with arms outstretched for Marigold.

"You may take the horses to the stable, Jake," he said. "We won't be needing them again tonight." The carriage immediately moved from the courtyard and disappeared behind the house.

Turning to Marigold, Shaun took her hand and led her up the steps to the massive cypress door. It was unlocked, and Shaun pushed it open and held it for Marigold to enter.

The air was cold, and the abrupt change from the warmth outside made the girl shudder. But the light coming through the windows diminished Marigold's sudden coldness, and she walked about in the great hall while Shaun stood back, observing her reaction.

The tapestry hanging from the wall, the crystal and brass chandelier with its dozens of candles ready to light the four corners of the baronial room—Marigold's tawny eyes observed it all.

She swallowed in awe at the richness, the obvious wealth and comfort. Far grander than Midgard, yet an undefinable something that was missing.

"You do not like it, Marigold?" The voice beside her caused her to jump.

"It . . . it is quite grand, Shaun," she replied hesitantly. "Far grander than Midgard," she added.

Shaun nodded. "That was my intention," he said.

"I . . . understand," Marigold whispered, her voice quivering with emotion.

"Do you, Souci?" Shaun asked softly, seeing disappointment cloud the girl's amber eyes.

"Yes. Because of my father . . ."

Shaun shook his head. "No. My revenge against Robert Tabor was short-lived. It is because of *you*, not your father, that I built this house."

"But the townhouse," she protested.

"Is already deeded back to him." Shaun's eyes, fierce and possessive, met Marigold's. "There was only one thing, Souci, that belonged to Robert Tabor that I coveted and was determined to have. From the first mo-

346

ment I saw you, I desired you and wanted you as my wife. I built this house for *you,* Souci, as a suitable setting for your beauty."

"Oh, Shaun." Marigold's face showed her happiness, and she stood on tiptoe to meet his kiss.

He drank long and deep from her soft, vulnerable mouth. And then gazing tenderly into her eyes, he smiled. "Our supper is waiting for us, Souci. But we'll have to serve ourselves. I have no wish to celebrate our wedding night with the servants underfoot."

The flames leaped from Marigold's eyes to ignite Shaun's passion. He crushed her to him, forgetting the food waiting for them, forgetting everything but his desire for her.

In a hoarse voice, Shaun murmured, "I want you now, Marigold. I can't wait any longer to make you mine."

Lifting her in his arms, Shaun carried an unprotesting Marigold up the stairs to the master bedroom—to the magnificent rosewood bed draped in silk.

His hands reached for the buttons of her snow white blouse, and she felt the contact of his hand upon her bare breast. Desire quickened and spread as Marigold felt his head move downward to trace the fragile pink nipple with his tongue.

Then, in haste, her skirt, her lace-embroidered petticoats, and her kid slippers were removed and discarded beside Shaun's own breeches and fine linen shirt.

"You are so beautiful," he murmured, staring at Marigold's supple young body waiting unashamedly for his caresses. His hands began their survey of every curve of her body, and Marigold closed her eyes as his flesh became her flesh, his hands a part of her—exploring her softness, knowing the most intimate parts of her body.

His weight pressed down upon her—shifting and teasing—until he moved upward, planting his hard flesh against hers. Her body responded, begging for release.

The thrust was gentle at first, tantalizingly sweet. But it grew more demanding with a rhythm that increased in tempo, until her hips began to move of their own accord, drawing him into her, again and again. Waves of sensuality swept over her, crashing in her ears, filling her mouth with the spreading sweetness of love and then ebbing in an overflow that moved to the very soles of her feet. Shaun, crying out with victory, refused to give her up, but shifted his weight, holding Marigold to him, until their positions were changed, with Marigold atop his strong, masculine body.

Afterward, satiated, Marigold clung to him, her long, golden hair spreading over his chest, her ear attuned to the rapidity of his heartbeat.

In a few minutes, his breathing was even, and Marigold stirred. But Shaun tightened his hold on her. "Not yet, Marigold. I have a great hunger for you that can't be appeased so easily."

"Shaun," she whispered, tasting his name on her lips. "I love you, Shaun."

The house came alive—listening to the sounds of love. Marigold wrapped her arms about the auburn-haired man with the emerald eyes. From the bed she could look out the window into the moonlit night. The constellation of the twins was visible in the evening sky. She thought of Maranta, so far away, and hoped, with all her heart, that her twin had also found love.

W0105-W

Dorothy Eden

One of today's outstanding novelists writes tales about love, intrigue, wealth, power—and, of course, romance. Here are romantic novels of suspense at their best.

☐ AN AFTERNOON WALK	24020-7	$1.95
☐ DARKWATER	23544-0	$1.95
☐ THE HOUSE ON HAY HILL	23789-3	$1.95
☐ LADY OF MALLOW	23167-4	$1.75
☐ THE MARRIAGE CHEST	23032-5	$1.50
☐ MELBURY SQUARE	24050-9	$1.95
☐ THE MILLIONAIRE'S DAUGHTER	23186-0	$1.95
☐ NEVER CALL IT LOVING	23143-7	$1.95
☐ RAVENSCROFT	23760-5	$1.75
☐ THE SALAMANCA DRUM	23548-9	$1.95
☐ THE SHADOW WIFE	23699-4	$1.75
☐ SIEGE IN THE SUN	23884-9	$1.95
☐ SLEEP IN THE WOODS	23706-0	$1.95
☐ SPEAK TO ME OF LOVE	23981-0	$1.95
☐ THE TIME OF THE DRAGON	23059-7	$1.95
☐ THE VINES OF YARRABEE	23184-4	$1.95
☐ WAITING FOR WILLA	23187-9	$1.50
☐ WINTERWOOD	23185-2	$1.75

Buy them at your local bookstores or use this handy coupon for ordering:

FAWCETT BOOKS GROUP
P.O. Box C730, 524 Myrtle Ave., Pratt Station, Brooklyn, N.Y. 11205

Please send me the books I have checked above. Orders for less than 5 books must include 75¢ for the first book and 25¢ for each additional book to cover mailing and handling. I enclose $_____ in check or money order.

Name_____

Address_____

City_____State/Zip_____

Please allow 4 to 5 weeks for delivery.

Victoria Holt

Here are the stories you love best. Tales about love, intrigue, wealth, power and of course romance. Books that will keep you turning the pages deep into the night.

☐ BRIDE OF PENDORRIC	23280-8	$1.95
☐ THE CURSE OF THE KINGS	23284-0	$1.95
☐ THE HOUSE OF A THOUSAND LANTERNS	23685-4	$1.95
☐ THE KING OF THE CASTLE	23587-4	$1.95
☐ KIRKLAND REVELS	23920-9	$1.95
☐ LEGEND OF THE SEVENTH VIRGIN	23281-6	$1.95
☐ LORD OF THE FAR ISLAND	22874-6	$1.95
☐ MENFREYA IN THE MORNING	23757-5	$1.95
☐ MISTRESS OF MELLYN	23924-1	$1.95
☐ ON THE NIGHT OF THE SEVENTH MOON	23568-0	$1.95
☐ THE PRIDE OF THE PEACOCK	23198-4	$1.95
☐ THE QUEEN'S CONFESSION	23213-1	$1.95
☐ THE SECRET WOMAN	23283-2	$1.95
☐ SHADOW OF THE LYNX	23278-6	$1.95
☐ THE SHIVERING SANDS	23282-4	$1.95

Buy them at your local bookstore or use this handy coupon for ordering

POPULAR LIBRARY
P.O. Box C730, 524 Myrtle Ave., Pratt Station, Brooklyn, N.Y. 11205

Please send me the books I have checked above. Orders for less than 5 books must include 75¢ for the first book and 25¢ for each additional book to cover mailing and handling. I enclose $_____ in check or money order.

Name_____

Address_____

City_____ State/Zip_____

Please allow 4 to 5 weeks for delivery.

Historical Romance

Sparkling novels of love and conquest against the colorful background of historical England. Here are books you will savor word by word, page by spellbinding page.

☐ TRUMPET FOR A WALLED CITY—Pala	23913-6	$1.75
☐ THE ARDENT SUITOR—Greenlea	23914-4	$1.75
☐ HONEY-POT—Stables	23915-2	$1.75
☐ SOPHIA AND AUGUSTA—Clark	23916-0	$1.75
☐ THE WITCH FROM THE SEA—Carr	22837-1	$1.95
☐ AFTER THE STORM—Williams	23928-4	$1.75
☐ ALTHEA—Robins	23268-9	$1.50
☐ AMETHYST LOVE—Danton	23400-2	$1.50
☐ AN AFFAIR OF THE HEART Smith	23092-9	$1.50
☐ AUNT SOPHIE'S DIAMONDS Smith	23378-2	$1.50
☐ A BANBURY TALE—MacKeever	23174-7	$1.50
☐ CLARISSA—Arnett	22893-2	$1.50
☐ DEVIL'S BRIDE—Edwards	23176-3	$1.50
☐ ESCAPADE—Smith	23232-8	$1.50
☐ A FAMILY AFFAIR—Mellow	22967-X	$1.50
☐ THE FORTUNE SEEKER Greenlea	23301-4	$1.50
☐ THE FINE AND HANDSOME CAPTAIN—Lynch	23269-7	$1.50
☐ FIRE OPALS—Danton	23984-5	$1.75

Buy them at your local bookstores or use this handy coupon for ordering:

FAWCETT BOOKS GROUP
P.O. Box C730, 524 Myrtle Ave., Pratt Station, Brooklyn, N.Y. 11205

Please send me the books I have checked above. Orders for less than 5 books must include 75¢ for the first book and 25¢ for each additional book to cover mailing and handling. I enclose $_____ in check or money order.

Name_____

Address_____

City_____State/Zip_____

Please allow 4 to 5 weeks for delivery.

FREE
Fawcett Books Listing

There is Romance, Mystery, Suspense, and Adventure waiting for you inside the Fawcett Books Order Form. And it's yours to browse through and use to get all the books you've been wanting . . . but possibly couldn't find in your bookstore.

This easy-to-use order form is divided into categories and contains over 1500 titles by your favorite authors.

So don't delay—take advantage of this special opportunity to increase your reading pleasure.

Just send us your name and address and 35¢ (to help defray postage and handling costs).

FAWCETT BOOKS GROUP
P.O. Box C730, 524 Myrtle Ave., Pratt Station, Brooklyn, N.Y. 11205

Name_____
(please print)

Address_____
City _____ State _____ Zip_____

Do you know someone who enjoys books? Just give us their names and addresses and we'll send them an order form too!

Name_____
Address_____
City _____ State _____ Zip_____

Name_____
Address_____
City _____ State _____ Zip_____